Book One of The Last Herald Mage

MAGIC'S PAWN

MERCEDES LACKEY

DAW BOOKS, INC.
DONALD A. WOLLHEIM, FOUNDER
375 Hudson Street, New York, NY 10014

ELIZABETH R. WOLLHEIM
SHEILA E. GILBERT
PUBLISHERS

First Printing, April 1989

40 39 38 37 36 35 34

DAW TRADEMARK REGISTERED
U.S. PAT. AND TM. OFF. AND FOREIGN COUNTRIES
—MARCA REGISTRADA
HECHO EN U.S.A.

PRINTED IN THE U.S.A.

Dedicated to:
Melanie Mar—just because
and
Mark, Carl, and Dominic
for letting me bounce things off them

One

"**Y**our grandfather," said Vanyel's brawny, fifteen-year-old cousin Radevel, "was crazy."

He has a point, Vanyel thought, hoping they weren't about to take an uncontrolled dive down the last of the stairs.

Radevel's remark had probably been prompted by this very back staircase, one that started at one end of the third-floor servants' hall and emerged at the rear of a linen closet on the ground floor. The stair treads were so narrow and so slick that not even the servants used it.

The manor-keep of Lord Withen Ashkevron of Forst Reach was a strange and patchworked structure. In Vanyel's great-great-grandfather's day it had been a more conventional defensive keep, but by the time Vanyel's grandfather had held the lands, the border had been pushed far past Forst Reach. The old reprobate had decided when he'd reached late middle age that defense was going to be secondary to *comfort*. His comfort, primarily.

Not that Vanyel entirely disagreed with Grandfather; he would have been one of the first to vote to fill in the moat and for fireplaces in all the rooms. But the old man had gotten some pretty peculiar notions about what he wanted where—along with a tendency to change his mind in mid-alteration.

There were good points—windows everywhere, and all of them glazed and shuttered. Skylights lighting all the upper rooms and the staircases. Fireplaces in nearly every room. *Heated* privies, part and parcel of the bathhouse.

Every inside wall lathed and plastered against cold and damp. The stables, mews, kennel, and chickenyard banished to new outbuildings.

But there were bad points—if you didn't know your way, you could *really* get lost; and there were an awful lot of places you couldn't get into unless you knew exactly how to get there. Some of those places were important—like the bathhouse and privies. The old goat hadn't much considered the next generation in his alterations, either; he'd cut up the nursery into servant's quarters, which meant that until Lord Withen's boys went into bachelor's hall and the girls to the bower, they were cramped two and three to a series of very tiny attic-level rooms.

"He was *your* grandfather, too," Vanyel felt impelled to point out. The Ashkevron cousins had a tendency to act as if they had no common ancestors with Vanyel and his sibs whenever the subject of Grandfather Joserlin and his alterations came up.

"Huh." Radevel considered for a moment, then shrugged. "He was still crazy." He hefted his own load of armor and padding a little higher on his shoulder.

Vanyel held his peace and trotted down the last couple of stone stairs to hold the door open for his cousin. Radevel was doing him a favor, even though Vanyel was certain that cousin Radevel shared everyone else's low opinion of him. Radevel was by far and away the best-natured of the cousins, and the easiest to talk round—and the bribe of Vanyel's new hawking gauntlet had proved too much for him to resist. Still, it wouldn't do to get him angry by arguing with him; he *might* decide he had better things to do than help Vanyel out, gauntlet or no gauntlet.

Oh, gods—let this work, Vanyel thought as they emerged into the gloomy back hall. *Did I practice enough with Lissa? Is this going to have a chance against a standard attack? Or am I crazy for even trying?*

The hallway was as cold as the staircase had been, and dark to boot. Radevel took the lead, feet slapping on the stone floor as he whistled contentedly—and tunelessly. Vanyel tried not to wince at the mutilation of one of his favorite melodies and drifted silently in his wake, his thoughts as dark as the hallway.

In three days Lissa will be gone—and if I can't manage to get sent along, I'll be all alone. Without Lissa . . .

If I can just prove that I need her kind of training, then maybe Father will let me go with her—

That had been the half-formed notion that prompted him to work out the moves of a different style of fighting than what he was *supposed* to be learning, practicing them in secret with his older sister Lissa: that was what had ultimately led to this little expedition.

That, and the urgent need to show Lord Withen that his eldest son wasn't the coward the armsmaster claimed he was—and that he *could* succeed on martial ground of his own choosing.

Vanyel wondered why he was the only boy to realize that there were other styles of fighting than armsmaster Jervis taught; he'd read of them, and knew that they had to be just as valid, else why send Lissa off to foster and study with Trevor Corey and his seven would-be sword-ladies? The way Vanyel had it figured, there was no way short of a miracle that he would ever succeed at the brute hack-and-bash system Jervis used—and no way Lord Withen would ever believe that another style was just as good while Jervis had his ear.

Unless Vanyel could *show* him. Then Father would *have* to believe his own eyes.

And if I can't prove it to him—

—oh, gods. I can't take much more of this.

With Lissa gone to Brenden Keep, his last real ally in the household would be gone, too; his only friend, and the only person who *cared* for him.

This was the final trial of the plot he'd worked out with Liss; Radevel would try to take him using Jervis' teachings. Vanyel would try to hold his own, wearing nothing but the padded jerkin and helm, carrying the lightest of target-shields, and trusting to speed and agility to keep him out of trouble.

Radevel kicked open the unlatched door to the practice ground, leaving Vanyel to get it closed before somebody yelled about the draft. The early spring sunlight was painful after the darkness of the hallway; Vanyel squinted as he hurried to catch up with his cousin.

"All right, peacock," Radevel said good-naturedly, dumping his gear at the edge of the practice ground, and snagging his own gambeson from the pile. "Get yourself ready, and we'll see if this nonsense of yours has any merit."

It took Vanyel a lot less time than his cousin to shrug into *his* "armor"; he offered tentatively to help Radevel with his, but the older boy just snorted.

"Botch mine the way you botch yours? No thanks," he said, and went on methodically buckling and adjusting.

Vanyel flushed, and stood uncertainly at the side of the sunken practice ground, contemplating the thick, dead grass at his feet.

I never botch anything except when Jervis is watching, he thought bleakly, shivering a little as a bit of cold breeze cut through the gambeson. *And then I can't do anything right.*

He could almost feel the windows in the keep wall behind him like eyes staring at his back. Waiting for him to fail—again.

What's wrong with me, anyway? Why can't I ever please Father? Why is everything I do wrong?

He sighed, scuffed the ground with his toe, and wished he could be out riding instead of trying something doomed to failure. He was the best rider in Forst Reach— he and Star had no equals on the most breakneck of hunts, and he *could*, if he chose, master anything else in the stables.

And just because I won't bother with those iron-mouthed brutes Father prefers, he won't even grant me the accolade there—

Gods. This time I have *to win.*

"Wake up, dreamer," Radevel rumbled, his voice muffled inside the helm. "You wanted to have at—let's get to it."

Vanyel walked to the center of the practice field with nervous deliberation, waiting until the last minute to get his helm on. He hated the thing; he hated the feeling of

being closed in, and most of all hated having his vision
narrowed to a little slit. He waited for Radevel to come
up to him, feeling the sweat already starting under his
arms and down the line of his back.

Radevel swung—but instead of meeting the blow with
his shield as Jervis would have done, Vanyel just moved
out of the way of the blow, and on his way past Radevel,
made a stab of his own. Jervis never cared much for
point-work, but Vanyel had discovered it could be really
effective if you timed things right. Radevel made a startled sound and got up his own shield, but only just in
time, and left himself open to a cut.

Vanyel felt his spirits rising as he saw this second
opening in as many breaths, and chanced another attack
of his own. This one actually managed to connect, though
it was too light to call a disabling hit.

"Light!" Vanyel shouted as he danced away, before
his cousin had a chance to disqualify the blow.

"Almost enough, peacock," Radevel replied, reluctant admiration in his voice. "You land another like that
with your weight behind it and I'll be out. Try *this* for
size—"

He charged, his practice blade a blur beside his shield.

Vanyel just stepped aside at the last moment, while
Radevel staggered halfway to the boundary under his own
momentum.

It was working! Radevel couldn't get *near* him—and
Vanyel was pecking away at him whenever he got an opportunity. He wasn't hitting even close to killing
strength—but that was mostly from lack of practice. If—

"*Hold, damn your eyes!*"

Long habit froze them both in position, and the armsmaster of Forst Reach stalked onto the field, fire in his
bloodshot glare.

Jervis looked the two of them up and down while Vanyel sweated from more than exertion. The blond, crag-
faced mercenary frowned, and Vanyel's mouth went dry.
Jervis looked angry—and when Jervis was angry, it was
generally Vanyel who suffered.

"Well—" the man croaked after long enough for Vanyel's dread of him to build up to full force. "—learning a new discipline, are we? *And whose idea was this?*"

"Mine, sir," Vanyel whispered.

"Might have guessed sneak-and-run would be more suited to *you* than an honest fight," the armsmaster sneered. "Well, and how did you do, my bright young lord?"

"He did all right, Jervis." To Vanyel's complete amazement Radevel spoke up for him. "I couldn't get a blow on 'im. An' if he'd put his weight behind it, he'd have laid me out a time or two."

"So you're a real hero against a half-grown boy. I'll just bet you feel like another Veth Krethen, don't you?" Jervis spat. Vanyel held his temper, counting to ten, and did *not* protest that Radevel was nearly double his size and certainly no "half-grown boy." Jervis glared at him, waiting for a retort that never came—and strangely, that seemed to anger Jervis even more.

"All right, *hero,*" he snarled, taking Radevel's blade away and jamming the boy's helm down over his own head. "Let's see just how good you really are—"

Jervis charged without any warning, and Vanyel had to scramble to get out of the way of the whirling blade. He realized then that Jervis was coming for him all-out—as if Vanyel was wearing full armor.

Which he wasn't.

He pivoted desperately as Jervis came at him again; ducked, wove, and spun—and saw an opening. This time desperation gave him the strength he hadn't used against Radevel—and he scored a chest-stab that actually rocked Jervis back for a moment, and followed it with a good solid blow to the head.

He waited, heart in mouth, while the armsmaster staggered backward two or three steps, then shook his head to clear it. There was an awful silence—

Then Jervis yanked off the helm, and there was nothing but rage on his face.

"Radevel, get the boys, then bring me Lordling Vanyel's arms and armor," the armsmaster said, in a voice that was deadly calm.

Radevel backed off the field, then turned and ran for

the keep. Jervis paced slowly to within a few feet of Vanyel, and Vanyel nearly died of fear on the spot.

"So you like striking from behind, hmm?" he said in that same, deadly quiet voice. "I think maybe I've been a bit lax in teaching you about honor, young milord." A thin smile briefly sliced across his face. "But I think we can remedy that quickly enough."

Radevel approached with feet dragging, his arms loaded with the rest of Vanyel's equipment.

"Arm up," Jervis ordered, and Vanyel did not dare to disobey.

Exactly what Jervis said, then—other than dressing Vanyel down in front of the whole lot of them, calling him a coward and a cheat, an assassin who wouldn't stand still to face his opponent's blade with honor—Vanyel could never afterward remember. Only a haze of mingled fear and anger that made the words meaningless.

But then Jervis took Vanyel on. His way, his style.

It was a hopeless fight from the beginning, even if Vanyel had been *good* at this particular mode of combat. In moments Vanyel found himself flat on his back, trying to see around spots in front of his eyes, with his ears still ringing from a blow he hadn't even seen coming.

"Get up," Jervis said—

Five more times Vanyel got up, each time more slowly. Each time, he tried to yield. By the fourth time he was wit-wandering, dazed and groveling. And Jervis refused to accept his surrender even when he could barely gasp out the words.

Radevel had gotten a really bad feeling in his stomach from the moment he saw Jervis' face when Van scored on him. He'd never seen the old bastard that angry in all the time he'd been fostered here.

But he'd figured that Vanyel was just going to get a bit of a thrashing. He'd *never* figured on being an unwilling witness to a deliberate—

—massacre. That was all he could think it. Van was no match for Jervis, and Jervis was coming at him all out—like he was a trained, adult fighter. Even Radevel could see that.

He heaved a sigh of relief when Vanyel was knocked flat on his back, and mumbled out his surrender as soon as he could speak. The worst the poor little snot had gotten was a few bruises.

But when Jervis had refused to accept that surrender—when he beat at Van with the flat of his blade until the boy *had* to pick up sword and shield just to get the beating to stop—Radevel got that bad feeling again.

And it got worse. Five times more Jervis knocked him flat, and each time with what looked like an even more vicious strike.

But the sixth time Vanyel was laid out, he *couldn't* get up.

Jervis let fly with a blow that broke the wood and copper shield right in the middle—and to Radevel's horror, he saw when the boy fell back that Vanyel's shield arm had been broken in half; the lower arm was bent in the middle, and that could only mean that both bones had snapped. It was pure miracle that they hadn't gone through muscle and skin—

And Jervis' eyes were *still* not what Radevel would call sane.

Radevel added up all the factors and came up with one answer: get Lissa. She was adult-rank, she was Van's protector, and no matter what the armsmaster said in justification for beating the crud out of Van, if Jervis laid one finger in anger on Lissa, he'd get thrown out of the Keep with both *his* arms broken. If Withen didn't do it, there were others who liked Liss a lot who would.

Radevel backed off the field and took to his heels as soon as he was out of sight.

Vanyel lay flat on his back again, breath knocked out of him, in a kind of shock in which he couldn't feel much of anything except—except that something was wrong, somewhere. Then he tried to get up—and pain shooting along his left arm sent him screaming into darkness.

When he came to, Lissa was bending over him, her horsey face tight with worry. She was pale, and the nostrils of that prominent Ashkevron nose flared like a frightened filly's.

"Don't move—Van, no—both the bones of your arm are broken." She was *kneeling* next to him, he realized, with one knee gently but firmly holding his left arm down so that he couldn't move it.

"Lady, get away from him—" Jervis' voice dripped boredom and disgust. "It's just his shield arm, nothing important. We'll just strap it to a board and put some liniment on it and he'll be fine—"

She didn't move her knees, but swung around to face Jervis so fast that her braid came loose and whipped past Vanyel's nose like a lash. "*You* have done quite enough for one day, Master Jervis," she snarled. "I think you forget your place."

Vanyel wished vacantly that he could see Jervis' face at that moment. It must surely be a sight.

But his arm began to *hurt*—and that was more than enough to keep his attention.

There wasn't usually a Healer at Forst Reach, but Vanyel's Aunt Serina was staying here with her sister during her pregnancy. She'd had three miscarriages already, and was taking no chances; she was attended by her very own Healer. And Lissa had seen to it that the *Healer,* not Jervis, was the one that dealt with Vanyel's arm.

"Oh, Van—" Lissa folded herself inelegantly on the edge of Vanyel's bed and sighed. "*How* did you manage to get into this mess?"

That beaky Ashkevron nose and her determined chin combined with her anxiety to make her look like a stubborn, mulish mare. Most people were put off by her appearance, but Vanyel knew her well enough to read the heartsick worry in her eyes. After all, she'd all but raised him.

Vanyel wasn't certain how clear he'd be, but he tried to explain. Lissa tucked up her legs, and rested her chin on her knees, an unladylike pose that would have evoked considerable distress from Lady Treesa. When he finished, she sighed again.

"I think you attract bad luck, that's all I can say. You don't do anything *wrong,* but somehow things seem to happen to you."

Vanyel licked his dry lips and blinked at her. "Liss—Jervis was really *angry* this time, and what you told him didn't help. He's going to go right to Father, if he isn't there already."

She shook her head. "I shouldn't have said that, should I? Van, all I was thinking about was getting him away from you."

"I—I know Liss, I'm not blaming you, but—"

"But I made him mad. Well, I'll see if I can get to Father before Jervis does, but even if I do he probably won't listen to me. I'm just a female, after all."

"I know." He closed his eyes as the room began to swing. "Just—try, Liss—please."

"I will." She slipped off the bed, then bent over and kissed his forehead. "Try and sleep, like the Healer told you, all right?"

He nodded.

Tough-minded and independent, like the grandmother who had raised *her,* Lissa was about the only one in the keep willing to stand up to Lord Withen now that Grandmother Ashkevron had passed on. Not surprising, that, given Grandmother. The Ashkevrons seemed to produce about one strong-willed female in every generation, much to the bemusement of the Ashkevron males, and the more compliant Ashkevron females.

Lady Treesa (anything but independent) had been far too busy with pregnancy and all the vapors she indulged in when pregnant to have anything to do with the resulting offspring. They went to the hands of others until they were old enough to be usefully added to *her* entourage. Lissa went to Grandmother.

But Vanyel went to Liss. And they loved each other from the moment she'd taken him out of the nursery. She'd stand up to a raging lion for his sake.

So Lissa went in search of their father. Unfortunately that left him alone. And unfortunately Lissa didn't return when she couldn't immediately find Lord Withen. And that, of course, left him vulnerable when his father chose to descend on him like the god of thunders.

Vanyel was dizzy with pain as well as with the medicines the Healer had made him drink when Lord Withen

stormed into his tiny, white-plastered room. He was lying
flat on his back in his bed, trying not to move, and still
the room seemed to be reeling around him. The pain was
making him nauseous, and all he wanted was to be left
in peace. The very last thing he wanted to see was his
lord father.

And Withen barely gave him enough time to register
that his father was *there* before laying into him.

"What's all this about your cheating?" Withen roared,
making Vanyel wince and wish he dared to cover his ears.
"By the gods, you whelp, I ought to break your other
arm for you!"

"I *wasn't* cheating!" Vanyel protested, stung, his voice
breaking at just the wrong moment. He tried to sit upright—which only made the room spin the more. He fell
back, supporting himself on his good elbow, grinding his
teeth against the pain of his throbbing arm.

"I was," he gasped through clenched teeth, "I was
just doing what Seldasen said to do!"

"And just who might this 'Seldasen' be?" his father
growled savagely, his dark brows knitting together.
"What manner of coward says to run about and strike
behind a man's back, eh?"

Oh, gods—now what have I done? Though his head
was spinning, Vanyel tried to remember if Herald Seldasen's treatise on warfare and tactics had been one of
the books he'd "borrowed" without leave, or one of the
ones he was *supposed* to be studying.

"*Well?*" When Lord Withen scowled, his dark hair
and beard made him look positively demonic. The drugs
seemed to be giving him an aura of angry red light, too.

Father, why can't you ever *believe* I *might be in the
right?*

The book *was* on the "approved" list, Vanyel remembered with relief, as he recalled his tutor Istal assigning
certain chapters to be memorized. "It's *Herald* Seldasen,
Father," he said defiantly, finding strength in rebellion.
"It's from a book Istal assigned me, about tactics." The
words he remembered strengthened him still more, and
he threw them into his father's face. "He said: 'Let every
man that must go to battle fight within his talents, and

not be forced to any one school. Let the agile man use his speed, let his armoring be light, and let him skirmish, but not close with the enemy. Let the heavy man stand shoulder to shoulder with his comrades in the shield wall, that the enemy may not break through. Let the small man of good eye make good use of the bow, aye, and let the Herald fight with his mind and not his body, let the Herald-Mage combat with magic and not the sword. *And let no man be called coward for refusing the place for which he is not fit.'* And I didn't *once* hit anybody from behind! If Jervis says I did—well—I *didn't!'*

Lord Withen stared at his eldest son, his mouth slack with surprise. For one moment Vanyel actually thought he'd gotten through to his father, who was more accustomed to hearing him quote poetry than military history.

"Parrot some damned book at me, will you?" Lord Withen snarled, dashing Vanyel's hopes. "And what does some damned lowborn Herald know about fighting? You *listen* to me, boy—you are my heir, my firstborn, and you *damned* well better learn what Jervis has to teach you if you want to sit in my place when I'm gone! If he says you were cheating, then by *damn* you were cheating!"

"But I *wasn't* cheating and I don't *want* your place—" Vanyel protested, the drugs destroying his self-control and making him say things he'd sooner have kept behind his teeth.

That stopped Lord Withen cold. His father stared at him as if he'd gone mad, grown a second head, or spoken in Karsite.

"Great good *gods,* boy," he managed to splutter after several icy eternities during which Vanyel waited for the roof to cave in. "What *do* you want?"

"I—" Vanyel began. And stopped. If he told Withen that what he wanted was to be a Bard—

"You ungrateful whelp—you will learn what I *tell* you to learn, and do what I *order* you to do! You're my heir and you'll do your duty to me and to this holding if I have to see you half dead to get you to do it!"

And with that, he stormed out, leaving Vanyel limp

with pain and anger and utter dejection, his eyes clamped
tight against the tears he could feel behind them.

*Oh, gods, what does he expect of me? Why can't I ever
please him? What do I have to do to convince him that I
can't be what he wants me to be? Die?*

*And now—now my hand, oh, gods, it hurts—how much
damage did they do to it? Am I ever going to be able to
play anything right again?*

"Heyla, Van—"

He opened his eyes, startled by the sound of a voice.

His door was cracked partway open; Radevel peered
around the edge of it, and Vanyel could hear scuffling
and whispers behind him.

"You all right?"

"No," Vanyel replied, suspiciously.

What the hell does he want?

Radevel's bushy eyebrows jumped like a pair of excited
caterpillars. "Guess not. Bet it hurts."

"It hurts," Vanyel said, feeling a sick and sullen anger
burning in the pit of his stomach.

*You watched it happen. And you didn't do anything to
stop it, cousin. And you didn't bother to defend me to
Father, either. None of you did.*

Radevel, instead of being put off, inched a little farther
into the room. "Hey," he said, brightening, "you should
have seen it! I mean, *whack,* an' that whole shield just
split—an' you fell down an' that arm—"

"*Will you go to hell?*" Vanyel snarled, just about ready
to kill him. "And you can take all those ghouls lurking
out there with you!"

Radevel jumped, looked shocked, then looked faintly
offended.

Vanyel didn't care. All that mattered was that Radevel—and whoever else was out there—took themselves
away.

Left finally alone, Vanyel drifted into an uneasy slumber, filled with fragmented bits of unhappy dreams. When
he woke again, his mother was supervising the removal
of his younger brother Mekeal and all Mekeal's belongings from the room.

Well, that was a change. Lady Treesa usually didn't

interest herself in any of her offspring unless she had
something to gain from it. On the other hand, Vanyel had
been a part of her little court since the day he'd evidenced
real talent at music about five years ago. She wouldn't
want to lose her own private minstrel—which meant she'd
best make certain he healed up all right.

"I won't have you racketing about," she was whispering to Mekeal with unconcealed annoyance on her plump,
pretty face. "I won't have you keeping him awake when
he should be sleeping, and I won't have you getting in
the Healer's way."

Thirteen-year-old Mekeal, a slightly shrunken copy of
his father, shrugged indifferently. " 'Bout time we went
to bachelor's hall anyway, milady," he replied, as Lady
Treesa turned to keep an eye on him. "Can't say as *I'll*
miss the caterwauling an' the plunking."

Although Vanyel could only see his mother's back, he
couldn't miss the frown in her voice. "It wouldn't hurt
you to acquire a bit of Vanyel's polish, Mekeal," Lady
Treesa replied.

Mekeal shrugged again, quite cheerfully. "Can't make
silk out 'o wool, Lady Mother." He peered through
dancing candlelight at Vanyel's side of the room. "Seems
m'brother's awake. Heyla, peacock, they're movin' me
down t' quarters; seems you get up here to yourself."

"Out!" Treesa ordered; and Mekeal took himself off
with a heartless chuckle.

Vanyel spent the next candlemark with Treesa fussing
and weeping over him; indulging herself in the histrion-
ics she seemed to adore. In a way it was as hard to deal
with as Withen's rage. He'd never been on the receiving
end of her vapors before.

Oh, gods, he kept thinking confusedly, *please make
her go away. Anywhere, I don't care.*

He had to keep assuring her that he was going to be
all right when he was not at all certain of that himself,
and Treesa's shrill, borderline hysteria set his nerves
completely on edge. It was a decided relief when the
Healer arrived again and gently chased her out to give
him some peace.

The next few weeks were nothing but a blur of pain

and potions—a blur endured with one or another of his mother's ladies constantly at his side. And they all flustered at him until he was ready to scream, including his mother's maid, Melenna, who should have known better. It was like being nursemaided by a covey of agitated doves. When they weren't worrying at him, they were preening at him. *Especially* Melenna.

"Would you like me to get you a pillow?" Melenna cooed.

"No," Vanyel replied, counting to ten. Twice.

"Can I get you something to drink?" She edged a little closer, and leaned forward, batting her eyelashes at him.

"No," he said, closing *his* eyes. "Thank you."

"Shall I—"

"No!" he growled, not sure which was worse at this moment, the pounding of his head, or Melenna's questions. At least the pounding didn't have to be accompanied by Melenna's questions.

Sniff.

He cracked an eyelid open, just enough to see her. She sniffed again, and a fat tear rolled down one cheek.

She was a rather pretty little thing, and the only one of his mother's ladies *or* maidservants who had managed to pick up Treesa's knack of crying without going red and blotchy. Vanyel knew that both Mekeal and Radevel had tried to get into her bed more than once. He also knew that she had her heart set on him.

And the thought of bedding her left him completely cold.

She sniffed a little harder. A week ago he would have sighed, and apologized to her, and allowed her to do something for him. Anything, just to keep her happy.

That was a week ago. Now— *It's just a game for her, a game she learned from Mother. I'm tired of playing it. I'm sick to death of all their games.*

He ignored her, shutting his eyes and praying for the potions to work. And finally they did, which at least gave him a rest from her company for a little while.

"Van?"

That voice would bring him out of a sound sleep, let

alone the restless drug-daze he was in now. He struggled up out of the grip of fever-dreams to force his eyes open.

Lissa was sitting on the edge of his bed, dressed in riding leathers.

"Liss—?" he began, then realized what *riding leathers* meant. "—oh, gods—"

"Van, I'm sorry, I didn't want to leave you, but Father said it was now or never." She was crying; not prettily like Lady Treesa, but with blotched cheeks and bloodshot eyes. "Van, please say you don't mind too much!"

"It's . . . all right, Liss," he managed, fighting the words out around the cold lump in his throat and the colder one in his gut. "I . . . know. You've got to do this. Gods, Liss, *one* of us has to get away!"

"Van—I—I'll find some way to help you, I promise. I'm almost eighteen; I'm almost free. Father *knows* the Guard is the only place for me; he hasn't had a marriage offer for me for two years. He doesn't dare ruin my chances for a post, or he'll be stuck with me. The gods know you're safe enough *now*—if anybody dared do anything before the Healer says you're fit, he'd make a protest to Haven. Maybe by the time you get the splints off, I'll be able to find a way to have you with me. . . ."

She looked so hopeful that Vanyel didn't have the heart to say anything to contradict her. "Do that, Liss. I—I'll be all right."

She hugged him, and kissed him, and then left him.

And *then* he turned to the wall and cried. Lissa was the only support he had had. The only person who loved him without reservations. And now she was gone.

After that, he stopped even pretending to care about anything. They didn't care enough about him to let Liss stay until he was well—so why should he care about anything or anyone, even enough to be polite?

"Armor does more than protect; it conceals. Helms hide faces—and your opponent becomes a mystery, an enigma."

Seldasen had that *right. Just like those two down there.*

The cruel, blank stares of the helm-slits gave no clues to the minds within. The two opponents drew their blades, flashed identical salutes, and retreated exactly twenty paces each to end at the opposite corners of the field. The sun was straight overhead, their shadows little more than pools at their feet. Twelve restive armored figures fidgeted together on one side of the square. The harsh sunshine bleached the short, dead grass to the color of light straw, and lit everything about the pair in pitiless detail.

Hmm. Not such enigmas once they move.

One fighter was tall, dangerously graceful, and obviously well-muscled beneath the protection of his worn padding and shabby armor. Every motion he made was precise, perilous—and professional.

The other was a head shorter. His equipment was new, the padding unfrayed, the metal lovingly burnished. But his movements were awkward, uncertain, perhaps fearful.

Still, if he feared, he didn't lack for courage. Without waiting for his man to make a move, he shouted a tremulous defiant battle cry and charged across the sun-burnt grass toward the tall fighter. As his boots thudded on the hard, dry ground, he brought his sword around in a low-line attack.

The taller fighter didn't even bother to move out of his way; he simply swung his scarred shield to the side. The sword crunched into the shield, then slid off, metal screeching on metal. The tall fighter swept his shield back into guard position, and answered the blow with a return that rang true on the shield of his opponent, then rebounded, while he turned the momentum of the rebound into a cut at the smaller fighter's head.

The pale stone of the keep echoed the sound of the exchange, a racket like a madman loose in a smithy. The smaller fighter was driven back with every blow, giving ground steadily under the hammerlike onslaught—until he finally lost his footing and fell over backward, his sword flying out of his hand.

There was a dull *thud* as he hit his head on the flinty, unforgiving ground.

He lay flat on his back for a moment, probably seeing stars, and scarcely moving, arms flung out on either side of him as if he meant to embrace the sun. Then he shook his head dazedly and tried to get up—

Only to find the point of his opponent's sword at his throat.

"Yield, Boy," rumbled a harsh voice from the shadowed mouth-slit of the helmet. "Yield, or I run you through."

The smaller fighter pulled off his own helm to reveal that he was Vanyel's cousin Radevel. "If you run me through, Jervis, who's going to polish your mail?"

The point of the sword did not waver.

"Oh, all right," the boy said, with a rueful grin. "I yield."

The sword, a pot-metal practice blade, went back into its plain leather sheath. Jervis pulled off his own battered helm with his shield hand, as easily as if the weight of wood and bronze wasn't there. He shook out his sweat-dampened, blond hair and offered the boy his right, pulling him to his feet with the same studied, precise movements as he'd used when fighting.

"Next time, you yield immediately, Boy," the arms-master rumbled, frowning. "If your opponent's in a hurry, he'll take banter for refusal, and you'll be a cold corpse."

Jervis did not even wait to hear Radevel's abashed assent. "You—on the end—Mekeal." He waved to Vanyel's brother at the side of the practice field. "Helm up."

Vanyel snorted as Jervis jammed his own helm back on his head, and stalked back to his former position, dead center of the practice ground. "The rest of you laggards," he growled, "let's see some life there. Pair up and have at."

Jervis doesn't have pupils, he has living targets, thought Vanyel, as he watched from the window. *There isn't anyone except Father who could even give him a workout, yet he goes straight for the throat every damned time; he gets nastier every day. About all he does give them is that he only hits half force. Which is still enough to set Radev on his rump. Bullying bastard.*

Vanyel leaned back on his dusty cushions, and forced his aching hand to run through the fingering exercise yet again. Half the lute strings plunked dully instead of ringing; both strength and agility had been lost in that hand.

I am never going to get this right again. How can I, when half the time I can't feel what I'm doing?

He bit his lip, and looked down again, blinking at the sunlight winking off Mekeal's helm four stories below. *Every one of them will be moaning and plastering horse liniment on his bruises tonight, and boasting in the next breath about how long he lasted against Jervis this time. Thank you, no. Not I. One broken arm was enough. I prefer to see my sixteenth birthday with the rest of my bones intact.*

This tiny tower room where Vanyel always hid himself when summoned to weapons practice was another legacy of Grandfather Joserlin's crazy building spree. It was Vanyel's favorite hiding place, and thus far, the most secure; a storage room just off the library. The only conventional access was through a tiny half-height door at the back of the library—but the room had a window—a window on the same side of the keep as the window of Vanyel's own attic-level room. Any time he wanted, Vanyel could climb easily out of his bedroom, edge along the slanting roof, and climb into that narrow window, even in the worst weather or the blackest night. The hard part was doing it unseen.

An odd wedge-shaped nook, this room was all that was left of the last landing of the staircase to the top floor—an obvious change in design, since the rest of the staircase had been turned into a chimney and the hole where the roof trapdoor had been now led to the chimney pot. But that meant that although there was no fireplace in the storeroom itself, the room stayed comfortably warm in the worst weather because of the chimney wall.

Not once in all the time Vanyel had taken to hiding here had anything new been added to the clutter or anything been sought for. Like many another of the old lord's eccentricities, its inaccessibility made it easy to ignore.

Which was fine, so far as Vanyel was concerned. He had his instruments up here—two of which he wasn't even supposed to own, the harp and the gittern—and any time he liked he could slip into the library to purloin a book.

At the point of the room he had an old chair to sprawl in, a collection of candle ends on a chest beside it so that he could read when the light was bad. His instruments were all safe from the rough hands and pranks of his brothers, and he could practice without anyone disturbing him.

He had arranged a set of old cushions by the window so that he could watch his brothers and cousins getting trounced all over the moat while he played—or tried to play. It afforded a ghost of amusement, sometimes. The gods knew he had little enough to smile about.

It was lonely—but Vanyel was always lonely, since Lissa had gone. It was bloody awkward to get to—but he couldn't hide in his room.

Though he hadn't found out until he'd healed up, the rest of his siblings and cousins had gone down to bachelor's hall with Mekeal while he'd been recovering from that broken arm. He hadn't, even when the Healer had taken the splints off. His brothers slandered his lute playing when they'd gone, telling his father they were just as happy for Vanyel to have his own room if he wanted to stay up there. Probably Withen, recalling how near the hall was to his own quarters, had felt the same. Vanyel didn't care; it meant that the room was his, and his alone—one scant bit of comfort.

His other place of refuge, his mother's solar, was no longer the retreat it had been. It was too easy for him to be found there, and there were other disadvantages lately; his mother's ladies and fosterlings had taken to flirting with him. He enjoyed that, too, up to a point—but they kept wanting to take it beyond the range of the game of courtly love to the romantic, for which he *still* wasn't ready. And Lady Treesa kept encouraging them at it.

Jervis drove Mekeal back, step by step. *Fools*, Vanyel thought scornfully, forcing his fingers through the exercise in time with Jervis' blows. *They must be mad, to let that sour old man make idiots out of them, day after day—maybe break their skulls, just like he broke my arm!* Anger tightened his mouth, and the memory of the shuttered satisfaction he'd seen in Jervis' eyes the first time Vanyel had encountered him after the "accident" roiled in his stomach. *Damn that bastard, he* meant *to break my arm, I* know *he did; he's good enough to judge any blow he deals to within a hair.*

At least he had a secure hiding place; secure because getting into it took nerve, and neither Jervis, nor his father, nor any of the rest of them would ever have put him and a climb across the roof together in the same thought—even if they remembered the room existed.

The ill-assorted lot below didn't look to be relatives; the Ashkevron cousins had all gone meaty when they hit adolescence; big-boned, muscled like plow horses—

—*and about as dense*—

—but Withen's sons were growing straight up as well as putting on bulk.

Vanyel was the only one of the lot taking after his mother.

Withen seemed to hold *that* to be his fault, too.

Vanyel snorted as Mekeal took a blow to the helm that sent him reeling backward. *That one should shake up his brains! Serves him right, too, carrying on about what a great warrior he's going to be. Clod-headed beanpole. All he can think about is hacking people to bits for the sake of "honor."*

Glorious war, hah. Fool can't see beyond the end of his nose. For all that prating, if he ever saw *a battlefield he'd wet himself.*

Not that *Vanyel* had ever seen a real battlefield, but he was the possessor of a far more vivid imagination than anyone else in his family. He had no trouble in visualizing what those practice blades *would* be doing if they were real. And he had no difficulty at all in imagining the "deadlie woundes" of the ballads being inflicted on *his* body.

Vanyel paid close attention to his lessons, if not to weapons work. He knew *all* of the history ballads and unlike the rest of his peers, he knew the parts about what happened *after* the great battles as well—the lists of the dead, the dying, the maimed. It hadn't escaped his notice that when you added up those lists, the totals were a lot higher than the number of heroes who survived.

Vanyel knew damned well which list *he'd* be on if it

ever came to armed conflict. He'd learned his lesson only too well: why even try?

Except that every time he turned around Lord Withen was delivering another lecture on his duty to the hold.

Gods. I'm just as much a brute beast of burden as any donkey in the stables! Duty. That's bloody all I hear, he thought, staring out the window, but no longer seeing what lay beyond the glass. *Why me? Mekeal would be a thousand times better Lord Holder than me, and he'd just love it! Why couldn't I have gone with Lissa?*

He sighed and put the lute aside, reaching inside his tunic for the scrap of parchment that Trevor Corey's page had delivered to *him* after he'd given Lissa's "official" letters into Treesa's hands.

He broke the seal on it, and smoothed out the palimpsest carefully; clever Lissa to have filched the scraped and stained piece that no one would notice was gone! She'd used a good, strong ink though; even though the letters were a bit blurred, he had no trouble reading them.

Dearest Vanyel; if only you were here! I can't tell you how much I miss you. The Corey girls are quite sweet, but not terribly bright. A lot like the cousins, really. I know I should have written you before this, but I didn't have much of a chance. Your arm should be better now. If only Father wasn't so blind! What I'm learning is exactly what we were working out together.

Vanyel took a deep breath against the surge of anger at Withen's unreasonable attitude.

But we both know how he is, so don't argue with him, love. Just do what you're told. It won't be forever, really it won't. Just—hold on. I'll do what I can from this end. Lord Corey is a lot more reasonable than Father ever was and maybe I can get him talked into asking for you. Maybe that will work. Just be really good, and maybe Father will be happy enough with you to do that. Love, Liss.

He folded the letter and tucked it away. *Oh, Liss. Not a chance. Father would* never *let me go there, not after the way I've been avoiding my practices. "It won't be forever," hmm? I suppose* that's right. *I probably won't live past the next time Jervis manages to catch up with me. Gods. Why is it that nobody ever asks me what I want—or when they do ask, why can't they mean it and listen to me?*

He blinked, and looked again at the little figures below, still pounding away on each other, like so many tent pegs determined to drive each other into the ground.

He turned restlessly away from the window, stood up, and replaced the lute in the makeshift stand he'd contrived for it beside his other two instruments.

And everywhere I turn I get the same advice. From Liss—"don't fight, do what Father asks." From Mother—crying, vapors, and essentially the same thing. She's not exactly stupid; if she really cared about me, she could manage Father somehow. But she doesn't care—not when backing me against Father is likely to cost her something. And when I tried to tell Father Leren about what Jervis was really like—

He shuddered. *The lecture about filial duty was bad enough—but the one about "proper masculine behavior"—you'd have thought I'd been caught fornicating sheep! And all because I objected to having my bones broken. It's like I'm doing something wrong somewhere, but no one will tell me what it is and why it's wrong! I thought maybe Father Leren would understand since he's a priest, but gods, there's no help coming from that direction.*

For a moment he felt trapped up here; the secure retreat turned prison. He didn't dare go out, or he'd be caught and forced into that despised armor—and Jervis would lay into him with a vengeful glee to make up for all the practices he'd managed to avoid. He looked wistfully beyond the practice field to the wooded land and meadows beyond. It was such a beautiful day; summer was just beginning, and the breeze blowing in his open window was heady with the aroma of the hayfields in the sun. He longed to be out walking or riding beneath those trees; he was as trapped by the things he didn't dare do as by the ones he had to.

Tomorrow I'll have to go riding out with Father on his rounds, he gloomed, *And no getting out of that. He'll have me as soon as I come down for breakfast.*

That was a new torment, added since he'd recovered.
It was nearly as bad as being under Jervis' thumb. He
shuddered, thinking of all those farmers, staring, staring—like they were trying to stare into his soul. This was
not going to be a pleasure jaunt, for all that he loved to
ride. No, he would spend the entire day listening to his
father lecture him on the duties of the Lord Holder to the
tenants who farmed for him and the peasant-farmers who
held their lands under his protection and governance. But
that was not the worst aspect of the ordeal.

It was the people themselves; the way they measured
him with their eyes, opaque eyes full of murky thoughts
that he could not read. Eyes that expected everything of
him; that *demanded* things of him that he did not want
to give, and didn't know how to give even if he had
wanted to.

I don't want *them looking to me like that! I don't* want
to be responsible for their lives! He shuddered again. *I
wouldn't know what to do in a drought or an invasion,
and what's more, I don't care! Gods, they make my skin
crawl, all those—people, eating me alive with their eyes—*

He turned away from the window, and knelt beside his
instruments; stretched out his hand, and touched the
smooth wood, the taut strings. *Oh, gods—if I weren't
me—if I could just have a* chance *to be a Bard—*

In the days before his arm had been hurt he had often
imagined himself a Court Bard, not in some out-of-the-
way corner like Forst Reach, but one of the Great Courts;
Gyrefalcon's Marches or Southron Keep. Or even the
High Court of Valdemar at Haven. Imagined himself the
center of a circle of admirers, languid ladies and jewel-
bedecked lords, all of them hanging enraptured on every
word of his song. He could let his imagination transport
him to a different life, the life of his dreams. He could
actually see himself surrounded, not by the girls of Treesa's bower, but by the entire High Court of Valdemar,
from Queen Elspeth down, until the visualization was
more real than his true surroundings. He could see, hear,
feel, all of them waiting in impatient anticipation for him
to sing—the bright candles, the perfume, the pregnant
silence—

Now even that was lost to him. Now practices were solitary, for there was no Lissa to listen to new tunes. Lissa had been a wonderful audience; she had a good ear, and knew enough about music to be trusted to tell him the truth. She had been the only person in the keep besides Treesa who didn't seem to think there was something faintly shameful about his obsession with music. And she was the only one who knew of his dream of becoming a Bard.

There were no performances before his mother's ladies, either, because he refused to let them hear him fumble.

And all because of the lying, bullying bastard his father had made armsmaster—

"Withen—"

He froze; startled completely out of his brooding by the sound of his mother's breathless, slightly shrill voice just beyond the tiny door to the library. He knelt slowly and carefully, avoiding the slightest noise. The *last* thing he wanted was to have his safe hiding place discovered!

"Withen, what *is* it you've dragged me up here to tell me that you couldn't have said in my solar?" she asked. Vanyel could tell by the edge in her voice that she was ruffled and not at all pleased.

Vanyel held his breath, and heard the sound of the library door being closed, then his father's heavy footsteps crossing the library floor.

A long, ponderous silence. Then, "I'm sending Vanyel away," Withen said, brusquely.

"*What?*" Treesa shrilled. "You—how—where—*why?* In the gods' names, Withen, *why?*"

Vanyel felt as if someone had turned his heart into stone, and his body into clay.

"I can't do anything with the boy, Treesa, and neither can Jervis," Withen growled. "I'm sending him to someone who can make something of him."

"You can't do anything because the two of you seem to think to 'make something of him' you have to force him to be something he can never be!" Treesa's voice was muffled by the intervening wall, but the note of hys-

teria was plain all the same. "You put him out there with
a man twice his weight and expect him to—"

"To behave like a man! He's a sniveler, a whiner,
Treesa. He's more worried about damage to his pretty
face and delicate little hands than damage to his honor,
and you don't help matters by making him the pet of the
bower. Treesa, the boy's become nothing more than a
popinjay, a vain little peacock—and worse than that, he's
a total coward."

"A *coward!* Gods, Withen—only *you* would say that!"
Lady Treesa's voice was thick with scorn. "Just because
he's too clever to let that precious *armsmaster* of yours
beat him insensible once a day!"

"So what does he do instead? Run off and hide because
once—just *once*—he got his poor little arm broken! Great
good gods, I'd broken every bone in my body at least
once by the time I was his age!"

"Is that supposed to signify virtue?" she scoffed. "Or
stupidity?"

Vanyel's mouth sagged open. *She's—my gods! She's
standing up to him! I don't believe this!*

"It signifies the willingness to endure a little discom-
fort in order to *learn*," Withen replied angrily. "Thanks
to you and your fosterlings, all Vanyel's ever learned was
how to select a tunic that matches his eyes, and how to
warble a love song! He's too damned handsome for his
own good—and you've spoiled him, Treesa; you've let
him trade on that pretty face, get away with nonsense and
arrogance you'd never have permitted in Mekeal. And
now he has no sense of responsibility whatsoever, he
avoids even a hint of obligation."

"You'd prefer him to be like Mekeal, I suppose," she
replied acidly. "You'd like him to hang on your every
word and never question you, never challenge you—"

"Damned right!" Withen roared in frustration. "The
boy doesn't know his damned place! Filling his head with
book-learned nonsense—"

"He doesn't know his *place?* Because he can think for
himself? Just because he can read and write more than
his bare name? *Unlike* certain grown men I could name—

gods, Withen, that priest of yours has you parroting every little nuance, doesn't he? And you're sending Van away because he doesn't measure up to *his* standards of propriety, aren't you? Because Vanyel has the intelligence to question what he's told, and Leren doesn't like questions!'' Her voice reached new heights of shrillness. ''That *priest* has you so neatly tied around his ankle that you wouldn't *breathe* unless he declared breathing was orthodox enough!''

—ah, Vanyel thought, a part of his mind still working, while the rest sat in stunned contemplation of the idea of being ''sent away.'' Now Treesa's support had a rational explanation. Lady Treesa did not care for Father Leren. Vanyel was just a convenient reason to try to drive a wedge between Withen and his crony.

Although Vanyel could have told her that this was *exactly* the wrong way to go about doing so.

''I expected you'd say something like that,'' Withen rumbled. ''You have no choice, Treesa, the boy is going, whether you like it or not. I'm sending him to Savil at the High Court. *She'll* brook no nonsense, and once he's in surroundings where he's not the only pretty face in the place he *might* learn to do something besides lisp a ballad and moon at himself in the mirror.''

''*Savil?* That old harridan?'' His mother's voice rose with each word until she was shrieking. Vanyel wanted to shriek, too.

He remembered his first—and last—encounter with his Aunt Savil only too well.

Vanyel had bowed low to the silver-haired stranger, a woman clad in impeccable Heraldic Whites, contriving his best imitation of courtly manner. Herald Savil—who had packed herself up at the age of fourteen and hied herself off to Haven without word to anyone, and then been Chosen the moment she passed the city gates—was Lissa's idol. Lissa had pestered Grandmother Ashkevron for every tale about Savil that the old woman knew. Vanyel couldn't understand *why*—but if Lissa admired this woman so much, surely there must be more to her than appeared on the surface.

It was a pity that Liss was visiting cousins the one week her idol chose to make an appearance at the familial holding.

But then again—maybe that was exactly as Withen had planned.

"So this is Vanyel," the woman had said, dryly. "A pretty boy, Treesa. I trust he's something more than ornamental."

Vanyel went rigid at her words, then rose from his bow and fixed her with what he hoped was a cool, appraising stare. Gods, she *looked* like his father in the right light; like Lissa, she had that Ashkevron nose, a nose that both she and Withen thrust forward like a sharp blade to cleave all before them.

"Oh, don't glare at me, child," the woman said with amusement. "I've had better men than you try to freeze me with a look and fail."

He flushed. She turned away from him as if he was of no interest, turning back to Vanyel's mother, who was clutching a handkerchief at her throat. "So, Treesa, has the boy shown any sign of Gift or Talent?"

"He sings beautifully," Treesa fluttered. "Really, he's as good as any minstrel we've ever had."

The woman turned and stared at him—stared through him. "Potential, but nothing active," Savil said slowly. "A pity; I'd hoped at least one of your offspring would share my Gifts. You can certainly afford to spare one to the Queen's service. But the girls don't even have potential Gifts, your four other boys are worse than this one, and this one doesn't appear to be much more than a clotheshorse for all his potential."

She waved a dismissing hand at him, and Vanyel's face had burned.

"I've seen what I came to see, Treesa," she said, leading Vanyel's mother off by the elbow. "I won't stress your hospitality anymore."

From all Vanyel had heard, Savil was, in many ways, not terribly unlike her brother; hard, cold, and unforgiving, preoccupied with what she perceived as her duty. She had never wedded; Vanyel was hardly surprised. He couldn't imagine *anyone* wanting to bed Savil's chill arrogance. He couldn't imagine why warm, loving Lissa wanted to be like her.

Now his mother was weeping hysterically; his father was making no effort to calm her. By that, Vanyel knew there was no escaping the disastrous plan. Incoherent hysterics were his mother's court of last resort; if *they* were failing, there was no hope for him.

"Give it up, Treesa," Withen said, unmoved, his voice rock-steady. "The boy goes. Tomorrow."

"You—unfeeling *monster*—" That was all that was understandable through Treesa's weeping. Vanyel heard the staccato beat of her slippers on the floor as she ran out the library door, then the slower, heavier sound of his father's boots. Then the sound of the door closing—

—as leaden and final as the door on a tomb.

Two

Vanyel stumbled over to his old chair and collapsed into its comfortable embrace.

He couldn't think. Everything had gone numb. He stared blankly at the tiny rectangle of blue sky framed by the window; just sat, and stared. He wasn't even aware of the passing of time until the sun began shining directly into his eyes.

He winced away from the light; that broke his bewildered trance, and he realized dully that the afternoon was gone—that someone would start looking for him to call him for supper soon, and he'd better be back in his room.

He slouched dispiritedly over to the window, and peered out of it, making the automatic check to see if there was anyone below who could spot him. But even as he did so it occurred to him that it hardly mattered if they found his hideaway, considering what he'd just overheard.

There was no one on the practice field now; just the empty square of turf, a chicken on the loose pecking at something in the grass. From this vantage the keep might well have been deserted.

Vanyel turned around and reached over his head, grabbing the rough stone edging the window all around the exterior, and levered himself up and out onto the sill. Once balanced there in a half crouch, he stepped down onto the ledge that ran around the edge of the roof, then reached around the gable and got a good handhold on the slates of the roof itself, and began inching over to his bedroom window.

Halfway between the two windows, he paused for a moment to look down.

It isn't all that far—if I fell just right, the worst I'd do is break a leg—then they couldn't send me off, could they? It might be worth it. It just might be worth it.

He thought about that—and thought about the way his broken arm had hurt—

Not a good idea; with my luck, Father would send me off as soon as I was patched up; just load me up in a wagon like a sack of grain. "Deliver to Herald Savil, no special handling." Or worse, I'd break my arm again, or both arms. I've got a chance to make that hand work again—maybe—but if I break it this time there isn't a Healer around to make sure it's set right.

Vanyel swung his legs into the room, balanced for a moment on the sill, then dropped onto his bed. Once there, he just lacked the spirit to even move. He slumped against the wall and stared at the sloping, whitewashed ceiling.

He tried to think if there was anything he could do to get himself out of this mess. He couldn't come up with a single idea that seemed at all viable. It was too late to "mend his ways" even if he wanted to.

No—no. I can't, absolutely can't face that sadistic bastard Jervis. Though I'm truly not sure which is the worst peril at this point in the long run, Aunt Ice-And-Iron or Jervis. I know what he'll do to me. I haven't a clue to her.

He sagged, and bit his lip, trying to stay in control, trying to think logically. *All* he knew was that Savil would have the worst possible report on him; and at Haven—the irony of the name!—he would have no allies, no hiding places. That was the worst of it; going off into completely foreign territory *knowing* that everybody there had been told how awful he was. That they would just be waiting for him to make a slip. All the time. But there was no getting out of it. For all that Treesa petted and cosseted him, Vanyel knew better than to rely on her for anything, or expect her to ever *defy* Withen. That brief flair during their argument had been the exception; Treesa's real efforts always lay in keeping her own life

comfortable and amusing. She'd cry for Vanyel, but she'd
never defend him. Not like Lissa might well have—

If Lissa had been here.

When the page came around to call everyone to dinner,
he managed to stir up enough energy to dust himself off
and obey the summons, but he had no appetite at all.

The highborn of Forst Reach ate late, a candlemark
after the servants, hirelings and the armsmen had eaten,
since the Great Hall was far too small to hold everyone
at once. The torches and lanterns had already been lit
along the worn stone-floored corridors; they did nothing
to dispel the darkness of Vanyel's heart. He trudged along
the dim corridors and down the stone stairs, ignoring the
servants trotting by him on errands of their own. Since
his room was at the servants' end of the keep, he had a
long way to go to get to the Great Hall.

Once there, he waited in the sheltering darkness of the
doorway to assess the situation in the room beyond.

As usual he was nearly the last one to table; as far as
he could tell, only his Aunt Serina was missing, and she
might well have eaten earlier, with the children. Carefully watching for the best opportunity to do so undetected, he slipped into his seat beside his brother Mekeal
at the low table during a moment when Lord Withen was
laughing at some joke of Father Leren's. The usually aus-
tere cleric seemed in a very good mood tonight, and Vanyel's heart sank. If Leren was pleased, it probably didn't
bode *Vanyel* any good.

"Where were *you* this afternoon?" Mekeal asked, as
he wiggled over to give Vanyel a place on the bench,
interrupting his noisy inhalation of soup.

Vanyel shrugged. "Does it matter?" he asked, trying
to sound indifferent. "It's no secret how I feel about that
nonsense, and it's no secret how Jervis feels about me.
So does it really matter where I was?"

Mekeal chuckled into his bowl. "Probably not. You
know Jervis'll just be harder on you when you do get
caught. And you're going to get caught one of these days.
You're looking for another broken arm, if you're lucky.
If that's the way you want it, on your head be it."

So Father hasn't said anything yet—Vanyel thought

with surprise, his spoon poised above the soup. He glanced over at the head table. Lady Treesa *was* in her accustomed place beside her lord. And she didn't look any more upset than she usually did; she certainly showed no signs of the hysterics Vanyel had overheard this afternoon.

Could she actually have stood up for me, just this once? Could she have gotten him to back down? Oh, gods, if only!

The renewal of hope did not bring a corresponding renewal of appetite; the tension only made his stomach knot up the more. The room seemed far too hot; he loosened the laces of his tunic, but that didn't help. The flames of the lamps on the wall behind him made the shadows dance on the table, until he had to close his eyes and take several deep breaths to get his equilibrium back. He felt flushed and feverish, and after only a few mouthfuls of the thick, swiftly cooling soup that seemed utterly tasteless, he signaled to a servant to take it away.

He squirmed uncomfortably on the wooden bench, and pushed the rest of his meal around on his plate with one eye always on the high table and his father. The high table *was* high; raised on a dais a good hand above the rest of the room, and set at the head of the low table like the upper bar of a "t." That meant that it overlooked and overshadowed the low table. Vanyel could feel the presence of those sitting there looming over him even at those few times when he *wasn't* watching them. With each course his stomach seemed to acquire another lump, a colder and harder one, until he finally gave up all pretense of eating.

Then, just at the dessert course, when he thought he might be saved, his father rose to his feet.

Lord Withen towered over the table as he towered over Vanyel and everything belonging to Forst Reach. He prided himself on being a "plain man," close enough in outlook to any of his men that they could feel easy with him. His sturdy brown leather tunic and linen shirt were hardly distinguishable from the garb of any of the hireling armsmen; the tunic was decorated with polished silver studs instead of copper, but that was the only token of his rank. The tunic strained across his broad shoulders—and across the barest hint of a paunch. His long, dark hair was confined in a tail at the nape of his neck by a silver band; his beard trimmed close to his square jawline.

Vanyel's changeling appearance, especially when contrasted with Mekeal's, may have been one reason why Withen seemed to be irritated whenever he looked at his eldest son. Vanyel was lean, and not particularly tall; Mekeal was tall and muscular, already taller than Vanyel although he was two years younger. Vanyel's hair was so black it had blue highlights, and his eyes were a startling silver-gray, exactly like his mother's—and he had no facial hair to speak of. Mekeal's eyes were a chestnut brown, he already had to shave, and his hair matched his father's so closely that it would not have been possible to tell which of them a particular plucked hair came from.

Mekeal made friends as easily as breathing—

I never had anyone but Lissa.

Mekeal was tone-deaf; Vanyel lived for music. Mekeal suffered through his scholastic lessons; Vanyel so far exceeded his brother that there was no comparison.

In short, Mekeal was completely his father's son; Vanyel was utterly Withen's opposite.

Perhaps that was all in Withen's mind as he rose and spared a glance for his first-and-second-born sons, before fixing his gaze on nothing in particular. The lanterns behind Withen danced, and his shadow reached halfway down the low table. As that stark shadow darkened the table, it blackened Vanyel's rising hope.

"After due consideration," Withen rumbled, "I have decided that it is time for Vanyel to acquire education of a kind—more involved than we can give him here. So tonight will be the last night he is among us. Tomorrow he will begin a journey to my sister, Herald-Mage Savil at the High Court of Valdemar, who will take official guardianship of him until he is of age."

Withen sat down heavily.

Treesa burst into a tearful wail, and shoved herself away from the table; as she stood, her chair went over with a clatter that sounded, in the unnatural silence that now filled the Great Hall, as loud as if the entire table were collapsing. She ran from the room, sobbing into her sleeve, as Withen maintained a stony silence. Her foster-lings and ladies followed her, and only Melenna cast an unreadable glance over her shoulder at Vanyel before trailing off in the wake of the others.

Everyone in the silent room seemed to have been frozen by an evil spell.

Finally Withen reached forward and took a walnut from the bowl before him; he nestled it in his palm and cracked it in his bare hands. Vanyel jumped at the sound, and he wasn't the only one.

"Very good nuts last year, don't you think?" Withen said to Father Leren.

That seemed to be the signal for the entire room to break out in frantic babbling. On Vanyel's right, three of his cousins began laying noisy bets on the outcome of a race between Radevel and Kerle on the morrow. On his right, Radevel whispered to Mekeal, while across the table from him his youngest brother Heforth exchanged punches and pokes with cousin Larence.

Vanyel was pointedly ignored. He might just as well have been invisible, except for the sly, sidelong looks he was getting. And not just from the youngsters, either. When he looked up at the high table once, he caught Father Leren staring at him and smiling slyly. When their eyes met, the priest nodded very slightly, gave Vanyel a look brimming with self-satisfaction, and only then turned his attention back toward Withen. During that silent exchange—which nobody else seemed to have noticed—Vanyel had felt himself grow pale and cold.

As the dessert course was cleared away, the elders left the hall on affairs of their own, and a few of the girls—more of Vanyel's cousins—returned; a sign that Lady Treesa had retired for the night.

The boys and young men remaining now rose from their seats; the young usually reigned over the hall undisturbed after dinner. With the girls that had returned they formed three whispering, giggling groups; two sets of four and one of eleven—all three groups blatantly clos-

ing Vanyel out. Even the girls seemed to have joined in
the conspiracy to leave him utterly alone.

Vanyel pretended not to notice the muttering, the jealous glances. He rose from the bench a few moments after
the rest had abandoned him, making it a point of honor
to saunter over to stare into the fire in the great fireplace.
He walked with head high, features schooled into a careful mask of bored indifference.

He could feel their eyes on the back of his neck, but
he refused to turn, refused to show any emotion at all,
much less how queasy their behavior was making him
feel.

Finally, when he judged that he had made his point,
he stretched, yawned, and turned. He surveyed the entire
room through half-closed eyelids for a long moment, his
own gaze barely brushing each of them, then paced lazily
across the endless length of the Great Hall, pausing only
to nod a cool good night to the group nearest the door
before—finally!—achieving the sanctuary of the dark
hallway beyond it.

"Ye gods, you'd think he was the Heir to the Throne!"
Sandar exclaimed, rolling his eyes and throwing up his
hands. "Queen Elspeth herself wouldn't put on such
airs!"

Eighteen-year-old Joserlin Corveau stared after the lad
for a long moment, putting his thoughts together. He was
the oldest of the fosterlings, and the latest-come. Really,
he wasn't properly a fosterling at all; nor a close cousin.
A true cousin, childless after many years, had decided
on Joserlin as his Heir and (as he himself was not in the
best of health) requested he be fostered to Lord Withen
to learn the ways of governance of one's Holdings. He
was broad and tall as any of the doors to the keep, and
even Jervis respected the power of his young muscles.
After a single practice session with young Jos, Jervis had
decreed that he was old enough to train with Withen's
armsmen. After seeing the way Jervis "trained" the boys,
Jos had been quite content to have it so.

Some of the younger boys had made the mistake of
thinking that his slow speech and large build meant that

he was stupid. They had quickly discovered their mistake when he'd gotten them with well-timed jokes.

He liked to say of himself that while he didn't think quickly, he *did* think things through all the way. And there were aspects of this vaguely disturbing evening that were not adding together properly in his mind.

Meanwhile the rest of his group continued dissecting Withen's least-beloved offspring.

"He thinks he *is* the Heir to the Throne," giggled Jyllian, swishing her skirts coquettishly. "Or at least, that the rest of us are that far below him. You should *see* him, lording it over us in the bower!" She struck her nose in the air and mimed looking down it while playing a make-believe lute. "But just *try* and get anything out of him besides a song! Brrr! Watch the snow fall! You'd think we were poison-vellis, the way he pulls away and goes cold!"

Mekeal snorted, tossing his head. "Thinks he's too good for you, I s'ppose! Nothing high enough for *him* but a lady of the blood-royal, no doubt! Think girls like you aren't lofty enough."

"Or not pretty enough," snickered Merthin. "Havens, give it a thought—none of you little lovelies are even a close match for His Majesty's sweet face. Can't have his lady less beautiful than *he* is, after all."

"I don't doubt." Larence put in his bit, coming up behind Merthin. "Well, he'll find he's not the only pretty face when he gets to the High Court. He *just* might find himself standing in somebody's shadow for a change! Take my word for it, dear little Vanyel is going to get a rude awakening when he gets to Haven."

"Dammit, it's not *fair*," Mekeal grumbled, face clouding at this reminder of Vanyel's destination. "I'd give my *arm* to go to Haven! I mean, think of it; the best fighters in the country are there—it's the center of everything!" He flung his hands wide, nearly hitting Merthin, in a gesture of total frustration. "How'm I ever going to get a—an officer's commission or any kind of position when nobody with any say at Court is ever going to see me? That's why they sent m'sister off to be fostered right near there! You have a chance to get *noticed* at Court!

She's going to be an officer, you can bet on it, an' best I'll ever get is *maybe* a Sector command, which means not one damn thing! I *need* to be at Court; I ain't going to inherit! *I'm* the one that should be going, not Vanyel! It's not *fair!*''

"Huh. You've got that right," Larence echoed, shifting his feet restlessly. "Dammit, we're all seconds, thirds—we *all* need a chance like that, or we'll be stuck doing nothing at the end of nowhere for the rest of our lives! We're never going to get anywhere, stuck off here in the back of beyond.''

"And think of the ladies," added Kerle, rolling his eyes up and kissing his hand at the ceiling. "All the loveliest darlings in the kingdom.''

He ducked, laughing, as Jyllian feinted a blow at his head, then shook her fist at him in mock-anger.

"Dammit, think a bit," Mekeal persisted. "What in Haven's name has he *done* to deserve getting rewarded like that? All he does around here is play he's a minstrel, look down that long nose of his at the rest of us, and shirk every duty he can!" Mekeal glowered and pounded his fist into the palm of his other hand to emphasize his words. "He's *Mother's* little darling, but—there's no way she'd have talked Father into sending him off, you all saw how she acted! So *why?* Why him, when the rest of us would *die* to get a chance to go to the capital?''

Joserlin continued to stare off into the dark; he was still putting together what he'd been observing. Everyone looked expectantly at him when Mekeal subsided and he cleared his throat. They all knew at this point that he was not the bright intellectual light among his brothers and cousins that Vanyel was, but he had a knack of seeing to the heart of things, and they wanted to hear if *he* had an answer for them. He usually did, and as they had half expected, this time was no exception.

"What makes you all think it's a reward?" he asked quietly.

The astonishment in the faces turned to his, followed by the light of dawning understanding, made him nod as he saw them come to the same conclusion he had made.

"You see?" he said, just as quietly as before. "It isn't a reward for Vanyel—it's an exile."

Vanyel didn't have to control his trembling when he reached the safe, concealing shelter of the hallway, but he didn't dare pause there. Someone might take it into his or her head to follow him.

But what he *could* do—now that he was out of the range of prying, curious eyes and ears—was run.

So he did, though he ran as noiselessly as he could, fleeing silently behind his shadow through the dim, uncertain light of the hallways. His flight took him past the dark, closed doorways leading to the bower, to bachelor's hall, to the chapel. His shadow sprang up before him every time he passed a lantern or torch, splaying out thin and spidery on the floor. He kept his head down so that if anyone should happen to come out of one of those doorways, they wouldn't see how close he was to tears.

But no one appeared; he reached the safe shelter of the servants' wing without encountering a single soul. Once there he dashed heedlessly up the stone staircase. Someone had extinguished the lanterns on the staircase itself; Vanyel didn't care. He'd run up these stairs often enough when half blind from trying not to cry, and his feet knew the way of themselves.

He hit the top landing at a dead run, and made the last few feet to his own door in a few heartbeats. He was sobbing for breath as he fumbled out his key in the dark and unlocked it—and the tears were threatening to spill.

Spill they did as soon as he got the door open. He shut and locked it behind him, leaning his back against it, head thrown back and resting against the rough wood. He swallowed his sobs out of sheer, prideful refusal to let *anyone* know of his unhappiness, even a servant, but hot tears poured down his cheeks and soaked into the neck of his tunic, and he couldn't make them stop.

They hate me. They all hate me. I knew they didn't much like me, but I never knew how much they hated me.

Never had he felt so utterly alone and nakedly vulnerable. At that moment if he could have *ensured* his death he'd have thrown himself out of his window. But as he'd noted earlier, it wasn't *that* far to the ground; and pain was a worse prospect than loneliness.

Finally he stumbled to his bed, pulled his clothing off, and crawled under the blankets, shivering with the need to keep from crying out loud.

But despite his best efforts, the tears started again, and he muffled his sobs in his pillow.

Oh, Liss—oh, Liss—I don't know what to do! Nobody cares, nobody gives a damn about me, nobody would ever risk a hangnail for me but you—and they've taken you out of reach. I'm afraid, and I'm alone, and Father's trying to break me, I know he is.

He turned over, and stared into the darkness above him, feeling his eyes burn. *I wish I could die. Now.*

He tried to will his heart to stop, but it obstinately ignored him.

Why can't they just leave me alone? He closed his burning eyes, and bit his lip. *Why?*

He lay in his bed, feeling every lump in the mattress, every prickle in the sheets; every muscle was tensed until it ached, his head was throbbing, and his eyes still burning.

He lay there for at least an eternity, but the oblivion he hoped for didn't come. Finally he gave up on trying to sleep, fumbled for the candle at his bedside, and slid out into the stuffy darkness of the room. He grabbed up his robe from the foot of the bed and pulled it on over his trembling, naked body, and began crossing the floor to the door.

Though the room itself was warm—too warm—the tiled floor was shockingly cold under his feet. He felt his way to the door, and pressed his ear against the crack at the side, listening with all his might for any sounds from the corridor and stairs beyond.

Nothing.

He cautiously slipped the inside bolt; listened again. Still nothing. He cracked the door and peered around the edge into the corridor.

It was thankfully empty. But the nearest lantern was all the way down at the dead end.

He took a deep breath and drew himself up; standing

as tall and resolutely erect as if he were Lord of the Keep himself. He walked calmly, surely, down the empty corridor, with just as much arrogance as if all his cousins' eyes were on him. Because there was no telling when one of the upper servants who had their rooms along this hall might take it into their heads to emerge—and servants talked. Frequently.

And they would *talk* if one of them got a glimpse of Vanyel in tears. It would be all over the keep in a candlemark.

He lit his candle at the lantern, and made another stately progress back to his room. Only when he had securely bolted the door behind him did he let go of the harpstring-taut control he'd maintained outside. He began shaking so hard that the candle flame danced madly, and spilled drops of hot wax on his hands.

He lit the others in their sconces by the door and over the bed as quickly as he could, and placed the one he was clutching in the holder on his table before he could burn himself with it.

He sat down heavily on the rucked-up blankets, sucking the side of his thumb where hot wax had scorched him, and staring at his belongings, trying to decide what his father was likely to let him take with him.

He didn't even bother to consider his instruments. They were far safer where they were. Maybe someday—if he survived this—he could come back and get them. But there was *no* chance, none at all, that he could sneak them out in his belongings. And if his father found them packed up—

He'd smash them. He'd smash them, and laugh, and wait for me to say or do something about it.

He finally got up and knelt on the chill stone beside the chest that held his clothing. He raised the heavy, carved lid, and stared down at the top layer for a long moment before lifting it out.

Tunics, shirts, breeches, hose—all in the deep, jewel-tones of sapphire and aquamarine and emerald that he knew looked so good on him, or his favorite black, silvery or smoky gray. All clothing he wore because it was one tiny way to defy his father—because his father could wear the same three outfits all year, all of them identical, and never notice, never care. Because his father didn't give a damn about what he or anyone else wore—and it angered him that Vanyel did.

Vanyel pondered the clothing, stroking the soft raime of a shirt without much thinking about what he was doing. *He won't dare keep me from taking the clothes, though I bet he'd like to. I'll have to look presentable when I get there, or I'll shame him—and the stuff Mekeal and the rest scruff around in is* not *presentable.*

He began rolling the clothing carefully, and stowing it into the traveling packs kept in the bottom of the chest. Though he didn't dare take an instrument, he managed to secrete some folded music, some of his favorite pieces, between the pages of the books he packed. *Bards are thick as birds in a cherry grove at Haven,* he thought with a lump in his throat. *Maybe I can get one to trade an old gittern for a cloak-brooch or something. It won't be the same as my lovely Woodlark, but it'll be better than nothing. Provided I can keep Aunt Unsavory from taking it away from me.*

It was all too quickly done. He found himself on the floor beside the filled packs with nothing more to do. He looked around his room; there was nothing left to pack that he would miss—except for those few things that he wanted to take but didn't dare.

Pretty fine life I've led, when all of it fits in four packs.

He got slowly to his feet, feeling utterly exhausted, yet almost too weary to sleep. He blew out all the candles except the one at his bedside, slipped out of his robe, tucked it into the top of the last pack, and climbed back into bed.

Somehow he couldn't bring himself to blow out the last candle. While there was light in the room he could keep the tears back. But darkness would set them free.

He lay rigid, staring silently at the candlelight wavering on the slanted ceiling, until his eyes burned.

All the brothers and fosterlings shared rooms; Mekeal had shared his with Vanyel until his older brother's broken arm had sent Mekeal down here a year early. And when Vanyel hadn't made the move down—Mekeal hadn't been particularly unhappy.

So for a while he had this one to himself, at which point he found that he really hadn't liked being alone after all. He liked company. Now, though—at least since late spring—he'd shared with Joserlin.

That had been *fine* with him. Jos was the next thing to an adult; Mekeal had been excited to have him move in, pleased with his company, and proud that Jos had treated him like an equal. And Jos talked to him; he didn't talk much, but when he did it was worth listening to. But he'd already said his say earlier tonight—so Mekeal had thought.

So he was kind of surprised when Jos' deep voice broke the silence right after they'd blown the candles out.

"Mekeal, why are you younglings so hard on your brother?"

Mekeal didn't have to ask *which* brother, it was pretty plain who Jos meant. But—"hard on him?" How could you be hard on somebody who didn't give a damn about anything but himself?

" 'Cause he's a—*toad*," Mekeal said indignantly. "He's got no more backbone than a mushroom! He's a baby, a coward—an' the only thing he cares about's hisself! He's just like Mama—she's gone and made him into a mama-pet, a shirker."

"Hmm? Really? What makes you so sure of that last?"

"Father says, and Jervis—"

"Because he won't let Jervis pound him like a set of pells." Joserlin snorted with absolute contempt. "Can't says as *I* much blame him, myself. If I was built like him, with Jervis on my back, reckon I'd find a hiding-hole, too. I sure's Haven wouldn't go givin' Jervis more chances t' hit on me."

Mekeal's mouth fell open in shock, and he squirmed around in his bed to face where Joserlin was, a dark bulk to his right. "But—but—Jervis—he's *armsmaster!*"

"He's a ham-handed lackwit," came the flat reply. "You forget, Meke, I was fostered with Lord Kendrik; I learned under a *real* armsmaster; Master Orser, and he's a good one. Jervis wouldn't be anything but another armsman if he hadn't been an old friend of your father's. He *don't* deserve to be armsmaster. Havens, Meke, he goes after the greenest of you like you was his age, his weight, and his experience! He don't pull his blows half the time; and he don't bother to show you how to take 'em, just lets you fumble it out for yourselves. An' he don't know but *one* bare style, an' that one's Holy Writ!''

"But—"

"But nothin'. He's no great master, let me tell you; by *my* way of thinkin' he's no master at all. If I was Vanyel, I'd'a poisoned myself before I let the old goat take his spleen out on me again! I *heard* what happened this spring—about how he took after Van an' beat him down a half dozen times, an' then broke his arm.''

"But—he was cheating!'' Mekeal protested.

"No such thing; Radevel told me what really happened. *Before* that bastard managed to convince you lot that you *didn't* see Van getting beaten up 'cause he bested the old peabrain. That weren't nothing but plain old bullying, an' if *my* old armsmaster had treated one of *his* pupils that way, he'd have been kicked off the top of the tower by Lord Kendrick hisself!''

Mekeal could hardly believe what he was hearing. "But—'' he protested again. "But Father—''

"Your father's a damn fool,'' Joserlin replied shortly. "An' I won't beg your pardon for sayin' so. He's a damn fool for keepin' Jervis as Master, an' he's a damn fool for treatin' young Vanyel the way he does. He's beggin' for trouble ev'ry time he pushes that boy. Half of what Vanyel does he *made* him do—to spite him. You mark my words; I seen this before, only the opposite. Place next to where I was fostered at your age, old Lady Cedrys at Briary Holding. Old Cedrys, she was big on scholarly stuff; nothin' would do but for *her* oldest t' be at the books night and day.'Cept her oldest was like you, mad for the Guard. And the more Cedrys pushed books, the more Liaven ran for the armsmaster at our place, till one day he kept right on running and didn't stop till he'd signed up with a common mercenary-company, an' she never saw him again.''

"But—Jos—you've *seen* him, the way he lords it over

us like he was King of the Gods or something—keeping his nose in the air every time he looks at us.''

"Uh-huh," Joserlin replied out of the dark, "And some of it's 'cause he's spoiled flat rotten by Lady Treesa. I won't deny that; he's one right arrogant little wart an' he sure knows he's the prettiest thing on the holding. Makes sure everybody else knows it, too. But I can't help but wonder how much he sticks that nose in the air around you lot 'cause you seem so bent on rubbin' it in the dirt. Hmm?''

Mekeal could find nothing to say in reply.

I could run away, Vanyel thought, almost dizzy with weariness, but still finding sleep eluding him. *I could run away—I think—*

He chewed his lip until it bled. *If I did, what could I do? Go for sanctuary? Gods, no—there is no way I was meant to be a priest! I don't write well enough to be a scribe, and besides, there isn't a lord would hire me once they found out who I was. Father would see to that, I know he would. Oh, gods, why didn't you make me a Bard?*

He licked the corner of his mouth, struck with a kindred thought. *I could try my hand at minstrelsy, couldn't I? I couldn't, I daren't show my face at any large courts, but there's a bit of coin to be had singing almost anywhere else.*

For a moment it seemed the way out. He need only slip across to the storeroom and get his instruments, then run off before dawn. He could be far away before anyone realized he was gone, and not just hiding again.

But—no.

My hand—my hand. Until it's working right, I can't do anything but the barest simple music. If I can't play right, there's no way I could look for a place in a household. And without the kind of noble patronage I can't look for, I won't be able to do much more than keep myself fed. I can't live like that, I just can't! I can't sing for farmers in the taverns and the folks in the fairs, I can't go begging like that, not to peasants. Not unless it looks like Savil is going to poison me, and I don't bloody think that's likely.

She's a Herald; Heralds don't do that sort of thing even to please their brothers. He sighed, and the candle went out. *No, it won't work. There's no way to escape.*

He waited, feeling the lump growing in his throat, threatening to undermine him again. The tears were going to come—going to weaken him still further, push him down into helplessness.

The darkness closed around him like a fist, and he fought against crying with such single-mindedness that he never quite knew when he passed from a half-daze into troubled, dream-haunted sleep.

He was alone, completely alone. For once in his life there was no one pushing him, no one mocking him. Above him was only dull gray sky; around him a plain of ice and snow stretched glittering to the horizon.

Everywhere he looked there was nothing but that barren, white plain. Completely empty, completely featureless. It was so cold he felt numb.

Numb. Not aching inside. Not ready to weep at a single word. Just—cold.

No pain. Just—nothing. He just stood, for several long moments, savoring the unfeeling, the lack of pain.

Safe. He was safe here. No one could touch him. As long as he stayed in this isolation, this wilderness, no one could touch him.

He opened his eyes wide in the dream, and breathed the words out. "If no one touches me—no one can hurt me. All I have to do is never care."

It was like a revelation, a gift from the hitherto-uncaring gods. This place, this wilderness of ice—if he could hold it inside him—if he could not-care enough—he could be safe. No matter what happened, who hated him, no one could ever hurt him again.

Not ever again.

Three

In the morning all he had to do was think of his dream, and he was cold inside, ice filling the place within him where the hurt and loneliness had been. He could be as remote and isolated as a hermit on a frozen mountaintop, any time he chose.

It was like taking a drug against pain. An antidote to loneliness.

Indifference was a defense now, and not just a pose.

Could this armor of indifference serve as an offensive weapon too? It was worth a try.

After all, he had nothing to lose; the worst had already occurred.

He dressed quickly; riding leathers that had originally been brown that he had ordered redyed to black—without his father's knowledge. He was very glad that he'd done so, now. Black always made him look taller, older—and just a little bit sinister. It was a good choice for a confrontation. It was also the color of death; he wanted to remind his father of just how often the man had Vanyel—elsewhere.

He had second thoughts about his instruments, at least the lute, which he *had* been permitted. He wouldn't pack it, but it should *be* here, else Lord Withen might wonder where it was.

Besides, if he could confront Withen *with* it, then force the issue by packing it in front of his eyes—

It might gain him something. So he slipped quickly across to his hiding place and back before the sun actually rose, and when Withen came pounding on his door, he was ensconced below the window with the instrument in his hands, picking out a slow, but intricate little melody. One where his right hand was doing most of the work. He had staged the entire scene with the deliberate intent to make it seem as if he had been there for hours.

Lord Withen had, no doubt, expected to find his oldest son still in his bed—had expected to rouse out a confused and profoundly unhappy boy into the thin, gray light of post-dawn. Had undoubtedly counted on finding Vanyel as vulnerable as he had been last night.

That would have pleased you, wouldn't it, Father—it would have given you such confirmation of my worthlessness. . . .

Instead, he flung the door open after a single knock— to find Vanyel awake, packed, and already dressed for travel, lute suddenly stilled by his entrance.

Vanyel looked up, and regarded his father with what he hoped was a cool and distant arrogance, exactly the kind of expression one would turn upon a complete stranger who had suddenly intruded himself without invitation.

His surprise and the faint touch of unease in his eyes gave Vanyel the first feelings of gratification he'd had in a long time.

He placed his lute on the bed beside him, and stood up slowly, drawing himself up as pridefully erect as he could. "As you see, sir—" he lifted a single finger and nodded his head very slightly in the direction of his four packs. "—I am prepared already."

Lord Withen was obviously taken further aback by his tone and abstracted manner. He coughed, and Vanyel realized with a sudden surge of vindictive joy that *he,* for once, had the advantage in a confrontation.

Then Withen flushed as Vanyel stooped quickly and caught up the neck of his lute, detuning it with swift and practiced fingers and stuffing it quickly into its traveling bag.

That was a challenge even Withen recognized. He glowered, and made as if to take the instrument from his son—

And Vanyel drew himself up to his full height. He said nothing. He only gave back Withen a stare that told him—

Push me. Do it. See what happens when you do. I have absolutely nothing to lose and I don't care what happens to me.

Withen actually backed up a pace at the look in his son's eyes.

"You may take your toy, but don't think this means you can spend all your time lazing about with those worthless Bards," Withen blustered, trying to regain the high ground he'd lost the moment he thrust the door open. "You're going to Savil to learn something other than—"

"I never imagined I would be able to for a moment—sir," Vanyel interrupted, and produced a bitter not-smile. "I'm quite certain," he continued with carefully measured venom, "that you have given my aunt very explicit instructions on the subject. And on my education. Sir."

Withen flushed again. Vanyel felt another rush of poisonous pleasure. *You know and I know what this is really about, don't we, Father? But you want me to pretend it's something else, at least in public. Too bad. I don't intend to make this at all easy on you, and I don't intend to be graceful in public. I have the high ground, Father. I don't give a damn anymore, and that gives me a weapon you don't have.*

Withen made an abrupt gesture, and a pair of servants entered Vanyel's room from the corridor beyond, each picking up two packs and scurrying out of the door as quickly as they could. Vanyel pulled the shoulder strap of the lute over his own head, arranging the instrument on his back, as a clear sign that he did not intend anyone else to be handling it.

"You needn't see me off, sir," he said, when Withen made no move to follow the servants with their burdens. "I'm sure you have—more important things to attend to."

Withen winced, visibly. Vanyel strolled silently past him, then turned to deliver a parting shot, carefully calculated to hurt as much as only a truth that should not be spoken could.

"After all, sir," he cast calmly over his shoulder, "It isn't as if I mattered. You have four other potential—and

far worthier—heirs. I *am* sorry you saw fit not to inform
my mother of my hour of departure; it would have been
pleasant to say farewell to someone who will miss my
presence.''

Withen actually flinched.

Vanyel raised one eyebrow. ''Don't bother to wish me
well, sir. I know what Father Leren preaches about the
importance of truth, and I would not want you to perjure
yourself.''

The stricken look on Withen's face made a cold flame
of embittered satisfaction spring up in Vanyel's ice-
shrouded soul. He turned on his heel and strode firmly
down the corridor after the scuttling servants, not giving
his father the chance to reply, nor to issue orders to the
servants.

He passed the two servants with his packs in the dim,
gray-lit hallway, and gestured peremptorily that they
should follow him. Again, he felt that blackly bitter satisfaction; obviously Lord Withen had intended that his
son should have scampered along in the servants' wake.
But the sudden reversal of roles had confused Withen and
left the servants without clear instructions. Vanyel seized
the unlooked-for opportunity and held to it with all his
might. For once, just this once, Vanyel had gotten the
upper hand in a situation, and he did not intend to relin-
quish it until he was forced to.

He led them down the ill-lit staircase, hearing them
stumbling blindly behind him in the darkness and thank-
ful that *he* was the one carrying his lute and that there
was nothing breakable in the packs. They emerged at the
end of the hall nearest the kitchen; Vanyel decided to
continue to force the issue by going out the *servants'*
door to the stables. It was closer—but that wasn't why he
chose it; he chose it to make the point that he *knew* his
father's thoughts about him.

The two servitors, laden as they were with the heavy
packs, had to stretch to keep up with him; already they
were panting with effort. As Vanyel's boots crunched in
the gravel spread across the yard between the keep and
the stables, he could hear them puffing along far behind
him.

The sun was barely over the horizon, and mist was rising from the meadows where the horses were turned loose during the day. It would likely be hot today, one of the first days of true high summer. Vanyel could see, as he came around the side of the stable, that the doors were standing wide open, and that there were several people moving about inside.

Couldn't wait to be rid of me, could you, Father dear? Meant to hustle me off as fast as you could throw me into my clothes and my belongings into packs. I think in this I will oblige you. It should keep you sufficiently confused.

Now that he had this set of barriers, for the first time in more than a year he was able to think clearly and calmly. He was able to make plans without being locked in an emotional morass, and carry them out without losing his head to frustration. Gods, it was so simple—just don't give a damn. Don't care what they do to you, and they do nothing.

If I were staying, I'd never have dared to say those things. But I'm not, and by the time Father figures out how to react, I'll be far beyond his ability to punish me. Even if he reports all this to Aunt Unsavory, it's going to sound really stupid—and what's more, it'll make him look a fool.

He paused in the open doors, feet slightly apart, hands on his hips. After a few moments, those inside noticed him and the buzz of conversation ceased altogether as they turned to gape at him in dumbfounded surprise.

"Why isn't my mare saddled?" he asked quietly, coldly. The only two *horses* bearing riding saddles were two rough cobs obviously meant for the two armsmen beside them, men who had been examining their girths and who had suddenly straightened to attention at the sound of his voice. There was another beast with a riding saddle on it, but it wasn't a horse—it was an aging, fat pony, one every boy on the holding had long since outgrown, and a mount that was now given to Treesa's most elderly women to ride.

"Beggin' yer pardon, m'lord Vanyel," said one of the grooms, hesitantly, "But yer father—"

"I really could not care less what my father ordered,"

Vanyel interrupted, rudely and angrily. *"He* isn't going to have to ride halfway to the end of the world on that hobbyhorse. *I* am the one being sent on this little exile, and I am *not* going to ride *that.* I refuse to enter the capital on a beast that is going to make me look like a clown. Besides, Star is *mine,* not his. The Lady Treesa gave her to *me,* and I intend to take her with me. Saddle her.''

The groom continued to hesitate.

''If you won't,'' Vanyel said, his eyes narrowing, his voice edged with the coldest steel, ''I will. Either way you'll have trouble. And if *I* have to do it, and my lady mother finds out, you'll have trouble from her as well as my father.''

The groom shrugged, and went after Star and her tack, leaving his fellow to strip the pony and turn it into the pasture.

Lovely. Put me on a mount only a tyro would have to ride, and make it look as if I was too much a coward to handle a real horse. Make me look a fool, riding into Haven on a pony. And deprive me of something I treasured. Not this time, Father.

In fact, Vanyel was already firmly in Star's saddle by the time Lord Withen made a somewhat belated appearance in the stableyard. The grooms were fastening the last of the packs on the backs of three mules, and the armsmen were waiting, also mounted, out in the yard.

Vanyel patted the proudly arched neck of his Star, a delicately-boned black palfrey with a perfect white star on her forehead, a star that had one long point that trailed down her nose. He ignored his father for a long moment, giving him a chance to absorb the sight of his son on his spirited little blood-mare instead of the homely old pony. Then he nudged Star toward the edge of the yard where Lord Withen stood; by his stunned expression, once again taken by surprise. She picked her way daintily across the gravel, making very little sound, like a remnant of night-shadow in the early morning light. Vanyel had had all her tack dyed the same black as his riding leathers, and was quite well aware of how striking they looked together.

So was she; she curved her neck and carried her tail like a banner as he directed her toward his father.

Lord Withen's expression changed as they approached; first discomfited, then resigned. Vanyel kept his the same as it had been all this morning; nonexistent. He kept his gaze fixed on a point slightly above his father's head.

Behind him, Vanyel could hear the mules being led out to have the lead rein of the first fastened to the cantle of one of the armsmen's saddles. He halted Star about then, a few paces from the edge of the yard. He looked down at his father, keeping his face completely still, completely closed.

They stared at each other for a long moment; Vanyel could see Withen groping for something appropriate to say. And each time he began to speak, the words died unspoken beneath Vanyel's cold and dispassionate gaze.

I'm not going to make this easy for you, Father. Not after what you've done to me; not after what you tried to do to me just now. I'm going to follow my sire's example. I'm going to be just as nasty as you are—but I'm going to do it with more style.

The silence lengthened almost unbearably; even the armsmen began picking up the tension, and shifted uneasily in their saddles. Their cobs fidgeted and snorted restlessly.

Vanyel and Star could have been a statue of onyx and silver.

Finally Vanyel decided he had prolonged the agony enough. He nodded, once, almost imperceptibly. Then, without a word, he wheeled Star and nudged her lightly with his heels. She tossed her head and shot down the road to the village at a fast trot, leaving the armsmen cursing and kicking at their beasts behind him, trying to catch up.

He reined Star in once they were past the Forst Reach village, not wanting her to tire herself so early in the journey, and not wanting to give the armsmen an excuse to order him to ride between them.

Father's probably told them that they're to watch for me trying to bolt, he thought cynically, as Star fought the

rein for a moment, then settled into a more-or-less sedate
walk. And indeed, that surmise was confirmed when he
saw them exchange surreptitious glances and not-too-well
concealed sighs of relief. *Huh. Little do they know.*

For once they got beyond the Forst Reach lands that
lay under the plow, they entered the completely untamed
woodlands that lay between Forst Reach and the nearest
eastward holding of Prytheree Ford. This forest land had
been left purposely wild; there weren't enough people to
farm it at either Holding, and it supplied all of the wood
products and a good half of the meat eaten in a year to
the people of both Holdings.

It took skilled foresters to make their way about in a
wood like this. And Vanyel knew very well that he had
no more idea of how to survive in wilderland than he did
of how to sprout fins and breathe water.

The road itself was hardly more than a rutted track of
hard-packed dirt meandering through a tunnel of tree
branches. The branches themselves were so thick overhead that they rode in a kind of green twilight. Although
the sun was dispersing the mist outside the wood, there
were still tendrils of it wisping between the trees and
lying across the road. And only an occasional sunbeam
was able to make its way down through the canopy of
leaves to strike the roadway. To either side, the track was
edged with thick bushes; a hint here and there of red
among the green leaves told Vanyel that those bushes were
blackberry hedges, probably planted to keep bears and
other predators off the road itself. Even if he'd been
thinking of escape, he was not fool enough to dare their
brambly embrace. Even less did he wish to damage Star's
tender hide with the unkind touch of their thorns.

Beyond the bushes, so far as he could see, the forest
floor was a tangle of vegetation in which *he* would be lost
in heartbeats.

No, he was not in the least tempted to bolt and run,
but there were other reasons not to run besides the logical
ones.

There were—or seemed to be—things tracking them
under the shelter of the underbrush. Shadow-shapes that
made no sound.

He didn't much like those shadows behind the bushes or ghosting along with the fog. He didn't at all care for the way they moved, sometimes following the riders on the track for furlongs before giving up and melting into deeper forest. Those shadows called to mind far too many stories and tales—and the Border, with all its uncanny creatures, wasn't all *that* far from here.

The forest itself was too quiet for Vanyel's taste, even had those shadows *not* been slinking beneath the trees. Only occasionally could he hear a bird call above the dull clopping of the horses' hooves, and that was faint and far off. No breeze stirred the leaves above them; no squirrels ran along the branches to scold them. Of course it *was* entirely possible that they were frightening all the nearby wildlife into silence simply with their presence; these woods *were* hunted regularly. That was the obvious explanation of the silence beneath the trees.

But Vanyel's too-active imagination kept painting other, grimmer pictures of what might be lurking unseen out there.

Even though it became very warm and a halt would have been welcome, he really found himself hoping they wouldn't make one. The armor that had so far been proof against pressure from without cracked just a little from the pressure within of his own vivid imagination. He was uneasy when they paused to feed and water the horses and themselves at noon, and was not truly comfortable until they saddled up and moved off again. The only way he could keep his nerves in line was to concentrate on how well he had handled Lord Withen. Recalling that stupified look he'd last seen on Withen's face gave him no end of satisfaction. Withen hadn't seen Vanyel the boy—he'd seen a man, in some sort of control over his situation. And he plainly hadn't enjoyed the experience.

It was with very real relief that Vanyel saw the trees break up, then open out into a huge clearing ahead of them just as the woods began to darken with the dying of the day. He was more than pleased when he saw there was an inn there, and realized that his guardians had been undoubtedly intending to stay there overnight.

They rode up the flinty dirt road to the facade of the inn, then through the entryway into the inn yard. That was where his two guardians halted, looking about for a stableboy. Vanyel dismounted, feeling very stiff, and a lot sorer than he had thought he'd be.

When a groom came to take Star's reins, he gave them over without a murmur, then paced up and down the length of the dusty stableyard, trying to walk some feeling back into his legs. While he walked, one of the armsmen vanished into the inn itself and the other removed the packs from the mules before turning them and their cobs over to more grooms.

It was at that point that Vanyel realized that he didn't even know his captors' names.

That bothered him; he was going to be spending a lot of time in their company, yet they hadn't even introduced themselves during the long ride. He was confused, and uncomfortable. Yet—

The less I feel, the better off I'll be.

He closed his eyes and summoned his snow-field; could almost *feel* it chilling him, numbing him.

He began looking over the inn, ignoring the other guard, and saw with mild surprise that it was huge; much bigger than it had looked from the road. Only the front face of it was really visible when he rode up to it; now he could see the entire complex. It was easily five times the size of the little village inn at Forst Reach, and two-storied as well. Its outer walls were of stone up to the second floor, then timber; the roof was thickly thatched, and the birds Vanyel had missed in the forest all seemed to have made a happy home here, nestling into the thatch with a riot of calls and whistles as they settled in for the night. With the stables it formed two sides of a square around the stable yard, the fourth side being open on a grassy field, probably for the use of traders and their wagons. The stables were extensive, too; easily as large as Lord Withen's, and he was a notable horsebreeder.

Blue shadows were creeping from the forest into the stableyard, although the sky above had not quite begun to darken very much. And it was getting quite chilly; something Vanyel hadn't expected, given the heat of the day. He was just as glad when the second armsman finally put in an appearance, trailed by a couple of inn servants.

Vanyel pretended to continue to study the sky to the west, but he strained his ears as hard as he could to hear what his guardians had to say to each other.

"Any problems, Garth?" asked the one who'd remained with Vanyel, as the first bent to retrieve a pack and motioned to the servants to take the ones Vanyel recognized as being his own.

"Nay," the first chuckled. "This early in th' summer they be right glad of custom wi' good coin in hand, none o' yer shifty peddlers, neither. Just like m'lord said, got us rooms on second story wi' his Highness there on t' inside. No way he gets out wi'out us noticin'. Besides we bein' second floor, 'f's needful we just move t' bed across t' door, an' he won't be goin' nowhere."

Vanyel froze, and the little corner of him that had been wondering if he could—perhaps—make allies of these two withdrew.

So that's why they're keeping their distance. He straightened his back, and let that cool, expressionless mask that had served so well with his father this morning drop over his features again. *I might have guessed as much. I was a fool to think otherwise.*

He turned to face his watchers. "I trust all is in order?" he asked, letting nothing show except, perhaps, boredom. "Then—shall we?" He nodded slightly toward the inn door, where a welcoming, golden light was shining.

Without waiting for a reply, he moved deliberately toward it himself, leaving them to follow.

Vanyel stared moodily at the candle at his bedside. There wasn't anything much else to look at; *his* room had no windows. Other than that, it wasn't that much unlike his old room back at Forst Reach; quite plain, a bit stuffy—not too bad, really. Except that it had no windows. Except for being a prison.

Inventory: one bed, one chair, one table. No fireplace,

but that wasn't a consideration given the general warmth of the building and the fact that it was summer. All four of his packs were piled over in the corner, the lute still in its case leaning up against them.

He'd asked for a bath, and they'd brought him a tub and bathwater rather than letting him go down to the bathhouse. The water was tepid, and the tub none too big—but he'd acted as if the notion had been his idea. At least his guardians hadn't insisted on being in the same room watching him when he used it.

One of them *had* escorted him to the privy and back, though; he'd headed in that direction, and the one called Garth had immediately dropped whatever it was he'd been working on and attached himself to Vanyel's invisible wake, following about a half dozen paces behind. That had been so humiliating that he hadn't spoken a single word to the man, simply ignored his presence entirely.

And they hadn't consulted him on dinner either; they'd had it brought up on a tray while he was bathing.

Not that he'd been particularly hungry. He managed the bread and butter and cheese—the bread was better than he got at home—and a bit of fresh fruit. But the rest, boiled chicken, a thick gravy, and dumplings, and all of it swiftly cooling into a greasy, congealed mess on the plate, had stuck in his throat and he gave up trying to eat the tasteless stuff entirely.

But he really didn't want to sit here staring at it, either.

So he picked up the tray, opened his door, and took it to the outer room, setting it down on a table already cluttered with oddments of traveling gear and the wherewithal to clean it.

Both men looked up at his entrance, eyes wide and startled in the candlelight. The only sound was the steady flapping of the curtains in the light breeze coming in the window, and the buzzing of a fly over one of the candles.

Vanyel straightened, licked his lips, and looked off at a point on the farther wall, between them and above their heads. "Every corridor in this building leads to the common room, so I can hardly escape you that way," he said, in as bored and detached a tone as he could muster. "And besides, there's grooms sleeping in the stables, and I'm certain you've already spoken with *them*. I'm scarcely going to climb out the window and run off on foot. You might as well go enjoy yourselves in the common room. You may be my jailors, but that doesn't mean you have to endure the jail yourselves."

With that, he turned abruptly and closed the door of his room behind him.

But he held his breath and waited right beside the door, his ear against it, the better to overhear what they were saying in the room beyond.

"Huh!" the one called Garth said, after an interval of startled silence. "Whatcha think of *that?*"

"That he ain't half so scatterbrained as m'lord thinks," the other replied thoughtfully. "*He* knows damn well what's goin' on. Not that he ain't about as nose-in-th'-air as I've ever seen, but he ain't addlepated, not a bit of it."

"Never saw m'lord set so on his rump before," Garth agreed, speaking slowly. "Ain't never seen him taken down like that by a *lord*, much less a grass-green youngling. An' never saw *that* boy do anythin' like it before, neither. Boy's got sharp a'sudden; give 'im that. Too sharp?"

"Hmm. No—" the other said. "No, I reckon in this case, he be right." Silence for a moment, then a laugh. "Y'know, I 'spect his Majesty just don't want to have t' lissen t' us gabbin' away at each other. Mebbe we bore 'im, eh? What th' hell, I could stand a beer. You?"

"Eh, if you're buyin', Erek—"

Their voices faded as the door to the hall beyond scraped open, then closed again.

Vanyel sighed out the breath he'd been holding in, and took the two steps he needed to reach the table, sagging down into the hard, wooden chair beside it.

Tired. Gods, I am so tired. This farce is taking more out of me than I thought it would.

He stared numbly at the candle flame, and then transferred his gaze to the bright, flickering reflections on the brown earthenware bottle beside it.

It's awful wine—but it is wine. I suppose I could get good and drunk. There certainly isn't anything else to

*do. At least nothing they'll let me do. Gods, they think
I'm some kind of prig. "His Majesty" indeed.*

He shook his head. *What's wrong with me? Why should
it matter what a couple of armsmen think about me? Why
should I even want them on my side? Who are they, anyway? What consequence are they? They're just a bare
step up from dirt-grubbing farmers! Why should I care
what they think? Besides, they can't affect what happens
to me.*

He sighed again, and tried to summon a bit more of
the numbing disinterest he'd sustained himself with this
whole, filthy day.

It wouldn't come, at first. There was something in the
way—

Nothing matters, he told himself sternly. *Least of all
what they think about you.*

He closed his eyes again, and managed this time to
summon a breath of the chill of his dream-sanctuary. It
helped.

After a while he shifted, making the chair creak, and
tried to think of something to do—maybe to put the
thoughts running round his head into a set of lyrics. Instead, he found he could hear, muffled, and indistinct,
the distracting sounds of the common room somewhere
a floor below and several hundred feet away.

The laughter, in particular, came across clearly. Vanyel
bit his lip as he tried to think of the last time he'd really
laughed, and found he couldn't remember it.

Dammit, I am better *than they are, I don't* need *them,
I don't* need *their stupid approval!* He reached hastily for
the bottle, poured an earthenware mug full of the thin,
slightly vinegary stuff, and gulped it down. He poured a
second, but left it on the table, rising instead and taking
his lute from the corner. He stripped the padded bag off
of it, and began retuning it before the wine had a chance
to muddle him.

At least there was music. There was always music.
And the attempt to get what he'd lost back again.

Before long the instrument was nicely in tune. That
was one thing that minstrel—*What was his name? Shanse,
that was it*—had praised unstintingly. Vanyel, he'd said,

had a natural ear. Shanse had even put Vanyel in charge of tuning *his* instruments while he stayed at Forst Reach.

He took the lute back to the bed, and laid it carefully on the spread while he shoved the table up against the bedstead. He curled up with his back against the headboard, the bottle and mug in easy reach, and began practicing those damned finger exercises.

It might have been the wine, but his hand didn't seem to be hurting *quite* as much this time.

The bottle was half empty and his head buzzing a bit when there was a soft tap on his door.

He stopped in mid-phrase, frowning, certain he'd somehow overheard something from the next room. But the tapping came a second time, soft, but insistent, and definitely coming from his door.

He shook his head a little, hoping to clear it, and put the lute in the corner of the bed. He took a deep breath to steady his thoughts, uncurled his legs, rose, and paced (weaving only a little) to the door.

He cracked it open, more than half expecting it to be one of his captors come to tell him to shut the hell up so that they could get some sleep.

"Oh!" said the young girl who stood there, her eyes huge with surprise; one wearing the livery of one of the inn's servants. He had caught her with her hand raised, about to tap on the door a third time. Beyond her the armsmen's room was mostly dark and quite empty.

"Yes?" he said, blinking his eyes, which were not focusing properly. When he'd gotten up, the wine had gone to his head with a vengeance.

"Uh—I just—" the girl was not as young as he'd thought, but fairly pretty; soft brown eyes, curly dark hair. Rather like a shabby copy of Melenna. "Just—ye wasn't down wi' th' others, m'lord, an' I wunnered if ye needed aught?"

"No, thank you," he replied, still trying to fathom why she was out there, trying to think through a mist of wine-fog. Unless—that armsman Garth might well have sent her, to make certain he was still where he was supposed to be.

The ties of the soft yellow blouse she was wearing had

come loose, and it was slipping off one shoulder, exposing the round shoulder and a goodly expanse of the mound of one breast. She wet her lips, and edged closer until she was practically nose-to-nose with him.

"Are ye sure, m'lord?" she breathed. "Are ye sure ye cain't think of nothin'?"

Good gods, he realized with a start, *she's trying to seduce me!*

He used the ploy that had been so successful with his mother's ladies. He let his expression chill down to where it would leave a skin of ice on a goblet of water. "Quite certain, thank you, mistress."

She was either made of sterner stuff than they had been, or else the subtler nuances of expression went right over her head.

Or, third possibility, she found either Vanyel or his presumably fat purse too attractive to let go without a fight.

"I c'd turn yer bed down fer ye, m'lord," she persisted, snaking an arm around the door to glide her hand along Vanyel's buttock and leg. He was only wearing a shirt and hose, and felt the unsubtle caress with a startlement akin to panic.

"No, please!" he yelped in shock; the high-pitched, strangled shout startled her enough so that she pulled back her arm. He slammed the door in her face and locked it.

He waited with his ear pressed up against the crack in the door; waited for an explosion of some kind. Nothing happened; he heard her muttering to herself for a moment, sounding very puzzled, then finally heard her retreating footsteps and the sound of the outer door opening and closing again.

He staggered back to the bed, and sat down on it, heavily. Finally he reached for the lute, detuned it, and put it back in its traveling case.

Then he reached for the bottle and gulped the wine as fast as he could pour it down his throat.

Oh, lord—oh, gods. A fool. After everything this morning, after I start to feel like I'm getting a grip on things, and I go and act like a fool. Like a kid. Like a baby who'd never seen a whore before.

He burned with humiliation as he imagined the girl telling his guards what had just passed between them. And drank faster.

He *did* remember to unlock his door and blow out the candle before he passed out. If Sun and Shadow out there decided to take it into their heads to check on him, he didn't want them breaking the door down. That would be even more humiliating than having them follow him to the privy, or laughing at him with the girl.

I've never been this drunk before, he thought muzzily, as he sank back onto the bed. *I bet I have a head in the morning. . . .*

He snorted then, a sound with no amusement in it. *At least if I'm hung over, it'll make Trusty and Faithful happy. If they can't report to Father that I tried to escape, at least they can tell him I made a drunken sot of myself at the first opportunity. Maybe I should have let the girl in after all. It wouldn't be the first time I've bedded something I didn't much care for. And it would have given them one more story to tell. Oh, gods, what's wrong with me? Mekeal would have had her tumbled before she blinked twice! What is* wrong *with me?*

He rolled over, and it felt a lot like his head kept on rolling after he'd stopped moving.

Then again—I don't think so. Not even for that. The wine's bad enough here. I hate to think where the girls came from . . . or where they've been.

But why can't I react the way everyone else seems to? Why am I so different?

His head hurt, but not unbearably. His stomach was not particularly happy with him, but he wasn't ready to retch his guts up. In short, he was hung over—though less than he'd expected. In an odd sort of way, he was feeling even more detached than before. Perhaps his intoxication had purged something out of him last night; some forlorn hope, some last grasping at a life no one would ever let him have.

He pulled on his riding leathers and groomed himself

as impeccably as he could manage without a mirror, leaving only the tunic off, since he intended to soak his aching head in cold water before he mounted Star—in the horse trough if he had to. He walked out into the morning light pouring in through the outer room, surveying the pathetic wrecks that had been his alert and vigilant guardians only the night before with what he hoped was cool, distant impassiveness.

And he spared a half a moment to hope that the girl *hadn't* told them—

His guards were in far worse case than he was, having evidently made a spectacular night of it. *Quite* a night, judging by their bleary eyes, surly, yet satiated expressions, and the rumpled condition of the bedding. And Vanyel was not such an innocent as to be unable to recognize certain—aromas—when he detected them in the air before Garth opened the window. He was just as pleased to have been so drunk as to be insensible when they had been entertaining their temporary feminine acquaintances. Could be the chambermaid had found what she'd sought in the company of Garth and Erek after being rebuffed by Vanyel.

They weren't giving him the kind of sly looks he'd have expected if the girl *had* revealed his panicked reaction.

Well—maybe she was too busy. Thank you, gods.

He managed to deal with his hangover in a fairly successful fashion. Willowbark tea came for his asking, hot from the kitchen; on the way to the privy, with the faithful Garth in queasy attendance, he managed to divert long enough to soak his head under the stable pump until his temples stopped pounding. The water was very cold, and he saw Garth wincing when he first stuck his head beneath it.

That dealt with the head; the stomach was easier. He drank nothing but the tea and ate nothing but bread, very mild cheese, and fruit.

He was perfectly ready to ride out at that point. His guards were not so fortunate. Or, perhaps, so wise, since *their* remedies seemed to consist of vile concoctions of raw eggs and the heavy imbibing of the ale that had *caused* their problem the night before.

As a result, their departure was delayed until mid-morning—not that this disturbed Vanyel a great deal. They'd be outside the bounds of the forest before dark; at least according to what the innkeeper told Garth. That was all *Vanyel* cared about.

Garth and Erek were still looking a bit greenish as they mounted their cobs. And neither seemed much inclined toward talk. That suited Vanyel quite well; it would enable him to concentrate on putting just a bit more distance between himself and the world. And it would allow him to do some undisturbed thinking.

The forest did not seem quite so unfriendly on the eastern side of the inn—perhaps because it was hunted more frequently on this side. The underbrush certainly wasn't as thick. The boughs of the trees overhead weren't, either, and Vanyel got a bit of nasty satisfaction at seeing Garth and Erek wincing out of the way of sunbeams that were *much* more frequent on this side of the woods.

But it was hotter than yesterday, and Vanyel finally stripped off his leather tunic and bundled it behind him.

Seeing no lurking shadows beneath the trees, he felt a bit easier about turning his attention inward to think about just what, exactly, he was heading toward.

I can guess at what Father's told the old bat. That's easy enough. The question is what she's likely to do about it.

He tried to dig everything he could remember out of the dim recesses of memory—not just about his aunt in particular, but about Heralds in general.

He'll tell her I'm to be weapons-schooled, that's for certain. But how—that's up to her. And now that I think of it—damn if it wasn't a Herald *that wrote that book that got me in such trouble! I may, I just* might *actually be better off in that area! Huh—now that I think about it, I can't see any way I'd be worse off.*

A bird called overhead, and Vanyel almost felt a bit hopeful. *No matter* who *I get schooled under, he can't* possibly *be worse than Jervis—because whoever he is, he* won't *have a grudge against me. The absolute worst I can get is a Jervis-type without a grudge. That might just be survivable, if I keep myself in the background, if I manage to convince him that I'm deadly stupid and clumsy. Stupid and clumsy are not possible to train away, and even Jervis knew that.*

Another bird answered, reminding him that there was, however, the matter of music.

He's bound to have issued orders that I'm not to be allowed anywhere near the Bards except right under Savil's eye—and if she's like Father, she has no ear at all. Which means she'll never go to entertainments unless she has no choice. He sighed. *Oh, well, there's worse. I won't be any worse off than I was at home, where I saw a real, trained Bard once in my entire lifetime. At least they'll be around. Maybe if I can get my fingering back and play where one is likely to overhear me—*

He sternly squelched that last. *Best not think about it. I can't afford hope anymore.*

Star fidgeted; she wanted her usual early-morning run. He reined her in, calmed her down, and went back to his own thoughts. *One thing for sure, Father is likely to have told Savil all kinds of things about how rotten I am. So she'll be likely looking for wrong moves on my part—and I'll bet she'll have her proteges and friends watching me, too. It's going to be hell. Hell, with no sanctuary, and no Liss.*

He studied Star's ears as he thought, watching her flick them back with alert interest when she heard him sigh.

Well, everyone else is going to hate me, but you still love me. He patted Star's neck, and she pranced a little.

To the lowest hells with all of them. I do not need them, I don't need anybody, not even Liss. I'll do all right on my own.

But there was one puzzle, one he was reminded of later, when they passed one of the remote farms, and Vanyel saw the farmer out in the field, talking with someone on horseback who was likely his overlord. *Huh*—he thought, *I can't figure how in Havens Father expects Savil to train me in governance. . . .*

Then he felt a cold chill.

Unless he doesn't really expect me to ever come home again. Gods—he could *try to work something out in the way of sending me off to a temple. He could do that—*

*and it bloody wouldn't matter if Father Leren could find
him a priest he could bribe into accepting an unwilling
acolyte. It would work—it would* work. *Especially if it
was a cloistered order. And with me out of the way in
Savil's hands, he has all the time he needs to* find *a compliant priest. He doesn't even have to tell Savil; just issue
the order to send me back home again when it's all arranged. Then spirit me off and announce to anyone who
asks that I discovered I had a vocation. And I would
spend the rest of my life in a little stone cave somewhere—*

He swallowed hard, and tried to find reasons to dismiss
the notion as a paranoid fantasy, but all he could discover
were more reasons why it was a logical move on Lord
Withen's part.

He tried to banish the fear, telling himself that it was
no good worrying about what might only be a fantasy
until it actually happened. But the thought wouldn't go
away. It kept coming back, not only that day, but every
day thereafter. It wasn't quite an obsession—but it wasn't
far off.

It was quite enough to keep him wrapped in silent,
apprehensive thought for every day of the remainder of
the journey, and to keep him sleepless for long hours
every night. And not even dreams of his isolate snow-
plain helped to keep it from his thoughts.

Four

"**A**ll right, Tylendel, that was passable, but it wasn't particularly smooth," Herald-Mage Savil admonished her protege, tucking her feet under the bottom rung of her wooden stool, and absently smoothing down the front of her white tunic. "Remember, the power is supposed to *flow;* from you to the shield and back again. Smoothly, not in spurts. You tell me why."

Tylendel, a tall, strikingly attractive, dark blond Herald-trainee of about sixteen, frowned with concentration as he considered Savil's question. She watched the power-barrier he had built about himself with her Mage-Sight, and Saw the pale violet half-dome waver as he turned his attention to her question and lost a bit of control over the shield. She could feel the room pulsing as he allowed the shield to pulse in time with his heartbeat. If he let this go on, it would collapse.

"Tylendel, you're losing it," she warned. He nodded, looked up and grimaced, but did not reply; his actions were reply enough. The energy comprising the half-dome covering him stopped rippling, firmed, and the color deepened.

"Have you an answer to my question yet?"

"I think so," he answered. "If it doesn't flow smoothly, I'll have times when it's weak, and whatever I'm doing with it will be open to interruption when it weakens?"

"Right," Savil replied with a brisk nod. "Only don't think in terms of 'interruption,' lad. Think in terms of 'attack.' Like *now.*"

She flung a levinbolt at his barrier without giving him any more warning than that, and had the satisfaction, not only of Seeing it deflected harmlessly upward to be absorbed by the Work Room shields, but Seeing that he shifted his defenses to meet it with no chance to prepare at all.

"Now *that* was good, my lad," she approved, and Tylendel's brown eyes warmed in response to the compliment. "So—"

Someone knocked on the door of the Work Room, and Savil bit off what she was going to tell him with a muffled curse of annoyance. *"Now* what?" she muttered, shoving back her tall stool and edging around Tylendel's mage-barrier to answer the door.

The Work Room was a permanently shielded, circular chamber within the Palace complex that the Herald-Mages used when training their proteges in the Mage-aspects of their Gifts. The shielding on this room was incredibly ancient and powerful. It was *so* powerful that the shielding actually muffled physical sound; you couldn't even hear the Death Bell toll inside this room. One of the duties of every Herald-Mage in the Circle was to augment the protections here whenever they had the time and energy to spare. This shielding had to be strong; strong enough to contain magical "accidents" that would reduce the sparse furniture within the room to splinters. Those "accidents" were the reason why the walls were stone, the furniture limited to a couple of cheap stools and an equally cheap table, and why *every* Herald-Mage put full personal shields on himself and his pupil immediately on entering the door of this room.

Those accidents were also the reason why anyone who disturbed the practice sessions going on in the Work Room had better have a damned good reason for doing so.

Savil yanked the door open, and glared at the fair-haired, blue-uniformed Palace Guard who stood there, at rigid and proper attention. "Well?" she said, letting a bit of ice creep into her voice.

"Your pardon, Herald-Mage," he replied, his expression as stiff as his spine, "But you left orders to be notified as soon as your nephew arrived.'' He handed her a folded and sealed letter. ''His escort wished you to have this.''

She took it and stuffed it in a pocket of her breeches without looking at it. ''Oh, bloody hell,'' she muttered. ''So I did.''

She sighed, and became a bit more civil. ''Thank you, Guard. Send him and whatever damned escort he brought with him to my quarters; I'll get with them as soon as I can.''

The Guard saluted and turned sharply on his heel; Savil shut the door before he finished his pivot, and turned back to her pupil.

''All right, lad, how long have we been at this?''

Tylendel draped an arm over his curly head and grinned. ''Long enough for my stomach to start growling. I'm sorry, Savil, but I'm hungry. That's probably why my concentration's going.''

She shook her finger at him. ''Tchah, younglings and their stomachs! And just what do you plan to do if you get hungry in the middle of an arcane duel? Hmm?''

''Eat,'' he replied impishly. She threw up her hands in mock despair.

''All right, off with you—ah, ah,'' she warned, wagging her finger at him as he made ready to dispel the barrier the quick and dirty way; by pulling the energies into the ground. *''Properly,* my lad—''

He bowed to her in the finest courtly manner. She snorted. ''Get on with it, lad, if you're in such a hurry to stuff your face.''

She Watched him carefully as he took down the barrier—properly—did so with quite a meticulous attention to little details, like releasing the barrier-energy back into the same flow he'd taken it from. She nodded approvingly when he stepped across the place where the border had been and presented himself to have the shields she'd put on him taken off.

''You're getting better, Tylendel,'' she said, touching the middle of his forehead with her index finger, and absorbing the shield back into herself. Her skin tingled for a moment as she neutralized the overflow. ''You're coming along much faster than I guessed you would. Another year—no, less, I think—and you'll be ready to try your hand at a Border stint with me. And not much longer than that, and I'll shove you into Whites.''

"It's my teacher," he replied impishly, seizing her hand and kissing it, his long hair falling over her wrist and tickling it. "How can I help but succeed in such attractive surroundings?''

She snatched her hand back, and cuffed his ear lightly. "Get on with you! Even if I *wasn't* old enough to be your grandmother, we *both* know I'm the wrong sex for you to find me attractive!''

He ducked the blow, grinning, and pulled the door open for her. "Oh, Savil, don't you know that the real truth is that I'd lost my heart to my teacher, knew I had no hope, and couldn't accept a lesser woman than—''

"Out!" she sputtered, laughing so hard she nearly choked. "Liar! Before I do you damage!''

He ran off down the wood-paneled hallway, his own laughter echoing behind him.

She closed the Work Room door behind her and leaned against the wall, still laughing, holding her aching side. *The imp. More charm than any five younglings, and all the mischief of a young cat! I haven't laughed like this in years—not the way I have since I acquired Tylendel as a protege. That boy is such a treasure—if I can just wean him out of that stupid feud his family is involved in, he'll make a fine Herald-Mage. If I don't kill him first!*

She gulped down several long breaths of air, and composed herself. *I'm going to have to deal with that spoiled brat of a nephew in a few minutes,* she told herself sternly, using the thought to sober herself. *And I haven't the foggiest notion of what to do with him. Other than have him strangled—no, that's not such a good notion, it would please Withen too much. Great good gods, the man has turned into such a pompous ass in the last few years! I hardly recognized him. That ridiculous letter a week ago could have come from our father.*

She smoothed her hair with her hands (checking to see that the knot of it at the base of her neck had not come undone), tugged on the hem of her tunic, and made sure that the door of the Work Room was closed and mage-locked before heading up the hall toward her personal quarters. The heels of her boots clicked briskly against the stone of the hallway, and she nodded at courtiers and other Heralds as they passed her.

If only Treesa hadn't spoiled the lad so outrageously, there might be something there worth salvaging. Now, I don't know. I certainly don't have the time to find out for myself. Huh. I wonder—if I put the buy into lessons with the other Herald-trainees, then leave him to his own devices the rest of the time, that just might tell me something. If he doesn't turn to gambling and hunting and wild parties—if he becomes bored with the flitter-heads in the Court—

She pushed open one half of the double doors to the new Heralds' quarters, and strode through. Her own suite was just at the far end and on the left side of the hall.

Changes, changes. Five years ago we were crammed in four to a room, and not enough space to throw a tantrum in. Now we rattle around in this shiny-new barracks like a handful of peas in a bucket. And me with a suite and not getting forlorn looks from Jays or Tantras because one of the rooms is vacant. I can't see how we'll ever get enough bodies to fill this place . . .

The door stood slightly ajar; she shoved it out of the way, and paused a few steps into her outer room, crossing her arms and surveying the trio on the couch beneath her collection of Hawkbrother featherwork masks at the end of the room.

Only one of them was actually *on* the couch; Vanyel. Beside him, only too obviously playing his jailers, stood a pair of Withen's armsmen. On Vanyel's right, a short, stocky man—axeman, if Savil was any judge. On his left, one about a head taller and very swarthy; a common swordsman. And Vanyel, sitting very stiffly on the edge of the couch.

Savil heaved a strictly internal sigh. *Lad, a year obviously hadn't improved you except in looks—and that's no advantage. You're too damned handsome, and you know it.*

Since she'd last seen him, Vanyel's face and body had

refined. It was a face that could (and probably did) break hearts—broad brow, high cheekbones, pointed chin, sensuous lips—fine-arched black brows, and incredible silver eyes; all of it crowned with thick, straight, blue-black hair most women would kill to possess. The body of an acrobat; nicely muscled, if not over-tall.

And the posture was arrogant, the mouth set in sullen silence; the eyes sulky, and at the same time, challenging her.

Lord and Lady. Do I believe my fool brother, or do I take the chance that a good portion of what's wrong with the boy is due to Withen trying to mold him into his own image?

While she tried to make up her mind, she nodded at the two armsmen. "Thank you, good sirs," she said, crisply. "You have performed your duty admirably. You may go."

The taller one coughed uneasily, and gave her an uncomfortable look.

"Well?" she asked, sensing something coming—something she wasn't going to like. Something petty and small-minded—

"The boy's horse—"

"Stays, of course," she interrupted, seeing the flash of hurt in Vanyel's eyes before he masked it, and reacting to it without needing to think about which way she was going to jump.

"But, Herald, it's a valuable animal!" the armsman protested, his mouth thinning unhappily. "Lord Withen—my lord—surely you've beasts enough here—"

"What do you think this is?" she snapped, turning on him with unconcealed anger. Gods, if this was symptomatic of the boy's trip here, no wonder he was sullen.

Take the boy's horse, will you? You bloody little— She took control of herself, and gave them irrefutable reasons to take back to their master. They were, after all, only following orders.

"You think we run a damned breeding farm here? We haven't horses to spare. The boy will be taking equitation lessons, of course, and he's hardly going to be able to go over the jumping course on foot!"

"But—" the armsman sputtered, not prepared to give up, "Surely the Companions—"

"Bear their *Chosen* and *no other.*" She took a deep breath and forced her temper to cool. The man was making her more than annoyed with his obstinacy, he was making her quite thoroughly enraged, and if this was a measure of what Vanyel had been subjected to over the past few years, well, perhaps the boy wasn't entirely to blame for his current behavior.

"I said," she told the men, glaring, "you may go."

"But—I have certain orders—certain things I am to tell you—"

"I am countermanding those orders," she answered swiftly, invoking all of her authority, not just as a Herald, but as one of the most powerful Herald-Mages in the Heraldic Circle, second only to Queen's Own, Seneschal's, and Lord-Marshal's Herald. "This is *my* place, and *my* jurisdiction. And you may tell my brother Withen that I will make up my own mind what is to be done with the boy. If he wants to deposit young Vanyel in my care, then he'll have to put up with my judgments. And you can tell him I said so. Good day, gentlemen." She smiled with honeyed venom. "Or need I call a Guard to escort you?"

They had no choice but to take themselves off, though they did so with extreme reluctance. Savil waited until they had gone, and were presumably out of hearing range, before taking the letter she'd been given out of her pocket. She held it up so that Vanyel could see that it had not been opened, then slowly, deliberately tore it in four pieces and dropped the pieces on the floor.

Margret is going to have my hide, she thought wryly. *If she's told me once not to throw things on the floor, she's told me a hundred times—*

"I don't know what Withen had to say in that letter," she told the strange and silent boy. Was that sullenness in the set of his mouth, or fear? Was that suspicion in the back of his eyes, or arrogance? "Frankly, I don't care. This much I can tell you—young man, you are going to stand or fall with me by your own actions. I tell you now that I very much resent what Withen has done; I have three proteges to train, and no time to waste on cosseting a daydreamer.'' *Might as well let him know the truth about how I feel right out and right now; he'll find out from the gossip sooner or later. I can't afford to have him pulling something stupid in the hopes I'll pull him out of it and give him some attention.* "I have no intention of trying to make you into something you aren't. But I also have no intention of allowing you to make a fool out of me, or inconvenience me.''

There was a whisper of sound at the door.

Without turning around, Savil knew from the brush of embarrassed Mindspeech behind her that Tylendel and her other two proteges, Mardic and Donni, had come in behind her, not expecting to find anyone except Savil here. They had stopped in the doorway—startled at finding their mentor dressing down a strange boy, and more than a bit embarrassed to have walked in at such a touchy moment.

And of course, now it would be even more embarrassing for them to walk back out and try to pretend it hadn't happened.

"You'll be taking lessons with some of the Herald-trainees and with some of the young courtiers as soon as I get a chance to make the arrangements,'' Savil continued serenely, gesturing slightly with her right hand for her three "children" to come up beside her. "Now—Vanyel, this is Donni, this Mardic, and this Tylendel. As Herald-trainees, they outrank you; let's get that straight right now.''

"Yes, Aunt,'' Vanyel said without changing his expression a hair.

"Now what that actually *means* is not one damned thing, except I expect you to be polite.''

"Yes, Aunt.''

"My servant Margret tends to us; breakfast and lunch are cold and left over on that table over there. Supper will be with the Court for you once I get you introduced. If you miss it, you can take your chances with us. Lessons, hmm. For now—oh—Donni, I want you to take him with you in the morning and turn him over to Kayla;

Withen was rather insistent on his getting weapons work, and for once I agree with him.''

"Yes, Savil,'' the short, tousle-haired trainee said calmly. Savil blessed the girl's soothing presence, and also blessed the fact that she was lifebound to Mardic. Nothing shook a lifebond except the death of one of the pair. Vanyel's handsome face wasn't going to turn *her* head.

She rather dreaded the effect of that face on the rest of the younglings at the Court, though.

"Mardic?''

The imperturbable farmer's son nodded his round head without speaking.

"Take him to Bardic Collegium in the afternoon for me, and get them to put him into History, Literature, and—'' she wrinkled her brow in thought as her three proteges arranged themselves around her.

"How about Religions?'' Tylendel suggested. He raised one dark-gold eyebrow and Mindspoke his teacher in Private-mode, his lips thinning a little. *:He's lovely, Savil. And he Feels like he's either an arrogant little bastard, or somebody's been hurting him inside for an awfully long time. Frankly, I couldn't tell you which. Is he going to be as much trouble as I think?:*

:Don't know, lad,: Savil Mindspoke soberly. *:But don't get wrapped up with him, not until we know. And* don't *fall in love with him. I have no idea where his preferences lie, but even Withen didn't hint he was* shay'a'chern. *I don't want to have to patch your broken heart up. Again.:*

:Not a chance, Teacher,: Tylendel mind-grinned. *:I've learned better.:*

:Huh. I should hope. Oh, Lord of Light—I did *give all of you grabs at Dominick's old room, didn't I? I don't want to start this off with hurt feelings—:*

:Yes, you did, and none of us wanted to move,: Tylendel mind-chuckled. *The garden door may be nice but it's drafty as the Cave of the Winds. If I had someone to keep me warm—:*

:I could get you a dog,: she suggested, and watched his lips twitch as he tried not to smile. *:Well, that's one worry out of the way.:* Then said aloud, "All right, Van-

yel, History, Literature and Religions it is, and weapons work with Kayla in the morning. She teaches the young highborns, and she's very good—and if I find out you've been avoiding her lessons, I'll take a strap to you.''

Vanyel flushed at that, but said nothing.

''Donni, Mardic, Tylendel, give Vanyel a hand with his things; we'll put him in the garden chamber. I had Margret get it ready for him this morning.''

As the three trainees scooped up a pack apiece, and Vanyel bent slowly to take the fourth, Savil added a last admonition.

''Vanyel, what you do with your free time is your own business,'' she said, perhaps a bit more harshly than she intended. ''But if you get yourself into trouble, and there's plenty of it to get into around here, don't expect me to pull you out. I can't, and I won't. You're an imposition. It's your job to see that you become less of one.''

Vanyel thanked the trainees for their help as they dropped his packs to one side of the door, speaking in a voice that sounded dull and exhausted even in his own ears.

The blond one hesitated for a moment—just long enough to give him what *looked* like a genuine smile, before slipping out the door.

But despite that smile, Vanyel was mortally glad when they didn't linger. He closed the door behind them, then leaned up against it with his eyes shut. The entire day had been confusing and wearying, an emotional obstacle course that he was just happy to have survived.

The worst of it had been the past couple of hours; first, being shuttled off to Savil's quarters with Erek and Garth suddenly deciding to act like the jailers that they were, then the interminable wait—then the Interview.

Her words had hurt; he willed them not to. He willed himself not to care.

Then he moved to the middle of his new room and looked around himself, and blinked in surprise.

It was—amazing. Warm, and welcoming, paneled and furnished in goldenoak, and as well-appointed as his

mother's private chamber. Certainly *nothing* like his room
back at Forst Reach. A huge bed stood against one wall,
a bed almost wide enough for *three* and covered with a
thick, soft red comforter. In the corner, a wardrobe, not
a simple chest, to hold his clothing. Beside it a desk and
padded chair—Havens, an *instrument* rack on the wall
next to the weapons-rack! Next to the window a second,
more heavily padded chair, both chairs upholstered in
red that matched the comforter. His own fireplace. A
small table next to the bed, and a bookcase. But that
wasn't the most amazing thing—

His room had its own private entrance, something that
was either a small, glazed door or an enormous window
that opened up on a garden.

I don't believe this, he thought, staring stupidly through
the glass at the sculptured bushes and the glint of setting
sun on the river beyond. *I just do not believe this. I expected to be in another prison. Instead—*

He tried the door/window. It was unlocked, and swung
open at a touch.

*—instead, I'm given total freedom. I do not believe
this!* His knees went weak, and he had to sit down on the
edge of the bed before he collapsed. The breeze that had
been allowed to enter when he opened the window made
the light material used as curtains flap lazily.

Gods—he thought, dazedly. *I don't know what to think.
She saves Star—then she humiliates me in front of the
trainees. She gives me this room—then she tells me I'm
the next thing to worthless and she threatens to beat me
herself. What am I supposed to believe?*

He could hear the murmuring of voices beyond the
other door, the one the tall blond had closed after himself. *They sound so comfortable out there, so easy with
each other,* he thought wistfully. They were terribly un-
alike, the three of them. The one called Donni could have
been Erek's twin sister; they looked to have been cast
from the same mold—dark, curly-haired, phlegmatic. The
shorter boy, Mardic, had the look of one of Withen's
smallholders; earthy, square, and brown. But the third—

Vanyel was experiencing a strange, unsteady feeling

when he thought about the tall, graceful blond called Tylendel. He didn't know why.

Not even the minstrel Shanse had evoked this depth
of—disturbance—in him.

There was a burst of laughter beyond the door. *They
sound so happy,* he thought a bit sadly, before his thoughts
darkened. *They're probably laughing at me.*

He clenched his teeth. *Damn it, I don't care, I won't
care. I don't need their approval.*

He closed his walls a little tighter about himself, and
began the mundane task of settling himself into his new
home. And tried not to feel himself left on the outside,
telling himself over and over again that nothing mattered.

The slender girl Vanyel's aunt had called "Donni"
looked askance at all the padding and armor Vanyel
picked off his armor-stand and weapons-rack. "Are you
really taking all that?" she asked, hazel eyes rather wide
with surprise.

He nodded shortly.

She shook her head in disbelief, her tight, sable curls
scarcely moving. "I can't see why you want all *that* stuff,
but I guess it's your back. Come on."

There'd been no one in the suite when Vanyel woke,
but there *had* been cider, bread and butter, cheese, and
fruit waiting on a sideboard in the central room. He had
figured that was supposed to be breakfast, seeing that
someone—or several someones, more like—had already
made hearty inroads on the food. He had helped himself,
then found a servant to show him the way to the bathing-
room and the privies, and cleaned himself up.

He'd pulled on some of his oldest and shabbiest clothing in anticipation of getting them well-grimed at the
coming weaponry-lesson. He was back in his own room
and in a very somber mood, sitting on the floor while
putting some new leather lacings on his practice armor,
when Donni came hunting him.

He gathered up his things and followed one step behind
her out through his garden door and into the sunlit, fra-
grant garden, trying not to let any apprehension seep into
his cool shell. She took him on a circuitous path that led

from his own garden door, past several ornamental grottoes and fish ponds, down to a graveled pathway that followed the course of the river.

They trudged past what looked like a stable, except that the stalls had no doors on them, and past a smaller building beside it. Then the path took an abrupt turn to the right, ending at a gate in a high wooden fence. By now Vanyel's arms were getting more than a little tired; he was hot, and sweating, and he hoped that this was at least close to their goal.

But no; the seemingly placid trainee flashed him what *might* have been a sympathetic grin, and opened the gate, motioning for Vanyel to go through.

"There," she said, pointing across what seemed to be an expanse of carefully manicured lawn as wide as the legended Dhorisha Plains. At the other end of the lawn was a plain, rawly new wooden building with high clerestory windows. "That's the salle," she told him. "That's where we're going. They just built it last year so that we could practice year 'round." She giggled. "I think they got tired of the trainees having bouts in the hallways when it rained or snowed!"

Vanyel just nodded, determined to show no symptoms of his weariness. She set off across the grass with a stride so brisk he had to really push himself to keep up with her. It was all he could do to keep from panting with effort by the time they actually reached the building, and his side was in agony when she slowed down enough to open the door for him.

Once inside he could see that the structure was one single large room, with a mirrored wall and a carefully sanded wooden floor. There were several young people out on the floor already, ranging in apparent age from as young as eleven or twelve to as old as their early twenties. Most of them were sparring—

Vanyel was too exhausted to take much notice of what they were up to, although the pair nearest him (he saw with a sinking heart) were working out in almost *exactly* the weapons style Jervis used.

"This him?"

A woman with a soft, musical contralto spoke from

behind them, and Vanyel turned abruptly, dropping a vambrace.

"Yes, ma'am," Donni said, picking the bracer up before Vanyel had a chance even to flush. "Vanyel, this is Weaponsmaster Kayla. Kayla, this stuff is all his; I guess he brought it from home. I've got to get going, or I'll miss my session in the Work Room."

"Havens forfend," Kayla said dryly. "Savil would eat me for lunch if you were late. Don't forget you have dagger this afternoon, girl."

Donni nodded and slipped out the door, leaving Vanyel alone with the redoubtable Weaponsmaster.

For redoubtable she was. From the crown of her head to the soles of her feet she was nothing but sinew and muscle. Her black hair, tightly braided to her head, showed not a strand of gray, despite the age revealed by the fine net of wrinkles around her eyes and mouth. Those gray-green eyes didn't look as if they missed much.

For the rest, Kayla's shoulders were nearly a handspan wider than his, and her wrists as thick as his ankles. Vanyel had no doubt that she could readily wield *any* of the blades in the racks along the wall, even the ones as tall or taller than she. He did *not* particularly want to face this woman in *any* sort of combat situation. She looked like she could quite handily take on Jervis *and* mop the floor with his ugly face.

Vanyel remained outwardly impassive, but was inwardly quaking as she in turn studied him.

"Well, young man," she said quietly, after a moment that was far too long for his liking. "You might as well throw that stuff over in the corner over there—" she nodded toward the far end of the salle, and a pile of discarded equipment. "—we'll see what we can salvage of it. *You* certainly won't be needing it."

Vanyel blinked at her, wondering if he'd missed something. "Why not?" he asked, just as quietly.

"Good gods, lad, that stuff's about as suited to you as boots on a cat!" she replied, with a certain amusement. "Whoever your last master was, he was a fool to put you in *that* gear. No, young man—you see Redel and Oden over there?"

She pointed with her chin at a pair of slender, androgynous figures involved in an intricate, and possibly deadly dance with very light, slender swords.

"I'll make Duke Oden your instructor; he'll be pleased to have a pupil besides young Lord Redel. That's the kind of style suited to you, so *that's* what you'll be doing, young Vanyel," she told him.

His heart rose to its proper place from its former position—somewhere in the vicinity of his boots.

Kayla graced him with a momentary smile. "Mind you, lad, Oden's no light taskmaster. You'll find you work up as healthy a sweat and collect just as many bruises as any of the hack-and-bashers. So let's get you suited for it, eh?"

If the morning was an unexpected pleasure—and it was; for the first time in his life he received *praise* for weapons work, and preened under it—the afternoon was an unalloyed disaster.

It started when he returned with equipment that weighed a third of what he'd carried over. He racked it with care he usually didn't grant to weaponry, and sought the central room of the suite.

Someone—probably the hitherto invisible Margret—had taken away the food left on the sideboard this morning and replaced it with meat rolls, more fruit and cheese, and a bottle of light wine.

Tylendel was sprawled on the couch, a meat roll in one hand, a book in the other, a crease of concentration between his brows. He didn't even look up as Vanyel moved hesitantly just into the common room itself.

Once again he got that strange, half-fearful, fluttery feeling in the pit of his stomach. He cleared his throat, and Tylendel jumped, dropping his book, and looking up with his eyes widened and his hair over one eye.

"Good gods, Vanyel, make some *noise*, next time!" he said, bending to retrieve his book from the floor. "I didn't know there was anyone here but me! That's lunch over there—"

He pointed with the half-eaten roll.

"Savil says to eat and get yourself cleaned up; she's

going to present you to the Queen before the noon recess. Then you'll be able to have dinner with the Court; the rest of us get it on the fly as our schedules permit. Savil will be back in a few minutes so you'd better move." He tilted his head to one side, just a little, and offered, "If you need any help. . . ."

Vanyel stiffened; the offer hadn't sounded at all unfriendly, but—it could be Tylendel was looking for a way to spy on him. Savil hadn't necessarily told the truth.

—*if only*—

"No," he replied curtly, "I don't need any help." He paused, then added for politeness' sake, "Thank you."

Tylendel gave him a dubious look, then shrugged and dove back into his book.

Savil *was* back in moments; Vanyel had barely time to make himself presentable before she scooped him up and herded him off to the Throne Room.

The Throne Room was a great deal smaller than he had pictured; long and narrow, and rather dark. And stuffy; there were more people crammed into this room than it had ever been intended to hold. Somewhere down at the farther end of it was the Throne itself, beneath a huge blue and silver tapestry of a rampant winged horse with broken chains on its throat and legs that took up the entire wall over the Throne. Vanyel could see the tapestry, but nothing else; everyone else in the room seemed to be at least a hand taller than he was, and all he could see were heads.

The presentation itself was a severe disappointment. Vanyel waited with Savil at his side for nearly an hour while some wrangle or other involving a pair of courtiers was ironed out. Then Savil's name was called; the two of them (Vanyel trailing in Savil's formidable wake) were announced by a middle-aged Herald in full Court Whites. Vanyel was escorted to the foot of the Throne by that same Herald, where Queen Elspeth (a thin, dark-haired woman who was looking very tired and somewhat preoccupied) nodded to him in a friendly manner, and said about five words in greeting. He bowed and was escorted back to Savil's side, and that was all there was to it.

Then Savil hustled him back to change *out* of Court

garb and into ordinary day-garb for his afternoon classes. Mardic practically flew in the door from the hallway and took him in tow. They traversed a long, dark corridor leading from Savil's quarters, out through a double door, to a much older section of the Palace. From there they exited a side door and out into more gardens—herb gardens this time, and kitchen gardens.

Mardic didn't seem to be the talkative type, but he could certainly move. His fast walk took them past an l-shaped granite building before Vanyel had a chance to ask what it was, and up to a square fieldstone structure. "Bardic Collegium," Mardic said shortly, pausing just long enough for a couple of youngsters who were running to get past him, then opening the black wooden door for him.

He didn't say another word; just left him at the door of his first class before vanishing elsewhere into the building.

He was finding it hard to believe that Savil was going so far in ignoring his father's orders as to put him in *lessoning* with the Bardic students. Nevertheless, here he was.

Inside Bardic Collegium. Actually inside the building, seated in a row of chairs with three other youngsters in a small, sunny room on the first floor.

More than that, pacing back and forth as he lectured or questioned them was a real, live Bard in full Scarlets; a tall, powerful man who was probably as much at home wielding a broadsword as a lute.

At home Vanyel had always been a full step ahead of his brothers and cousins when it came to scholastics, so he began the hour with a feeling of boredom. History was the proverbial open book to him—or so he had always thought. He began the session with the rather smug feeling that he was going to dazzle his new classmates.

The other three boys looked at him curiously when he came in and sat down with them, but they didn't say anything. One was mouse-blond, one chestnut, and one dark; all three were dressed nearly the same as Vanyel, in ordinary day-clothing of white raime shirt and tunic and breeches of soft brown or gray fabric. He couldn't tell if they were Heraldic trainees or Bardic; they wore no uniforms the way their elders did. Not that it mattered, really, except that he would have liked to impress them with his scholarship if they *were* Bardic students.

The room was hardly bigger than his bedroom in Savil's suite; but unlike the Heralds' quarters, this building was old, worn, and a bit shabby. Vanyel had a moment to register disappointment at the scuffed floor, dusty furnishings, and fuded paint before the leonine Bard at the window-end of the room began the class.

After that, all he had a chance to feel was shock.

"Yesterday we discussed the Arvale annexation; today we're going to cover the negotiations with Rethwellan that followed the annexation." With those words, Bard Chadran launched into his lecture; a dissertation on the important Arvale-Zalmon negotiations in the time of King Tavist. It was fascinating. There was only one problem.

Vanyel had never even heard of the Arvale-Zalmon negotiations, and all he knew of King Tavist was that he was the son of Queen Terilee and the father of Queen Leshia; Tavist's reign had been a quiet one, a reign devoted more to studied diplomacy than the kind of deeds that made for ballads. So when the Bard opened the floor to discussion, Vanyel had to sit there and try to look as if he understood it all, without having the faintest idea of what was going on.

He took reams of notes, of course, but without knowing why the negotiations had been so important, much less what they were about, they didn't make a great deal of sense.

He escaped that class with the feeling that he'd only just escaped being skinned and eaten alive.

Religions was a *bit* better, though not much. He'd thought it was Religion, singular. He found out how wrong he was—again. It was, indeed, Religions in the plural sense. Since the population of Valdemar was a patchwork quilt of a dozen different peoples escaping from various unbearable situations, it was hardly surprising that each one of those peoples had their own religion. As Vanyel heard, over and over again that hour, the law of Valdemar on the subject of worship was "there is no 'one, true way.' " But with a dozen or more "ways" in practice, it would have been terribly easy for a Bard—or Herald—to misstep among people strange to him. Hence this class, which was currently covering the "People of the One" who had settled about Crescent Lake.

It was something of a shock, hearing that what *his* priest would have called rankest heresy was presented as just another aspect of the truth. Vanyel spent half his time feeling utterly foolish, and the other half trying to hide his reactions of surprise and disquiet.

But it was Literature—or rather, an event just before the Literature class—which truly deflated and defeated him.

He had been toying with the idea of petitioning one of the Bards to enroll him in their Collegium before he began the afternoon's classes, but now he was doubtful of being able to survive the lessons.

Gods, I—I'm as pig-ignorant compared to these trainees as my cousins are compared to me, he thought glumly, slumping in the chair nearest the door as he and the other two with him waited for the teacher of Literature to put in her appearance. *But—maybe this time. Lord of Light knows I've memorized every ballad I could ever get my hands on.*

Then he overheard Bard Chadran talking out in the hallway with another Bard; presumably the teacher of this class. But when he heard his own name, and realized that they were talking about *him*, he stretched his ears without shame or hesitation to catch all that he could.

"—so Savil wants us to take him if he's got the makings," Chadran was saying.

"Well, has he?" asked the second, a dark, sensuously female voice.

"Shanse's heard him sing; says he's got the voice and the hands for it, and I trust him on that," said Chadran, hesitantly.

"But not the Gift?" the second persisted.

Chadran coughed. "I—didn't hear any sign of it in class. And it's pretty obvious he doesn't compose, or we'd have heard about it. Shanse would have said something, or put it in his report, and he didn't."

"He has to have two out of three; Gift, Talent, and Creativity—you *know* that, Chadran," said the woman. "Shanse didn't see any signs of Gift either, did he?"

Chadran sighed. "No. Breda, when Savil asked me about this boy, I looked up Shanse's report on the area. He *did* mention the boy, and he *was* flattering enough about the boy's musicality that we could get him training as a minstrel if—"

"If—"

"If he weren't his father's heir. But the truth is, he said the boy has a magnificent ear, and aptitude for mimicry, and the talent. But no creativity, and no Gift. And that's not enough to enroll someone's heir as a mere minstrel. Still—Breda, love, *you* look for Gift. You're better at seeing it than any of us. I'd really like to do Savil a favor on this one. She says the boy is set enough on music to defy a fairly formidable father—and we owe her a few."

"I'll try him," said the woman, "But don't get your hopes up. Shanse may not have the Gift himself, but he knows it when he hears it."

Vanyel had something less than an instant to wonder what they meant by "Gift" before the woman he'd overheard entered the room. As tall as a man, thin, plain—she still had a *presence* that forced Vanyel to pay utmost attention to every word she spoke, every gesture she made.

"Today we're going to begin the 'Windrider' cycle," she said, pulling a gittern around from where it hung across her back. "I'm going to begin with the very first 'Windrider' ballad known, and I'm going to present it the way it should be dealt with. Heard, not read. This ballad was *never* designed to be read, and I'll tell you the truth, the flaws present in it mostly vanish when it's sung."

She strummed a few chords, then launched into the opening to the "Windrider Unchained"—and he no longer wondered what the "Gift" could be.

Because she didn't just *sing*—not like Vanyel would

have sung, or even the minstrel (or, as he realized now, the *Bard*) Shanse would have. No—she made her listeners *experience* every word of the passage; to feel every emotion, to see the scene, to live the event as the originals must have lived it. When she finished, Vanyel knew he would never forget those words again.

And he knew to the depths of his soul that he would never be able to do what she had just done.

Oh, he tried; when she prompted him to sing the next Windrider ballad while she played, he gave it his best. But he could tell from the look in his fellow classmates' eyes—interest, but *not* rapt fascination—that he hadn't even managed a pale imitation.

As he sat down and she gestured to the next to take a ballad, he saw the pity in her eyes and the slight shake of her head—and knew then that *she* knew he'd overheard the conversation in the hallway. That this was her way of telling him, gently, and indirectly, that his dream could not be realized.

It was the pity that hurt the most, after the realization that he did not have the proper material to be a Bard. It cut—as cruelly as any blade. All that work—all that fighting to get his hand back the way it had been—and all for nothing. He'd never even had a hope.

Vanyel threw himself onto his bed, his chest aching, his head throbbing—

I thought nothing would ever be worse than home—but at least I still had dreams. Now I don't even have that.

The capper on the miserable day was his aunt, his competent, clever, selfless, damn-her-to-nine-hells aunt.

He flopped over onto his stomach, and fought back the sting in his eyes.

She'd pulled him aside right after dinner; "I asked the Bards to see if they could take you," she'd said. "I'm sorry, Vanyel, but they told me you're a very talented musician, but that's all you'll ever be. That's not enough to get you into Bardic when you're the heir to a holding."

"But—" he'd started to say, then clamped his mouth shut.

She gave him a sharp look. "I know how you probably

feel, Vanyel, but your duty as Withen's heir is going to have to come first. So you'd better resign yourself to the situation instead of fighting it.''

She watched him broodingly as he struggled to maintain his veneer of calm. "The gods know," she said finally, *"I* stood in your shoes, once. I wanted the Holding—but I wasn't firstborn son. And as things turned out, I'm glad I didn't get the Holding. If you make the best of your situation, you may find one day that you wouldn't have had a better life if you'd chosen it yourself.''

How could she *know?* he fumed. *I hate her. So help me, I hate her. Everything she does is so damned perfect! She never says anything, but she doesn't have to; all she has to do is give me that* look. *If I hear one more word about how I'm supposed to* like *this trap that's closed on me, I may go mad!*

He turned over on his back, and brooded. It wasn't even sunset—and he was stuck here with his lute staring down at him from the wall with all the broken dreams it implied.

And nothing to distract him. Or was there?

Dinner was over, but there were going to be people gathered in the Great Hall all night. And there were plenty of people his age there; young people who *weren't* Bard trainees, nor Herald proteges. Ordinary young people, more like normal human beings.

He forgot all his apprehensions about being thought a country bumpkin; all he could think of now was the admiration his wit and looks used to draw at the infrequent celebrations that brought the offspring of several Keeps and Holdings together. He needed a dose of that admiration, and needed its sweetness as an antidote to the bitterness of failure.

He flung himself off the bed and rummaged in his wardrobe for an appropriately impressive outfit; he settled on a smoky gray velvet as suiting his mood and his flair for the dramatic.

He planned his entrance to the Great Hall with care; waiting until one of those moments that occur at any gathering of people where everyone seems to choose the same moment to stop talking. When that moment came, he seized it; pacing gracefully into the silence as if it had been created expressly to display *him*.

It worked to perfection; within moments he had a little circle of courtiers of his own flocking about him, eager to impress the newcomer with their friendliness. He basked in their attentions for nearly an hour before it began to pall.

A lanky youngster named Liers was waxing eloquent on the subject of his elder brother dealing with a set of brigands. Vanyel stifled a yawn; this was sounding *exactly* like similar evenings at Forst Reach!

"So he charged straight at them—"

"Which was a damn fool thing to do if you ask me," Vanyel said, his brows creasing.

"But—it takes a *brave* man—" the young man protested weakly.

"I repeat, it was a damn fool thing to do," Vanyel persisted. "Totally outnumbered, no notion if the party behind him was coming in time—great good gods, the *right* thing to do would have been to turn tail and run! If he'd done it convincingly, he could have led them straight into the arms of his own troops! Charging off like that could have gotten him killed!"

"It worked," Liers sulked.

"Oh, it worked all right, because nobody in his right mind would have done what he did!"

"It was the *valiant* thing to have done," Liers replied, lifting his chin.

Vanyel gave up; he didn't dare alienate these younglings. They were all he had—

"You're right, Liers," he said, hating the lie. "It was a valiant thing to have done."

Liers smiled in foolish satisfaction as Vanyel made more stupid remarks; eventually Vanyel extricated himself from *that* little knot of idlers and went looking for something more interesting.

The fools were as bad as his brother; he could *not*, would *never* get it through their heads that there was nothing "romantic" about getting themselves hacked to bits in the name of Valdemar or a lady. That there was nothing uplifting about losing an arm or a leg or an eye. That there was nothing, *nothing* "glorious" about warfare.

As soon as he turned away from the male contingent, the female descended upon him in a chattering flock; flirting, coquetting, each doing her best to get Vanyel's attention settled on *her*. It was exactly the same playette that had been enacted over and over in his mother's bower; there were more players, and the faces were both different and often prettier, but it was the identical script.

Vanyel was bored.

But it was marginally better than being lectured by Savil, or longing after the Bards and the Gift he never would have.

"—Tylendel," said the pert little brunette at his elbow, with a sigh of disappointment.

"What about Tylendel?" Vanyel asked, his interest, for once, caught.

"Oh, Tashi is in love with Tylendel's big brown eyes," laughed another girl, a tall, pale-complected redhead.

"Not a chance, Tashi," said Reva, who was flushed from a little too much wine. She giggled. "You haven't a chance. He's—what's that word Savil uses?"

"*Shay'a'chern,*" supplied Cress. "It's some outland tongue."

"What's it mean?" Vanyel asked.

Reva giggled, and whispered, "That he doesn't like girls. He likes boys. Lucky boys!"

"For Tylendel I'd turn into a boy!" Tashi sighed, then giggled back at her friend. "Oh, what a waste! Are you sure?"

"Sure as stars," Reva assured her. "Only just last year he broke his heart over that bastard Nevis."

Vanyel suppressed his natural reaction of astonishment. Didn't—like girls. He knew at least that the youngling courtiers used "like" synonymously with "bedding." But—didn't "like" girls? "Liked" boys?

He'd known he'd been sheltered from some things, but he'd never even guessed about this one.

Was this why Withen—

"Nevis—wasn't he the one who couldn't make up his mind *which* he liked and claimed he'd been seduced every time he crawled into somebody's bed?" Tashi asked in rapt fascination.

"The very same," Reva told her. "I am *so* glad his parents called him home!"

They were off into a dissection of the perfidious Nevis then, and Vanyel lost interest. He drifted around the Great Hall, but was unable to find anything or anyone he cared to spend any time with. He drank a little more wine than he intended, but it didn't help make the evening any livelier, and at length he gave up and went to bed.

He lay awake for a long time, skirting the edges of the thoughts he'd had earlier. From the way the girls had giggled about it, it was pretty obvious that Tylendel's preferences were something short of "respectable." And Withen—

Oh, he knew now what Withen would have to say about it if he knew that his son was even sharing the same quarters as Tylendel.

All those times he went after me when I was tiny, for hugging and kissing Meke. That business with Father Leren and the lecture on "proper masculine behavior." The fit he had when Liss dressed me up in her old dresses like an overgrown doll. Oh, gods.

Suddenly the reasons behind a great many otherwise inexplicable actions on Withen's part were coming clear.

Why he kept shoving girls at me, why he bought me that—professional. Why he kept arranging for friends of Mother's with compliant daughters to visit. Why he hated seeing me in fancy clothing. Why some of the armsmen would go quiet when I came by—why some of the jokes would just stop. *Father didn't even want a hint of this to get to me.*

He ached inside; just ached.

I've lost music—no; even if Tylendel is to be trusted, I can't take the chance. Not even on—being his friend. If he didn't *turn on me, which he probably would.*

All that was left was the other dream—the ice-dream. The only dream that couldn't hurt him.

* * *

The chasm wasn't too wide to jump, but it was deep. And there was something—terrible—at the bottom of it. He didn't know how he knew that, but he knew it was true. Behind him was nothing but the empty, wintry ice-plain. On the other side of the chasm it was springtime. He wanted to cross over, to the warmth, to listen to bird-song beneath the trees—but he was afraid to jump. It seemed to widen even as he looked at it.

"Vanyel?"

He looked up, startled.

Tylendel stood on the other side, wind ruffling his hair, his smile wide and as warm and open as spring sun-shine.

"Do you want to come over?" the trainee asked softly. He held out one hand. "I'll help you, if you like."

Vanyel backed up a step, clasping his arms tightly to his chest to keep from inadvertently answering that ex-tended hand.

"Vanyel?" The older boy's eyes were gentle, coaxing. "Vanyel, I'd like to be your friend." He lowered his voice still more, until it was little more than a whisper, and gestured invitingly. "I'd like," he continued, "to be more than your friend."

"No!" Vanyel cried, turning away violently, and run-ning as fast as he could into the empty whiteness.

When he finally stopped, he was alone on the empty plain, alone, and chilled to the marrow. He ached all over at first, but then the cold really set in, and he couldn't feel much of anything. There was no sign of the chasm, or of Tylendel. And for one brief moment, lone-liness made him ache worse than the cold.

Then the chill seemed to reach the place where the loneliness was, and that began to numb as well.

He began walking, choosing a direction at random. The snow-field wasn't as featureless as he'd thought, it seemed. The flat, smooth snow-plain that creaked be-neath his feet began to grow uneven. Soon he was having to avoid huge teeth of ice that thrust up through the crust of the snow—then he could no longer avoid them; he was having to climb over and around them.

They were sharp-edged; sharp as glass shards. He cut himself once, and stared in surprise at the blood on the snow. And, strangely enough, it didn't seem to hurt—
There was only the cold.

Five

Tylendel was sprawled carelessly across the grass in the garden, reading. Vanyel watched him from behind the safety of his window curtains, half sick with conflicting emotions. The breeze was playing with the trainee's tousled hair almost the same way it had in his dream.

He shivered, and closed his eyes. *Gods. Oh, gods. Why me? Why now? And why, oh why, him? Savil's favorite protege—*

He clutched the fabric of the curtain as if it were some kind of lifeline, and opened his eyes again. Tylendel had changed his pose a little, leaning his head on his hand, frowning in concentration. Vanyel shivered and bit his lip, feeling his heart pounding so hard he might as well have been running footraces. No girl had ever been able to make his heart race like this. . . .

The thought made him flush, his stomach twisting. *Gods, what am I? Like him? I must be. Father will—oh, gods. Father will kill me, lock me up, tell everyone I've gone mad. Maybe I have gone mad.*

Tylendel smiled suddenly at something he was reading; Vanyel's heart nearly stopped, and he wanted to cry. *If only he'd smile at me that way—oh, gods, I can't, I can't, I daren't trust him, he'll only turn on me like all the others.*

Like all *the others.*

He turned away from the window, invoking his shield of indifference with a sick and heavy heart.

If only I dared. If only I dared.

* * *

Savil locked the brassbound door of her own private version of the Work Room with fingers that trembled a little, and turned to face her favorite protege, Tylendel, with more than a little trepidation.

Gods. This is not going to be easy. She braced herself for what was bound to be a dangerous confrontation; both for herself and for Tylendel. She didn't *think* he was going to go for her throat—but—well, this time she was going to push him just a little farther than she had dared before. And there was always the chance that it would be *too* far, this time.

He stood in the approximate center of the room, arms folded over the front of his plain brown tunic, expression unwontedly sober. It was fairly evident that he had already gathered this was not going to be a lesson or an ordinary discussion.

There was nothing else in this room, nothing at all. Unlike the public Work Room, this one was square, not circular; but the walls here were stone, too, and for some of the same reasons. In addition there was an inlaid pattern of lighter-colored wood delineating a perfect circle in the center of the hardwood floor. And there was an oddness about the walls, a sense of presence, as if they were nearly alive. In a way, they were; Savil had put no small amount of her own personal energies into the protections on this room. They were, in some senses, a part of her. And because of that, she should be safer here than anywhere else, if something went wrong.

"You didn't bring me in here to practice," Tylendel stated flatly.

Savil swallowed and shook her head. "No, I didn't. You're right. I wanted to talk with you; I have two subjects, really, and I don't want anyone to have a chance at overhearing us."

"The first subject?" Tylendel asked. "Or—I think I know. My family again." His expression didn't change visibly, but Savil could sense his sudden anger in the stubborn setting of his jaw.

"Your family again," Savil agreed. "Tylendel, you're a Herald, or nearly. Heralds *do not* take sides in anyone's fight, not even when their own blood is involved. Your people have been putting pressure on you to do something. Now *I* know you haven't interfered—but I also know you want to. And I'm afraid that you might give in to that temptation.''

His mouth tightened and he looked away from her. ''So Evan Leshara can pour his poison into the ear of anyone at Court who cares to listen—and I'm not allowed to do or say anything about it, is that it? I'm not even allowed to call him a damned liar for some of the things he's said about Staven?'' He pulled his gaze back to her, and glared at her as angrily as if she were the one responsible for his enemy's behavior. ''It's more than just my blood, Savil, it's my *twin*. By all he believes, by all he holds true, we've got blood-debt to pay here—and *Staven*, for all that he's young, is the Lord Holder now. It's his decision; the rest of us Frelennye must and *will* support him. And besides all that, he's in the *right*, dammit!''

''Lord Holder or not, *young* or not, *right* or not, he's a damned hotheaded fool,'' Savil burst out, flinging up both her hands before her in a gesture of complete frustration. ''Blood-debt be hanged, it's that kind of fool thinking that got your people and the Leshara into this *stupid* feud in the first damned place! *You can't bring back the dead with more blood!*''

''It's honor, dammit!'' He clenched his hands into fists. ''Can't you even *try* to understand that?''

''It has nothing to do with *real* honor,'' she said scornfully. ''It has everything to do with plain, obstinate pride. 'Lendel, you *cannot* be involved.''

She froze with her heart in her mouth as he made one angry step toward her.

He saw her reaction, and halted.

She plowed onward, trusting in the advice she'd gotten. *Please, Jaysen, be right this time, too.*

''This whole feud is *insanity*! 'Lendel, listen to me— it has got to be stopped, and if it goes on much longer it's the Heralds who'll have to stop it and you *cannot* take sides!''

All right so far, she hadn't said anything new. Now for

the fresh goad. And hope it wasn't too much of a goad, too soon.

" 'Lendel, I know you've never been able to figure out why both you *and* Staven weren't taken by Companions— well, dammit, it's *exactly* this insanity that's the reason your beloved twin *didn't* get Chosen and *you* did. You at least can *see* the futility of this when you aren't busy defending him—he's too full of vainglory and too damned stubborn to *ever* see any solution to this but crushing the Leshara, branch and root! Your twin is an *idiot*, 'Lendel! He's just as much an idiot as Wester Leshara, but that doesn't change the fact that he's going to get people killed out of plain stupidity! And I will not permit this to go on for very much longer. If I have to denounce Staven to end your involvement with this, I will. *Never* doubt it. You have more important things to do with your life than waste it defending a fool."

Tylendel's fists clenched again; he was nearly rigid with anger, as his eyes went nearly black and his face completely white with the force of his emotions—and for one moment Savil wondered if he'd strike her this time. Or strike *at* her, that is; if he came for her, she didn't intend to be where his fist landed. Or his levinbolt, if it came to that.

Please, Lord and Lady, don't let him lose it this time, let him stay in control—I've never pushed him this far before. And don't let him try magic. If he hits out, I may not be able to save him from what my protections will do.

She prayed, and looked steadfastly (and, she hoped, compassionately) into those angry eyes.

She could Feel him vibrating inside, caught between his need to strike out at the one who had attacked his very beloved twin and his own conscience and good sense.

Savil continued to hold her ground, refusing to back down. The tension in the room was so acute that the power-charged walls picked it up, reverberating with his rage. And that fed back into Savil, will-she, nill-she. It was all *she* could do to hold fast, and maintain at least the appearance of calm.

Then he whirled and headed blindly into a corner. He rested his forehead against the cool stone of the wall with one arm draped over his head, pounding the fist of his free hand against the gray stones, cursing softly under his breath.

Now Savil let him alone, saying absolutely nothing.

Once you get him worked into a rage, let him deal with his anger and his internal turmoil in his own way, had been Jaysen's advice. *Leave him alone until he's calmed* himself *down.*

Finally he turned back to the room and her, bracing himself in the corner, eyes nearly closed; breathing as hard as if he'd been running a mile.

"You'll never get me to agree to stop supporting Staven, you know," he said in a perfectly conversational tone. "I won't interfere with the Heralds, I won't help with the feud, and I won't call Evan Leshara a damned liar—but I *will* defend Staven and what he thinks is right, if only to you. I love him, and I will not give that up."

There was no sign that a moment before he'd been in—literally—a killing rage.

"I know," Savil replied, just as calmly, giving no indication that *she* was still shaking inside. "I'm not asking you to give up loving Staven. All I want is for you to *think* about this mess, not just react to it. If it was only your two families, it would be bad enough, but you're involving the whole region in your feuding. We know very well that you've both been looking for mages to escalate this thing—and 'Lendel, I do not want to hear a single word about which side started *that*. The important thing is that you've done it. The *important* thing is that if either side involves magic in this, the Heralds must and *will* take a hand. We can't afford to have wild magic loose and hurting innocent people. You are a Herald, or nearly. You have to remember that you *cannot* take a side. You *have* to be impartial. No matter what Evan Leshara does or says."

Tylendel shrugged, but it was *not* an indifferent shrug. His pain was very real, and only too plain to his mentor; she hurt *for* him. But this was one of the most important lessons any Herald had to learn—that he *had* to be impartial, no matter what the cost of impartiality was. And no matter whether the cost was to himself, or to those he cared for.

"All right," he said, tonelessly. "I'll keep out of it. So. Now that you've turned my guts inside out, what else did you want to discuss?"

"Vanyel," Savil said, relaxing enough that her voice became a little dulled with weariness. "He's been here for more than a month. I want you to tell me what you think."

"Gods." He sagged back against the wall, and opened his eyes completely. They had returned to their normal warm brown. "You would bring up His Loveliness."

"What's the matter?" Savil asked sharply, and took a closer look at him; he was wearing a most peculiar half-smile, and she smelled a rat—or at least a mouse. " 'Lendel, *don't* tell me you've gone and fallen in love with the boy!"

He snorted. "No, but the lad is putting a lot of stress on my self-control, let me tell you that! When I don't want to smack that superior grin off his face, I want to cuddle and reassure him, and I don't know which is worse."

"I don't doubt," Savil replied dryly, walking over to where he leaned, and draped herself against the wall opposite him. "All right, obviously you've had your eye on him; tell me what you've figured out so far. Even speculation will do."

"Half the time I think you ought to drown him," her trainee replied, shaking his golden head in disgust. "That miniature Court he's collected around himself is sickening. The posing, the preening—"

Savil made a little grimace of distaste. "You don't have to tell *me*. But what about the other half?"

"In my more compassionate moments, I'm more certain than ever that he's hurting, and all that posing is just that—a pose, a defense; that the little Court of his is to convince *himself* that he's worth something. But I've made overtures, and he just—goes to ice on me. He doesn't hit at me, he just goes unreachable."

"Well—" Savil eyed her protege with speculation.

"That particular scenario hadn't occurred to me. I thought that now he'd been given his head, he was just showing his true colors. I was about ready to wash my hands of him. Foster him with—oh—Oden or somebody—somebody with more patience, spare time, and Court connections than me."

"Don't," Tylendel said shortly, a new and calculating look on his face. "I just thought of something. Didn't you tell me one of the things his father was absolutely livid about was his messing about with music?"

"Yes," she said, slowly, pretending to examine the knuckles of her right hand as if they were of intense interest, but in reality concentrating on Tylendel's every word. The boy was a marginal Empath when he wasn't thinking about it. She didn't want to remind him of that Gift just now; not when she needed the information she could get from it. "Yes," she repeated. "Point of fact, he told me flat I was to keep the boy away from the Bards."

"And you told me Breda let him down gently, or as gently as she could, about his ambitions. *How often has he played since then?*"

Now Savil gave him a measuring look of her own. "Not at all," she said slowly, "Not a note since then. Margret says there's dust collecting on that lute of his."

"Lord and Lady!" Tylendel bit his lip, and looked away, all his attention turned inward. "I didn't know it was that bad. I thought he might at least be playing for those social butterflies he's collected."

"Not a note," Savil repeated positively. "*Is* that bad?"

"For a lad who's certainly good enough to get a lot of praise from his sycophants? For one whose *only* ambitions lay with music? It's bad. It's worse than bad; we broke his dream for him. Savil, I take back the first half of what I said." Tylendel rubbed his neck, betraying a growing unease. He looked up at the ceiling, then back down at her, his eyes now frank and worried. "We have a problem. A serious problem. That boy is bleeding inside. If we can't get him to open up, he may bleed himself to death."

"How do we get at him?" Savil asked, taking him at

his word. Her weakness—and what made her a *bad* Field Herald, although it was occasionally an asset in training proteges—was in dealing with people. She didn't read them well, and she didn't really know how to handle them in a crisis situation. This business with Tylendel and his twin and the feud, for instance—

I would never have thought of this solution—desensitizing him, weaning him into thinking about it logically by bringing him to the edge over and over but never letting him slip past that edge. Bless Jaysen. And damn him. Gods, every time we play this game it wreaks as much damage on me as it does on poor 'Lendel. I'm still vibrating like a harpstring.

Tylendel pondered her question a long time before answering, his handsome face utterly quiet, his eyes again turned inward. "I just don't know, Savil. Not while he's still rebuffing every overture he gets. We need some time for this to build, I think, and then some event that will break his barricades for a minute. Until that happens, we won't get in, and he'll stay an arrogant bastard until he explodes."

She felt herself grow cold inside. "Suicidal?"

To her relief, Tylendel shook his head. "I don't think so; he's not the type. It wouldn't occur to him. Now *me*—never mind. No, what he'll do is go out of control in one way or another. He'll either do it fast and have some kind of breakdown, or slowly, and debauch himself into a state where he's got about the same amount of mind left as a shrub."

"Wonderful." She placed her right hand over her forehead, rubbing her eyebrows with thumb and forefinger. "Just what I wanted to hear."

Tylendel made one of his expressive shrugs. "You asked."

"I did," she said reluctantly. "Gods, why me?"

"If it's any comfort, it's not going to happen tomorrow."

"It better not. I have an emergency Council session tonight." She sighed, and rubbed her hands together. "I'll probably be up half the night, so don't wait up."

"Does that mean the interview is over?" he asked quirking one corner of his mouth.

"It does. You can have the suite all to yourself tonight—just don't leave crumbs on the floor or grease on the cushions. *I* wouldn't care, but Margret will take your hide off in one piece. And don't look for the lovebirds, either—they're out on a fortnight Field trial with Shallan and her brood. So you'll be all alone for the evening."

"Oh, gods, all alone with the beautiful Vanyel—you *really* want to test my self-control, don't you!" He laughed, then sobered, shoving away from the wall and straightening. "On the other hand, this might give me the chance I was talking about. If I get him alone, maybe I can get him to open up a bit."

Savil shrugged and pushed away from the wall herself. "You're better than I with people, lad, that's why I asked your advice. If you think you have an opportunity, then take it. Meanwhile, *I* have to go consult with the Queen's Own."

"And from there, straight to the meeting? No time for a break?" Tylendel asked, sympathetically. She nodded.

He reached for her shoulders and embraced her closely. "See that you eat, teacher," he murmured into her hair. "I want you to stay around for a while, not wear yourself into another bout of pneumonia, and maybe kill yourself this time. Even when I hate you, you old bitch, you know I love you."

She swallowed down another lump in her throat, and returned the embrace with a definite stinging in her eyes.

"I know, love. Don't think I don't count on it." She swallowed again, closed her eyes, and held him as tightly, a brief point of stability in a world that too often was anything but stable. "I love you, too. And don't you ever forget it."

The *emptiness* of the suite almost oppressed Tylendel. With the "lovebirds" gone, Savil due (so the dinnertime rumor in the kitchens had it) for a till-dawn Council session in her capacity as speaker for those Heralds teaching proteges, and Vanyel presumably entertaining his little coterie of followers, there was nothing and no one to break the stifling silence. It closed around him like a shroud, until the very beating of his heart was audible. Outside the windows it was as dark as the heart of sin, and so overcast not even a hint of moon came through. His scalp was damp, hot, and prickly. Sweat trickled down the back of his neck and soaked into his collar. It felt a whole lot later than it actually was; time was crawling tonight, not flying.

Tylendel gave up trying to read the treatise on weather-magic Savil had assigned him and switched to a history instead. A handwritten pamphlet on weatherworking was *not* what he needed to be reading right now, anyway; not with a storm threatening. His energy control often wasn't as good as he'd like, and he didn't want to inadvertently augment what was coming in. He was a lot better at controlling his subconscious than he *had* been, but there was no point in taking chances with Savil out of reach.

That storm was at least part of what was making the suite seem stuffy; Tylendel Sensed the thunderheads building up in the west even though he couldn't see them from where he was sprawled on the couch of the common room. That *was* the Gift that made him a Herald-Mage trainee and not just a Herald-trainee; the ability to See (or otherwise Sense) and manipulate energy fields, both natural and supernatural. His Gifts had come on him early and a long time before he was Chosen; they'd given him trouble for nearly half of his short life, and only his twin's support had kept him sane in the interval between their onset and when his Companion Gala finally appeared—

:Are you tucked safe away, dearling?: he Mindspoke to her. *:When this blow comes, it's going to be a good one.:*

The drowsy affirmative he got told him that she was half-asleep; heat did that to her.

Heat mostly made *him* irritable. He had propped every window and door wide open (and to hell with bugs), but there wasn't even a whisper of breeze to move the air around. The candle flames didn't even waver, and the honey-beeswax smell of the candles placed all around the common room was almost choking him with its sweetness.

He shook back his damp hair, rubbed his eyes, and tried to concentrate on his book, but part of him kept hoping for a flash of lightning in the dark beyond the windows, or the first *hint* of cooling rain. And part of him kept insisting that all he had to do was *nudge* it a little. He told *that* part of himself to take a long walk, and waited impatiently for the rain to come of itself.

Nothing happened. Just an itchy sort of tension building.

He gave up trying to concentrate, got up and went to the sideboard for a glass of wine; he needed to get centered and calmed, and a little less sensitive, and he wasn't going to be able to do it on his own. The only wine left was a white, and it was a bit dry for his taste, but it did accomplish what he wanted it to. With just that hint of alcohol inside him, he finally managed to relax and get *into* the blasted book.

He got so far into it, in fact, that when the first simultaneous blast of wind and thunder came, he nearly jumped off of the couch.

Half the candles—the ones not sheltered in glass chimney-lamps—blew out. Wind whipped through the suite, sending curtains flying and carrying with it a welcome chill and the scent of rain. The shutters in Mardic's and Donni's room banged monotonously against the walls; not hard enough to shatter the glass yet, but it was only a matter of time. He dropped the book and got up to head for their door just as Vanyel stumbled in through the corridor door and into the brightness of the common room.

The boy stood as frozen as a statue, blinking owlishly at the light. Tylendel's stomach gave a little lurch; Vanyel looked like death.

It was bad enough that the boy was light-complected; bad enough that he was wearing stark black tonight, which only accentuated his fair skin. But his face had *no* color at the moment; it was so white it was almost transparent. His eyes looked sunken, and his expression was of someone who has seen, but been denied, the Havens.

"Vanyel—" Tylendel said—whispered, really—his voice barely audible above the banging shutter and the sound of the storm. He cleared his throat and tried again. "Vanyel, I didn't expect you back so—uh—soon. Is something wrong?"

For one moment—for one precious moment—Tylendel thought he had him; he was sure that the boy was going to open up to him. His eyes begged for pity; his expression, so hungry and haunted, nearly cracked Tylendel's own calm. The trainee made a tentative step toward him—

It was the wrong move; he knew that immediately. Vanyel's face shuttered and assumed his habitual expression of flippant arrogance. "Wrong?" he said, with false gaiety. "Bright Lady, no, of course there's nothing wrong! Some of the Bards just came over from their Collegium and started an impromptu contest; it got so damned hot in the Great Hall with all those people crowded in that I gave up—"

Just then the shutters in both the lifebonded's room *and* Savil's crashed against the walls with such force that it was a wonder that the windows *didn't* shatter.

"Havens!" Vanyel yelped, "She'll kill us!" and dove for Savil's room. Tylendel dashed into the other, mentally cursing his own clumsiness, and cursing himself for letting *his* reaction to the boy cloud his reading of him.

By the time he got everything secured and returned to the common room, Vanyel had retreated into his *own* room and the door was firmly and irrevocably shut.

"Vanyel," the trainee said, softly, his eyes dark with compassion and understanding, "Is something wrong?"

"I—" Vanyel began, then closed his eyes as a fit of trembling hit him. "I—the music—I—"

Suddenly Tylendel was beside him, holding him, quieting his shivering. "It's all right," he murmured into Vanyel's ear, his breath warm and like a caress in his hair. "It's all right, I understand."

Vanyel stood as unmoving as a dead stick, hardly daring to breathe, afraid to open his eyes. Tylendel stroked his hair, the back of his neck, his hands warm and light— and Vanyel thought his heart was going to pound itself to pieces. "I understand," he repeated. "I know what it's like to want something, and know you'll never have it."

"You—do?" Vanyel faltered.

Tylendel chuckled. It was a warm, rich sound.

And his fingers traced the line of Vanyel's spine, slowly, sensuously. Vanyel started to relax in Tylendel's arms— and his eyes popped open in startlement when his own hands at Tylendel's chest encountered, not cloth, but skin.

The trainee was starkly, gloriously nude.

"Then again," Tylendel whispered, looking deeply into Vanyel's eyes. "Maybe I will get it."

Vanyel made a strangling noise, wrenched himself away, and fled into darkness, into cold—

Into the middle of his old dream.

First there had been the snow-plain, then as he walked across it, the teeth of ice had begun poking their way up through the granular snow. They'd grown higher as he walked, but what he hadn't known was that they were growing behind him as well. Now he was trapped inside a ring of them. Trapped inside walls of ice, smoother than the smoothest glass, colder than the coldest winter. He couldn't break out; he pounded on them until his arms were leaden, to no effect. Everywhere he looked—ice, snow, nothing alive, nothing but white and pale blue and silver. Even the sky was white. And he was so alone—so terribly alone.

Nothing soft, nothing comforting. Nothing welcoming. Only the ice, only the unyielding, unmoving ice and the white, grainy snow.

He was cold. So appallingly cold—so frozen that he ached all over.

He had to get out.

Hoping to climb over the barrier, he reached for the top of one of the ice-walls, and pulled back his hands as pain stabbed through them. He stared at them stupidly. His palms were slashed nearly to the bone, and blood oozed sluggishly from the cuts to pool at his feet.

There was blood on the snow; red blood—but as he stared at it in numb fascination, it turned blue.

Then his hands began to burn with the cold, yet fiery pain of the wounds. He gasped, and tears blurred his vision; he wanted to scream, but could only moan. Gods, it hurt, he'd give anything to make it stop hurting!

Suddenly, the pain did stop; his hands went numb. His eyes cleared and he looked down at his injured hands again—and saw to his horror that the slashes had frozen over and his hands were turning to ice; blue, and shiny, and utterly without feeling. Even as he gazed at them, the ice crept farther up; over his wrists, crawling up his forearms—and he cried out—

Then he wasn't there anymore, he was somewhere else. It was dark, but he could see; by the lightning, by a strange blue glow about him. Lightning flickered overhead, and seemed to be controlled by what he did or thought; he was standing on a mound of snow in the center of a very narrow valley. To either side of him were walls of ice that towered over his head, reaching to the night sky in sheer, crystalline perfection. Behind him—there was nothing—somehow he knew this. But before him—

''Vanyel!''

Before him an army; an army of mindless monsters—creatures with only one goal. To get past him. Already he was wounded; he twisted to direct the lightning to lash into their ranks, and felt pain lancing down his right side, felt the hot blood trickling down his leg into his boot and freezing there. There were too many of them. He was doomed. He gasped and wept at the horrible pain in his side, and knew that he was dying. Dying alone. So appallingly alone—

''Vanyel!''

He struggled up out of the canyon of ice, out of the depth of sleep; shaken out of the nightmare by hot, almost scorching hands on his shoulders and a commanding voice in his ears.

He blinked; feeling things, and not connecting them. His eyes hurt; he'd been crying. His hair, his pillow were soggy with tears, and he was still so cold—too cold even to shiver. That was why Tylendel's hands on his bare shoulders felt so hot.

''Vanyel—'' Tylendel's eyes were a soft sable in the light of the tiny bedside candle; like dark windows on the night, windows that somehow reflected concern. His hands felt like branding irons on Vanyel's skin. "Gods, Vanyel, you're like ice!"

As he tried to sit up, Vanyel realized that he was still leaking tears.

As soon as he started moving he began shivering so hard he couldn't speak. "I—" he said, and could get nothing more out.

Tylendel snagged his robe from the foot of the bed without even looking around, and wrapped it about his naked shoulders. It wasn't enough. Vanyel shook with tremors he could not stop, and the robe wasn't doing anything to warm him.

"Vanyel," Tylendel began, then simply wrapped his arms around Vanyel and held him.

Vanyel resisted—tried to pull away.

He blinked.

The snow-plain stretched all around him, empty—but not asking anything of him. Cold, but not a threat. But lonely, lonely—oh, gods, how empty—

But not asking, not hurting—

He blinked again, and Tylendel was still there, still staring into his eyes with an openness and a concern he could not doubt.

"Go away!" he gasped; waiting for pain, waiting to be laughed at.

"Why?" Tylendel asked, quietly. "I want to help you."

He was turning to ice; soon there would be no feeling and nothing to feel—and he would be trapped.

Tylendel took advantage of his distraction to get his arms around him. "Van, I wouldn't hurt you. I *couldn't* hurt you."

He closed his eyes and gasped for breath, his chest tight and hurting. *—oh, gods—I want this—*

"I'm just trying to get you warm again," Tylendel said with a hint of impatience. "That's *all*. Relax, will you?"

He *did* relax; he couldn't maintain his indifference—and to his shame, began crying again—and he couldn't stop the tears any more than he could the shivering.

But not only did Tylendel not seem to mind—

"Come on, Vanyel," he soothed, pulling him into a

comfortable position on his shoulder, supporting him like a little child. "It's all right, I told you I won't hurt you. I wouldn't *ever* hurt you. Cry yourself out, it's just you and me, and I'll never tell anyone. On my honor. Absolutely on my honor."

It was already too late to save his battered dignity anyway—

Vanyel surrendered appearance, self-respect, everything. He sagged against Tylendel's shoulder, burying his face in Tylendel's soft, worn, blue robe. He let the last of his pride dissolve, releasing all the tears he'd been keeping behind his walls of indifference and arrogance. Soon he was crying so hard he couldn't even think, just cling to Tylendel's shoulders and sob. He didn't really hear what Tylendel was saying, only the tone of his voice registered in his sleep-mazed grief; comforting, compassionate, caring.

He cried his eyes sore and dry; he cried until his nose felt swollen to the size of an apple. All the time he shivered with the terrible cold that seemed to have become one with his very bones; shivered until the bed shook.

Finally there just weren't any tears left—and he wasn't shivering anymore, he was warm—and more than warm; protected. And completely exhausted. Tylendel held him as carefully as if he was made of spun glass and would shatter at a breath; just held him. That was all.

It was enough. It was more than he ever remembered having. He wished it could last forever.

—*may the gods help me. I've always wanted this*—

"Done?" Tylendel asked, very quietly, a good while after the last of the sobs and the tremors had finished shaking his body.

He nodded, reluctantly, and felt the arms holding him relax. He sat up again, and Tylendel cupped both his hands around his face, turning him into the light. He winced away from it, knowing what he must look like; the trainee chuckled, but it had a kindly, not a mocking, sound.

"You're a mess, peacock," he said, somehow making the words a joke to be shared between them. Vanyel smiled, tentatively, and Tylendel dabbed at his eyes with the corner of the sheet.

"Do you have so common a thing as a handkerchief around here?" he asked, quite casually. Vanyel nodded, and fumbled at the drawer of the bedside table until Tylendel patted his hand away and got the square of linen out of it himself.

"Here," he gave it to Vanyel, then settled back a little. "I couldn't sleep; got up to get some wine and heard you. Do this often?"

Vanyel blew his nose, and looked up at the older boy through half-swollen eyes. "Often enough," he confessed.

"Nightmare?"

He nodded, and looked down at his hands.

"Know why?"

"No," he whispered. But he did. He did. It was hearing the Bards—hearing what he'd never, ever have—and then encountering Tylendel and knowing—

Gods.

"Want to tell me about it?"

He dared another glance at the trainee; the quiet face of the older boy was not easy to read, but there were no signs of deception there that Vanyel could see.

But—

"You'll laugh at me," he said, ready to pull away again.

"No. On my honor. Van, *I don't lie*. I won't laugh at you, and nothing you tell me will go outside this room unless you want it to."

Vanyel shivered again, and without any warning at all, the words came spilling out.

"It's—ice," he said, sniffing, studying his hands and the handkerchief he had twisted up in them. "It's all around me; I'm trapped, I can't get out, and I'm so cold—so cold. Then I cut myself, and *I* start to turn into ice. Then—sometimes, like tonight—I'm somewhere else, and I'm fighting these things, and I know I'm going to die. And the worst of it isn't the pain, or the dying—it's that—that—" he faltered, "—I'm—all alone. So totally alone—"

It sounded so banal, so incredibly foolish, just put into words like that. Especially when he didn't, *couldn't*, tell Tylendel the rest, the part about *him*. He looked up, expecting to see mockery in the older boy's face—and froze, seeing nothing of the kind.

"Van, I think I know what you mean," Tylendel said slowly. "There are times when—when being alone is a hurt that's worse than dying. When it's easier to die than to be alone. Aren't there?"

Vanyel blinked, caught without words.

Tylendel's voice was so soft he might well have been speaking to himself. "Sometimes, maybe it's better to have had someone and lost them than to have never had anyone—"

Then Tylendel's eyes focused for a moment on Vanyel. And Vanyel's heart spasmed at the flash of emotion he saw. A longing he'd not *ever* dreamed to see there. Directed at him.

—oh—gods. I never—I thought—he can't—
He does. He is. Father will—
I don't care!

He snatched at what was proffered before it could be taken away.

"Vanyel—" the blond began.

" 'Lendel—" Vanyel interrupted, urgently, daring the nickname he'd heard his aunt use. "Stay with me—please. Please." His words tumbled over one another as he hurried to get them out before Tylendel could interrupt; he caught hold of the older boy's wrist. "The ice is still there, I *know* it is, it's inside me and it's freezing me from the inside out—it's killing my—feelings. I think it's killing me. Please, please, don't leave me alone with it—"

"You *don't* know what you're asking," Tylendel said, almost angrily; pulling his hand out of Vanyel's, his eyes no longer readable. "You can't know. You don't know what *I* am."

"But I *do*," Vanyel protested desperately. "I do, the girls tell me things to get my attention—they told me you're—uh—*shay'a'chern*, they said. That you don't sleep with girls; that you—" He felt himself blush, the rush of blood almost painful, his cheeks were so sore from crying.

"Then *dammit,* Vanyel, what do you think I'm made of?" Tylendel cried harshly, his face twisted and his eyes reflecting internal pain. "What do you think I am? Marble? You're *beautiful,* you're bright, you're everything I'd ever ask for—you think I can stay here and not want you? Good gods, I *won't* take advantage of an innocent, but what you're asking of me would try the control of a saint!"

"You don't understand. I *know* what I'm asking," Vanyel replied, catching his wrist again before he could get up and stalk off into the dark. "I *do* know."

Tylendel shook his head violently and looked away.

"'Lendel—look at me," Vanyel pleaded, pouring his heart out in a confession he'd never have dared to make before this. "Listen—I don't like girls either. I'm *not* an innocent, I know what I want, 'Lendel, please, listen—I've been—I've *bedded* enough of them to know that they don't do anything for me. It's—about as mechanical as dancing, or eating. They just don't *mean* anything to me."

Tylendel stopped trying to pull away, and turned a face to Vanyel that was so full of dumbfounded surprise that the younger boy had to fight hysterical laughter.

"And I do? You—" Tylendel began, then his face hardened. "Don't play with me, Vanyel. Don't toy with me. I've had that game played on me once already—and I don't want to hear you crying to Savil in the morning that I seduced you."

Vanyel bit his lip, and looked directly into Tylendel's eyes, pleadingly. "I'm not playing, 'Lendel. Please." He felt his eyes sting, and this time didn't try to hide the two tears that spilled down his raw cheeks. "I—I've been thinking about this for a long while. Almost since I got here, and they—told me about you. And you never laughed at me. You—were—kind to me. You kept being kind to me even when I was pretty rude. It meant a lot to me. And I didn't know how to thank you. I—started feeling—things around you. I was scared. I didn't dare let you guess. I didn't want to admit what I wanted; now I do.''

The older boy looked at him sideways. ''Which is?''

Vanyel gulped. ''I want to be with you, 'Lendel. And if you go—I won't have any choice but the ice—''

Once again Tylendel cupped his face between his strong hands, and gently brushed the tears away with hesitant fingers. He stared deeply into Vanyel's eyes for so long, and so searchingly, that Vanyel thought he surely must be reading right down to the depths of his soul. Vanyel held his gaze, and tried to make his own eyes say that he meant every word he'd said. Tylendel finally nodded, once, slowly.

Then he reached out, quite deliberately, and snuffed the candle before taking Vanyel back into his arms.

It was very dark; no light outside, no sound but the rain falling. After a moment, Tylendel chuckled with what sounded like surprise, and said softly into Vanyel's ear, ''I'm beginning to wonder just who's taking advantage of who, here.''

Then, a bit later, another chuckle to tell Vanyel that he was teasing. ''Move over, you selfish little peacock, I'm about to freeze to death.''

Then no words at all.

Then again, they didn't need words.

The halls were totally deserted, chill, and lit by lamps that were slowly flickering out as they used up the last of the night's oil. Savil's slow, weary footsteps echoed before and behind her without disturbing so much as a spider. At one point on the long walk back to her quarters from the Council Chamber, Savil wasn't entirely certain she was going to make it. She was so damned tired she was about ready to give up and lie down in the middle of the cold hall.

I'm getting too old for this, she told herself. *No more younglings after this lot. I can't take the emotional ups and downs. And I truly cannot take these all-night sessions with a lot of stubborn old goats.*

She grinned a little ironically at herself.

Of which I am one of the most stubborn. But gods—

hours like this are for the young. I hurt. And I think I'm going to beg off 'Lendel's weather working lesson today, else my bones are going to ache more. Gods bless—the door at last.

She pushed open the door to the suite; Tylendel had left a night-candle burning, but it, too, was guttering. No matter, there was the pearly gray light of an overcast dawn creeping in through the windows of her room, the lifebonded's, and Tylendel's—

She froze. Tylendel's bed was unoccupied; she could see it through the door.

Don't panic, old woman— she cautioned herself. *Just do a bit of a trace, first—you've shared magic; you've got the line to his mind. See where it leads.*

She found the little energy-link that said *Tylendel* and followed it back to where Tylendel himself was. It wasn't very far. Still in the suite, in fact. In Vanyel's room.

Vanyel's room?

Her first reaction was to fling the door open and demand to know what was going on. Her second was to chuckle; with aura overtones like *that* she bloody well *knew* what was going on!

But—*Vanyel?* Gods have mercy. No sign he was *shay'a'chern*—

Then again, given Withen's prejudices, he *might* have feared for a long time that the boy was fey. And Withen's answer to that fear would have been—

Exactly what he'd been doing. Keeping the boy sheltered at home rather than fostering him out and trying to shove him in the direction Withen wanted. Trying to force the boy into a mold he was totally unsuited for. And he also might well have protected the boy from even the *idea* that same-sex pairings were possible. So the boy himself wouldn't have known what he was—until he first found out about 'Lendel.

Which answered a great many questions indeed. The question now was—what had led to this, and what was it going to mean for the future?

She took a deep breath of the chilly, damp air, and groped her way back to her own room. No use rushing things; questioning could be done just as easy with herself lying in her own warm bed. Easier, actually, given how she felt.

She stripped herself down to the skin, promised her weary bones a bath *later,* and dragged on a bedgown before crawling into the blankets. The *warm* blankets, and she blessed Tylendel's thoughtfulness for putting the warming spell on her bed before he'd taken to his own. Or—whatever.

She settled herself comfortably, and reached out a thin tendril of Mindspeech in Private-mode. If the imp was awake—

He was.

:Savil?: came the sleep-blurred thought, dense with a feeling of contentment. *:Thought I heard you come in. Found me, hmm?:*

:Aye. And I have a pile of questions.: She shifted herself until her left shoulder stopped aching quite so much. *:The only important one is, how did you talk him into it?:*

:I didn't. It was all Van's idea.:

She almost lost the Mindspeech thread with her start of surprise, and had to grope after it. *:Sounds like I really missed something! What in the name of the Havens happened last night?:*

:Too much to talk about now.: There were overtones of mental and physical weariness to his Mind-voice. *:But he's going to be all right, Savil. We did more than—just the physical. I think we must have talked for hours, before and after. He handed me the key to himself, and he wanted me to have it.:*

She raised a sardonic mental eyebrow. *:'Lendel—I don't want to drench you with cold water, but may I remind you of what happened the last time morning arrived with you in someone else's bed?:*

:It's all right, Savil, it really is this time.: A feeling of faint surprise. *:You know, you're always teasing me about falling in love—but—I don't know, this feels different.:*

Savil snorted. *:Right; it always does. No, don't let an old cynic disturb you.:*

:Teacher—I think this is going to be something more than just a one-time; I think he needs me.:

:Oh, Havens. All right, if that's the way you think it's going—just let me know in the morning if you plan to move in with him. Or him with you, though his is the better chamber. We could use a spare for guests.:

Flavor of laughter like crisp apples. *:You just want my room back.:*

:If you aren't using it—seriously, 'Lendel, this is important. I want to have a long talk with him when I get up, and I want you there. He really should know what he's letting himself in for as shay'a'chern. I don't think we should let that get out, and I'll Mindspeak with you on that before we talk with him. Hmm—cancel your classes this morning; I'm too tired, and I have the feeling you weren't exactly early to sleep:

Another apple-feeling of laughter, and the mind-link faded. And she let exhaustion pull her down into a slumber that she really didn't *want*, not anymore.

One last thought before sleep came.

Great good gods, what am I going to tell Withen?

Tylendel raised himself up on his elbow and looked down at the slumbering boy beside him. Rest had repaired the damages that several hours of soul-wrenching weeping had done to Vanyel's face; relaxed, and with all his barriers down, he looked as innocent as an unawakened child—

—which he was, as Tylendel now knew quite intimately, *not*. Not in any way; except, perhaps, his vulnerability.

"Van," he whispered, touching his shoulder, and feeling just a faint chill of apprehension despite his words to his mentor, "can you wake up a little?"

Vanyel stirred, wrinkled his nose, and half-opened his eyes. And when he saw who was beside him, he smiled with heart-stopping sweetness. With all his masks gone, he was as charming as he was beautiful.

"Hmm?" he said, blinking, as Tylendel felt a surge of relief and gratitude that this was *not* going to be a repeat of the infamous Nevis affair.

"Want a roommate?"

"You—why?"

He grinned; he knew now that you had to *show* Van that something was a joke, or often he'd taken it seriously. "Savil seems to want my room back—for guests, she says. Besides, I like your company."

Vanyel's reply, though not verbal, was a definite and unmistakable affirmative.

"We have," Savil said dryly, "several problems, here."

She'd had that Mindspeech conference with Tylendel as she'd gotten herself put together for the day. Nice thing, Mindspeech; let you cover more than one thing at once. And after giving it thorough consideration while she bathed, she decided to have her "little talk" with Vanyel in *his* room. With any luck, he'd feel less threatened there.

She did usurp the most comfortable chair in the room, though. *The privilege of age,* she told herself, waiting for the two young men to settle themselves. Without seeming to consult about it, Tylendel sat on the edge of the bed, and Vanyel arranged himself cross-legged on the floor at his feet.

And the flexibility of youth. Would that I could still do that! The body language gave her spirits a lift, though; the way Vanyel had positioned himself was interesting. At Tylendel's feet, below both her head and his lover's. That could well show he'd given up that pose of arrogant superiority. Very interesting.

I wonder if having a steady lover at his side might well give 'Lendel something to think about besides his twin and that damned feud. On the other hand—this lad's been so affection-starved—this could be another sort of trouble.

"Yes, indeed, we have quite a few little problems here," she repeated.

Tylendel nodded at her words; Vanyel looked puzzled, at first, then thoughtful.

"The first problem and the one that's going to tie in to all the others, Vanyel, is your father." She paused, and Vanyel bit his lip. "I'm sure that you realize that if he finds out about this, he is going to react badly."

Vanyel coughed, and bowed his head, hiding his face for a moment. When he looked back up, he was wearing a weary, ironic half-smile; a smile that had as much pain in it as humor. It was, by far and away, the most open expression Savil had ever seen him wear.

" 'Badly' is something of an understatement, Aunt," he replied, rubbing his temple with one finger. "He'll— gods, I can't predict what he'll do, but he'll be in a rage, that's for certain."

"He'll pull you home, Van," Tylendel said in a completely flat voice. "And he can do it; you're not of age, you aren't Chosen, and you aren't in Bardic."

"And *I* can't protect you," Savil sighed, wishing that she could. "I can stall him off for a while, seeing as he officially turned guardianship of you over to me, but it won't last more than a couple of months. Then—well, I'll give you my educated guess as to what Withen will do. I *think* he'll put you under house arrest long enough for everybody to forget about you, then find himself a compliant priest and ship you off to a temple. Probably one *far* away, with very strict rules about outside contact. There are, I'm sorry to say, several sects who hold that *shay'a'chern* are tainted. They'd be only to happy to 'purify' you for Withen and Withen's gold. And under the laws of this kingdom, none of us could save you from them."

Vanyel nodded; by the startled agreement in his eyes, Savil reckoned that this was a speculation he'd entertained before this, although for different causes. "So is there *anything* I can do?" he asked quietly.

"Obviously," she said, "Or I wouldn't be talking to you now. But you aren't going to like the solution to your problem. It's pretty heartbreakingly simple. Outside of this room, Vanyel, *nothing is to change.*"

"But—" He twisted his head around to see what Tylendel thought about this, only to find that his lover was nodding, in complete agreement with her.

"Savil's right, Van," Tylendel said sadly.

"But—" Vanyel protested, holding out one hand toward him in entreaty, then turning the same pleading eyes on Savil when Tylendel shook his head.

"Mardic and Donni are discreet, and I'd trust Margret to keep what she knows behind her teeth even under torture, but if you want to *stay* here, Vanyel, you won't say or do anything to betray your relationship to 'Lendel. The moment people start to talk, it'll get back to your father."

"The quickest way to make them talk, love," Tylendel said in what was almost a whisper, "is to change. Is to even be *friendlier* to me than you have been. You told me the girls told you I was a pervert." Vanyel's eyes widened at Tylendel's directness. "It can't have escaped your notice how they sniggered and giggled about it, and they were being *polite*. My preferences are not generally socially acceptable. There are only two reasons why I have as little trouble as I do. The first is that I'm a Herald-trainee, and Heralds are allowed a bit more license than ordinary mortals. And my patron is Savil. She just happens to outrank everybody in the Circle except the Queen's Own."

"And the other reason?" Vanyel said in a very subdued voice.

What stretched Tylendel's mouth was something less than a smile. "The fact that I took a couple of the worst offenders on and kept knocking them down until they didn't get up."

"Oh."

Tylendel caught up one of his hands in both of his own. "I *know* you want everyone to know about us. I can't tell you how much that means to me. But it will mean a lot more to me to know you were going to be able to *stay* with me."

"And to do that, young Vanyel," Savil said, intruding into the intense interaction between them, "you are going to have to begin a performance a Master Player couldn't equal. 'Lendel and I have been talking about you this afternoon."

From the complete astonishment on his face, Savil could tell that he *hadn't* guessed they'd been in conference via Mindspeech. For that matter, it might be that he didn't know they both had that Gift.

"We share the Mindspeech Gift, lad, and it's damned

useful at times like this. He's told me some of what you told him, and it rather changed my mind about you. But I will not lie to you; I'm going to help you because *he* wants it, because he wants you here. So now I'm going to *order* you; outside of this suite you are to be the same arrogant little bastard that arrived here. And if you can manage to be *slightly* rude to 'Lendel, that's even better. And in return, I'll make this suite a little sanctuary for the two of you. Is it a bargain?''

Vanyel, who had gone rather pale, gulped, and nodded.

Savil smiled for the first time since she'd begun this conference.

''That's a good lad. If you're half of what 'Lendel claims for you, I'm going to come to like you a great deal, and I'm sorry for the treatment you've had from your father. I'll tell you that he *isn't* the same person I knew when I was Chosen. He's gone stiff and stubborn, and altogether hidebound. Maybe it's age; maybe it's that a lot of his old friends have taken the Long Walk and he's seeing Death looking for him, too. Maybe it's that priest he's gotten tied up with—I just don't know.'' She coughed. ''Well, that's not to the point; what *is* to the point is that you'll only have to keep up this charade until you're eighteen; you'll be your own man then, and can do what you please. And I'll see to it that 'Lendel begins having trouble with his Mage-lessons.'' She winked, and Tylendel chortled. ''I think we can keep him out of Whites until you're of age. After that,'' *if this love affair lasts that long* ''you'll have to make your decisions on your own. Fair enough?''

''More than fair, Aunt Savil.'' Vanyel looked very subdued, and quite unlike the boy that had faced her something like a month ago. She couldn't quite pinpoint why.

:*'Lendel, what is it about him?*: she Mindspoke, letting her puzzlement drift over.

:*No masks,*: came the immediate answer. :*This is the real Vanyel, dearheart. The one nobody but me—and maybe his sister—has seen. Now see why I love him?*:

The last thought stopped her cold. :*Are you that sure, ke'chara? Are you really that sure?*:

His eyes caught hers over Vanyel's head; caught and held them. *:I'm that sure.:*

:And him?:

:I don't know; but he was willing to defy his father for me, and I think that says something.:

She closed her own eyes against that burning, intense gaze. *:Then may the gods help and guard you.:*

She turned her attention back to Vanyel, and quickly. He was still looking toward Tylendel, and the very same look was in his eyes—and a vulnerability and apprehension that cut at her heart.

"I'll help you all I can, son," she said quietly. "I'll help you all I can."

Six

"Don't go yet," Tylendel said abruptly, as Vanyel picked himself up off the floor. Vanyel gave him a look of uncertainty. He was still too new to this—being open. He was still waiting for blows that never came.

But Tylendel seemed to know that.

"It's all right, Van," he said softly. "It's really all right. I have a good reason."

"I've got a lesson," he protested. "History, and I'm still behind the other three."

Tylendel made a wry face. "You're a law unto yourself, remember? At least that's what you're supposed to be acting like. You skipped your lessons this morning, skip the rest of them today; tell 'em you were sick. Tell 'em the storm last night gave you a headache."

"But—"

"It's important," Tylendel coaxed. "Really, it is. More important than that history lesson. If you're behind, I'll coach you. Please?"

It didn't take much encouragement from Tylendel to get him to do what he already *wanted* to do; lessons were hardly as attractive as more of Tylendel's company. *Here* he wasn't going to be hurt. Here—someone cared for him. It was as heady as a little too much wine, only without the hangover.

Vanyel closed the door to his room, then turned an expectant face toward his lover, poised with one hand still on the latch.

Tylendel stretched lazily, reaching for the ceiling with his head tilted back. Then he dropped his arms, rose from his seat on the bed, and walked over to put his hand behind Vanyel's shoulder.

"There's somebody I want you to meet," he said, gently pushing Vanyel in the direction of the room's outside door.

"But—" Vanyel protested weakly, "I thought—"

"You're awfully fond of that word 'but,' love," Tylendel chuckled. "What does it take to get you to say something else?"

He opened the door, still without enlightening Vanyel as to the reason why he was going to introduce Vanyel to someone after Savil had just got done telling them both that they were to keep the relationship a secret—

—and Tylendel had agreed with her.

Vanyel started to protest again, realized that the only thing he could think of to say was "but," and subsided, as Tylendel guided him out the door to the gardens beyond.

"You see that bridge?" Tylendel pointed northward to the first of the two bridges crossing the Terilee River on the Palace grounds. "And that stand of pines on the other side?"

Vanyel nodded; it was quite a healthy grove, in fact, and the trees extended a good distance back into the Field. They were tall, very thick, and a deep green that was almost black, with huge branches that drooped beneath their own weight until they touched the ground.

"You count to fifty after you see me go in there, then you follow," Tylendel ordered. "In case anybody happens to come by, though, or looks out a window, you'd better try your hand at acting the arrogant little prig."

Vanyel nodded again; completely mystified, but willing to go along with about anything that Tylendel wanted. He posed himself carefully, leaning against the doorframe with his arms crossed over his chest, attempting to look as if he were simply idling about in the gardens, while Tylendel sauntered off.

This is going to be harder than it was before, he thought somberly, trying to look anywhere except after Tylendel. *I didn't have anything to lose, before. Now I have everything to lose if I slip.* He closed his eyes, and turned his face up to the sun, as if he were savoring the warmth. *But if I don't slip—oh, gods, whichever one of you is responsible for this—it's worth anything. I swear, it's worth anything you ask of me!*

He chanced a sideways glance across the river; Tylendel was only just reaching the pine grove. He looked away, strolled over to a stand of daylilies, admired them for a moment, then glanced across the river again. Tylendel's blond hair gleamed against the dark boughs like a tangled skein of spun sunlight, then vanished as the branches closed behind him.

Vanyel transferred his admiration to a bed of rose vines, languidly bending to inhale their perfume, all the while counting to the requisite fifty. He had no sooner reached the required number, though, when a giggling flock of his admirers rounded a hedge, saw him, and altered their course to intersect with his.

Oh, no! he thought, dismayed, and looked surreptitiously about for an escape route, but saw no way to avoid them. Sighing, he resigned himself to the inevitable, and waited for their arrival.

"*Van*yel, what are you doing out here?" asked slim, barely-adolescent Jillian, batting her sandy lashes at him. "Aren't you supposed to be at lessons?"

Vanyel covered a wince. *It* would *have to be Jillian. No common sense, and the moral fiber of a hound in heat. And after me with all the dedication you'd see in a hawk stooping on a pigeon. Lord. I hope her father marries her off quick, or she'll be sleeping her way around the Court before long.*

But he smiled at her, a smile with a calculated amount of pain in it. "A rotten headache, pretty one. It took me last night when the storm came in, and I *cannot* be rid of it. I tried sleeping in, but—" he shrugged. "My aunt *suggested* I take a long walk."

The entire covey giggled in near-unison. "Suggested with a stick, I'll bet," dark Kertire said sardonically, squinting into the sunlight. "Sour Savil. Well, we'll walk with *you* then, and keep you from being bored."

Vanyel bit his lip in vexation and thought quickly. "She *suggested* my course, as well," he told them, grimacing.

"To the end of Companion's Field and back. And I have no doubt she's watching from her window."

He pouted at them. "Much as I would adore your company, my pretties, I rather doubt those slippers you're wearing are equal to a hike across a field full of—er—"

"Horseturds," said Jesalis inelegantly, wrinkling her nose and tossing her blonde curls over her shoulder. "Bother. No, you're right," she continued, sticking her foot out a little, and surveying the embroidered rose-satin slipper on it with regret. "I *just* finished the embroidery on these and got them back from the cobbler; I don't want them spoiled, and they would be before we'd gotten half across." The others murmured similar sentiments as their faces fell. "We're *never* going to forgive you for deserting us, Vanyel."

"Now *that's* unfair," he exclaimed, assuming a crushed expression. "Blaming me for the orders of my crotchety old aunt!" He rolled his eyes mournfully at them.

Jesalis giggled. "We'll only forgive you if you promise to make it up to us tonight after dinner."

"Tonight?" he asked, pained by the idea of spending the evening with them instead of with Tylendel as they'd planned this morning.

They mistook his expression for headache. "Well, not if you still aren't feeling well," Jesalis amended.

"After a tramp across a perilous obstacle course like *that*," he gestured flamboyantly at the Field across the river, "I much doubt I'm going to be feeling *better*."

"Well—"

"A bargain; if you'll forgive me, I'll come and play for you while you're doing finework tomorrow morning," he said, quite desperately, willing to promise them almost anything to avoid losing his evening, and recalling that they'd all been pestering him to play for them. Before it hadn't been possible; it would have hurt too much. Now, though—well, becoming—or not becoming—a Bard didn't seem all that important anymore. And consequently the thought of music didn't hurt anymore. Or not as much. Certainly it was a small price to pay for having his evening free.

"You will?" squealed Wendi, whose older sister was fostered with Vanyel's mother. "Really? Ratha told me you were as good as a Bard!"

"Well," he shrugged, then smirked, "I won't say I'm a bad hand at the lute. And I know a ballad and a dance or two."

"Done," said Jesalis. "A bargain."

"Bless you, my dear," he replied, with honest thankfulness. "I wouldn't be able to live without your forgiveness. Now, if you'll all excuse me—the sooner I get this nonsense over, the sooner I'll be able to go back to my bed."

They giggled and turned back, retracing their footsteps. While he watched them, they disappeared behind the hedge again, heading in the direction of the maze.

When they were safely out of sight, he trudged—to all appearances, *most* unwillingly—across the bridge and up a little rise, heading a little indirectly for the pine grove.

He went past it, walking through soft grasses that ranged from knee-high to closely cropped. And despite what he had told the girls, there were no "traps" lurking beneath the grass for the unwary. That *did* surprise him, a bit; he was no stranger to long walks across pastureland and the hazards thereof.

What on earth do the Companions do—drop it all in one corner? I suppose—the stories say they're as intelligent as a human. I suppose it's possible. Likely, really. They still eat grass, like horses, and who'd want to eat in the privy?

After first making certain that there was no one about to see him, Vanyel doubled back to the pine grove, and pushed aside the heavy, scratchy boughs. He almost had to force his way past them; the needles caught in his hair and clothing and the branches closed over his head almost immediately, shutting off most of the sunlight. A few feet inside the grove there was no direct light; he walked through a pine-scented twilight gloom, with boughs lacing together just barely above his head, and a thick carpet of dry needles at his feet. The needles crunched a little, releasing more piny scent, but otherwise his own footsteps were almost noiseless. Somewhere in the distance he could hear birds calling, but their songs seemed to be furlongs away. This place looked enormous now that he was inside it, much larger than it had appeared from outside; magical, almost mystical, and far removed from the bright green-and-gold Field just a few feet away.

This wasn't *the* Grove; that was a good deal farther into the Field—but this stand of ancient pines was giving Vanyel a pleasant, shivery sort of feeling, making him feel somehow more aware and alive.

" 'Lendel?'' he called softly into the blue-green quiet under the pine boughs, his voice muffled by the rows of straight, columnar trunks of shaggy ebony all about him. He turned, slowly, trying to see past the shadows; peering beneath the feathery branches.

"Right here," came the reply from slightly behind him, and a white shape ghosted up on his right, resolving itself into—

A Companion. The first that Vanyel had ever seen at close range. And Tylendel beside her, one hand on her snowy, arched neck.

"This is who I wanted you to meet. Van—this is Gala. She already knows about you, Van, she knew last night. We're mind-linked; I told her everything, and she wanted to see you right away."

Vanyel felt strange and awkward. Those sapphire eyes held an intelligence that was rather frightening, but the *form* was a horse. How in the *Havens* did you introduce yourself to a horse?

The silence grew; he stared into Gala's eyes, swallowed, and finally made the attempt.

"Hullo," he said, shyly, looking straight into those eyes and hoping to speak directly to the intelligence there; trying to ignore the fact that he was feeling more than a bit intimidated and foolish. "I—I hope you don't mind—"

Gala snorted, and Tylendel chuckled. "She says to tell you that she's been hoping I'd 'find a nice mate and give her a chance for a little peace' for a long time. She says it's altogether disconcerting to be sidling up to a handsome stallion and find *me* in her head asking for bedtime stories!''

That was the *last* response he'd expected. Vanyel choked down a laugh. '' 'Lendel, you didn't!''

He nodded, as Gala tossed her own head. "I most certainly did, but *only* once. It was after Nevis, and I was,'' he faltered, and looked to the side, "rather lonely.''

Vanyel touched the hand still resting on Gala's neck. "Not anymore, I hope.''

Tylendel glanced from the hand resting lightly on his own to Vanyel's face, and half-smiled into his eyes. "No,'' he replied quietly. "Not anymore.''

The quiet, the peace of the shadowed grove let them ignore everything except each other. Caught in the spell of that place and that pose, neither paid any attention to the passing of time—

Until Vanyel stumbled forward, propelled by a hard shove in the small of his back. Tylendel grabbed him to keep him from falling, both of them too startled to do more than emit rather undignified squeaks of surprise.

Gala danced backward a few steps, making sounds Vanyel would have been willing to stake his life were *laughter*. It was pretty obvious that she'd shoved him into Tylendel's arms with her nose.

Tylendel burst into gales of laughter; he clutched his stomach, nearly incoherent, and gasping for breath. Gala snorted and bobbed her head, and he doubled over again.

They're talking, Vanyel finally realized, as Tylendel wheezed. *Or—well, I guess she's teasing him. Gods above and below, all the stories are* true! *I wish I could hear them.*

His stomach fluttered uncertainly, and he tasted the sour bite of what could only be jealousy. Tylendel and Gala were sharing something he never could—something they'd had for years before he had come along. In this, he was, he would always be, the outsider. That realization condensed into a hard, cold lump in his throat, and besides the bitter taste of jealousy, he shivered in a sudden chill of loneliness. And just a touch of doubt.

He could really have about anyone he wanted, couldn't

*he? So why should he bother with me? How can I know
if he means what he told me?*

But before he could throw himself into a mire of de-
pression he found he had his hands full; keeping the
trainee from falling over, while Tylendel struggled to
breathe around his laughter, and gasped like a stranded
fish.

"You wouldn't!" Tylendel choked, as tears ran down
his cheeks, and he pulled away from Vanyel to advance
on his Companion in mock threat—the effect somewhat
spoiled by the fact that he had to catch hold of a tree
trunk as something she "said" made him bend over again
with laughter. "Don't you dare! Gala, I'll do *no* such
thing! You *rude* little bitch!"

Gala danced in place, her hooves making no sound at
all in the thick carpet of needles. Her eyes sparkled with
mischief, and Vanyel had, for one moment, a disconcerting double-vision image of the prancing Companion
and an equally mischievous young woman of about Tylendel's age, laughing soundlessly at her Chosen.

This was worse than before. Vanyel felt *completely*
alone—and left altogether on the outside.

Tylendel, not noticing his distress in the least, managed to get himself back under control, and wiped his
eyes with the back of his hand as he straightened up.

He assumed a stern expression. "Now see here, you
wicked young lady," he began, when she turned the tables on him by whickering and reaching out to nuzzle his
cheek.

Vanyel saw his eyes soften as he folded immediately.
"Oh, all right, I forgive you," he sighed in defeat, putting his arms around her neck and resting his cheek
against hers. "But you had damn well *better* not—"

What it was Gala had "better not" do, Tylendel did
not verbalize; nor was Vanyel entirely certain he wanted
to know. He had the sneaking suspicion that it would be
no little embarrassing.

Finally Gala shook herself free and shoved her Chosen
in Vanyel's direction—a good bit more gently than she'd
shoved the latter. And as if in apology, she paced forward and gave Vanyel a brief caress with her nose, rather

like a soft kiss, before trotting off into the blue twilight under the pine boughs and out of sight among the trunks.

Silence followed her going.

"Well," Tylendel said, at last. "That was Gala."

Vanyel replied with the first thing that came into his head. "You really love her, don't you?"

"More than anything or anybody except you and Staven," Tylendel replied, almost apologetically. "I'm not sure I can explain it—" He bit off what he was saying, as if something in Vanyel's expression told him how depressed this meeting had made him.

"Van," he reached out hesitantly toward Vanyel's shoulder, then pulled his hand back, as if unsure whether to touch him. "I didn't bring you here to hurt you."

His very real distress forced Vanyel to pull himself together and try to *analyze* his feelings, instead of just wallow in them.

They were, to say the least, mixed. "I think I'm jealous," he said, after an uncomfortable pause. "I know it's stupid, she can't ever have you the way I do—but I can't ever share your thoughts the way she does."

"Huh. You wouldn't *want* to—" Tylendel began.

"But that's not the point," Vanyel interrupted, backing a few steps away. "I can't *know* that. You can tell me, but I can't ever *know* that, can I?" He wasn't sure what to do or what else to say, and so fell silent, turning away slightly and looking out past Tylendel into the shadows that had swallowed the Companion.

"Van," he felt Tylendel's hand fall lightly on his shoulder, and turned to look into his eyes. "Do you want to talk about this? Do you want to hear about what it's like for us, how it started? Do you think that will help you understand?"

Not trusting his voice, Vanyel nodded.

"This will take a while; pick a spot to sit. Unless you'd rather go back to the room?" Tylendel raised one eyebrow inquiringly.

"No, I like it here; it somehow seems more private." Vanyel faltered, and covered his hesitation by looking around for a good place. He finally chose a spot at the base of one of the bigger trees beside them, between two roots that were each as thick as his leg. He put his back against the trunk and slid down it to be cradled where the roots joined the tree.

Tylendel pondered his choice for a moment. "Well, I can only see two ways I can talk and look at you at the same time, and since I don't fancy shouting across the clearing—"

Before Vanyel had time to react, he'd stretched himself out along the ground and put his head in Vanyel's lap. "—*much* better," he sighed.

Vanyel froze.

"Van," Tylendel said quietly, closing his eyes, *"I won't hurt you.* Not for any reason. I like being near you, with you. I need to touch people; and I won't *ever* hurt you."

Vanyel relaxed a little.

"I like this grove, too, though hardly anyone else seems to. It feels like there's no time in here." He kept his eyes closed, and Vanyel saw a little pain-crease between his eyebrows.

He gets those headaches; he told me last night—I wonder—if he'd mind—if it would help—

Vanyel hesitated for a moment, then began massaging Tylendel's temples with gentle fingertips.

The trainee chuckled and Vanyel felt his shoulders relax. "You have about a hundred years to stop doing that," he said. "I think I have the headache you claimed."

"You were going to tell me about you and Gala and being Chosen," Vanyel prompted, though the thought made him a little uncomfortable still. "I mean, you practically got my whole life story last night, and I still don't know that much about you."

"To begin at the beginning—I have a twin, Staven. He's the elder by about an hour. Nothing like me, by the way; he's taller, thinner, darker, and *much* handsomer. He's the leader, I'm the follower. We've had a primitive sort of mind-link ever since we were born. Things happened between us all the time. Things like—oh, I blacked out when he fell down the well; he acted like he'd broken his leg when I broke *mine.* We always knew what the other one was up to." He took a deep breath. "People

knew all about *that*, but I had other Gifts, too, that I could use. Besides that mind-link, from the time I was about nine I had a touch of Thought-sensing for people besides Stav, and I had an ability to—make accidents happen to people I didn't like.''

"Did that cause you problems?" Vanyel asked. "With other people, I mean. I should think they wouldn't much appreciate that last.''

Tylendel shook his head slightly. "It didn't crop up often enough for people to really notice—or if they did, they were too afraid of my father to say anything about it. I didn't do it often, the accident-causing, I mean; it made me sick, after. Staven sometimes tried to egg me on, but it wasn't something I'd give in to him about.'' Tylendel paused, and bit his lip; his expression flickered briefly into one both dark and brooding before it lightened again. "It was the link between me and Staven that was the strongest and most predictable of the Gifts; it was pretty much limited to physical sensations, but once we figured out how to use it—''

Vanyel chuckled. "I bet you were unholy terrors.''

Tylendel echoed the chuckle, and winked at him. "I wouldn't mind having a link like that with you.''

Vanyel blushed, but answered with exactly what he was thinking. "I wouldn't mind either.''

Tylendel's expression sobered. "Now comes the part where things got odd. Staven matured pretty early; by twelve he was as tall as most at fifteen, and all the girls were starting to flirt with him. And not just the girls, but grown women as well. I think he got all his share of female-attraction *and* mine, if you want to know the truth. That summer we were hosting a tournament and everything from goosegirls to visiting highborn were after him and he was acting like a young and randy rooster in a henyard. It all climaxed—if you'll forgive the expression—when one of the ladies who'd come to visit Mother dropped him a note that said in no uncertain terms that she'd be quite pleased to find him in her bed that night—well—''

He closed his eyes for a moment, then looked up into Vanyel's face, his own expression ironic. "Understand,

I was just as curious as any twelve year old about what
Doing It was like. *I* said I'd cover for him if *he* let me—
uh—eavesdrop.''

"Something tells me it didn't go according to plan,"
Vanyel guessed.

"Dead in the black," Tylendel said soberly. "I was
'with' him for about as long as it took for things to get
interesting. I had been feeling odd from the start, but I
tried to ignore it, and concentrated on the link. Then
things got—I don't know how to describe it, except that
I started losing my grip on *me* and started merging with
him. And the more I concentrated, the stranger it all got.
It was a bit like those times I'd made accidents happen;
the room faded in and out, I was in a kind of sickish
fever, my heart was racing—and I couldn't tell what was
'me' and what was Stav. Under any other circumstances
I think I would have quit and shut everything down, but
I was stubborn and I was a little afraid of Stav making
fun of me for diving out, after this was over. I kept holding to that link, figuring that if I could just weather it
out, things would get fun again. Then—'' He shook his
head a bit, and his mouth twitched. "Just as things were
about to come to the cusp for Staven, something—broke
loose in me. I just barely remember the start of it; like
I'd suddenly been dropped into a fire. I was in unbeliev-
able pain. It felt like being in the middle of a lightning
storm, and from the wreck I made of our room, that's
exactly what I may have created. Something about what
was going on, something about the link I had with Staven,
triggered *all* my potential Gifts—explosively. I was unconscious for about a day, and when I woke up—''

He shuddered. "—nothing would ever be the same."

He closed his eyes, and Vanyel stroked his forehead.
His mouth was tight, with lines of unhappiness at the
corners. Far off in the distance, Vanyel could hear mea-
dowswifts crying like the lost souls of ghost-children.

"So there I was;" Tylendel continued, his voice thin
and strained. "I had the Mage-Gift, Thought-sensing,
Fetching, a bit of Empathy—none of it predictable, none
of it controlled, and all of it likely to burst out at any
moment.'' He took a look at Vanyel's face and read the

puzzlement there. "Gods, I keep forgetting you aren't a
trainee. Fetching—that means I can move things without
touching them; Empathy means I can feel what someone
else is feeling, which is why I knew when you had that
nightmare last night. Thought-sensing—if someone isn't
shielding, I can tell what they're thinking. The Mage-Gift
is harder to explain, but it's what makes it possible for a
Herald-Mage to do magic."

"You can tell what I'm thinking?" Vanyel said dubiously. He would have liked being able to share Tylendel's
thoughts the way Gala did, but wasn't entirely sure he
wanted the relationship to hold that kind of one-sided
intimacy.

"I can, but I *won't*," Tylendel said, with such firmness
that Vanyel couldn't find it in his heart to doubt him.
"Even if it wasn't so unfair to you, it's counter to all the
ethics that go with being a Herald. Basically I just use it
to talk with Gala and Savil."

Vanyel nodded, comforted. "So you had all these—
Gifts—sort of thrown at you, and no way to control
them."

"Exactly," Tylendel said soberly. "And all this at
twelve. It was *two years* before Gala came for me. If it
hadn't been for Staven, I'd have gone mad."

"Why?" Vanyel whispered. "What was happening?"

"What *wasn't?* I'd drop into a fit—when I'd wake up
again, I'd be in the middle of a fifty-foot circle of wreckage. That was the Mage-Gift and Fetching working together in a way Savil and I haven't been able to duplicate
under control. Seems I have to go berserk."

He frowned, and reached up to rub his forehead between his eyebrows. "Staven was the only one who could
get near me—who was *willing* to stay near me, in or out
of a fit. They said I'd been taken by a demon. They said
that because of what Staven and I had tried to share, I
had been possessed. When I—started to show signs of
being *shay'a'chern,* they said I was cursed, too."

"That's—that's stupid!" Vanyel cried indignantly.

"They still said it; if they'd dared, they'd have outcaste
me. But they didn't; Staven swore if they did he'd go with
me, and *he* was the heir, the only possible heir with me

acting the way I was. Mother wasn't capable of having
any more children, Father wouldn't remarry, and he'd
been completely faithful to her, so there weren't any bastards around. They didn't have a choice. They had to
allow me to stay, but they didn't have to make it comfortable for me.''

Vanyel thought with wonder that Tylendel's situation
was actually worse than his own.

"They kept me pretty well isolated; even when I was
fine they avoided me. But when everyone else abandoned
me in one of my fits, *he* stayed, *he* took care of me,
absolute and unshakable in the belief that I would never
hurt him. Positive that, despite what was whispered, what
had happened was *not* that I'd been possessed, but was
something that would somehow be worked out.''

Tylendel shuddered again, his eyes haunted, and plainly
seeing another time and place. Vanyel, feeling *his* pain,
put both his hands on his shoulders, trying to just be a
comforting presence without disturbing him; Tylendel
looked up at him, patted his hand, and half-smiled.

"You see? I think maybe that's why we understand
each other. Well, finally Gala came—gods. I cannot ever
tell you what it was like, looking into her eyes for the
first time. It was—like souls touching. And the relief—
knowing that I *wasn't* mad, that I *wasn't* demon-
possessed—I went from hell to the Havens in the space
of a heartbeat.''

He sighed and seemed to sink into his own thoughts
for a long while.

"What did she do?'' Vanyel asked.

"For one thing, she put me under her shielding; got
me controlled until we arrived here and Savil took me
under her wing. That's more than enough reason to love
her, even without the bond to her. She's my very best
friend and the sister of my soul.''

He reached up, and touched Vanyel's cheek. His hand
was cool; almost cold. "But she'll never be what you
are. Can you understand what I'm saying, love? I owe
her my sanity, but in a lot of ways she's *more* than I am;
I love her the way I love Savil or my mother—inferior to

superior. *Not* brother to sister, or lover to lover; not *ever* as equals.''

Vanyel put his own hand over the one touching his cheek, and held it, warming it in his own. "What am I, then?"

"You're my partner, my equal, my friend—and my love. Vanyel, I didn't say this in so many words last night—but I *do* love you."

Those words were *not* expected; certainly the implied level of commitment was not what Vanyel had expected. "But—" he stuttered, not sure whether what he was feeling was joy or fear.

"Van, I know we haven't known each other long, but I do *love* you," Tylendel said, ignoring the 'but,' holding Vanyel's gaze with his own. "And I love you because I love you; not because I owe you anything, or because some god somewhere decided I was going to be a Herald, or because you're a beloved teacher. I love you because you're Vanyel, and we belong together, and together we can stand back-to-back against anything."

Much to his confusion, Vanyel felt his eyes start burning. "I don't know—really know what to say," he replied awkwardly, blinking hard. "Except—'Lendel, I think after last night—I can't ever remember being this *happy*. I've never loved anyone, I don't know what it's like, but if—" he tried to say what he felt. "—if wanting to die for you is love—"

His eyes burned; he rubbed at them with his free hand, and tried to put his feelings into coherent words. He groped after his thoughts, totally awkward and altogether out of his depth, but he *needed* to articulate his bewildering emotions. He'd never felt so vulnerable and exposed in his life. "I'd do anything for you; I'd take the sneers, the pointed fingers—I wouldn't care, so long as they didn't take me away from you. If I could, I'd give you anything. I'd do anything I could to make *you* happy. And—I'll gladly share you with Gala."

"Havens, don't say that," Tylendel chuckled, though his voice sounded suspiciously thick and *his* eyes glistened in the shadows. "*She* wanted to 'eavesdrop,' you know. She'd take you up on that, the randy little bitch."

Vanyel's face flamed hotly, and he laughed, using his own embarrassment to get past that moment of complete vulnerability. "I *knew* she was saying something that would make me blush, I just *knew* it!"

"Well, she is *not* going to have her prurience satisfied, I promise you," Tylendel said firmly. "*I* am not going to share *you*, and that's that."

Vanyel entered their room through the garden door, blinking until his eyes adjusted to the semidarkness after the noontide sunlight of the gardens. He was carrying his lute by the neck in his right hand, and holding his left, wrapped in a handkerchief, curled against his chest.

Ye gods, I should have known better, he thought ruefully, as his left hand throbbed. *I am such a damned fool.*

" 'Lendel?" he called into the outer room, racking the lute with care, still using only his right hand. "Are you out there?"

"Of course I am." Tylendel strolled in, a half-eaten slice of bread and cheese in one hand. "It's lunchtime, you know I'm always here when the food is!"

Vanyel began unwrapping his hand—slowly—

Tylendel stopped chewing, then tossed his lunch, forgotten, onto the table. "Gods, Van—what did you do to yourself? Sit!"

The ends of Vanyel's fingers were blistered, and the blisters had broken and were bleeding. The muscles of the hand were cramped so hard he couldn't have gotten his fingers uncurled to save his soul. He looked at the wreckage he'd made of his hand with a kind of pained disbelief.

Tylendel pushed him down onto the bed, and took the injured hand in both his own.

"I made a fool of myself, is what I did," Vanyel told him, regretfully. "I told the girls yesterday that if they'd leave me alone I'd play for them this morning. I forgot how long it's been since I played—and, well, I'll tell you the truth, I forgot I lost some feeling in those fingers when the arm got broken. I didn't even realize what I'd done to my finger-ends until *after* the muscles in my hand started to cramp."

"Stay right there." Tylendel went to the little chest at the foot of the bed that he'd moved into Vanyel's room with the rest of his things, bent over it for a moment, and came back with bandages and a little pot of salve. "I'm no Healer," he said, sitting down and taking Vanyel's hand back into his, "but I've banged myself up a time or two, and this is good stuff."

He took some of it on the ends of his fingers and massaged it into the palm of Vanyel's hand. A pleasant, sharp odor came from it, both green and spicy, and his fingers began to relax from their cramped position, both from the warming effect of the salve and the massage.

"What is that?" Vanyel asked, sniffing. "I'm going to smell sort of like a pastry."

Tylendel laughed. "Don't tempt me this early in the day, Vanyel-*ashke*. It's cinnamon and marigold. Good for the cramped muscles *and* the poor, battered fingers."

He had worked all the way out to the ends of Vanyel's fingers; the cramps were mostly gone, and the salve, rather than burning as Vanyel had half feared it would, was numbing the areas where Tylendel was spreading it.

"Now just let me get you bandaged up."

"What was that you just called me?"

"*Ashke?* It's *Tayledras*. Hawkbrother-tongue. All those feathered faces and masks Savil has on the wall out in the common room are from the *Tayledras;* she studied with one of their Adepts, Starwind k'Treva, and they made her a Wingsister. That's like a blood brother for them."

Tylendel was wrapping each finger carefully and taking his time about it. Vanyel didn't mind in the least. Now that he wasn't in much pain, there was something a bit sensual about Tylendel's ministrations.

"She uses a lot of their expressions when there isn't a good word for the thing in our tongue. Like *shay'a'chern*—it translates as—oh—'one whose lover is like self,' with a sexual connotation to the word 'self' that makes it clear that they aren't talking about incest *or* similar interests. It's a very complicated language." He looked up from his bandaging, and Vanyel could see laughter-glints lurking in the depths of his eyes. "You smell delicious; are you *sure* you have lessons this afternoon?''

"We promised Savil we'd be virtuous today," Vanyel reminded him, feeling greatly tempted anyway.

Tylendel heaved an exaggerated sigh. "Too true. Well, *ashke* translates simply to 'beloved.' And it's part of your name already—*ashke,* Ashkevron. See?''

He tied off the last bit of bandage with a flourish.

"Ashke," Vanyel mused. "I—like it."

"It suits you, *ashke;* Savil says the Hawkbrothers seldom go by their born-names, they take use-names when they become mages. Maybe that's the name you always should have had. Now let's go eat lunch and be virtuous—before I decide to break my sworn word to Savil!"

Savil looked up from her book and rubbed her tired, blurring eyes. Tylendel and Vanyel had taken over the couch across from her to study. Candlelight from the lantern beside them made a halo of Tylendel's dark gold curls and highlighted the golden brown of his tunic; beside him, in deep blue, Vanyel seemed to be an extension of his shadow. They shared Vanyel's history text; it rested on their knees with each holding a corner. Tylendel's arm was around Vanyel's shoulder, their heads nestled closely together. From time to time Savil could catch the murmur of a question from her nephew and Tylendel's slightly higher reply.

Strange that it's the older who has the tenor voice and the younger who's the deeper, she mused, blinking sleepily at them. *Though the pairing is strange all around. I would never have reckoned Vanyel for* shay'a'chern. *Not with Withen for a father.*

She yawned silently, and half-closed her eyes. The two young ones across the room from her blurred into a haze of gold and darkest blue. *He's got 'Lendel thinking about something other than that damned feud, at least; for that I'd warm to him. Even if I want to knock him into the wall occasionally for being a little prig. 'Lendel does seems to be getting some notion of responsible behavior into his head. And a bit more politeness. Though it's a damn good thing Mardic and Donni are inclined to take everything he says generously, or they might have knocked him into the wall for me! Bless them. He can be so damned rude sometimes—and not mean it.*

She worried a hangnail with the end of her thumb. *He's been so isolate I suppose I shouldn't be surprised. Gods be thanked 'Lendel seems to be civilizing him. There's more patience there than there was before—and I think, maybe, a little more kindness. Less arrogance, for certain. Withen should be pleased enough with the reports he's getting to let him stay.* She noted Vanyel's intense concentration on his book, and restrained the corners of her mouth from quirking up. *Looks like he's enjoying himself. Can't say that I'd mind studying with my 'Lendel coaching! Poor little lad; when he gives his heart to a thing, he certainly doesn't do it halfway. Still, I'm not certain I like the way he's becoming so dependent on 'Lendel. That isn't healthy, not for either of them. It could make for trouble later on.*

A thin tendril of contact reached for her from across the room, although Tylendel's eyes remained on the book. :*A silver for your thoughts, teacher-mine.*:

:*How pretty you look together, young demon.*: she replied the same way. :*And how grateful I am that you've managed to stay discreet.*:

:*Discipline, discipline,*: came the laughter-tinged answer. :*Seriously, you've heard no gossip?*:

:*Only that I'm likely to find you two at knife-point one day.*:

The aura of amusement deepened. :*Well, well, so it worked. I owe Van a forfeit.*:

Savil raised her eyebrows in surprise, and opened her eyes again to catch Tylendel looking at her with a smile lurking in the corners of his mouth. :*How so, demon-child?*:

:*He's been insulting me behind my back. Popinjay pecking. Mostly on my proclivities. So if anything gets back to Withen . . . We decided I should "find out about it" and go for him if the insults got noticed.*:

:*Great good gods!*: She bit her lip to keep from laughing. :*Pot calling kettle, oh my hope of the Havens! What were you planning on doing? Are you going to call him out? I'd rather you didn't have at each other with anything sharp.*:

:Oh, probably I'll make a major confrontation, with as many witnesses as possible. But not with blades, teacher-love; he's too good for me, and we figured he should lose so he gets the sympathy of his flock of doves. Bare-handed, we think. Wrestling; we'll try to keep fists out if it as much as possible too. We had some vague notion of trying it the next time it rains, in the mud. It should be lots of fun.:

Savil had to drop the mind-link for a moment until she got herself back under control. *Lots of fun indeed—great good gods, both of them tussling in the open in front of everyone and no one guessing how much they're enjoying it.*

:Demon-child, I think I'll put you in for envoy when I grant you your Whites; you have altogether too twisted a mind!:

:Well, doing it that way we can avoid the chance of hurting each other, and I've already established that I go after people very directly. Poor Van is going to have to decide which outfit of his I'm going to ruin, though. I intend to rip it to rags for verisimilitude.:

Savil nearly choked to death, trying not to laugh at the mind-pictures and overtones that came across with that last sending. *:Verisimilitude, my behind! You just want—:*

:Why, Savil!: The eyes across from her were wide with assumed innocence. *:How could you think such a thing?:*

:Easy enough,: she replied, her own mental tone so dry that it had a metallic taste. *:Given who I've got for a protege.:*

:Well—:

Well, indeed. 'Lendel—just a word of caution, and I may be being reactionary—but I don't like the way Van is coming to lean on you for everything. It isn't healthy; he needs to learn how to depend on himself a little.:

:Oh, Savil.:

:I'm serious.:

:It's just a phase. He's young, and he needs so badly. Great good gods, nobody's ever bothered to love him ex-

*cept his sister. After he's had me around for a bit and
knows I won't vanish on him, he'll grow out of it.*:

:*'Lendel, I'm not the expert on people that Lancir is,
but in my experience people don't grow out of a habit of
dependence.*: She glanced at the time-candle. :*Ah, we'll
just leave it at that, all right? Keep it in mind. And that's
enough study for one night. Both of you to bed.*:

Again the mental laughter. :*Why, Savil—:*

:*To sleep, dammit!:*

Tylendel nudged the other boy, and closed the book,
then looked across the room at his mentor with that ironic
half-smile she knew so well. "Let's pack it up for the
night, Van," he said quietly—

—and :*Of course, teacher. To sleep,:* she Mindheard.
Then, as they disappeared into their room—
:*Eventually.:*

Savil had forgotten all about the planned "fight" by
the time a good, soaking rain actually put in an appearance, nearly a fortnight later. She had reserved the Work
Room for Mardic and Donni that afternoon; for all that
they were lifebonded they were having a tremendous difficulty in working together, magically speaking. Donni
had a tendency to rush into something at full tilt; Mardic
was entirely the opposite, holding reserves back until the
very last moment and dithering about full commitment.
That meant that when they worked together their auras
pulsed and had some serious weak spots, and their shields
never quite meshed. Savil was putting them through an
exercise designed to force them to synchronize their
energy-levels and work as a unit rather than as an uneven
team, when someone pounded urgently on the door.

The union of energy fields disintegrated at the first
knock; dissipating with a "pop" into a shower of visible
sparks and separating into the auras—green for Donni,
yellow for Mardic—surrounding each of her crestfallen
students. Savil swore an oath sufficiently heated to blister
paint. She looked the couple over with OtherSight and
swore another nearly as strong.

Dammit, their concentration's gone completely. Look

at those auras pulse! Oh, hellfires! *If this isn't important, I'll* kill *whoever's out there!*

She banished the violet shield she had placed about the pair with an abrupt gesture, and stalked to the door, yanking it open and glaring at the agitated Guard standing just outside.

"*Yes?*" she said, with an edge to her voice that was sharp enough to shave with.

"Herald Savil, your nephew and your protege Tylendel—they're fighting—" the man gulped, stepping back involuntarily at the sight of her angry face. "Tylendel's put up a barrier and we can't get at them to break it up; he's got your nephew down and we're afraid he may do him true harm—"

"*Damn!*" the word exploded from her, as for one moment she thought that something had *really* happened between the pair and the fight was *serious.*

Then she recalled the plan, and almost ruined it for them all by laughing in the man's face.

She schooled her expression to the one she would have been wearing if this had been a *genuine* fight; mouth tight and eyes narrowed in feigned anger. "Show me," she barked. "I'll deal with this nonsense right now."

The Guard scurried ahead of her down the hallway; she followed at a near-trot, wincing a little at the aches the rain had called up in the depths of her joints.

I'll bet 'Lendel put up the mage-barrier to keep people from seeing that he and Van aren't really hitting each other, she decided, hastening her pace a bit as the Guard pulled ahead. *And to keep folks from breaking up the fight too soon. I'd better make a major scene over this or he'll never forgive me.*

There was no doubt of where the fight was taking place—Herald-proteges, young courtiers, Bard-trainees and other assorted young people were clustered tightly around the door to the gardens on the southeast side of the Palace, all of them babbling like a pack of fools. The Guard pushed his way through them with no regard for rank or ceremony whatsoever; Savil followed behind him and peered out the door into the pouring rain.

The combatants were about fifty paces beyond the door,

in a spot beside the paved path where all the grass had been worn away. There was, indeed, a mage-barrier over the area where they were struggling, a place that looked more like a pig-wallow at this point. The barrier and the rain were blurring the combatants badly enough that it was hard to see exactly what was going on. Vanyel was down, on his back; at least Savil assumed it was Vanyel, since the current loser was slightly smaller and his hair was mostly dark under the mud. Tylendel was sitting on his chest, and if Savil hadn't known better, she'd have sworn he was strangling the younger boy.

"You take that back, you little bastard!" Tylendel roared. "You take that back, unless you want another pound of mud shoved down your throat!"

Savil steeled herself and barked—in her best stop-a-mob-in-full-cry voice—a single word.

"ENOUGH!"

Instantly the fighters froze.

Savil strode out into the deluge, her dignity somewhat diminished when her feet squelched instead of coming down firmly, and the rain immediately plastered her hair to her skull, sending tendrils of it straggling into her eyes and mouth.

Nevertheless, she reckoned she looked imposing enough, since all the babbling behind her ceased as she reached the edge of Tylendel's mage-barrier and stopped.

"Take it down, trainee," she said, her tone so cold it could have turned the rain into snow.

Tylendel scrambled to his feet and dismissed the barrier. Now that he could be seen clearly, he truly looked as if he'd been through the wars. His hair was full of mud and straggling around his face in dirty coils. One eye was turning black and starting to swell; his lower lip was split and bleeding. His tunic was torn and muddy and so were his breeches; one of his boots had come unlaced and sagged around his ankle. He wore a very un-Tylendel-like expression; sullen and full of barely-smothered anger.

Vanyel remained prone for several moments longer with his chest heaving as he gulped for air; long enough that Savil began to think he might *really* be hurt. She breathed a little easier when he levered himself up out of the mud and got slowly to his feet.

He was in worse case than Tylendel; his tunic had been all but stripped from his body, there wasn't much left of it, and what there was hung in strips from his belt and his wrists. He had several angry-looking scratches on his arms and chest, and a split lip to match Tylendel's; but more seriously, he was favoring his right foot, wincing in real pain when he had to put any weight on it.

He didn't move, once he'd gotten to his feet; just stood with his hands clasped before him, wearing an expression so like Tylendel's that Savil began to be alarmed.

:'Lendel?: she Mindspoke, layering the name with her anxiety and distress.

Tylendel's expression didn't change by so much as a twitch of an eyelid, but the Mindvoice was as cheerful and amused as his face was angry and sullen. :No fear, teacher-mine. It's still going mostly as planned.:

She sighed mentally with relief. :Mostly?:

:Well, we couldn't practice this much, so we made some miscalculations. Van got me in the eye with his elbow, we both managed to sock each other in the mouth somehow, and I think I made him sprain his ankle when I tackled him. Hurry up and lecture us, I can't keep a straight face much longer!:

She straightened, and looked down her long nose at both of them, ignoring the water dripping off the end of it. "A fine thing," she said acidly, "when I can't trust my protege and ward to conduct themselves like civilized adults in my absence! What am I to do with you? Find you keepers?"

Tylendel made as if to say something, but shrank under her icy glare, the rain slowly washing the mud out of his hair.

"Trainee Tylendel, *you* should have known better! You are a Herald-in-training; I expect you to act in accordance with the dignity and honor of our office. I do *not* expect to find you thrashing about in the mud like a six-year-old brat with no manners and no sense! No matter how much Vanyel provoked you, you should have come to *me* first, not taken the matter into your own hands!"

Tylendel hung his head and mumbled something in the direction of the puddle around his feet.

"Louder, trainee," she snapped. "I can't hear you."

"Yes, Herald Savil," he repeated, his voice harsh, and full of suppressed emotion. "I was wrong."

"Go—back to your quarters. Now. Make yourself presentable. I'll deal with you when I'm done with Vanyel."

Tylendel bowed slightly, and without another word, walked past her and through the crowd at the doorway. Savil didn't turn around to watch his progress, but even above the steady beat of the rain she could hear the sound of the crowd parting behind her to let him through. One or two in the group snickered a little, but that was all.

She turned her dagger-gaze on Vanyel, who was glaring at her from under a wet comma of black hair that was obscuring one eye.

"And *you*. Fine state of affairs *this* is." She walked forward a bit and folded her arms, trying not to shiver in the cold rain. "I've heard about those snide little comments of yours, the backbiting, and all the rest of it. You've been picking at 'Lendel ever since you arrived here, young man, and I won't have it!"

Vanyel raised his head, glaring back at her with every bit of the arrogance he'd ever shown. "He's nothing but a—"

"He outranks *you*, young man, and you'd do well to remember that!" she snapped. "Consider yourself confined to your quarters for the duration! If I learn you've set one foot out of the suite when you aren't at lessons, I'll ship you back to your father so fast the wind of your passing will tear the thatch from the roofs! Now *march!*"

Vanyel set his jaw, and pivoted where he stood, setting off toward Savil's suite through the rain—taking the opposite course that Tylendel had followed. He was more than half staggering, and it made Savil's ankle ache in sympathy to to see him struggling through the mud, but she made no move to help him. Instead, she stalked along behind him, as if making certain that he reached his goal.

But once they had rounded the corner and were out of sight of the doorway, she dropped her pose and her dignity and scrambled through the slippery grass to reach his side.

"Lean on me, lad," she said, coming up beside him, and pulling his arm over her shoulder. "I've been called an old stick before this, I might as well act like one."

"Aunt—thank the gods—" he gasped. "I thought we'd never get out of sight." He stumbled and nearly fell, all of his weight suddenly landing on Savil, making her stagger. "Please, I've got to rest a minute. Gods above, this *hurts.*"

"How bad is it?" she asked, as he shivered beside her in the cold rain.

"Don't know." He managed a wan grin. "Hurts more than a thorn in the toe, less than when I broke my arm. That tell you anything?"

"Hardly," she snorted. "Come on, the sooner I get you inside, the happier I'll be. And I hope my protege has the sense to *think* and not come running out to help."

The lights of Savil's windows were in sight—and her heart sank for a moment when she *did* see someone running toward them through the rain. Then she saw a second silhouette beside the first, and realized that it was not Tylendel who was coming to help them in, but Mardic and Donni.

The youngsters took over the task of supporting Vanyel. That left Savil free to go on ahead of them; for which she was truly grateful. She was chilled right down to the bone, and those bones were starting to ache rather persistently.

She stepped in through Vanyel's outer door; almost as soon as she'd stepped across the threshold she found herself enveloped in a warm blanket and practically carried into the common room. It was Tylendel, of course; he stayed with her just long enough to settle her in her favorite chair and put a mug of mulled wine in her hand, then he was gone.

He was back again in a moment, Vanyel's arm around his shoulder, the latter hopping awkwardly beside him.

There was already a blanket waiting on the couch; Tylendel got Vanyel bundled into it and pressed another mug of the wine into his hands.

Mardic and Donni piled in right behind them; giggling, shaking the rain out of their hair, and heading straight for the kettle of wine on the hearth. Vanyel was more interested in his lover's black eye and swollen lip than the wine.

"Gods—'Lendel, I did *not* mean that—" he mourned, reaching out hesitantly to touch the edge of the bruise. "Oh Lord and Lady, *why* do I have to be so clumsy?"

"Oh, you just fight like a girl," Tylendel teased. "All flying knees and elbows. It was *my* own stupid fault for getting my face in the way. It's your ankle I'm worried about." He started unlacing Vanyel's boot, fighting the wet laces and swearing under his breath when they wouldn't cooperate.

"I'm all—*ouch!*"

Tylendel froze. "Did I—"

"No," Vanyel said around clenched teeth. "Just get that damned boot off before you have to cut it off."

But Tylendel dithered over the task until Mardic pushed him out of the way and took over, getting the boot off with an abrupt yank that blanched Vanyel to the color of pure beeswax. He clutched Tylendel's hand while Mardic examined the ankle, pronounced it "probably not broken," and bound it up.

"Havens, teacher," Mardic laughed, rescuing his cup from Donni and returning to sit at her feet across from Savil, "Were *we* as moonstruck as that? Gods, I feel like I'm being smothered in syrup!"

He nodded at the two on the couch, each assuring the other that his own hurts were less than nothing and fussing over the other's injuries.

"For at least the first five or six months," Savil replied dryly, after sipping her wine. "Just as moonstruck, and just as cloying. And even more sentimental." She raised her voice a bit. "You two *might* thank me."

"Certainly, Savil," Tylendel replied, craning his head around. "If you'd tell us what we're thanking you for."

"Gods. Vanyel, don't you ever listen?"

"I'm sorry, Aunt," he said, looking confused, his hair still trailing over one eye. "My foot hurt so much I wasn't paying any attention; it wasn't a *real* lecture, after all."

She cast her eyes up to the ceiling. "Give me strength. I just confined you completely to the suite for as long as I care to enforce my decision, you little ninny. I just got you *away* from the girl-gaggle and gave you *orders* to stay here indefinitely. Except for lessons, you'll be here waking and sleeping. That includes taking meals here."

"You did?" he said, dazed. "I am? You mean I can stay here?"

"With 'Lendel, and not arouse any suspicions," she interrupted. "That's exactly what I mean. Fact of the matter is, your damnfool father will probably be pleased to hear that you were—"

She broke off, seeing that she no longer had the attention of either of them. Across from her she heard Mardic snicker.

She favored the lifebonded with a sardonic glance. "Don't feel too smug," she told them. "Or I'll start trotting out tales about *you* two."

"Yes, Savil," Mardic replied, not in the least repentant. "Whatever you say. Would you care for honey in that wine?"

Savil spared a glance back toward the couch. Tylendel was rebandaging Vanyel's ankle, treating it as if it were as fragile as an insect's wing. She made a face.

"I think not," she replied. "We've got enough sweetness around here for one night."

Tylendel looked up, and stuck his tongue out at her, while Vanyel blushed.

Savil chuckled and sat back in her chair, well content with her world. *At least for the moment,* she thought, taking another sip of spiced wine, *which is all any Herald can reasonably hope for. I'll worry about tomorrow when tomorrow gets here.*

Seven

Tylendel sprawled in his favorite chair, and watched Vanyel restringing his lute, sitting cross-legged on the bed. Candlelight reflected in a honey-colored curve along the round belly of the instrument.

Is it time? he wondered. *He plays for the girls, but they don't matter. He doesn't care if he plays well or badly for them. Will he play for someone he loves, someone who* does *matter? Can he? Has he recovered enough?*

Only one way to find out, though.

"*Ashke,*" he said quietly, extending his little Gift of Empathy as far as it would go. Van lifted his head from his work; he looked rather comical with the old strings dangling from his mouth like the feelers on a catfish.

"Mph?" he replied.

"When you get Woodlark in tune, would you play for me?"

Vanyel froze. Tylendel *Felt* the startlement—and the ache. And reacted to them.

"Please? I'd like it."

Vanyel took the strings out of his mouth, and Tylendel could sense his withdrawal. "Why?" he asked, bitterly, his eyes shining wetly. "There's dozens better than I am right here at Bardic. Why listen to a half-crippled amateur?"

Tylendel restrained his natural reaction—which was to go to him, hold him, ease his hurt that way. That would ease it all right, but it wouldn't cure it. "Because you *aren't* half-crippled anymore," he replied. "Because you aren't an amateur. You're good; the Bards all say so."

"But not good enough to be one of them." Vanyel turned away, but not before Tylendel saw tears in his eyes. And Felt the anguish.

"That's not true," he insisted gently. "Look, Van, it's *not* that you aren't good enough. It's that you just don't have the Gift. Can a blind man paint?"

Vanyel just shook his head, and Tylendel could sense his further withdrawal. "It's not the same thing," he said, tightly. "The blind man can't see a painting. But there's nothing wrong with my ears."

Tylendel searched for something that might reach this wounded corner of his beloved, and finally found it.

"Ashke, why do you think there are minstrels trained at Bardic? Why do you think that people welcome minstrels when there are Bards about?" He'd asked that same question of Breda, who had all three Bardic Talents: the Gift, the Skill, and the Creativity. Her answer had been enlightening.

Vanyel shook his head, still tightly bound up inside himself. "Because there aren't enough Bards to go around, just like there aren't enough Heralds or Healers."

"Wrong," Tylendel said firmly, "and I have this from Breda. *There are times when the Gift gets in the way of the music."*

"What?" Vanyel's head whipped around in startlement, and Tylendel saw the shine of tears on his cheek. "What do you mean by that?"

"Just what I said." *Now* was the time to rise and go to Vanyel's side, and Tylendel did just that. "Listen to me; just what is the Bardic Gift, hmm? It's the ability to make others *feel* the things you want them to through music. But when a Bard does that, you can't keep your mind on the music, can you? You never really hear how beautiful it is; you're too busy with what the Bard is doing. You never really hear it for itself, and when you remember it, you don't remember the music, you remember the emotions. There's another reason; when the Bard performs, you put nothing of yourself into the listening. But when a minstrel performs, or a Bard without the Gift, you get out of the music exactly what you put into the listening.'' He chuckled, and reached for Vanyel's limp hands. "Breda said that in some ways it's a little like making love with a paid courtesan or with your lover. Your lover may not be as expert, but the experience is a lot more genuine.''

"Breda said that?" Vanyel faltered.

"In her cups, yes.'' He didn't add it had been here, in Savil's quarters, the evening she'd tested and failed Vanyel. Breda had a very soft heart beneath that bony chest; she'd not enjoyed destroying Vanyel's hopes, even indirectly. "They do say that there's truth in the bottom of every wine bottle.'' He paused, and raised one eyebrow at his lover. "She also said that if you *weren't* your father's heir, they'd snap you up so fast you'd leave your boots behind.''

"She did?" He could Feel Vanyel uncoiling from around that lump of hurt.

"She did.'' He picked up the lute and put it back in Vanyel's hands. "And since my personal preference is *not* for courtesans, however expert—will you play for me?''

"Just—'' Vanyel swallowed, and finally met his eyes. The hurt was still there, but already fading. "—just let me get her in tune.''

To Vanyel Ashkevron from Lord Withen Ashkevron: greetings. I have received good reports of you from Herald Savil, except for the instance of your quarrel with her protege. While I cannot condone your actions, I can understand that it may be irritating to share the same roof with the young man. You must keep your temper and not provoke him further, as it is obvious that he cannot be relied upon to keep his. I am also given to understand that you have abandoned your pretensions as a musician and relegated such nonsense to its proper place; an amusing hobby, no more. I am pleased with this development; it seems to me this is evidence of maturity and acceptance of your proper place in life, and I have sent a small token of my approval. Inscribed by Father Leren Benevy, By my hand and seal, Lord Withen Ashkevron.

* * *

*To Lord Withen Ashkevron from Vanyel Ashkevron:
greetings. I have received your letter and your token, for
which my thanks. I am endeavoring to follow all of Herald Savil's instructions to the best of my ability. I have
found her to be a wise and knowledgeable mentor, and
hope to better please her in the future. By my hand, Vanyel Ashkevron.*

*Dearest Son: I Pray with all my Heart that this finds
you Well, and that you were not Hurt by that Brutal Boy.
I Feared that something of this Nature would Occur from
the Instant your Father Told me of this Foolish Scheme
and have had Dark and Fell Dreams from the moment
you Departed. Savil is plainly Not To Be Relied Upon to
keep her Creatures in Order. I pray you, do not Provoke
the Barbarian further; I am endeavoring to Persuade your
Father to fetch you Home again, but thus far it is All In
Vain. I am Prostrate with Worry—and if your Absence
were not enough, I have been visited with a Further Grief.
My maid Melenna has been rendered With Child—and by
your Brother Mekeal! So she Claims, and so Mekeal Ad-
mits. Your Father is No Help; he seems to Think it is All
Very Amusing. Indeed, I am at my Wit's End and I know
not What To Do! But even in my Extremity, I have not
forgotten my Beloved Child, nor that your Birthday is this
very day. I enclose a Small Token—All that I could Manage, and not Nearly your Desert. I Beg you that if you
are in Need that you will Tell Me at Once. I shall Manage
something More from your Father, Hard-Hearted as he
is. Your Loving Mother, Lady Treesa Ileana Brendywhin-
Ashkevron.*

"Purple ink?" Tylendel said incredulously, looking
over Vanyel's shoulder. "Am I really seeing purple ink?
And *pink* paper?"

"Costs a fortune, and it's all she'll use," Vanyel answered absently, pondering how to reply without setting
his mother off again. The pink page lay on the blotter of
the desk, its very existence a maternal accusation that he
hadn't written since he arrived here. Beside it were two
piles of silver coins—absolutely equal in value.

One reward for beating up a pervert, one consolation for getting beaten up by a pervert. He sighed. *Gods, there are times I wish I was an orphan.*

"May I?" Tylendel asked.

Vanyel shrugged. "Go ahead. You'll encounter her eventually, I'm sure. You ought to know what she's like."

Tylendel worked his way through the ornamented and scrolled calligraphy, and gave it back to Vanyel with a grimace that said more than words could have.

"You think this is bad—you should see the letters she writes to friends, or worse, people she thinks have slighted her. Three, four, and five pages, purple ink and tear-blotches, and everything capitalized." He sighed again. "And *appalling* grammar. When she gets really hysterical, she goes into formal mode and she *cannot* seem to keep her 'thees' and 'thous' straight."

He contemplated the letter for a moment. "What's really awful, she *talks* like that, too."

Tylendel laughed, threw himself down on the bed, and got back to the book he'd been reading.

Dear Mother: I really am all right. Please don't worry about me—worry about yourself. If you don't take care of yourself, if you let your fine sensibilities get the better of you, you'll make yourself ill. Savil is quite kind, and the problems I had with Tylendel have been taken care of. Every rumor that comes out of this Court is an exaggeration at best and an outright lie at worst, so pay no attention to what your friends are telling you. I am sorry to hear about Melenna; this must be a terrible burden for you. Your present was very kind, and very much appreciated, and far in excess of my needs. I love you, and I think about you often. Be well, Vanyel.

Dear Vanyel; What in Havens is going on? Are you all right? If it's unbearable, for the gods' sake let me know and I'll lead the Seven Corey Swordmaids to your rescue—they're dying to play avenging angels, although given their figures, it's more like avenging angles. All my love, Lissa.

* * *

Vanyel laughed aloud, and passed the note to Tylendel.

Tylendel grinned broadly and handed it back to him. "Now *this* one I like. What's my chances of meeting her?"

"Pretty good," Vanyel replied, stretching. "Once the secret's out about us, Father will disinherit me, Mother will have vapors, and Lissa will show up, sword in hand, to defend me from Father's wrath. She's gotten a lot spunkier since she went over to the Coreys to foster. Lord Trevor has just about promised her a commission in the Guard."

"Which he can give her, since he's in charge of recruitment for the Guard," Tylendel said thoughtfully. "Is that your last letter?"

"One more after this—"

Dearest Lissa; Don't worry, it's all right. I'm fine, and I'm happier than I've been in my life here. Savil is on my side against Father, and some of what you've been hearing is to keep him happy. Trust me, it really is all right. I love you, and I miss you, Van.

To Vanyel Ashkevron from Evan Leshara; greetings. I believe we have mutual interests and I would be honored and pleased if we could meet to discuss them. I am at your disposal any evening. By my hand and seal, Evan Leshara.

" 'Lendel—" Vanyel said slowly, sorely puzzled by this last note, which had been delivered to the suite by a page that very afternoon. "Who is Evan Leshara?"

Tylendel paced the confines of the bedroom, as restless as a caged wolf. Savil thought both of them were in here; he hadn't told her that Vanyel had slipped his leash to go see what Evan Leshara wanted. He glanced over at the time-candle; it hadn't burned down any since the last time he'd looked at it.

I shouldn't have let him go. If Leshara figures out the fight was all a ruse—

Up and back, up and back. It was damned hot for an autumn night, or was it being on edge that was making him sweat? His scalp prickled, and he felt a headache beginning just under his right eye. Shadows cast by the light of the time-candle danced and flickered, shrank and grew.

—if he figures out the game we're playing, he'll be able to use blackmail on Van against me, and me against Staven. Oh. gods, I shouldn't have let him go. I should have told him to ignore Leshara's invitation. I should have. I—

The creak of the garden door broke into his worries, and his tensions evaporated when Vanyel slipped in from the darkness and latched the door behind himself.

"*Ashke?*" Tylendel began, then hesitated, seeing the troubled expression in Vanyel's eyes.

"He's a damned persuasive man, this Leshara," Vanyel said softly, sitting himself in the chair in front of the cold fireplace.

"That's why he's here," Tylendel replied grimly. "It's the Leshara countermove to my being here. Since they can't buy into the Heralds, they've sent the one of their kin with the sweetest tongue to get the ear of the Queen, if he can."

"He says he's got it. He said a lot of things. 'Lendel, there was an awful lot of what he said that made sense."

"Of course there was!" Tylendel interrupted. "I'll be willing to bet that half of what he told you was the absolute truth even by *my* standards. It's the *way* he said it, the context, and what he was prompting you to infer from what he told you that counts! You ought to know yourself from what you've been writing home that the best possible lie is to tell only the truth—just not all of it!"

"But 'Lendel," Vanyel still looked uncertain. " 'Lendel, he says his people have been willing to settle for months now, a settlement the Queen approves, and yours refuse to go along with it—"

"He didn't tell you what that 'plan' was, did he?"

Vanyel shook his head.

"To marry my thirty-year-old maiden-cousin who's never been outside of a cloister to a fifty-year-old lecher, take Staven out of being Lord Holder and put *her* in," he said savagely, "which effectively means putting *him* in, since there's no way she'd ever be able to stand up to him. She'd dry up and blow away the first time he spoke harshly to her. *That's* the Leshara notion of an equitable settlement." He glared at Vanyel, angry and a little hurt that Vanyel would even *consider* taking Evan Leshara's word as the whole truth. "He's using the fact that Staven's only seventeen as a way to imply that he's incompetent, too young to make any kind of rational decisions. And a lot of the powers at Court, being old goats themselves, are buying into the idea. After all, seventeen's only old enough to be told you have to go fight and die for something—it's *not* old enough to have any say in the matter!"

Vanyel's eyes had gotten very distressed, and he had shrunk back into the chair as far as he could. " 'Lendel," he faltered. "I didn't mean—I wasn't doubting you—"

Tylendel gave himself a mental kick in the posterior for upsetting him. *"Ashke,* I didn't mean to shout at you," he said, kneeling beside the chair and putting one hand on Vanyel's knee. "I'm sorry—I'm just so damned frustrated. He can say any damned thing he wants, and because I'm a Herald-trainee, I can't even refute him. It makes me a little crazy, sometimes."

Vanyel brightened, and put his hand over Tylendel's. "That's all right. I know how you feel. Like me and Father and Jervis."

"Something like it."

" 'Lendel, would you," Vanyel hesitated, "would you tell me your side?"

Tylendel took a deep breath. "If I do, I'll be breaking a promise I made to Savil, not to get you involved."

"I'm already involved. I—why? That's what I really want to know. What's keeping this thing going?"

"Something Wester Leshara did," Tylendel replied, fighting down the urge to get up, grab a horse, and ride out to strangle Wester with his bare hands. The white-hot rage that always filled him whenever he called that particular memory up was very hard to control. "Savil says I have to be absolutely fair—so to be absolutely fair,

I'll tell you that this was in retaliation for a raid that accidentally killed his youngest son. We—our people—went in to stampede his cattle. The boy fell off his horse and wound up under their hooves. But I don't think that excuses what Wester did.''

"Which was?''

"My father had just died; he hired some kind of two-copper conjuror to convince Mother that Father's ghost wanted to speak with her. She wasn't very stable—which Wester was damned well aware of, and this pushed her over the edge. We got rid of the charlatan, but not before he'd gotten her convinced that if she found just the right formula, she'd be able to communicate with Father's spirit. She started taking all manner of potions, trying to see him. Finally she *did* see him—she ate Black Angel mushrooms.''

He did not add that he and Staven had been the ones to find her. Vanyel looked sick enough. Tylendel got a lid on his anger, and changed the subject. "What did the bastard want, anyway?''

"He wanted me to let him know any time I heard anything about you or your family, and he wanted me to talk my father 'round to his side.''

"What did you tell him?''

Vanyel grimaced. "I guess I was playing the same game of telling not all of the truth. I told him that I heard more about your people directly from you than I heard casually, and let him draw his own conclusions.''

Tylendel relaxed, and chuckled. Vanyel brightened a little more. "What about your father?''

"I told him the truth; that I had been sent here as punishment, because I wouldn't toe the line at home, and that father would take advice from a halfwit before he'd take it from me. He was rather disappointed.''

Now Tylendel laughed, and hugged him. *"Ashke, ashke,* you couldn't have done better if I'd given you a script!''

"So I did all right?'' Now Vanyel was fairly glowing.

"You did better than all right.''

Gods, he thought, seeing Vanyel so elated, *he fades like an unwatered flower when he thinks I'm angry at him—and now this—you'd have thought I'd offered him a Bard's laurel. Does my opinion mean so much to him? Do I mean so much to him?*

The thought was a sobering one. And it was followed inevitably by another. *Maybe Savil's right. . . .*

"He said he wants to stay in touch with me anyway, just in case I hear something. I told him that was all right with me. In fact, I acted pretty eager about it." He turned his head a little to one side, and offered, tentatively, "I thought we could sort of tell him what we wanted him to hear."

Ha. "We," not "you." No, Savil's not right. He depends on me, but I depend on him, and if he's leaning on me a little, well, that isn't going to hurt anyone. He's just not used to making decisions on his own, that's all.

"That's perfect," he said, leaning on the arm of the chair. "Absolutely perfect. Now, after facing off the dragon for me, oh noble warrior, in what way can I *ever* reward you?" He batted his eyelashes at Vanyel, who laughed, and drew himself up as if he sat in a throne. "I'll do *anything*—"

"Oh?" Vanyel replied archly. "*Anything?*"

"Savil told me something funny today," Tylendel murmured quietly into Vanyel's ear. His voice roused Vanyel out of the sleepy half-dream he'd been in ever since he and Tylendel had settled into their favorite spot in all of the Field.

It was the first time either of them had broken the silence since they'd entered the pine copse.

The suite had seemed far too stuffy for the warm autumnal evening, even with all the windows open. And Vanyel had scarcely left it since they'd staged their "fight"—except for lessons and the obligatory evenings with Evan Leshara to feed him misinformation. And the appearances he *had* to make at Court to keep his circle of admirers happy and deceived.

It was moon-dark, and the chance of anyone seeing them heading out into Companion's Field together was practically nonexistent. So when Vanyel had looked up from his Religions text and tentatively suggested a walk,

Tylendel had shut his own book and flung the garden door open with a mocking bow and a real grin.

It was inevitable that Gala should join them when they crossed the river; Vanyel had come to take her presence for granted on the precious few joint excursions they'd judged safe from detection. It was equally inevitable that they should seek "their" pine grove; it drew them as no other place within walking distance could.

It was blacker than Sunsinger's despair beneath the branches on this moonless night, but Tylendel had made a tiny mage-light once they'd gotten past the first line of trees and were safely out of sight. They'd just rambled for a long time, from one end of the peaceful grove to the other and back again; not speaking, but not needing to. Not touching, either—but again, not needing to.

It wasn't until they'd walked out the last of their end-of-the-day tensions that they'd finally decided to settle next to the oldest tree in the grove and just relax in silence. Gala provided a willing backrest, and the two of them leaned up against her soft warmth, with Vanyel resting his head on Tylendel's shoulder. Tylendel had put out the mage-light, leaving them in near-total darkness. There were still a few crickets that hadn't been killed by the first frost, calling from a dozen different directions, and once Vanyel had heard geese crying by high overhead. But other than that, and the sigh of Gala's breathing, they might have been the only two living creatures in an endlessly empty, pine-fragrant universe.

Which was exactly the way Vanyel wanted it. This continual charade of theirs was proving to be both harder and easier than he'd thought it would. Easier, because he was no longer trying to block out his feelings, no longer trying to convince himself that he didn't need anyone. Easier, because the arrogant pose, the flirtation games, were no longer anything more than an elaborate set of games. But harder, because one single slip, one hint getting back to Withen of what was really going on, and he'd lose everything that was making his life something more than a burden to be endured. And harder, because of the double-game he was playing with Leshara. One slip *there* and Leshara would know what was really going on—and it would be child's play for him to use that knowledge as a double-weapon against Vanyel *and* Tylendel.

And there was no way of knowing how much—or how little—Evan Leshara believed out of all the things Vanyel was telling him. All he could do was trust that 'Lendel knew enough to seed the falsehoods with exactly the right amount of truth—because *he* certainly didn't know enough.

The pretense was a constant drain on his emotional energy, and it wasn't often that he felt safe enough to forget and enjoy the moment. The insecurity of the situation was the first thing on his mind when waking and the last when going to sleep.

That wasn't the only strain. Since the fight, he'd been virtually ostracized by the Bards, Heralds, and all their trainees. Tylendel was (somewhat to his own surprise) highly-regarded among the "working" members of Queen Elspeth's High Court. But that meant that Vanyel was bearing the burden of *their* scorn for provoking the fight. And while his teachers remained within the bounds of polite civility, they were making no secret of their disdain. Lessons had become ordeals, and only Tylendel's insistence that he was going to *have* to continue if the charade was going to work had kept Vanyel persisting in the face of the hostility he was facing. The only one of his teachers that seemed oblivious to the whole mess was Lord Oden—possibly because the Lord-Marshall's second-in-command was pretty well indifferent to anything not involving the martial arts. Vanyel had ample occasion to reflect on the irony that his situation was now precisely the opposite of what he had endured at Forst Reach. There he'd been the pet of his tutors, except for the armsmaster, and despised by everyone his own age. Here—discounting the trainees—his peers were fawning on him, but his teachers were doing their icily gracious best to get him to give up and drop out of their lessons—except for his armsmaster. It was *not* his imagination that they were being harder on him than the others being lessoned; Mardic was in his Religions group now, and had confirmed his suspicions.

"So what did Savil say?" he replied, closing his weary eyes, and shifting a bit so that he wasn't resting so much of his weight on Tylendel's arm. Tylendel responded by holding him a little closer.

"That she can't understand why we haven't had at least one fight," Tylendel said, laughing a little. "She says we're sickening."

"She has a point," Vanyel conceded, with a ghost of a chuckle. "We are, a bit."

"She told me she can't understand how we stay so dotingly devoted to each other. She says we act like a couple of spaniels—you know, kick 'em, and they just come back begging to be kicked again—only worse, because we aren't kicking each other."

"She just doesn't realize," Vanyel said, sobered by a moment of introspection. " 'Lendel, there is no way I'd fight with you, when any moment my father might find out about us and pull me home. I couldn't bear the idea of our last words being angry ones. I have to make every moment we have together a good memory."

"Don't let it eat at you," Tylendel interrupted. "You're sixteen now; I'm seventeen. It's only two years before you're of age. We'll be all right so long as you can keep your end of things going with Lord Evan."

Vanyel sighed. "Gods, gods, two years—it seems like forever. It seems like it's been years already. I just can't imagine coming to the end of this."

Tylendel stroked his hair, his hand as light as a breath of wind. "You'll manage, *ashke*. You're stronger than you think. I sometimes think you're stronger than I am. I doubt I could be dealing successfully with the plate you've been handed. And whether or not you believe this, I think I depend as much on you as you do on me. Gala says so."

"She does?" Vanyel's voice rose with his surprise. "Really?"

"Frequently." He sighed, and Vanyel wondered why. There were times when it seemed that there were some serious points of disagreement between Gala and her Chosen, usually involving Tylendel's tacit and unshakable support of his twin. Vanyel personally couldn't see what all the fuss was about. Even if 'Lendel *hadn't* had the close bond he did with Staven, even if Wester Leshara *hadn't* connived the painful suicide of 'Lendel's mother, it would still have been his duty to support Staven. Even though Vanyel himself had a rather bitter and uncomfortable relationship with his own brother, Mekeal, if it came to an interHouse confrontation there was no doubt in his mind where *he* would stand, and he knew Mekeal was likely to feel the same. And given how much Tylendel owed to his brother for supporting *him* in the face of all opposition—well, Vanyel couldn't see what else he *could* do, in all decency and honor.

But then, there was a great deal about all this "Herald" business he didn't understand. For instance—

" 'Lendel, if we make it that far—all the way to when you get your Whites—"

" 'If?' Don't think in terms of 'if,' love," Tylendel chided, softly. "It may not be easy, but we'll make it. Havens, I should talk about not being easy, when it's you that is having to take the worse share on your shoulders. But I'll help you, I'll help you all I can, and we *will* see this through to the other side."

"Well, what's going to happen with us? When you get your Whites and I'm of age—what then?"

There was a long pause, and Tylendel's hand stopped moving, resting on the back of his neck. "That's the easy part, really. First thing, you make up your mind about exactly what you want to do about Lord Withen. I mean, you could flat tell him about us, or you could just—let him find out. Whichever way you want. At that point the worst he could do is disown you, and you *know* everything I have is yours for the asking. The Circle won't stint me; I'll have more than enough to support two."

"He probably will disown me," Vanyel said bitterly. "Which will mean I'll *have* to ask, 'Lendel."

"So? We're partners, aren't we? It won't be charity, *ashke;* it'll be sharing."

Vanyel squelched the automatic retort that it would still *feel* like charity. "All right, assume I've told my father and I'm free to do what I want. Then what?"

"After that, Savil will turn the lovebirds over to an-

other Herald and take me—us—out on a Field assign-
ment. Us, because obviously I won't go without you;
Savil knows that, so it's a given. That's a year, or there-
abouts. But then—I don't know. I'm a Herald-Mage
trainee; they usually give us permanent positions rather
than having us ride circuit like the straight Heralds do.
They'll probably put me either here at Haven, or out along
the Border at the places where magic is needed. Down
by White Foal Pass, around the edge of the Pelagirs—''

"Why? That's something that has me baffled. Why?''
Vanyel asked. "I mean, why are you going to do what
somebody else wants? Why do you have to go where *they*
say? Who *are* 'they,' anyway?''

" 'They'—that's the Heraldic Circle. Queen's Own,
Seneschal's Herald, Lord-Marshal's Herald, the speaker
for the Heralds with trainees—that's Savil—the speaker
for the Herald-Mages and the speaker for the Heralds on
circuit. And the Queen, of course, and the Heir. They're
the ones who decide where Heralds and Herald-Mages
will serve and what they'll do. That's—that's just the way
it is. Van, I don't understand *you* now.'' There was hurt
in Tylendel's voice. "Don't you *want* to go with me?''

"Oh, gods—'' Vanyel groped for Tylendel's free hand,
and held it tightly. " 'Lendel, I didn't mean that. I'd
rather lose my arms and legs than lose you. I'll go wherever you go, and glad to. I'm just trying to get all this to
make sense. *Why* are you doing this, going where they
tell you, doing what they tell you to do? Why is this—
Herald stuff—so important to you?''

Vanyel could almost feel Tylendel fumbling after the
right words. "It's, I don't know, it's a kind of hunger. I
can't help it. I've got these abilities, these Gifts, and I
can't *not* use them. I couldn't sit here, knowing that there
were people out there who need *exactly* the kind of help
I can give them and not make the effort to find them and
take care of them. It's like backing Staven—it's just something I could not even see myself *not* doing. I can't explain it, Van, I can't. I have to, or—or I'm not me
anymore.''

Vanyel just shook his head a little. "All right, I'll accept that. But I still can't really grasp it,'' he confessed.

"Giving up everything to play nursemaid to a pack of people you don't even know. Won't you have any life of your own? Who are these hypothetical people that need you, that you're sacrificing your whole life for them?"

"Huh," Tylendel said, "You sound just like Stav—"

Suddenly he went rigid; "Staven?" he whispered. "Stav—"

Then his entire body convulsed as he screamed Staven's name. And the night erupted into chaos around them.

The scream went on and on, filling the entire universe with pain and loss. An unbearable pressure rose around them, and shattered, all in the moment, the eternity of that scream. The still air churned, and began pummeling them with fists of heat and turbulence.

Gala scrambled to her feet; Vanyel caught and held his lover, trying to support him as he thrashed in uncontrolled spasms. Tylendel's forehead cracked against the bridge of his nose; he saw stars and tasted blood, but gritted his teeth against the pain and held on.

A gale-force wind sprang up out of the confusion and chaos. It went howling about them, moving outward in a spiral, nearly tearing the clothes from Vanyel's body as it passed. Tylendel was—glowing; angry red light pulsed around him. In it, Vanyel could see his face set in a mask of madness. His teeth were clenched in a grimace of pain, and there was no sense in his eyes, no sign of intelligence.

The trees closest to them literally exploded in a shower of splinters; those farther away spasmed in convulsions much like Tylendel's before they began tearing themselves apart.

The wind picked up in strength; trees farther away began thrashing and the wind spiraled outward a little farther than it had a moment before. The light surrounding Tylendel—and now Vanyel—throbbed, ebbing and strengthening with each paroxysm of his body. And something frighteningly like lightning was crackling off the edges of that glow, striking at random all about them. Where it hit, the effect was exactly like natural lightning; trees split, and the ground was scorched and pitted.

The wind was scouring the earth bare, making projectiles of dead needles and bits of wood. Even the ground was shuddering, heaving like a horse trying to throw a rider.

Vanyel held Tylendel as tightly as he could, looking wildly about for Gala. Finally he saw her, off on the edge of the circle of chaos. She, too, was glowing, bluely; the edge of her glow seemed to be deflecting the debris and the lightning, but it looked as if she was unable to *do* anything. Not that she wasn't trying—she stretched her neck out toward her Chosen, her eyes bright and terrible with distress—but all she seemed able to do was shield herself. She couldn't even get *near* them.

"Gala!" Vanyel shouted, over the screaming of the wind, restraining Tylendel as his lover spasmed in another convulsion. "Get help! Get Savil!" He couldn't think. If Gala were helpless to do anything, Savil was the only possible source of aid.

She shook her head; tried to force her way through the gale toward them, but was actually pushed back by whatever force was controlling the raging wind. She tried twice more; twice more was shoved farther back, as the circle of destruction grew. Finally she reared, screamed like a terrified human, and pivoted on her hind feet, then sprang off into the darkness.

Vanyel closed his eyes and clasped Tylendel against his chest, trying to protect him from the wind, trying to keep him from hurting himself as he continued to convulse. He was well beyond fear; his mind numb, his mouth dry, his heart pounding—praying for an end to this, praying for help. He couldn't think, couldn't move—all he could do was *stay*.

'Lendel, I'm here—he thought, as hard as he could, hoping somehow that Tylendel would "hear" him. *'Lendel, come back to me*—

The trainee spasmed once more, his back arcing—and suddenly, it was over. The light vanished, and with it, the wind. The ground settled—and there was nothing but a deadly silence, hollow darkness, and the weight of his lover's unmoving body in Vanyel's arms.

" 'Lendel?" He shook Tylendel's shoulders, and bit back a moan when he got no response. "Oh, gods—"

Tylendel was still breathing, but it was strange, shallow breathing—and the trainee's skin was clammy and almost cold.

A moment later Savil and two other Heralds came pounding up on their Companions, mage-lights glowing over their heads. By their light, Vanyel could see that Tylendel was limp and completely unconscious, his head lolling back, his eyes rolled up under half-open lids. He swallowed down fear, as Savil slid off Kellan's back without waiting for her to come to a full stop, landing heavily and stumbling to them. As the light of the pulsing balls strengthened, Vanyel saw with shock that there was not so much as a single pine seedling left standing in what had been a healthy grove of trees.

"I—I—I d-d-don't know what h-h-happened," he stuttered, as Savil went to her knees beside them, pulled open Tylendel's eyelids and checked his pulse, her face gray and grim in the blue light of her globe. The other two Heralds dismounted slowly, looking about them at the destruction with expressionless faces. "He was a-a-all right one minute, and then—Aunt Savil, please, *I* d-d-didn't do this t-t-to him—did I?"

"No, lad," she said absently. "Jaysen, come over here and confirm, will you?"

The taller of the two Heralds knelt beside Savil and made the same examination she had. "Backlash shock," he said succinctly. "Bad. Best thing we can do for him is get him in a bed and put someone he trusts with him."

"What I thought," she replied, getting to her feet and motioning to the older Herald to come help Jaysen take up the unconscious trainee. "No, Vanyel, it had nothing to do with you." She finally *looked* at him. "Did you know your nose is broken?"

"It is?" he replied, mind still fogged with fear for Tylendel.

"It is. Hold still; Jaysen's got just about enough of the Healing Gift to do something—"

The tall, bleached-looking Herald freed a hand from his task just long enough to touch his face. There was an odd tugging sensation, and a flash of pain that sent him blind for a moment, then numbness.

Savil looked him over briefly. "Good enough; it'll hurt like hell for the next few days, but it'll heal up straight. We'll wash the blood off your face later. Jaysen, Rolf, get 'Lendel back to my quarters; this isn't anything a Healer's going to be able to treat. We'll take care of him ourselves."

"Aunt, please, what happened?" He staggered to his feet, holding Tylendel's hand tightly as the other two picked him up, still limp as a broken doll and showing no signs of consciousness. He was not willing to let go until he *knew* what was wrong.

Savil gently loosed his fingers from their grip. "If what we got from Gala is right—the moment he went mad is the moment someone assassinated his twin," she said angrily. "You know the bond he had with Staven."

Vanyel nodded, and his whole face throbbed.

"He felt it; felt the death, knew what had happened. Lost all control, lost his mind for a while, like the fits he used to have—only, I think, worse this time. Now he's depleted himself down to next to nothing, his whole body's in collapse from the energies he put through it, his mind's in trauma from Staven's death. That's backlash shock."

Vanyel wasn't sure he understood, but nodded anyway.

Savil's face darkened to pure rage. "May all the gods damn those fools and their feuding! Death after death, and *still* they aren't satisfied! Van, our job is to see we don't lose Tylendel as well."

"Lose him?" Vanyel's voice broke, and he looked wildly after the Heralds and their unconscious burden. "Oh no—oh gods—Aunt, tell me what to *do,* I can't let him—"

"I don't intend to let him die," she interrupted him. pushing him after the other Heralds. "The masquerade has been canceled, and to hell with what your father finds out; I'll deal with Withen myself, and I'll keep you here if I have to get the Queen's order to do it. You go with them, and don't you leave him, no matter what happens." Savil bit her lip, and gave Vanyel another push when he looked at her with a fear that held him nearly paralyzed. "Go—go on. He needs you, lad—like he's never needed anyone before. You're my only hope of getting him through this sane.''

The two Heralds that Savil had called Jaysen and Rolf got Tylendel stripped and into bed without the trainee giving any sign of returning consciousness. Vanyel hovered at the edge of the room, his hands clenched, his face throbbing and feeling as if it were nearly as white as Tylendel's. When they left—after giving him more than one dubious and curious glance—he installed himself in a chair at Tylendel's side, took his lover's limp, cold hand in his own, and refused to be moved.

He stayed there for the rest of the night; unable to sleep, unable to even think very clearly. Tylendel looked ghastly; his skin had gone transparent and waxy, there was no muscle tone in the hand Vanyel held, and the only thing showing he was alive was the shallow movement of his chest as he breathed.

Savil looked in once or twice during the night, but said nothing. Mardic came in at dawn to try to persuade him to get some rest, but Vanyel only shook his head stubbornly. He would not, he *could* not, rest; until he knew that Tylendel would be all right.

Savil left for a Council session—probably dealing with the feud—right after sunrise; with some reluctance, Mardic and Donni departed for their lessons a couple of candlemarks later. When Mardic failed to convince Vanyel to rest, Donni had tried to talk him into some food. He'd refused that as well, suspecting that—with all the best intentions in the world—she might have slipped something into it to make him sleep.

'' 'Lendel, they've gone,'' he said, when he heard the door open and close, just to have some other sound in the room besides Tylendel's breathing. ''It's just you and me. 'Lendel, you have to come back—please. I *need* you, 'Lendel.'' He laughed, right on the edge of hysteria. ''Look, you know yourself that I'm too far behind on my History for Mardic to help me.''

He thought—maybe—he saw a flicker of response. His heart leapt, and he continued talking, coaxing, reciting bits of Tylendel's favorite poems—anything to bring him out of that unnatural sleep. He talked until his mouth and throat were dry, talked his voice into a harsh croak, left just long enough to get water, and returned to begin the monologue again. He lost track of what he was saying, somewhere around mid-afternoon; he was vaguely aware of someone checking on them, but ignored the other presences to keep up the flow of words. For by afternoon, there was no doubt; there *was* some change going on in Tylendel's condition, and for the better. He didn't know if it was the talking that was doing it, but he couldn't take any chances. He just kept holding to Tylendel's hand, saying anything that came into his head, however foolish-sounding.

Sunset arrived, turning the river beyond the windows briefly to a sword of flame; the light faded, the room darkened, and still he refused to move. Savil came in long enough to light the candles and whisper something—that he was doing the right thing, he thought, he wasn't sure. He didn't care; his whole world had narrowed to the white face resting on the pillow, and the slowly warming hand in his.

His eyes grew heavy, and his whole body ached, and his voice had thinned down to a whisper not even he could make out. He finally put his head down on his arms, intending to just rest for a moment—

And woke, feeling a hand tentatively caressing his hair. He started, jerking his head up off the coverlet, making his face pulse with pain.

Tylendel regarded him out of blue-ringed, weary eyes; eyes so full of anguish and loss that Vanyel nearly started weeping. "I heard you," he whispered. "I heard you, I just didn't have the strength to answer. Van—Staven—"

His face crumpled, and Vanyel slid off the chair and onto the side of the bed, talking him into his arms and holding him as tightly as he could; supporting him against his shoulder, giving him what little comfort his presence would give. Tylendel's body shook with sobs and he clung to Vanyel as to the only source of consolation left to him in the entire world, and Vanyel wept with him.

They finally fell asleep like that; true sleep, not the state of shock Tylendel had been in—Vanyel still fully

clothed and sprawled between his chair and the side of
the bed; Tylendel clinging to him like a heartbroken child.

"Eat," Vanyel ordered, setting the tray down in Tylendel's blanket-covered lap.

Tylendel looked nauseated and shook his head.
"Can't," he whispered hoarsely.

"You mean 'won't,' " Vanyel retorted almost as
hoarsely, trying to ignore the fact that talking made the
whole of his face ache. "You've gone all day without
food. Savil says if you don't get something down, you'll
go into backlash shock again. I didn't spend all that time
talking you out to have you drop back in again. Now *eat*,
dammit!" He crossed his arms over his chest and glared
down at Tylendel. The trainee eased a little higher up on
the pillows supporting him in a sitting position and tried
to shove the tray away. Unfortunately he was so weak he
couldn't even lift it; he just moved it a palm-length away.
Vanyel put it back precisely where he had placed it the
first time.

Tylendel gave the perfectly good soup on the tray a
look that would have been better bestowed on a bowl of
pig swill, but picked up the spoon anyway. He swallowed
the first spoonful with the air of someone who expects
what he's just eaten to make a precipitate reappearance,
but when nothing happened, gingerly ventured a second
mouthful, and a third.

Vanyel sat warily on the edge of the bed, careful not
to overset the tray between them. There was something
very different about Tylendel since he'd reawakened—
something secretive, but at the same time, impassioned.
He could sense it in every word they'd exchanged. He
thought he knew what it was, but he wanted to be sure.

"They're afraid I'm going to go mad, you know," Tylendel whispered in a matter-of-fact tone when he was
about halfway through the bowl.

"I know," Vanyel replied, just as matter-of-factly,
sensing that the secret was about to be revealed. "That's
why they have me here. Are you?"

Tylendel looked up from his meal, and there was that
strange, burning *something* Vanyel had felt searing sul-

lenly at the back of his eyes. "They might think so. Van, you've got to help me."

"You didn't have to ask," Vanyel replied soberly. "Tell me what you want, and I'll get it for you.'

"Vengeance." The thing at the back of his eyes flared for a moment, before subsiding into half-hidden, secretive smoldering again.

Vanyel nodded. This was rather what he had expected. If Tylendel wanted revenge— "Tell me. If I can do it, I will."

Tylendel slumped back on the pillows piled behind him, his head tilted back a little, his eyes closed, his features gone slack with relief. "Oh, gods—Van—I thought—"

"Eat," Vanyel growled. "I've told you before this that *I* understand, even if Savil doesn't. The only question *I've* got is how you think two half-grown, half-trained younglings are going to get revenge on people who live a good fortnight away by fast horse. I assume you've got an answer for that problem."

Tylendel opened his eyes and nodded soberly, but the spoon was still lying in the bowl of soup where he'd left it—and Vanyel was concentrating on the more immediate goal of getting him back on his feet. He'd worry about this plan when Tylendel was in shape to execute it, and not before.

"Dammit, 'Lendel, if you *don't* eat, I *won't* help you!"

Tylendel started guiltily, and leaned forward again to finish his meal.

Vanyel stole his mug long enough to get a sip of wine. His face hurt as badly as it looked, and when he'd taken one glance in the mirror, he'd had to look away again. His circle of admirers would have little to sigh over at the moment. He looked like he was wearing a black-and-blue domino mask and a putty nose. And he hurt. Gods, he hurt. The only reason he'd slept at all, once he'd comforted Tylendel last night, was because he'd been utterly, utterly exhausted.

"Did I do that?" Tylendel asked softly, finally *looking* at his face, as he scraped the last spoonful of soup from the bottom of the bowl.

Vanyel nodded, seeing no reason to deny it. "You weren't exactly yourself," he said, taking the tray away and stretching across Tylendel to put it on the table beside the bed.

"Oh, gods—Van, I'm sorry—" The smothered fury faded from Tylendel's eyes for a moment, and was replaced by concern as he reached in the direction of Vanyel's nose. The concern was replaced by hurt as Vanyel winced away.

"Touch me anywhere but *there;* it hurts bloody awful and it wasn't your fault, all right?" To counteract that flash of hurt in Tylendel's eyes, he moved closer, close enough to give 'Lendel a quick hug before taking his hand in both his own. "Now—you want to talk? I think maybe it's my turn to listen."

The deeply-buried fire returned, warring with anguish in his expression. "That link between Staven and me—it was different from what they think. Most of the time distance matters in a link like that, distance makes it weaker. It never did, for us. But Savil thought it did, and I let her go on thinking that. She would have been on me to break it, otherwise." He tensed, and closed his eyes; Vanyel held his hand a little more tightly. "All I ever had to do was think about him for him to be *with* me; it was the same for him. They—the Leshara—they ambushed him; killed his escort. Killed him. And it wasn't just an assassination, Van. *They used magic.*"

Vanyel felt his mouth drop open. "They what? How? How could a Herald—"

"It wasn't a Herald. They've hired a mage from outKingdom. They turned some—*things*—loose on the Holding. Magic monsters, maybe from the Pelagirs. Staven went after them with an escort; but when he got there, they were gone. He must have spent all day trying to track them down, and just exhausting himself, the fighters, and their horses. That's when the mage brought them back and ambushed Staven with them." Tylendel's eyes were horrible, like he was looking into hell. "These things, they *hurt* him before they killed him; hurt him awfully. On purpose; on their master's orders. I think on Leshara's orders. I can't tell you—"

He shuddered. "Stav reached for me—he reached for me through the link—Van, I was *with* him, I *felt* him die!"

He gripped Vanyel's hand so tightly that *both* their hands went white, and his voice quavered.

"He knew I was there with him; he knew it the moment I linked. Thank the gods—he knew he wasn't alone. But the last thing, the very last thing he did was to beg me, plead with me, to *pay them back.*" His eyes opened, and they no longer smoldered; they flamed with fury and pain. "I promised him, Van. I *promised* him. Those bastards killed Staven—but they *won't* get away with it."

Vanyel met that fury, and bowed before it. "I told you, 'Lendel," he replied quietly. "Just ask."

"Oh, love—" the voice broke on a sob, and Vanyel looked up to see tears trickling down Tylendel's cheek. "I shouldn't get you into this—gods, I shouldn't. It isn't fair, it isn't right. You've got no stake in this."

"You told me yourself that we're partners, that whatever you had I'd share," Vanyel replied, as forcefully as he could. "That means the bad as well as the good, by *my* way of thinking." Now it was his turn to fumble in the drawer of the bedside table for a handkerchief. "Here," he said, pressing it into Tylendel's hand. "Now, tell me what you want me to do."

Tylendel scrubbed the tears away, his hand shaking. "We can't let Gala know what we're doing; she'd try to stop me. I can block her from knowing, I've already blocked her from knowing about the link to Staven. I'll—play sick—"

"You *are* sick; look at your hand shake."

Tylendel looked at the trembling of his hands with a certain amount of surprise. "Sicker, then. Too sick to do anything but lie here. What I need you to do is to sneak into Savil's room and get me two books. They're proscribed; nobody except very high-level Herald-Mages are even supposed to know they exist, and Savil is one of only three here at Haven who have copies."

Vanyel felt stirrings of misgiving. "In that case, won't they be locked up?"

The corner of Tylendel's mouth twitched. "Oh, they

are. She's got them under protections. *But the protections don't work against someone with no Mage-Gift.*''

"What?" Vanyel's jaw dropped again.

"Margret has to get in there and clean, so Savil only put up a protection against someone with a Mage-Gift touching them. That way Margret can handle them and put them away if she leaves them out by accident. She figured nobody without the Gift would ever know what to look for. So *you* can get them, even though I can't."

"Now?" Vanyel asked dubiously.

Tylendel shook his head. "No, I can't—can't handle much of anything right now. Later—" He choked, and whispered, "Oh, gods—Staven—"

His breath caught again, and this time he couldn't control himself. He dissolved into hopeless sobbing, and Vanyel turned his attention instantly from plans of revenge to comfort.

"You'll have to turn the pages," Tylendel told him, looking down at the plain, black-bound book lying on the coverlet between them. "I don't dare touch them."

Vanyel shrugged, and obliged, opening the ordinary-looking book to the first page.

The ruse had worked admirably well; Tylendel had feigned a far greater weakness than he actually felt, and all Savil had shown was simple concern that he rest as much as possible. She hadn't evidenced any signs that she thought his recovery was taking overlong; she hadn't even brought in a Healer when Vanyel had tentatively suggested (as a test) that Tylendel didn't seem to be improving that much.

"Backlash is a nasty thing, lad," she'd said with a sigh. "Takes weeks to bounce back from it; months, sometimes. I didn't expect him to come out of this as well as he did, and I think perhaps I've got *you* to thank for it."

Vanyel had blushed, and mumbled something deprecating. Savil had ruffled his hair and told him to get back to his charge, and not be an idiot. In a way, he'd felt a bit guilty at that moment, knowing what he knew, knowing that they were plotting something she wouldn't have permitted.

But she couldn't possibly understand, he told himself for the hundredth time. *She couldn't possibly. She cut her family ties long ago, and they were never that strong to begin with.* From time to time the strength of Tylendel's desire for revenge frightened him a little, but he told himself that it was *Tylendel* who was within his rights in this.

And when the thought occurred that his lover had grown to be obsessed with his revenge, he dismissed the thought as unworthy. Unworthy of 'Lendel, of Staven. This wasn't revenge—it was justice. Certainly the Heralds hadn't made any move toward dealing with the Leshara.

This afternoon Savil had scheduled Donni and Mardic for the Work Room, and threatened murder on anyone who interrupted her *this* time. With the coast thus completely cleared, Vanyel had slipped into her room.

The books, so Tylendel had told him, would be in a small bookcase built into the wall beside the door that led to her own work room. He'd felt a chill of apprehension when he'd found the two volumes Tylendel wanted on the top shelf. He'd reached for them, expecting any moment to be flung across the room or fried by a lightning bolt.

But nothing had happened.

He'd returned to the bedroom where Tylendel waited, tucked up in bed with pen and paper. He slipped in furtively, clutching the books to his chest and shutting the door behind him.

Tylendel's fierce look of joy as he placed the books on the coverlet sent a shiver down his spine that he told himself was a thrill of accomplishment.

"What are you looking for?" he asked curiously, turning the pages slowly, Tylendel nodding to signal when he should.

"Two spells. We don't use spells a lot, but that doesn't mean they don't work," Tylendel said absently. "They do, and they work really well for somebody with a Mage-Gift as strong as the one I've got. Savil says I can pull

energy out of rocks—well, most of us can't, so that's why
we don't use spells much. The first one I want is something called a 'Gate'; it'll let us cover that distance from
here to the Leshara lands in under an hour.''

"You have *got* to be joking," Vanyel replied in disbelief. "I've never heard of anything like that."

"Herald-Mages would rather that people didn't know
they could do that—really, only the best of them can;
Savil can, and she said once that I should be able to, and
Mardic and Donni if they ever learn how to work together. Most of the ones that can, *won't*, if they're on
their own. That's because to do it, you need a lot of
energy; it takes everything a mage has, and then what's
he going to do when he gets where he wants to go?''

"Good point; what *are* you going to do?"

"I'm going to borrow *your* energy—if—you'll let
me—" Tylendel faltered, and looked up from the book
in entreaty.

Vanyel firmed his chin. "What do you mean, 'if'? *Of
course* you can borrow it, what other good am I going to
do?''

"Gods—*ashke, ashke,* I don't deserve you," Tylendel
said softly, half-smiling, his voice shaking in a way that
told Vanyel he was on the verge of tears again.

"It's the other way around, love," Vanyel replied, cutting him off. "Who was it kept me from—killing myself
by inches? Who showed me what happiness was about?
Who loves me when nobody else does? Hmm?''

"Who blacked your eyes, broke your nose, and nearly
fractured your ankle?''

"Well, that proves it, doesn't it?" Vanyel retorted, trying to make a feeble joke. "They say if you don't hurt,
you don't love.''

Tylendel shook his head. "I—gods, don't let me go all
to pieces again. Vanyel-*ashke,* I could *never* hope to do
this without you. There's no one else that I would trust
in this that could help me with a Gate-spell—and Van, I
should warn you, you're going to feel damn seedy afterward; like you've had a case of backlash to match mine.''

"*Can* you borrow this stuff?" Vanyel interrupted dubiously. "I mean, I don't have any Mage-Gifts or anything."

"Not active; you've got something, you've got the potential, but it's locked. I wouldn't have known, but I think we're linking a little, on a deeper level than Savil and I have—or even Gala and I. It's more like what I had with my twin; it isn't conscious, but—I know you know when I'm—"

"—unhappy," Vanyel finished for him, thoughtfully. "And other things. Uh-huh, I think you're right. I thought it might just be because I'm worried about you, but it seems to be going farther than that. Like last night, when I woke you up before you'd barely started to nightmare."

Tylendel nodded. "So I think we're linking, I think it happened some time between when I started the fit and when I came out of the backlash coma. I can feel—something—in you. Something very deep, but very strong. That's when I thought about the Gate-spell, and I used OtherSight on you. I sort of felt the link, and then I saw you had Mage-energies I could tap into using that link."

"Gods—'Lendel, don't tell me I'm going to turn into a Herald-Mage," he said, alarmed by the very idea.

"If you haven't by now, it isn't too bloody likely," Tylendel replied, to his profound relief. "Savil says a lot of people have the potential, but nothing ever triggers it. You've just got the potential."

"So don't trigger it," Vanyel replied, shivering with an unexplained chill. "I don't want to be a Herald or a Herald-Mage, or anything like them."

Tylendel gave him an odd look, but only said, "I doubt I could, even if you wanted it. There's stories that there's a couple of Mage-schools that know how to trigger potential, but nobody I know has ever seen it done, so even if it's possible the people that can do it are keeping the means a deep secret."

"Good," Vanyel replied, still fighting down his chill of apprehension. "That's exactly the way I want it. So— you make this Gate thing. Then what?"

"When we get to the other side of the Gate, we'll be on Leshara land; right on top of the keep, if I can manage it. I'll use the other spell I'm looking for—and that will be the end of it.''

Vanyel suddenly *knew*, without knowing how he knew, that he did not *want* to know what this ''other spell'' was.

''Fine,'' he replied shortly, turning another page. ''You keep looking. Just tell me when to stop.''

Eight

Vanyel stared nervously at his own reflection in the window—a specter, pale and indistinct; ghostlike, with dark hollows for eyes. Beyond the glass, night blanketed the gardens; a moonless night, a night of wind and cloud and no light at all, not even starlight.

Sovvan-night; the night of celebration of the harvest, but also the night set apart for remembering the dead of the year past. The night when—so most traditions held—the Otherworld was closer than on any other night. A night of profound darkness, like the one a moon ago when Staven had been slain.

Savil was with the rest of the Heralds, mourning *their* dead of the year. Donni and Mardic, having no one in need of remembrance, were with some of the other trainees at a Palace fete, indulging in a certain amount of the superstitious foolery associated with Harvestfest that was also a part of Sovvan-night, at least for the young.

Lord Evan Leshara had gone home to Westrel Keep. Presumably well satisfied with himself. There was no doubt in Vanyel's mind that Lord Evan had somehow extracted enough good information from what had been fed to him to deduce exactly what bait would serve best to lure Staven to his death. They had tried to use him—and had ended up being used by him.

And that was a blackly bitter thought.

Tylendel and Vanyel had been left alone in the suite—

Tylendel and Vanyel would not be mewed up in the suite much longer.

"Are you ready?" Tylendel asked from the door behind him.

Vanyel nodded, and pulled the hood of his dark blue cloak up over his head, trying not to shiver at his own reflection. With the hood shrouding his face, he looked like an image of Death itself. Then Tylendel moved silently to his side, and there were *two* of the hooded figures reflected in the clouded glass; Death, and Death's Shadow.

He shook his head to free it of such ominous thoughts, as Tylendel opened the door and they stepped out into the cold, blustering night.

This morning he had slipped out into Haven and bought a pair of nondescript horses from a down-at-the-heels beast-trader, using most of the coin he and Tylendel had managed to scrape together over the past three weeks. He'd taken them off into the west end of the city and stabled them at an inn just outside the city wall.

Tylendel had told Vanyel that before he worked the spell to take them within striking distance of the Leshara holding, he wanted to be out of the easy sensing range of the Herald-Mages. They needed transportation, but it didn't matter how broken-down the beasts were; their horses only needed to last long enough to get them an hour's ride out of the city. After that it wouldn't matter what became of them.

Obviously, riding Gala was totally out of the question. They weren't taking Star or "borrowing" any of the true horses from the Palace stables, because if their absence were noticed, Tylendel didn't want any suspicions aroused until it was too late to stop them. Vanyel had concurred without an argument; if they couldn't force their mounts through Tylendel's Gate—and the trainee had indicated that they might not be able to or might not want to—they were going to have to turn them loose to fend for themselves. He didn't want to lose Star, and he didn't want to be responsible for the loss of anyone else's prized mount, either.

The ice-edged wind caught at their cloaks, finding all the openings and cutting right through the heavy wool itself. Vanyel was shivering long before they slipped past the Gate Guard at the Palace gates and on out into the streets of the city. The Guard was preoccupied with warming himself at the charcoal brazier beside the gate; he didn't seem to notice them as they hugged the shadows of the side of the gate farthest from him and took to the cobblestoned street beyond.

Now they were out in the wealthiest district of the city. The high buildings on either side of them served only to funnel the wind right at them. or so it seemed. Tylendel, who was still not entirely steady on his feet, grabbed Vanyel's arm and hung on. Vanyel could feel him shivering, partly with cold, but from the way his eyes were gleaming in the shadows of his hood, partly also with excitement.

These mansions of the wealthy and highborn were mostly dark tonight; the inhabitants were either at Temple services or attending the Harvestfest gathering at the Palace. Vanyel had *not* received an invitation—and although he was anything but displeased, he wasn't entirely certain why he had not. His apparent about-face with regard to Tylendel had confused not only his own little circle, but the trainees and Heralds as well. And no one had enlightened them; Savil had reckoned that keeping the rumormongers confused would keep the real story from reaching Withen for a while and buy them additional time.

Assuming Lord Evan hadn't told him, just for the pure spite of making things difficult for Tylendel and Tylendel's lover. It would suit the man's character.

Vanyel thought briefly of the Sovvan-fete he was missing. It was possible that those in charge of the festivities had assumed he would be staying at Tylendel's side, especially tonight. It was also possible that they blamed him for Tylendel's condition (Mardic had reported several stories to that effect) and were "punishing" him for his conduct.

Whatever the reason, this had proved to be too good an opportunity to slip out undetected to let pass by.

They turned a corner, and the buildings changed; now they were smaller, crowded closer together, and no longer hidden behind walls. Each had candles in the otherwise darkened windows—another Sovvan-custom. It was by the light of these candles that the two were finding their way; the torches that usually illuminated the street by night had long since blown out.

Tylendel had been growing increasingly strange and withdrawn in the past several days since Vanyel had purloined Savil's magic books for him. Vanyel would wake up in the middle of the night to find him huddled in the chair, studying his handwritten copies of the two spells with fanatic and feverish concentration. During waking hours he would often stare for hours at nothing, or at a candleflame, and his conversation had become monosyllabic. The only time he seemed anything like his old self was when he'd begin a nightmare and Vanyel would wake him from it; then he would cry for a while on Vanyel's shoulder, and afterward talk until they both fell asleep again. *Then* he sounded like the old Tylendel—not afraid to share his grief or his fears with the one he loved. But when day arrived, he would be back inside his shell, and nothing Vanyel would do or say could seem to crack that barrier.

Vanyel had long since begun to think that he would *never* be his old self again until his revenge had been accomplished, and he had begun to long for that moment with a fervor that nearly equaled his lover's.

They reached the sector of shops and inns long before they saw another human out on the streets, and that was only the Nightwatch. The patrol of two men gave them hardly more than a passing glance; they were obviously unarmed except for knives, were too well-dressed to be street-toughs, and not flashy enough to be young highborns out to find some trouble. The two men of the Watch gave them nearly simultaneous nods, curt and preoccupied, nods which they returned as the light from the Watchlantern in the hands of the rightmost one fell on them. Satisfied by what they saw, the Watch passed on, and so did they, bootheels clattering on the cobbles.

Here the buildings were only one or two stories tall, and the wind howled and ramped about them unimpeded. The quality and state of repair of these buildings—mostly shops, inns, lodging-houses and workshops—declined steadily and rapidly as they neared the west city-wall of Haven.

The Guards on the great gates of Haven were not in evidence tonight, although there was a viewport in the wall, and Vanyel could almost feel eyes on him as they passed below it. Obviously the Guards found as little to alarm them in the two younglings as the Watch had; they passed out under the wall with no challenge whatsoever.

Once outside the west wall, they were in the lowest district in the city. Vanyel led the way to the ramshackle inn where he'd left their sorry nags; fighting the wind every inch of the way, as it nearly tore the edges of his cloak out of his half-frozen hands.

The Red Nose Inn was brightly lit and full to bursting with roisterers; Vanyel heard their out-of-tune singing and hoarse laughter even over the moaning of the wind as they passed by the open door. Smoke and light alike spilled out that door, and the wind carried a random puff of the smoke into their eyes as they passed, a noisome smudge that made them cough and their eyes water for a moment before cleaner air whipped it out of their faces again. They ignored that open door and passed around the side of the inn to the dirty courtyard and the stabling area.

There was a single, half-drunk groom on duty, slumped on a stack of hay bales by the stable door, illuminated by a feebly burning lantern. His head lolled on his chest as he snored, smelling, even in this wind, as if he'd fallen into a vat of cheap beer. Tylendel waited in the shadows beyond reach of the light from the smoking lantern that had been hung in the lee of the stable door, while Vanyel shook the man's shoulder until he roused up.

"Eh?" the man grunted, peering into the shadows under Vanyel's hood in an unsuccessful attempt to make out his features. His breath was as foul as his clothing; his face was filthy and unshaven, and his hair hung around his ears in lank, greasy ringlets. "What ye want, then? Where be yer nags?"

"Already here," Vanyel replied, in a tone as adult, brusque, and gruff as he could manage. "Here—" He shoved the claim-chits at the groom, together with two silver pieces. The man stared stupidly at them for a moment, blinking in surprise, as if he were having trouble telling the chits from the coins. Then he grinned in sudden comprehension, displaying a mouthful of half-rotten teeth, and nodded.

" 'Nuff celebratin', eh, master? Just ye wait, just ye wait right here." He shoved the coins and chits together into the pocket in the front of his stained, oily leather apron, heaved himself up off his couch of hay bales, and staggered inside the stable door. He emerged a great deal sooner than Vanyel would have thought possible, leading a pair of scruffy-looking, nondescript brown geldings that were already saddled and bridled with patched and worn tack. Vanyel squinted at them in the smoky light, trying to make out if they were the same ones he'd bought this morning, then realized that it didn't matter if they were or not. It wasn't as if the horses he'd purchased were any kind of prize specimens—in fact, if these *weren't* "his" horses, they were likely as not to be an improvement over the ones he'd bought!

He took the reins away from the groom without another word, turned, and led them across the dirt court to where Tylendel was waiting, huddled against the inn wall in a futile attempt to avoid the biting wind. When he looked back over his shoulder, he could see that the groom had already flopped down on the straw bales and resumed his interrupted nap.

He handed Tylendel the reins of the best of the two mounts, and scrambled into his own saddle. His flea-bitten beast skittered sideways in an attempt to avoid being mounted, and gave a half-hearted buck as Vanyel settled into his seat. Vanyel made a fist and gave it a good rap between the ears; the nag stopped trying to rid itself of its rider and settled down.

The spine of his saddle was broken; the horse itself was swaybacked, and its gait was as rough as he'd ever had the misfortune to encounter. He hoped, as Tylendel took the lead and they headed down Exile's Road into the west, that they wouldn't be riding for too very long.

* * *

The wind had died down—at least momentarily—when Tylendel finally stopped. It was so dark that the only way he really knew that Tylendel pulled up was because the sound of hooves on the hard surface of the road ahead of him stopped. They'd trusted to the fact that Exile's Road was lined on either side with hedges to keep their sorry beasts on the roadway. He kicked at his own mount and forced it forward until he could feel the presence of Tylendel and his horse bulking beside him.

There was a flare of light; Vanyel winced away from it—it was quite painful after the near-total darkness of the last candlemark or so. When he could bear to look again, he saw that Tylendel had dismounted and was leading his horse, a red ball of mage-light bobbing along above his head.

He scrambled off of his own mount, glad enough to be out of that excruciatingly uncomfortable saddle, snatched the reins of the beast over its head, and hastened to catch up.

"Are we far enough away yet?" he asked, longing for even a single word from the trainee to break the silence and tension. Tylendel's face was drawn and fey, and strained; Tylendel's attention was plainly somewhere else, his whole aspect wrapped up in the kind of terrifying concentration that had been all too common to him of late.

"Almost," he replied, after a long and unnerving silence. His voice had a strange quality to it, as if Tylendel was having to work to get even a single word out past whatever it was he was concentrating on. "I'm—looking for something. . . ."

Vanyel shivered, and not from the cold. "What?"

"A place to put the Gate." They came to a break in the hedge. No—not a break. When Tylendel stopped and led his horse over to it, Vanyel could see that it was the remains of a gated opening in the hedge, long since overgrown. Beyond the gap something bulked darkly in the dim illumination provided by the mage-light. Tylendel nodded slightly. "I thought I remembered this place," he muttered. He didn't seem to expect a response, so Vanyel didn't make one.

It was obvious that the horses were not going to be

able to force themselves through so narrow a passage; Tylendel stripped the bridle from his, hung it on the saddlebow, and gave the gelding a tremendous slap on the hip that made it snort with surprise and sent it cantering off into the darkness. Vanyel did the same with his, *not* sorry to see it go, and turned away from the road to see that Tylendel had already forced his way past the gap in the hedge and was now out of sight. Only the reddish glow of the mage-light through the leafless branches of the hedgerow showed where he had gone.

Vanyel shoved his way past the branches, cursing as they caught on his cloak and scratched at his face. When he emerged, staggering, from the prickly embrace of stubborn bushes, he found that he was standing knee-deep in weeds, in what had been the yard of a small building. It could have been anything from a shop to a cottage, but was now going to pieces; the yard was as overgrown as the gate had been. The building seemed to be entirely roofless and the door and windows were mere holes in the walls. Tylendel was examining the remains of the door with care.

The gap where the door had been was a large one, easily large enough for a horse and rider to pass through. Tylendel nodded again, and this time there was an expression of dour satisfaction on his face. "This will do," he said softly. "Van, think you're ready?"

Vanyel took a deep breath, and tried to relax a little. "As ready as I'm ever likely to get," he replied.

Tylendel turned and took both Vanyel's hands in his; he looked searchingly into Vanyel's eyes for a long moment. "Van, I'm going to have to force that link between us wide open for this to work. I may hurt you. I'll try not to, but I can't promise. Are you still willing to help me?"

Vanyel nodded, thinking, *I've come this far; it would be stupid to back out at this point. Besides—he needs this. How can I not give it to him?*

Tylendel closed his eyes; his face froze into as impassive a mask as Vanyel had ever worn. Vanyel waited, trembling a little, for something to happen.

For a long while, nothing did. Then—

Rage flamed up in him; a consuming, obsessive anger that left very little room for anything else. One thing mattered: Staven was dead. One goal drove him: deal the same painful death to Staven's murderers. There was still a tiny corner of his mind that could think for itself and wonder at the overwhelming power of Tylendel's fury, but that corner had been locked out of any position of control.

The truism ran "Pain shared is pain halved"—but this pain was doubled on being shared.

He turned to face the ancient doorway without any conscious decision to do so, Tylendel turning even as he did. He saw Tylendel raise his arms and cast a double handful of something powderlike on the ground before the door; heard him begin a chant in some strange tongue and hold his now empty hands, palm outward, to face that similarly empty gap.

He felt something draining out of him, like blood draining from a wound; and felt that it was taking his strength with it.

The edges of the ruined doorway were beginning to glow, the same sullen red as the mage-light over Tylendel's head; like the muted red of embers, as if the edge of the doorway smoldered. As more and more of Vanyel's energy and strength drained from him, the ragged border brightened, and tiny threads of angry scarlet wavered from them into the space where the door had stood. More and more of these threads spun out, waving like water-weeds in a current, until two of the ends connected across the gap.

There was a surge of force out of him, a surge that nearly caused his knees to collapse, as the entire gap filled with a flare of blood-red light—

Then the light vanished—and the gap framed, not a shadowed blackness, but a garden; a formal garden decorated for a festival, and filled with people, light and movement.

He had hardly a chance to see this before Tylendel grabbed his arm and pulled him, stumbling, across the threshold. There was a moment of total disorientation, as though the world had dropped from beneath his feet, then—

Sound: laughter, music, shouting. He stood, with Tylendel, facing that garden he had seen through the ruined doorway, and beyond the garden, a strange keep. Lanterns bobbed gaily in the branches of a row of trees that stood between them and the gathered people, and trestle tables, spread with food and lanterns, were visible on the farther side. Near the trees was a lighted platform on which a band of motley musicians stood, playing with a vigor that partially made up for their lack of skill. Before the platform a crowd of people were dancing in a ring, laughing and singing along with the music.

Vanyel's knees would not hold him; as soon as Tylendel let go of his arm, his legs gave way, and he found himself half-kneeling on the ground, dizzy, weak and nauseated. Tylendel didn't notice; his attention was on the people dancing.

"They're *celebrating*," Tylendel whispered, and the anger Vanyel was inadvertently sharing surged along the link between them. "Staven's *dead*, and they're *celebrating!*"

That small, rational corner still left to Vanyel whispered that this was *only* a Harvestfest like any other; that the Leshara weren't particularly gloating over an enemy's death. But that logical voice was too faint to be heard over the thunder of Tylendel's outrage. A wave of dizziness clouded his sight with a red mist, and he could hear his heart pounding in his ears.

When he could see again, Tylendel had stepped away from him, and was standing between him and the line of trees with his hands high over his head. From Tylendel's upraised hands came twin bolts of the same vermilion lightning that had lashed the pine grove a moon ago. Only *this* lightning was controlled and directed; and it cracked across the garden and destroyed the trees standing between him and the gathered Leshara-kin in less time than it took to blink.

In the wake of the thunderbolt came startled screams; the music ended in a jangle of snapped strings and the squawk of horns. The dancers froze, and clutched at each other in clumps of two to five. Tylendel's mage-light was blazing like a tiny, scarlet sun above his head; his face was hate-filled and twisted with frenzy. Tears streaked his face; his voice cracked as he screamed at them.

"He's *dead*, you bastards! He's *dead*, and you're *laughing*, you're *singing! Damn you all, I'll teach you to sing a different song! You want magic? Well*, here's *magic for you—*"

Vanyel couldn't move; he seemed tethered to the still-glowing Gate behind him. He could only watch, numbly, as Tylendel raised his hands again—and this time it was not lightning that crackled from his upraised hands. A glowing sphere appeared with a sound of thunder, suspended high above him. About the size of a melon, it hung in the air, rotating slowly, a smoky, sickly yellow. It grew as it turned, and drifted silently away from Tylendel and toward the huddled Leshara-folk, descending as it neared them, until it came to earth in the center of the blasted, blackened place where the trees had been a moment before.

There it rested; still turning, still growing, until it had swelled to twice the height of a man.

Then, between one heartbeat and the next, it burst.

Another wave of disorientation washed over him; Vanyel blinked eyes that didn't seem to be focusing properly. Where the globe had rested there seemed to be a twisting, twining mass of shadow-shapes, shapes as fluid as ink, as sinuous as snakes, shapes that were *there* and *not there* at one and the same time.

Then they slid apart, those shapes, separating into five writhing mist-forms. They solidified—

If some mad god had mated a viper and a coursing-hound, and grown the resulting offspring to the size of a calf, the result *might* have looked something like the five creatures snarling and flowing lithely around one another in the gleaming of Tylendel's mage-light. In color they were a smoky black, with skin that gave an impression of smooth scales rather than hair. They had long, long necks, too long by far, and arrowhead-shaped heads that were an uncanny mingling of snake and greyhound, with yellow, pupilless eyes that glowed in the same way and

with the same shifting color that the globe that had birthed
them had glowed. The teeth in those narrow muzzles were
needle-sharp, and as long as a man's thumb. They had
bodies like greyhounds as well, but the legs and tails
seemed unhealthily stretched and unnaturally boneless.

They regarded Tylendel with unwavering, saffron eyes;
they seemed to be waiting for something.

He quavered out a single word, his voice breaking on
the final, high-pitched syllable—and they turned as one
entity to face the cowering folk of Leshara, mouths gaping in unholy parodies of a dog's foolish grin.

But before they had flowed a single step toward their
victims, a shrill scream of equine defiance rang out from
behind Vanyel.

And Gala thundered through the Gate at his back,
pounding past him, then past Tylendel, ignoring the
trainee completely.

She screamed again, more anger and courage in her
cry than Vanyel had ever thought possible to hear in a
horse's voice, and skidded to a halt halfway between Tylendel and the things he had called up. *She* was glowing,
just like she had during 'Lendel's fit; a pure, blue-white
radiance that attracted the eye in the same way that the
yellow glow of the beasts' eyes repelled. She continued
to ignore Tylendel's presence entirely, turning her back
to him; rearing up to her full height and pawing the air
with her forehooves, trumpeting a challenge to the five
creatures before her.

They reversed their positions in an instant as her hooves
touched the ground again, facing her with silent snarls
of anger. She pawed the earth, and bared her teeth at
them, daring them to try to fight her.

"Gala!" Tylendel cried in anguish, his voice breaking
yet again. *"Gala! Don't—"*

She turned her head just enough to look him fully in
the eyes—and Vanyel heard her mental reply as it rang
through Tylendel's mind and heart and splintered his soul.

:I do not know you: she said coldly, remotely. *:You are
not my Chosen.:*

And with those words, the bond that had been between
them vanished. Vanyel could feel the emptiness where it

had been—for he was still sharing everything Tylendel
felt.

Tylendel's rage shattered on the cold of those words.

And when the bond was broken, what took its place
was utter desolation.

Vanyel moaned in anguish, sharing Tylendel's agony,
and the torment and bereavement as he called after Gala
with his mind and received not even the echo of a reply.
Where there had been warmth and love and support there
was now—nothing; not even a ghost of what had been.

The link between them surged with loss, and Vanyel's
vision darkened.

He heard Tylendel cry out Gala's name in utter despair,
and willed his eyes to clear.

And to his horror he watched her fling herself at the
five fiends, heedless of her own safety.

They swarmed over and about her, their darkness ex-
tinguishing her light. He heard her shriek, but this time
in pain, and saw the red splash of blood bloom vividly
on her white coat.

He tried to stagger to his feet, but had no strength; his
ears roared, and he blacked out.

He barely felt himself falling again, and only Tylendel's scream of anguish and loss penetrated enough to
make him fight his way back to consciousness.

He found himself half-sprawled on the cold ground.
He shoved himself partially erect despite his spinning
head, and looked for Gala—

But there was no Companion, no fight. Only a muti-
lated corpse, sprawling torn and ravaged, throat slashed
to ribbons, the light gone from the sapphire eyes. Tylendel was on his knees beside her, stroking the ruined head,
weeping hoarsely.

Beside her lifeless body lay one of the five monstrosi-
ties, head a shapeless pulp. The others flowed around the
Companion's body, as if waiting for the corpse to rise
again so that they could attack it. Two of the others
limped on three legs—but two were still unharmed, and
given what they had done to Gala in a few heartbeats,
two would be more than enough to slaughter every man,
woman, and child of the Leshara.

Finally they left off their mindless, sharklike circling, and turned to face the terrified celebrants. They took no more notice of Tylendel than of the dead Companion.

A man bolted from the crowd. With a start, Vanyel recognized him for Lord Evan. Whether he meant to attack the beasts, or simply to flee, Vanyel couldn't tell. It really didn't matter much; one of the beasts that was still unhurt flashed across the intervening space and caught him. He did not even have time to cry out as it disembowled him.

A woman screamed—and that seemed to signal the beasts to move again. They began to ooze in a body toward their victims—

And a bolt of brilliantly white lightning cracked from behind Vanyel to scorch the earth before the leader.

There was a pounding of hooves from the Gate. Vanyel was momentarily blinded by the light and by another surge of weakness that sent him sagging back to the ground.

When his eyes cleared again, there were three white-clad Heralds and their three Companions closing on the fiends, lightnings crackling from their upraised hands. They were using the lightnings to herd the beasts into a tight little knot and barring their path to their prey.

He barely had time to recognize two of the three as Savil and Jaysen before battle was joined.

Once again he started to black out, feeling as if something was trying to pull his soul out of his body. He fought against unconsciousness, though he felt as if he had nothing left to fight *with;* both the rage and the despair were gone now, leaving only an empty place, a void that ached unbearably.

He felt a tiny *inflowing* of strength; it wasn't much, but it was enough to give him the means to fight the blackness away from his eyes, to fight off the vertigo, and to finally get a precarious hold on the world again.

The first thing he saw was Tylendel; still on his knees, but no longer weeping. He was vacant-eyed, white as bleached linen, and staring at his own blood-smeared hands. Where the five creatures had been there was now nothing; only the mangled body of Gala and the burned and churned-up earth.

Taking her hand away from his shoulder was Savil—her face an unreadable mask.

Savil pulled her attention away from Tylendel, who was slumped in a kind of trance of despair beside her, and back to what Vanyel was telling the other two Heralds.

". . . then she said, 'I don't know you, you aren't my Chosen,'" the boy whispered, eyes dull and mirroring his exhaustion, voice colorless. "And she turned her back on him, just turned away, and charged those things."

"Buying time for us to get here," Jaysen murmured, his voice betraying the pain he would not show. "Oh, gods, the poor, brave thing—if she hadn't bought us those moments, we'd have come in on a bloodbath."

"She *repudiated* him," said Lancir, the Queen's Own, as if he did not believe it. "She repudiated him, and then—"

"Suicided," Savil supplied flatly, her own heart in turmoil; aching for Tylendel, for the loss of Gala, for all the things she should have seen and hadn't. "Gods, she *suicided*. She knew, she *had* to know that no single Companion could face a pack of *wyrsa* and survive."

Tylendel sat where they had left him; unseeing, unspeaking—all of hell in his eyes. Mage-lights of their own creation bobbed overhead, pitilessly illuminating everything.

Jaysen contemplated Savil's trainee for a long moment, but said nothing, only shook his head slightly. Then he spared a glance for Vanyel, and frowned; Savil heard his thought. *:The boy is still tied to the Gate, sister. He grows weaker by the moment. If you want him undamaged—:*

Unspoken, but not unfelt, was the vague thought that perhaps it would be no bad thing if Vanyel were to be "forgotten" until it was too late to save him from the aftereffects of the Gate-magic. That undercurrent of thought told Savil that Jaysen placed all of the blame for this squarely on Vanyel's shoulders.

:It wasn't his fault, Jaysen: she answered, heartsick, and near to weeping, but unable to be anything other than

honest. :*He didn't do anything worse than go along with what 'Lendel wanted without telling me. What happened was as much due to my negligence as anything he did.*:

Jaysen gave a curt nod, but a skeptical one. :*In that case, we need to get that Gate closed down as soon as possible, or the boy will sicken—or worse.*:

No need to ask what that "worse" was; Vanyel was already looking drawn, almost transparent, as the Gate pulled more and more of his life-force from him. How Tylendel, half-trained, and Vanyel, unGifted, had managed that, Savil had no notion—but they dared not break the link until they didn't need the Gate anymore.

:*Fine, but what are we going to do about all* that *mess?*: Savil asked, nodding her head at the milling crowd, the mangled corpse of the single victim the *wyrsa* had killed, and the pathetic body of the Companion. :*Somebody had better take them in hand, or no telling what they'll get up to. Go in for a wholesale slaughtering-party on Tylendel's people, make up some kind of tale about Heralds being in on this—*: Even a hair away from breaking down into tears, she was still *thinking;* she couldn't help it.

:*I'll stay here,*: Lancir volunteered. :*Elspeth can do without me for a moon or so. I'll take care of the Leshara and see to—*: his thought faltered. :*—Gala.*:

:*And you'll get home how?*: Jaysen asked, concerned. :*We're going to shut the Gate from the other side as soon as we're through, and you aren't up to Gating by yourself these days.*:

:*Like ordinary mortals,*: he replied, with a deathly seriousness. :*On our feet.*:

:*What—what are we going to do about—*: Savil's eyes flicked to Tylendel and back; the boy was still staring vacantly into space, his face pale and blank, his eyes so full of inward-turned torment that she could scarcely bear to look into them for fear she *would* break down and cry.

:*I don't know,*: Lancir replied bleakly. :*I just don't know. There's no precedent. Get the boy home; worry about it when you've got time to think about it. Ask your Companions; it was one of their number that died. That's all I can think of. But you'd better get on with it if you expect to leave the other boy with a mind.*:

"Jays, take Tylendel, will you?" Savil said aloud, reaching for Vanyel's arm and pulling him to his feet. "Lance—"

"Gods with you, heart-sibs," said the Queen's Own, pity and compassion momentarily transforming his homely face into something close to saintly, like that of a beautiful carved statue. "You'll need their help. Taver?"

His Companion sidled up to him and held rock-still for Jaysen to help him to mount; like the Queen, like Savil, Lancir was feeling his age these autumn days, and needed the boost into place that Jaysen gave him. But once in the saddle, he resumed the strength and dignity of a much younger Queen's Own—the man he had been twenty years ago. Taver tossed his head, and walked with calm and quiet steps toward the shocked, confused mob of Leshara at the other end of the garden.

Jaysen tugged on Tylendel's arm; the boy rose, but with the automatic movements of someone spellbound, his attention still turned within himself. The Seneschal's Herald led the way to the Gate, followed closely by his Companion, and guiding the boy with a hand at his shoulder.

He cast a look back at Savil. "I don't fancy the notion of the ride we have ahead of us—too many things to go wrong on the way. You know more about this spell than I do—do you think you can reset this Gate to bring us out at the Palace?"

She wrenched her attention away from the unanswerable problem of what to do about the boys, and contemplated the structure of the Gate. The portal at *this* end was an ornamental gazebo in the center of the blasted garden. Through the arch of the entrance lay the dark of the ruinous cottage yard.

"I don't see any problem," she replied, after study. "I can bring us out in the Grove Temple, if that's all right."

"That should do," Jaysen said, eyeing the sky on the other side of the portal, which was flickering with lightnings. "Good gods—why did *that* blow in? There wasn't a storm due."

"Don't look so surprised, Jays," she growled, needed to lash out at *something* and using his absentmindedness to make him the target. "I've told you a dozen times that Gating plays merry cob with the weather. That's why I don't like to use Gates. It's going to get worse when I reset it, and all hell will break out when I collapse it."

He pursed his lips and frowned, but didn't reply, just waved at her with his free hand. She let go of Vanyel, who sagged back to his knees, too weakened to stay standing without her support. She raised both her hands high above her head, and made an intricately weaving little gesture. Filaments of dull red light floated from the Gate toward her, and were caught up on her fingers by that complex weaving. When she had them fast, she clenched her hands on them and sent her will coursing down them in a surge of pure, commanding power, the filaments turning from red to white as *her* will flowed back along them.

When the wave of white reached the Gate, the portal misted over, then flared incandescently. When the light died, the scene framed in the gazebo arch was that of Companion's Field, seen by the fitful flashes of lightning, as viewed from the porch of the Grove Temple.

Savil reached down and caught the fabric of Vanyel's tunic, pulling him to his feet again. She dragged him with her as she followed closely on Jaysen's heels. He hurried across the Gate threshold, pushing Tylendel before him; she half-ran a step behind him, dragging Vanyel with her by main force.

The Gate-crossing hit her with its all-too-familiar, sickening sensation of falling. Then—hard, smooth marble was beneath her feet, and they were home.

Lighting struck a nearby tree, and thunder deafened her for a moment. She cleared out of the path of the Gate and Kellan and Felar darted across, ears laid back, as soon as she and Vanyel were out of the way.

She let go of Vanyel, who stumbled the two steps to one of the pillars and clung to it. She turned to face the Gate even as another bolt struck nearby. The Gate was going unstable, wavering from red to white and back again, the instability in the energy fields mirrored in the increasing fury of the lightning storm overhead. She raised her hands and began the dismissal—and encountered unexpected resistance.

She tried again, wincing at the crack of thunder directly above her. There was something wrong, something very wrong. The Gate was fighting her.

"Jays—" she shouted over the growl of thunder and the whine of the wind. "—I need a hand, here."

Jaysen let go of Tylendel to add his strength to hers—their united wills worked at the spell-knot, forcing it to unravel faster than it could knit itself back up again.

With a surge of wild power that brought a half-dozen lightning strikes down on the Belltower of the Temple itself, the Gate collapsed—

Then again the unexpected; the Gate-energy, instead of dissipating back into the air and ground, flared up, and surged back down the one conduit left to it. The force-line that had tied it into Vanyel. Savil Saw it—but not in time to stop it.

Vanyel screamed in agony, convulsing, clutching the pillar as the released power arced back into him—and from him, a second, weaker arc leapt to Tylendel.

Tylendel jerked into sudden alertness—and uttered the most painful cry of despair Savil had ever heard; it was a cry that would haunt her nightmares for the rest of her life.

She pivoted and grabbed for him as quickly as she could as Vanyel collapsed in a moaning heap at the foot of the pillar.

But it was too late. No longer held in deceptive docility by his shock, he dodged her outstretched hand. She saw his face in another of the lightning flashes; his eyes were all pupil, his face a twisted mask of nothing but pain. He looked frantically about him with those terrible eyes that held no sanity at all, dodged her again, and then dashed past her into the tangled trees of the Grove.

Jaysen gave chase; Savil limped after both of them. Lightning was striking so often overhead now that the sky was almost as bright as day. She tried to use the line of their shared magic to get at Tylendel's mind as she ran, hoping to bring him back to her, but stumbled in shock and fell when she touched his thoughts. There was nothing to get a hold on—the boy was a chaotic, aching void of grief and loneliness. It was so empty, so unhuman, that for a moment she could only crouch in the cold, dry grass and listen to her overworked heart beat in panic. It took every ounce of discipline she had to get her own mind back under control after touching that terrible, all-consuming sorrow.

Belatedly she thought of Vanyel. If anyone could reach Tylendel, surely *he* could.

She lurched painfully to her feet and stumbled back toward the Temple. In the lightning flashes she could make out the younger boy staggering blindly out of the Temple, clutching himself as if he were freezing—saw him stumble and fall on his shoulder, without trying to save himself.

Then she saw Tylendel dart out of the tree-shadows to her right and race past her, past his fallen lover, and back into the Temple itself.

And her heart went cold with a sudden premonition of disaster.

She forced her exhausted legs into a stumbling parody of a run, but she wasn't fast enough.

Just as she reached the place where Vanyel lay, panting and moaning in pain, she saw his head snap up as if in response to a call only he could hear. He seemed to be looking up at the Tower that held the Death Bell. She heard him cry out something unintelligible, and followed his horror-stricken glance—

—and saw Tylendel poised against the lighting-filled sky, arms spread as if to fly—

—and saw him leap—

He seemed to hang in the air for a moment, as if he *had* somehow mastered flight.

But only a moment; in the next heartbeat he was falling, falling—she couldn't tell if the scream she heard was hers, or Vanyel's or both. It wasn't Tylendel's; his eyes were closed, and his mouth twisted and jaw clenched in a rictus of pure grief.

She felt the impact of his body with the unforgiving ground as if it had been her own body that had fallen—

—and the scream ended.

Jaysen stopped dead beside her, frozen in mid-step.

She whimpered in the back of her throat, and Jaysen walked slowly to the crumpled thing lying on the ground, not twenty paces from where she now stood. He went to his knees beside it, then looked up, and she saw him shake his head slowly, confirming what she already knew.

And at that moment, the Death Bell began solemnly tolling.

She stumbled to Jaysen's side, each step costing her more in pain than she had felt in a lifetime of sacrifice to Queen and Circle. She went heavily to her knees, and gathered up the limp, pitiable body to her breast.

She held him, cradling him against her shoulder, gently rocking a little as if she held a small child. Tears coursed silently down her face to mingle with the rain that was pouring from the sky; it seemed that the whole world echoed her grief. Jaysen knelt beside her, his head bowed, his shoulders shaking with sobs, as the Companions gathered about them and the Death Bell tolled above them.

It was only when the rest of the Heralds arrived to take their burden from them that they thought of Vanyel, and sent someone to look for him.

But the boy was gone.

Nine

Vanyel stumbled through the pouring, frigid rain. He was half-blinded with grief, with no hope of finding comfort anywhere in this world. There was nothing left for him—nothing.

He's dead—oh, gods, he's dead, and it's all my fault—

His whole body seemed to be on fire, a slow, smoldering pain that was burning away at him from the inside the way the ice of his dream had chilled him.

There was no reason to fight ice *or* fire anymore. Let either or both eat him, he couldn't care.

Rain pounded him, hail struck like slung stones. His head reeled and pounded with his pulse. He hurt, but he welcomed the pain.

It's all I deserve. It was all my fault—

He couldn't see where he was going, and he didn't give a damn. He tripped and fell any number of times, but bruises and cuts didn't matter; he just picked himself back up and kept running in whatever direction he happened to be facing.

His whole universe had collapsed the moment Tylendel had thrown himself off that tower. Somewhere down in the depths of his soul was the dim thought that if he ran far enough, ran fast enough, he might run off the edge of the world and into an oblivion where there would be no more feeling, and no more pain.

He didn't run off the edge of the world, quite. He ran off the bank into the river.

The ground just disappeared under his feet, and he

flailed his arms wildly as he half-fell, half-tumbled down the bank and somersaulted at the bottom into the icy water. It closed over his head, and the cold shocked him into an instant of forgetfulness; he lost the desire for oblivion as instinct took over, and he fought back to the surface.

He gulped air, shook water out of his eyes, and in a flash of lightning saw an oncoming tree limb too late to dodge it. He managed to turn away from it, but it hit him across the back of the head and knocked him under again. The second time his head broke the surface, he was dazed and unthinking; in another glare of lighting he saw the branches of a bush beside him and grabbed at them—

They were too far away, far out of his frantic reach—

Then the bush shook violently, and seemed to stretch toward *him*. He snatched at the ends of the branches—

He caught them, somehow; they cut into his hand, but he managed to pull himself into the shallows.

He had just enough strength left to crawl halfway up into the rain-slick bank, and just enough mind left to wonder why he'd bothered to save himself.

He lay facedown in the sodden, dead grass on the bank; chilled and numb, and growing colder, and wracked with anguished guilt and mourning.

'Lendel, 'Lendel, it was all my fault—oh, gods, it was all my fault—I should have told Savil. I should have tried to stop you.

He sobbed into the rough grass, the damp-smelling earth, longing inarticulately for the power of a god to reverse time, to unmake all that had happened.

I'm sorry—oh, please, someone, take it all back! If you have to have someone, take me instead! Make it a dream, oh, gods—please—

But it wasn't a dream; no more than the rain that was diluting his tears, or the icy water that tugged at his legs. And no god intervened to unmake the past. The wintry cold was closing in on him, chilling the fire along his veins; he was too weak to move, and too tired, and far too grief stricken to care. It occurred to him then that he might die here, as alone as Tylendel had died.

It was no less than his deserts, and he changed his

prayers. *Please*— he asked, desperately, of powers that were not answering. *Please—let me die.*

He thought of every mistake he had made, every wrong turning, and moaned. *I deserve to die*, he thought in anguish, closing his eyes. *I want to die.*

:No.: The mind-voice was bright, bright as a flame, and sharp as steel, piercing his dark hope for death. *:No, you must not. You must live, Chosen.:*

He raised his head a little, but couldn't get his eyes open, and really didn't want to. *:You don't know,:* he thought bleakly back at the intruder. *:Let me alone. No one wants me, nobody should want me; I kill everything I care for.:*

But someone grabbed him by the back of the collar and half-dragged him up the bank. He tried to twist away, but his body wouldn't work right anymore, and all he did was thrash feebly. Heartbeats later the rain was no longer pounding his back, and the green-smelling, soft moss under his weakly moving hands was dry; he'd been pulled into some kind of shelter. Whatever had him let go of his collar, after lowering him gently down onto the moss; he managed to get his eyes open, but with the lightning fading off in the distance, he could see nothing but darkness.

Something warm and large lay down beside him with a sigh. A soft nose nuzzled his cheek—

—like Gala had—

The sensation brought up memories that cut him into little shreds. He brought his knees up under his chest and curled up on himself, sobbing uncontrollably, driven to the edge of sanity by grief and loneliness.

:—but I am here—:

He brought his head up a little, and looked for the speaker with vision blurred by tears—and in a last glare of the lightning met a pair of glowing sapphire eyes— eyes so full of compassion and love that he knew their owner would forgive him anything. That love reached out for him, and flowed over into him. It couldn't erase his loss, but it could share the pain—and it didn't blame him for what had happened.

He uncurled, and groped for the smooth white neck

and shoulder the way he had seized on the branches of the bush to keep from drowning.

He sobbed himself into exhaustion on that shoulder, wept until he hadn't the strength to shed another tear, and into a kind of fevered half-sleep. And all the while, that bright voice murmured, like a litany, over and over, into his mind—

:*I am here, my Chosen. I love you. I will never leave you.*:

"Savil, we found him." Mardic burst into the room that had been Vanyel's and Tylendel's, dripping from head to toe, and shivering in the draft from the door behind him.

As he turned to close the door, Savil dredged up energy she hadn't dreamed she still possessed, and started to rise. Jaysen and Healer Andrel simultaneously seized her shoulders and pushed her back down into her chair.

"Where?" she demanded, in a voice hoarsened by weeping. "Who found him? Is he all right?"

"I dunno, the Companions found him; Yfandes did, anyway," Mardic replied vaguely, swaying with weariness, looking colorless with exhaustion in the yellow candlelight. "She found him on the garden side of the river and dragged him into a grotto. Tantras thinks he's sick, something like backlash, but he can't tell for sure. He's trying to persuade her to let him bring Van back here so Andrel can take care of him."

Savil shook her head, trying to make sense of his words. "Mardic, what are you trying to tell me? What has Yfandes got to do with anything?"

"She won't let anyone lay a finger on him, Savil," Mardic replied, blinking, and still shivering despite the warmth of the room. "She's adamant about it; damned near took Tantras' hand off when he tried to get at Van. She told my Fortin that she doesn't trust us to protect him and keep him under shield properly—that we won't understand what we've got—that he's hurt, all torn up inside his mind, and we can't begin to help him—"

"Mardic," Jaysen said, slowly, "are you saying that Yfandes *Chose* Vanyel? The only full-grown Companion in the Field that hasn't Chosen—the Companion that hasn't Chosen for over ten years—and *now* she's Chosen Vanyel?''

''She didn't come out and say so, but I guess she did,'' Mardic said, fatigue slurring his words as he slumped against the doorframe. ''I dunno why in hell she'd be curled up around him like he was her foal otherwise, and not letting us near him. We think he's unconscious; he isn't moving, and he isn't responding when we talk to him, but Yfandes won't let anyone close enough to get a good look at him.''

Savil exchanged startled looks with the Seneschal's Herald, but it was Healer Andrel who put their thoughts into words.

''By the Lady Bright,'' he murmured, green eyes gone round with consternation, ''what in the Havens is *this* going to mean?''

Vanyel swam up out of a feverish, fitful nightmare, prodded by an insistent voice in his head. He moaned, and opened dry, hot eyes that ached and burned. His head still pounded, and moving it even a little made his vision blur. He felt as if his whole body was a hot, tight, painfully constrictive garment; it felt like it didn't belong to him.

Sunlight gleamed weakly in through a rocky opening; he could see the river gurgling by just a few paces beyond it. It looked as if he were in a cave, but there were pink marble benches beside the entrance. Caves didn't have pink marble benches. They didn't have cultivated, moss-covered floors, either.

Then he recognized the place for what it was—one of the garden grottoes set into the riverbank. They were popular with courting couples or people seeking a moment of solitude from the Court. Tylendel had often wistfully expressed the wish that they dared to use one—

Tylendel. Grief closed around his throat and stopped his breath.

:No, Vanyel, Chosen. Not now. Mourn later; now get up.:

Without knowing quite how he had gotten there, Vanyel found himself on his feet, leaning heavily on the silky shoulder of a Companion.

His Companion. Yfandes.

He tried to make sense of that, but his head spun too much and he couldn't get a good grip on any of the thoughts that half-formed and then blew away.

:You are ill,: said the worried voice inside his mind. *:I cannot care for you. I did not wish to let you away from my protection, but I cannot help you. You have fever, you need a Healer. Move your foot. One step. Another—:*

He discovered that he was shaking, and clung a little tighter to the Companion's back. Obedient to that voice in his head, he put one hesitant foot in front of the other, learning quickly that he had to rest most of his weight on the arm clinging to Yfandes' shoulder. He had to close his eyes after the first couple of steps and trust to her to guide him; he was so dizzy and nauseated he couldn't make any sense out of what he was seeing.

They emerged into sunlight that was far too much for his eyes; he opened them once, and shut them again, quickly. The Companion suddenly stepped away from him, and he literally fell into the arms of a strange Herald; and once out of contact with Yfandes there were *dozens* of voices in his head, all of them clamorous, all of them confusing. He whimpered, tried to pull away, and hid his head in his arms. They hurt, they *hurt,* and he couldn't make out which were his own thoughts and which belonged to someone else.

:Tell your fool Chosen to shield him, Delian!:

That voice he recognized, although Yfandes had never spoken that sharply to him. The stranger bit off a curse and touched Vanyel's forehead, and the voices cut off. Vanyel opened his eyes again, and wished he hadn't; the world was spinning around with him as the center of the chaos. He shut them immediately, vowing not to reopen them.

"Let me, Tantras." The soft voice was that of yet another stranger.

Two cool hands rested lightly on his head, and brought with them the promise of comfort and the peace of sleep.

He took what they offered, falling into oblivion gratefully.

With any luck, he'd never wake up.

The bed looked far too big for the boy; never tall, he seemed to have collapsed in on himself. He was as pale as the sheets and—it might have been his dark hair and naturally fair complexion, but it seemed to her that he looked worse than Tylendel had after his fit. That was something Savil had not thought possible until now.

Tylendel. Oh, my 'Lendel, my poor, poor, 'Lendel.

Unshed tears made a hard knot in her throat and misted her eyes. So she missed the moment that Andrel took his hand away from the boy's forehead and sagged back into his chair with a sigh of weariness, his graying red hair damp with sweat, his freckles twice as evident with his skin so washed out and pale.

It was that sigh that brought her back to the urgent present.

"Andrel?" she said softly. "Can you tell me anything?"

"I did what I could for him—and more, I've got a line established," the Green-robed Healer to the Heralds replied, without looking up. "I want you to follow it—or if you feel you can't, find me a Herald-Mage your equal. I don't believe what I Saw, to be frank, and I want a confirmation."

Savil tightened her jaw, and told herself again that none of this had been Vanyel's fault. Besides, she was the only Herald-Mage at the Palace who was likely to have *any* feelings of charity toward the boy.

"I'll follow it. Have you got more to say, or—"

"I want you in there first. What I have to say is going to depend on whether you think I've gone over the edge or not."

Savil raised one eyebrow in surprise, but moved in to stand beside the Healer. She reached out for Andrel's soothing Presence as easily as she could have reached for his hand; they'd been lovers, once, and had worked together often, both before and since.

They meshed auras exactly as hand would close on

hand, and Savil followed the "line" the Healer had established down past the churning chaos of Vanyel's sleeping surface mind to the dark, grief-stricken core of him. The measure of that grief would have reconciled her to him even had she felt him blameworthy; she'd known the depth of Tylendel's feelings, but it seemed as if Vanyel's had run at least as deep. Certainly his grief and loss were as profound as her own. More—

Oh, gods—it's just what I warned 'Lendel against. He's lost, he's utterly lost without 'Lendel—

But that was not what rocked her back onto her heels with real shock.

Savil had spent most of the past twenty years of her life as the one Herald-Mage most intimately involved in training young Herald-Mages, and the one most often set to identify youngsters with active Gifts and the potential of being Chosen. She had seen children with one, two, or (most commonly) no Gifts. Tylendel had been unusual in having Mindspeech, Fetching, Empathy and the Mage-Gift, all at near-equal strength. Most Heralds or Herald-Mages had one or two strong Gifts—and few had as many as three.

Vanyel had them all. Each channel she tested—with the sole exception of Healing—was open; most of them had been forced open to their widest extent. The boy had Mindspeech, Fetching, FarSight, ForeSight, as much Empathy as Tylendel had shown, even enough Fire-starting to ensure he'd never need to use a tinderbox again, and the all-important Mage-Gift. His Mindspeech was even of both types, Thought-sensing and Projecting.

And—irony of ironies—as if the gods were taking with one hand and offering a pittance as compensation—the Bardic Gift.

This boy had more Gifts than any five full Heralds—and all of them had come into full activity in less than a day.

To her horror she could See that all the channels were as raw and sensitive as so many open wounds. The channels had not been "opened," they'd been *blasted* open. It was a wonder the boy wasn't mad with the pain alone.

Savil came up out of Vanyel's mind with a rush like a

startled fish jumping out of a stream, and looked from the boy to the Healer and back in a state of surprise that closely resembled shock.

"Great good *gods*," she said, "What the hell happened to do *that?*"

Andrel shook his head. "Your guess would be better than mine. I never cared much where our powers came from, I was just concerned with learning to use them effectively. But do you see what I'm up against with this boy?"

"I think so," Savil replied, groping for the bedpost and sitting down carefully on the foot of the bed. "Let me add this up. You've got backlash trauma from when the Gate-energy got pulled from him, and more trauma from when we sent it back *into* him; you've got the problems inherent when you wake Gifts late or early. You've got the problems with them being at full power from the moment they woke. Worst of all, you've got channels that were *burned* open or *torn* open instead of opening of themselves."

"That, and more mundane emotional trauma and physical shock. I hope to the Havens that he doesn't come down with pneumonia on top of it all. I already fought off one fever, one his own body produced when it couldn't handle the energy-overload." Andrel touched the back of his hand to the boy's waxen cheek, checking his temperature. "So far, so good, but it's a real possibility. And I'm fighting off the effects of exposure, too. Savil, the child is a mess."

"Lover, you have a talent for understatement." Savil contemplated Vanyel's pinched, grief-twisted face.

Even in sleep he doesn't lose his pain.

"Now I see why Yfandes was so reluctant to let him out of her care. Until she gets him firmly bonded to her, he's going to have to be in physical contact with her for her to protect him. But what can we do? I can't fit her in here, I can't put him in the stables, not with the weather being what it is."

"Try, and I'll call you up on charges," Andrel replied, and Savil could tell that he was not joking. "Do that in this chill, and you'll kill him. It's going to be touchy enough with him tucked up in a warm bed.''

''Well, how in hell do I protect him from his own powers?''

''Put your own shields on him, and hope nothing gets through.''

''I can't keep them up forever,'' Savil reminded him acidly. ''I'm fairly well fagged out myself. A couple of hours is about all I can manage at this point.''

''Then go order two *graves, dammit!''* the Healer snarled in sudden frustration. ''Because you're going to lose *this* one, too, if you don't do *everything* right with him!''

Savil pulled back, taken very much aback by the sudden explosion of temper. ''I,'' she faltered, then as his words penetrated, and she thought of what was lying in the Grove Temple at this moment, lost her own precarious hold on calm.

She got up, stumbling a little; turned away from him and leaned against the doorframe, her shoulders shaking with her silent weeping.

''Savil—''

Strong but trembling hands on her shoulders turned her back to face the room, and pulled her into an embrace against a bony chest covered in soft, green wool. ''Savil, I'm sorry,'' Andrel murmured into her hair. ''I shouldn't have said that. You're exhausted, I'm exhausted, and neither of us are up to facing the problem this boy represents. Is there *anyone* you can turn him over to, for a day, at least? Long enough for you to get some rest and a chance to think?''

A white square of linen appeared just when she needed it. She mopped at her eyes with the handkerchief he offered, and blew her nose. ''Under any other circumstances I'd just let *any* of the others spell me—but I don't know, Andy. A lot of them still think he's responsible for all this. Even if they shield—with Gifts like his, what's he going to pick up? *You* of all people should know how leaky we all are to a new, raw Gift, even when we aren't stressed.''

Andrel sighed. ''Dearheart, I don't think you have a

real choice. You'll just have to hope that if surface
thoughts leak past, he won't be able to understand them
yet. If you don't get some rest, *you're* going to collapse,
and even a novice Healer would be able to tell you that.''

She bowed her head, feeling the weight of all her years
and all her sorrows falling on her back. ''All right,'' she
said, acting against her better judgment, but unable to
see any other option open to her. ''See if you can round
up Tantras for me, will you? At least he didn't know poor
'Lendel all that well.''

Vanyel woke from a dream in which Tylendel was alive
again, and had teased him gently about how much he had
been grieving. For a confused moment after waking, he
wasn't certain which had been the dream, and which the
reality.

Then he opened his eyes, and found that he was in his
own bed, and his own room, now illuminated by carefully shaded candle-lanterns. And there was something
odd about the room.

After a long moment, he finally figured out what it
was. The feeling of ''Tylendel,'' the sense of his being
there even when he wasn't physically present, was missing.

That told him. He swallowed a moan of despair, and
closed his eyes against the resurgence of tears—and just
in time, for the door opened softly and closed again, and
he felt a new presence in the room with him.

He froze for a moment, then sighed, as if in sleep, and
turned onto his side, hiding his face away from the light.

He was hearing things—like someone talking to himself, only—only, *inside* his head, the way Yfandes' voice
had been inside his head. It hurt to listen, but he couldn't
stop the words from coming in. And from the feel of that
mind-voice, he knew who it was that was sitting by his
bedside, too; it was one of the Heralds that had been with
Savil, the one called Jaysen.

And Jaysen did not in the least care for Vanyel.

:—*gods*—: Vanyel heard, a little garbled by the pain
that came with the words. :—*trade this arrogant little
toad for Tylendel. Damn poor bargain.*:

Vanyel could feel brooding eyes on him, and the words in his head came clearer, more focused. :*No matter what Savil said, I'll never believe he didn't have something to do with the boy's death. If they'd been all that close, Tylendel would have listened to him, and even if 'Lendel was crazed on revenge, this one wasn't. 'Lendel may have loved him, but he could never have cared for the lad in the same way, or he'd have stopped him. 'Lendel was just one more little addition to his stable of admirers. If he'd left 'Lendel alone, if he hadn't played on his—weaknesses—:*

Vanyel cringed beneath the pitiless words, and the vision of himself that came with them; arrogant, self-centered, self-serving. Using Tylendel, not caring for him. And worse; worse than that, feeding him what he craved, like feeding a perpetual drunk the liquor he shouldn't have.

Without thinking about it, he reached beyond his room; it was a little like straining his ears to hear a conversation in the distance, and the pain that came with the effort felt like muscles pulling against a broken bone, but he found he could catch other snatches of—it must be thoughts—that touched on him.

They could have been echoes of Jaysen's thoughts.

He pulled his awareness back, as a child pulls its singed hand from the fire that has burned it. There were only two creatures in all the world that he could be certain cared for him despite what he was; Tylendel and Yfandes. Neither were to be trusted to know the truth about him. The second was besotted by whatever magic had made her Choose him; the first was—

The first was dead. And it was his fault. Jaysen was right; if he'd really *cared* for 'Lendel, he'd have stopped him. It wouldn't even have been hard; if he hadn't agreed to get those books, if he hadn't agreed to help with that spell, Tylendel would be alive at this moment. And if he hadn't seduced 'Lendel with his own needs, none of this ever would have happened.

Bad on top of worst; now he was a burden on the Heralds, who hated him, but felt honor-bound to take him in Tylendel's place. And he could *never* replace Tylendel, not ever; even *he* knew that. He had none of Tylendel's virtues, and *all* of his vices and more.

He *listened* to the mind-voice of the one beside him with all his strength, ignoring the pain it cost, hoping beyond hope that the Herald would somehow give him the chance to get away—get away and do something to make this right. If the Herald would just—go away for a moment, or—or better yet, fall asleep—

Jaysen *was* tired; though he'd done less magic than Savil, and had more time to rest, he was still very weary. He'd set himself up in the room's really comfortable chair; the one Tylendel had sometimes fallen asleep in. Vanyel could feel Jaysen's mind drifting over into slumber, and held his breath, hoping he'd drift all the way.

Because he'd gleaned something else from those minds out there—

Because the Death Bell had rung for him, despite what he'd done, Tylendel was being accounted a full Herald and tomorrow would be buried with all the honors.

Tomorrow. But tonight—he was in the Temple in the Grove. And if he could get that far, Vanyel was going to try to right the wrongs he had done to all of them, atoning with the only thing he had left to give.

Jaysen's thoughts slipped into the vague mumbles of sleep, and in the next moment a gentle snore from the chair beside the bed told Vanyel that he was completely gone.

Vanyel turned over, deliberately making noise.

Jaysen continued to snore, undisturbed.

Vanyel sat up, slowly, taking stock of himself and his surroundings.

About a candlemark later, he was dressed; even if he had *not* needed to move slowly for fear of waking the Herald, he would have had to for weakness. He had even needed to hold onto the furniture at first, because his legs were so unsteady. Even now his legs trembled with every step he took, but at least he was moving a bit more surely.

He stole soundlessly across the floor and unlatched the door, opened it just enough to squeeze himself through, and shut it again. It was dark out here, a still, cloudless night. He wouldn't be seen, but it was a long way to the Grove.

He steeled himself and stepped shakily onto the graveled path that ran from his door through the moonlit garden.

But someone had been waiting for him.

Yfandes glided out of the darkness to his side almost before he had made five steps along that path.

:No—: she said, sternly, barring his way. *:You are ill; you should be in bed.:*

For a moment he was ready to collapse right where he stood.

—gods, she's going to stop me—

Then he saw a way to get Yfandes to help him—without her knowing she was doing so.

:Please—: He directed everything he could on part of the truth. He couldn't lie mind-to-mind, he knew that, but he *didn't* have to reveal everything unless Yfandes should ask a direct question about it. And besides that, the link to her was fading in and out (and it hurt, like everything else) and he would bet she wouldn't want to force anything. *:Pleased, Yfandes, I have to—:* he faltered *:—to say—good-bye.:*

She bowed her head almost to the earth as he let his grief pour out over her. *:Very well,:* he heard, the mind-voice heavy with reluctance. *:I will help you. But you must rest, after.:*

:I will,: he promised, meaning it, though not in the way she had intended.

She went to her knees so that he could mount; he, once the best rider at Forst Reach, could not drag himself onto her back without that help. His arms and legs trembled with weakness as he clung to her back, and if it had not been that she could have balanced a toddler there and not let it fall, he would have lost his seat within the first few moments.

He concentrated on his weariness, on how physically miserable he was feeling, and spent not so much as an eyeblink on his real intentions. He closed his eyes, both to concentrate, and because seeing the ground move by so fast in the moonlight *was* making him nauseated and disoriented again.

He had had no notion of how fast the Companions could travel at a so-called walk. She was stepping carefully up to the porch of the Grove Temple long before he had expected her to get there; the clear ringing of her hooves on the marble surprised him into opening his eyes.

:We are here,: she said, and knelt for him to dismount.

The marble of the Temple porch glistened wetly in the moonlight, and he could see candlelight shining under the door. He slid from Yfandes' back, and "listened" with this new, mental ear for other minds within the Temple.

None.

He shivered in the cold wind; he'd dressed carefully, in the black silk tunic and breeches Tylendel had thought he looked best in, and once off Yfandes' warm, broad back the wind cut right through his clothing.

:Not for long,: she admonished, as he clung to the doorframe and negotiated unlatching the door into the Temple itself.

:No, Yfandes,: he said, sincerely. *:Not for long.:*

He got the door open and closed again—then, as quietly as he could, locked it.

There was no clamor from the opposite side, so he assumed she had not heard the bolt shoot home. He turned, bracing himself for what he was about to do, and faced the altar.

The Temple itself was tiny; hardly bigger than the common room of their suite. It had been built all of white marble, within and without. The walls took up the candlelight, and reflected it until they fairly glowed. There were only two benches in it, and the altar. Behind the altar were stands thick with candles; behind the candles, the wall had been carved into a delicate bas-relief; swirling clouds, the moon, stars and the sun—and in the clouds, suggestions of male and female faces, whose expressions changed with the flickering of the candles.

Before the altar stood the bier.

Vanyel's legs trembled with every step; he made his

way unsteadily to that white-draped platform, and looked down on the occupant.

They'd dressed Tylendel in full Whites; his eyes were closed, and there was no trace of his grief or his madness in that handsome, peaceful face. His hands were folded across his waist, those graceful, strong hands that had held so much of comfort for his beloved. He looked almost exactly as he had so many mornings when Vanyel had awakened first. His long, golden curls were spread against the white of the pallet, a few of them tumbled a little untidily over his right temple; long, dark-gold lashes lay against his cheeks. Only the pose was wrong. Tylendel had never, in all the time Vanyel had known him, slept in anything other than a sprawl.

Vanyel reached out, hesitantly, to touch that smooth cheek—almost believing, even now, that he had only to touch him to awaken him.

But the cheek was cold, as cold as the marble of the altar, and the eyes did not flutter open at his touch. This was no child's tale, where the sleeping one would wake again at the magic touch of the one who loved him.

"Please, 'Lendel, forgive me," he whispered to the quiet face, and took the knife from the white sheath on Tylendel's belt. "I—I'm going to try to—pay for all of what I did to you."

His hands shook, but his determination remained firm.

Quickly, before he could lose his courage, he bent and kissed the cold lips—hoping that this, too, would be forgiven, and caught in a grief too deep for tears. Then he knelt on the icy white marble of the floor beside the bier, and braced the hilt of the dagger between his knees, clasping his hands with the dagger between his wrists, resting them on either side of the blade-edge.

" 'Lendel, there's nothing without you. Forgive me— if you can," he whispered again, both to Tylendel and the brooding Faces behind the altar.

And before he could begin to be afraid, he pulled both wrists up along the knife-edges, slashing them simultaneously.

The dagger was as sharp as he had hoped—sharper than he had expected. He cut both wrists almost to the bone; gasped as pain shot up his arms, and the knife fell clattering to the marble, released when his legs jerked involuntarily.

He sagged with sudden dizziness, and fell forward over his bent knees; his head bowed over his hands, his arms lying limp on the marble floor. Blood began to spread on the white marble; pooled before him under his slashed wrists. He stared at it in morbid fascination.

Red on white. Like blood on the snow—

It was only at that moment that Yfandes seemed to realize what it was he was doing.

She screamed, and began kicking at the door.

But it was far too late; his eyes were no longer focusing properly anymore, and his wrists didn't even hurt.

But he was feeling so cold, so very cold.

:I'm sorry,: he thought muzzily at the frantic Companion, beginning to black out, and feeling himself falling over sideways. *:Yfandes, I'm sorry . . . you'll find someone . . . better than me. Worthy of you.:*

''Gone?'' Savil's voice broke. ''What the hell do you mean, *gone?*''

''Savil, I swear to you, the boy was asleep. I dozed off for a breath or two, and when I woke up he was gone,'' Jaysen answered, one hand clutched at the side of his head on a fistful of hair, his expression frantic and guilt-ridden. ''I thought maybe he'd gone to the privy or something, but I can't find him anywhere.''

Savil swung her legs out of the bed and rubbed her eyes, trying to think. Where would Vanyel have gone, and in the name of the gods, *why?*

But in a heartbeat she had her answer—the frightened, frantic scream of a Companion rang across the river, and her Kellan's voice shrilled into her head.

:Savil—the boy—: and an image of where he was and what he had done.

From the stricken look on Jaysen's face, his own Felar had given him the same information.

''*Gods!*'' Savil snatched her cloak from the chair beside her bed and ran out in her bare feet, through the

common room, and headed for the door of Vanyel's room,
Jaysen breathing down her neck.

She hit the garden door at a dead run, and it was a
damned good thing that it wasn't locked, because if it
had been, she'd have broken it off the hinges. The cold
of the night slapped her in the face like an impious hand;
that stopped her for a moment, but *only* a moment. In
the next instant Felar and Kellan pounded up at a gallop.
Felar skidded around in a tight pivot, presenting his hind-
quarters to his Chosen, who leapfrogged up into his seat
with an acrobatic skill that would have had Savil muttering about "show-offs" had the situation been less precarious. Instead, she waited for Kellan to come to a dead
halt, and clambered onto her back anyhow, her bedgown
rucked up around her legs. Kellan launched herself into
a full, frantic gallop as Savil clung on as best she could.

Now Savil was a breath behind Jaysen, as the young
Seneschal's Herald led the way across the nearest bridge
and up the Field to the Temple of the Grove. Nor were
they the only two summoned by the frantic screaming,
mind and voice, of Yfandes. Heralds and trainees were
boiling out of the Palace like aroused fire ants, rendez-
vousing with their Companions, and heading across the
river at breakneck speed.

But Jaysen and Savil were the first two on the scene;
it was their dubious privilege to see Yfandes trying to
batter down the solid bronze door of the Temple single-
handedly, and not budging it by so much as a thumbs'-
breadth. Her hooves were screeching across the metal,
leaving showers of sparks in their wake, and her anguished screams were far too like a human's for comfort.

Jaysen vaulted off Felar's back and hit the ground at a
run, ducking fearlessly under Yfandes' flying hooves to
make a trial of the door himself.

"It's locked from the inside," he shouted unnecessar-
ily, as Savil slid from Kellan's back to limp to his side.
He put his shoulder against the door, and rammed it,
with no more luck than Yfandes had had.

"Vanyel!" Savil put her mouth up against the crack
between door and frame, and shouted through it. "Van,
lad, let us in!"

She put her ear to the crack and listened, but heard nothing.

:Kellan—:

:Yfandes says he's still alive, but unconscious and weakening,: came the grim reply, as Yfandes danced in place, her sapphire eyes gone nearly black with anguish.

"*Somebody get me a mage-light on that damned tower!*"

It was Mardic; he had his hands on Donni's shoulders and was staring up at the tower. Donni was holding a crossbow with a bulky missile cocked and ready.

Savil responded first, running far enough back from the door that she could see the top of the Belltower. It was glowing faintly, but obviously too faintly for Donni to make out a target. Savil raised her hands, and sent up such a burst of power that the entire top of the tower flowered with light.

While Mardic closed his eyes and scowled in concentration, Donni raised the crossbow, squinted carefully along it, and fired.

The oddly-shaped arrow flew strangely, and slowly, trailing something light colored behind it—and in a moment, Savil realized why and what it was. Donni had been a bright little apprentice-thief when she'd been Chosen; this was a grapnel-arrow, meant to carry a light, but strong line through an open window and catch on the sill. Mardic had a very weak, but usable Fetching-Gift; he had invoked it to help the arrow carry something heavier than a light line. A climbing-rope.

It lobbed through the loop of the Bell-house, clanging ominously off the Death Bell itself. Savil felt a chill, and made a warding-gesture, nor was she the only one. She could see most of the others shivering at the least, and Yfandes moaned like a dying thing at the sound of the Bell.

Donni, normally mobile face gone blank, was paying no attention to anything other than her arrow and line; all her concentration was on the task in her hand. She drew the rope to her with agonizing slowness; Savil fought down the urge to shout at her to hurry. Finally

Donni's careful pulling met resistance; she tugged, then pulled harder, then yanked on the rope with all her might.

Then, before Savil had time to blink, she was swarming up it like a squirrel.

One or two of the trainees gave a ragged cheer; Donni ignored them. She reached the opening and squeezed through, and Savil saw to her surprise that Mardic was following her. She'd been so intent on Donni's progress that she'd missed seeing him altogether until he got into the glow of the mage-light.

Savil sprinted back for the door—the crowd there parted to let her through—and waited, trembling with impatience, with the rest.

:Hang on, Savil,: she heard Mardic's mind-voice, in Broadsend-mode. *:He's alive; thank the gods he didn't know the right way to slit his wrists. Donni's got the blood stopped, but we'll need a Healer, fast. 'Fandes warped the door pounding on it; it's going to take a bit of work to get it open.:*

A tall figure in Healer's Greens pushed through to Savil's side as Mardic began pounding on the door, forcing the bolt back thumb-length by thumb-length; Andrel opened his arms and wrapped Savil inside the warmth of his fur-lined cloak with him.

Finally the door creaked open; Andrel deserted her, leaving her suddenly in sole possession of the heavy cloak. She followed inside, hard on his heels.

Donni knelt in front of the bier; there was a frighteningly wide scarlet stain on the marble of the floor, and her hands looked as if she had dipped them in vermilion dye. She was holding Vanyel's wrists; the boy was sprawled on the floor beside her at the foot of the bier, his face as transparently white as the marble under his head, and slackly unconscious. Andrel was just beginning to kneel in the pool of blood on the other side of the boy, heedless of his robes, and as Savil limped across the floor toward them, followed by the rest of the would-be rescuers, he reached out and set his hands firmly over Donni's bloodstained ones.

His face was fixed in a mask of absolute concentration, and Savil could feel the power beginning to flow from him. But he'd been hard-pressed today, and had little time to rest. And she knew that his few reserves were not going to be enough—

She ran the last few steps and placed her hands on his shoulders as he began to falter, sending energy coursing down into his center. And in a moment, she felt herself joined by Jaysen—then Mardic—then Donni. The four of them meshed in a union that was as nearly perfect as any magic she'd ever witnessed, and sent Andrel all he needed and more, in a steady, steadfast, stream.

Finally the Healer sighed, and lifted his hands away from Donni's; the other three disengaged with something that was a little like reluctance. It wasn't often that even Heralds experienced the peace that came with a perfect Healing-meld; it was nearly a mystical experience, and as close to the peace of the Havens as Savil ever wanted to get until she was Called.

Donni lifted her hands away from Vanyel's wrists, and Savil could see that the skin, veins, and tendons beneath were whole again. For a moment the wrists were marred by angry red scars, then gradually those scars faded to thin white lines.

Jaysen moved swiftly to gather the unconscious boy in his arms; blood from the boy's sleeves stained the front of his Whites, but Jaysen didn't seem to notice.

Vanyel's head sagged against the Herald's chest. Despite being moved, he showed no signs of reviving.

Savil helped Andrel to rise and go to him. The Healer reached out a hand that shook uncontrollably and checked the pulse at the hinge of Vanyel's jaw, lifted an eyelid, then shook his head.

"Nearer than I like, and he lost too much blood, given what he's been through," Andrel said, grimacing. "Jays, can you and Felar get him back into his bed as of a candlemark ago?"

"No," Savil interrupted. "No, you leave that to me and Yfandes. Jays, give him to me as soon as I get mounted."

She pushed her way through the silent, shocked crowd and found Yfandes waiting as close to the open door as she could get. The Companion looked deeply into Savil's eyes, her own eyes back to a quiet, depthless sapphire, then went to her knees for the Herald to mount.

Savil mounted, and Yfandes rose gracefully to her feet, not in the least unsteady on the smooth marble. Savil held out her arms, amazed by her own calm, and Jaysen lifted the limp form of Vanyel up into place before her. She cradled the boy against her shoulder, wrapping Andrel's cloak about both of them; he was no burden at all, really—almost *too* light a weight for the ease of her heart and conscience.

Oh, lad, lad— she sighed, nudging Yfandes lightly with her heels to tell her to go on. *Poor little lad—we've made a right mess of your life, haven't we? And all for lack of listening to you. I don't know who is guiltier, me or Withen.*

She held him a bit tighter as Yfandes headed at a gentle walk toward the beckoning beacon of the open door of her suite. He was all the legacy Tylendel had left to her, and she pledged the silent sleeper in the Temple behind her that she would take better care of him from this moment on.

And the first task is to put you back together, my poor, bewildered, heart-broken lostling. If ever I can.

Ten

Years later—or so it seemed—Savil finally crawled into some clothing. She wanted, she needed, to collapse somewhere; wanted rest as a starving man wants bread, but dared not leave Vanyel alone. She finally dragged the chair Jaysen had been using close to the bedside and wrapped herself in the first warm thing that came to hand (which turned out to be Andrel's fur-lined cloak), intending, despite her exhaustion, to stay awake as long as possible.

But she dozed off, some time around dawn, and woke at the sound of a strangled sob.

She fought her way out of the tangled embrace of the cloak; when she got her head free of the folds of the hood, the first things she saw were Vanyel's silver eyes looking at her with a kind of accusative sorrow.

"Why?" he whispered mournfully. "Why did you stop me?"

Savil finally untangled the rest of her, sat up in her chair, and took a quick look around. As she'd ordered, Mardic was still standing weary guard over the door to the rest of the suite, and Donni was drowsing, slumped against the door to the garden. Vanyel was not going to give them the slip a second time, however unlikely the prospect seemed. It hadn't seemed possible the *last* time.

She gave Mardic a jerk of her head and a Mindsent order; :*Out, love, this needs privacy,*: and woke Donni with a quick Mindtouch. Donni came completely awake as soon as Savil touched her, a talent the Herald-Mage envied. She pulled herself to her feet with the help of the doorframe at her back. Then both of them left for their own quarters, closing the door into the common room of the suite behind them.

Savil got up stiffly, every joint aching, and sat on the side of the bed, taking both of Vanyel's hands in her own. They were like ice, and bloodless-looking. "I stopped you because I had to," she replied. "Because—Vanyel, self-destruction is no answer. Because we've already lost one we loved—and I couldn't lose you, too, now—"

"But I deserve to die—" His voice was weak, and broke on the last word.

And he wouldn't look her in the eyes.

Oh, gods—what was going through that head of his? What had he convinced himself of? "For what?" she asked, her voice sounding rough-edged even to her. "Because you made some mistakes? Gods, if *that* was worthy of a death sentence, I should have been sharing that knife!"

His hands were chilling hers; she tried to warm them, chafing them as gently as she could. "Listen to me, Vanyel—this whole wretched mess was one mistake piled on top of another. *I* made mistakes; I should have watched 'Lendel more carefully, I should have insisted he talk to Lancir when his brother was killed. That's one of Lancir's jobs; to keep our heads clear and our minds able to think straight. Dammit, *I* knew what 'Lendel was capable of where Staven was concerned! And he would *not* have been able to hide that obsession from a MindHealer! 'Lendel made mistakes—the gods themselves know that. He should have thought before he acted; I'd been trying to get him to do that. We—the Heralds—accept mental evidence! All he had to do was ask for a hearing, and we'd have had the material we needed from his own mind to put the Leshara down. You made mistakes, yes, but you made them out of love. He needed help, asked you for it, and you tried to help him the only way anyone had ever taught you was right. And, gods, even *Gala* made mistakes!"

Her voice was harsh with tears, and with her own guilt, and she was not ashamed to let him hear it. "Van, Van, we're only simple, fallible mortals—we aren't saints, we

aren't angels—we fall on our faces and make errors and
sometimes people die of them—sometimes people we
love dearly—''

She choked on a sob, and bowed her head.

He freed a hand and touched her cheek hesitantly; his
fingers were still snow-cold. She caught and held it, and
looked back up into his eyes, seeing worse than grief
there before he dropped them.

''You thought the world would be better with you out
of it, is that it?''

He nodded, dumbly, and his hands trembled in hers.

''Did you stop to think how *I* would feel? You were
'Lendel's love. Didn't you think I'd come to care for you
at least a bit, if only for his sake?''

How was she to reach him—when she'd *never* been
good with words? ''I've buried him today. Did you think
I'd be indifferent about burying you as well? What about
Jaysen? I'd left him to watch you. How do you think *he*
feels right now about his carelessness? What do you think
he'd have felt if you'd died? And—gods help us—what did
you think Yfandes would do?''

''I thought—I thought she'd find somebody better,'' he
faltered, his voice quavering a bit.

''She'd *die*, lad; Companions very seldom outlive their
Chosen. And she Chose *you*. If you die, she dies; she'd
probably pine herself to death, and she does *not* deserve
that.''

He shrank into himself, pulling even farther away from
her, and she cursed her clumsy words, her inability to
tell him what she really meant without hurting him further. ''Van—oh, *hell*—I'm not saying any of this the way
I wanted to. Listen to me; you're sick, you need to rest
and get well. We'll deal with this later, all right? Just—
don't take yourself out of this world right now, there are
folks who'll have holes in their lives if you go. And I'm
one of them.''

He nodded; he didn't look convinced, but now she had
exhausted what little eloquence she possessed, and didn't
know what else to say to him.

So she tried one last tactic. *Let me just keep him alive—
if I can do that, maybe we can help him.*

"Will you promise me, on your word of honor, that you won't try to do yourself in again? If you will, I'll trust you, and I won't leave guards on your doors."

He swallowed, pulled his hands out of hers, and whispered, haltingly, "I—promise. Word of honor." He still wouldn't look her in the face, but she trusted that sworn word.

She nodded. "Accepted. Now is there anything, anything at all, that I can do for you?" *Maybe*— "Need to talk?"

He shook his head, and she sensed his complete withdrawal, and cursed again. *Dammit, just when I need Lance the most, he's not here.*

"Sure?" She persisted, even in the face of defeat; that was her nature. "Vanyel—Vanyel, you're the only person I've got who knew 'Lendel from the inside the way I did. If—if you need somebody to mourn with. . . ."

He shook his head again, avoiding her eyes altogether, and she sighed, giving up. "If you change your mind— well, rest, lad. Get better. Call, if you need anything— mind or voice, either, I'll hear you."

He nodded slightly, and closed his eyes again, leaning back and turning his face to the wall. That face was as white as the pillows beneath it, and it made her hurt all over again to see that lost look of his. She waited for another response or a request of some kind, but he slipped right back into an uneasy, shallow slumber. Finally she eased off the bed, gathered up Andrel's cloak from the chair, and left him alone.

Andrel arrived at sunset in response to her invitation to fetch his cloak and share food and thoughts. They'd had more than one intimate little supper in their lives, many of them in this very room, but none so gloom-ridden. Mardic and Donni had gone off to cautiously interview some of Vanyel's circle of admirers, to see if there was someone else they could contact that might help to bring him out of this mental abyss.

Savil's Hawkbrother masks on the wall behind Andrel's left shoulder gazed at her from dispassionate and empty eyeholes. Candles flickered on the table between them.

Neither of them had much interest in food at the moment; both their minds were on the boy sleeping behind the closed door behind Savil's chair. "What we need," she told Andrel glumly, eating a dinner she did not taste, "is Lancir. We need his MindHealing; the boy's pulling farther away from *touching* with every moment he's awake, and I cannot get him to let me inside. He's barricading himself again; a different kind of barricade than that old arrogance, but it's there all the same. And Lance bloody *would* be out of touch right now."

He sighed, his breath making the candleflame flutter, and pushed his own food around on his plate with his fork. "I have to agree with you. Is there no chance you can get Lance back via Gate?"

She shook her head, shoving her frustration back down out of her way. She'd already been over this with Jaysen. "Not without knowing where he is, and he's not a strong enough Thought-senser to read a Broadcast-sending. And we don't know what route he's taking home; could be one of half a dozen. If something were wrong with Elspeth we could afford to send out half-a-dozen Heralds to look for him, but—Vanyel just is not that important." Her tone turned acid. "Or so I've been told."

Andrel frowned, and his eyebrows met. "He may become that important; I'm shielding him as much as I can, but his trauma is still leaking through. Half the trainees are depressed to the point of tears right now, Gifted Bardic, Healer, *and* Herald, and it's all due to Vanyel's leakage."

"Well what do you expect?" she countered, letting him see her very real anger. "*You* saw the strength and depth of his Gifts. Even with raw channels he's Broadsending without knowing it, and he has no more notion of how to shield than how to fly! And it's not every day you've got one half of a lifebonded pair left after the other half suicides. If he were *trained*, he'd be leaking. But nobody else believes how strong he is; they all think I'm letting my affection for Tylendel magnify everything that was connected with him out of all proportion to reality."

"Gods!" he looked up from his plate with the ex-

pression of a stunned sheep. "Vanyel and Tylendel—
lifebonded?"

She nodded unhappily. "I'm pretty damned sure of it;
what's more, so are Mardic and Donni, and if anyone
would recognize a bonding, it would be another bonded
pair. I expected grief, mourning; the natural responses
for a youngster who's lost his first love under rotten bad
circumstances—I did *not* expect to find the kind of gaping
emotional wounds I saw before he started shutting me
out today. I've never seen that depth of feeling before in
anyone, Herald, or no, *except* Mardic and Donni. So tell
me; what the hell do I do about a broken lifebond?"

He shook his head, obviously at a loss. "I can't tell
you; I don't know. I don't Heal minds, I Heal bodies.
And I don't know of anyone who Heals hearts."

She sighed, and looked down at her congealing dinner.
"That's what I was afraid you'd tell me. I have more bad
news; the relationship between them was one where
'Lendel was the leader and Van the follower. Van had
gotten totally dependent on 'Lendel for all his emotional
needs. I tried to warn 'Lendel, but—" She shrugged.
"And to put the snow on the mountain, Van's got some
guilt he's hiding from me, and all I can think is that he's
convinced he cursed 'Lendel because he seduced Tylendel. Mind you, he didn't; from all I know I'm positive
the seduction, if seduction it was, was mutual, but—there
it is."

"Jaysen," Andrel said positively.

She nodded. "Good bet, my friend. Jays has got all
those Kleimar prejudices about same-sex pairings. He accepted 'Lendel, but mostly after I rammed his prejudices
right up in his face. But Vanyel? Vanyel wasn't even a
Herald-candidate when he and 'Lendel paired. Jays hasn't
said a word, but you can bet on what he was thinking
when he was keeping watch on him. Resentment that Van
is alive and 'Lendel dead would be the least of it."

"And Vanyel picked it up," Andrel said sadly.

"Probably." She took a bite, found it catch in her
throat, and gave up trying to eat, shoving the plate away.
"From what I can tell, he's sensitive enough to pick up

things *you've* forgotten for years and do it right through your shielding. Ah, gods.''

She rested both elbows on the table, and covered her sore eyes with her hands. A moment later she felt one of Andrel's hands stroking her hair, and dropped her own back on the table, giving him a good long look across the candleflames. His deeply green eyes were fixed on her face, reflecting a profound concern.

"And what about you?" he asked, barely above a whisper.

"I am *trying* to reach out to him," she said, feeling old and tired and about ready to give up. "I think I've convinced myself that none of this was any more his fault than it was anyone else's. I bloody well hope so, or he's going to be getting knives in the gut from me, too. And he doesn't deserve that. The rest—gods, I don't know what to do."

"That isn't what I meant," he replied, taking his hand away from her hair, and reaching for her wrist. "I want to know how *you're* weathering this. Need a shoulder?"

"Want the truth?" She tensed all over, trying to keep from bawling like a little child. "Yes, I need a shoulder, and no, I am *not* taking this well. I want 'Lendel back, Andy—he was my soul-son, and I loved him, and I want him back with me."

Her voice cracked; she lost her veneer of calm, and just dissolved into tears. Andrel got up, gracefully, and without letting go of her wrist; he moved around the table, and pulled her to her feet, then led her over to the couch and gave her that shoulder she needed so badly.

The peaceful night rocked; Vanyel convulsed, wailing—

His cry sounded like something in its death agonies, and made Savil's hair stand on end.

The room trembled; literally. The walls shook as Vanyel's muscles spasmed.

His eyes were wide open, but saw nothing, and his pupils dilated with fear. He convulsed again, and the very foundation of the Palace rocked. The bed shook as if it were alive. His lute fell from the wall, landing with a sickening crack that surely meant it was broken past all repair; his armor-stand crashed over and scattered his equipment across the floor, and Savil was tossed from his bedside to the floor before she realized it.

She picked herself up off the floor beside his bed without thinking about safety or bruises, and flung herself at him again.

He thrashed beneath her, fighting her with a paranormal strength; he couldn't know where he was or who she was. All she could read from him was terrible agony—and beneath the pain, confusion, panic, entrapment. She caught his wrists and tried to pinion them against the pillows; then tried to pin him down with the blankets. His chest arched against hers, he screamed, and the walls shook again.

Mardic lay in the corner behind her, quite unconscious; Donni had his head in her lap and she was trying to protect him from falling objects with her own body. Vanyel had thrown him against the wall when this nightmare—or whatever it was—had started, and Mardic had made the mistake of trying to touch his mind to wake him.

:Donni—: Savil used a moment of lull to Mindtouch her pupil, taking a tiny fragment of her attention from the attempt—*attempt,* for it wasn't succeeding—to shield Vanyel, to get him under some kind of control. *:—Donni, how's Mardic?:*

:He's all right, just stunned,: came the reassuring reply. *:—I can spare you something. Catch this, quick—:*

The girl "threw" her a mental line, and began sending additional, sorely-needed energy down it as soon as Savil "caught" it.

It helped to keep Savil from blacking out as Vanyel lashed out with *his* mind, but that was about all.

Jaysen was coming on the run; Savil could Feel him reaching out to find out what the hell was going on, and Felt the panic in *his* mind when he realized they had a powerful Gifted trapped in a pain-loop and hallucination. He all but broke down the door, trying to get in, and flung himself into the affray without a second thought.

"*Shield* him, dammit," he shouted, throwing himself

across Vanyel's legs, as the walls (but, thank the gods, not the foundations again) shook.

"I'm *trying*," she snapped back, giving up on the uneven struggle to pin Vanyel down, and settling for securing his arms. "He breaks them as fast as I get them up!"

Jaysen succeeded in getting Vanyel physically restrained where she, being lighter, had failed. He added his strength to Savil's and Donni's on the crumbling shields they were trying to get on the boy. But it wasn't even stalemate; they were losing him to his own nightmares.

Andrel appeared. Savil didn't even see or Sense him run in; he was just *there* all in an instant. But instead of flinging himself into the melee, he grabbed their arms and pulled both of them *off* the boy.

Then he reached down for something at his feet, and came up with a bucket of icy water. He doused the boy, bed and all, without a heartbeat of hesitation.

The convulsions stopped as Vanyel came abruptly awake.

He sat up—stared—then he suddenly went limp.

The room stopped shaking.

"Savil, get me a blanket," Andrel ordered quietly. "Jays, help me get him out of that wet bed before he goes into shock, then get the bedding stripped before the mattress gets soaked,"

By the time Savil returned with the goosedown comforter from her bed, the two men had pulled the half-stunned boy from the tangled mess of water-soaked bedcoverings, and the bedding was piled on the floor. Andrel was carefully shaking the boy's shoulders while Jaysen supported him.

Behind them, Mardic was groggily climbing to his knees, Donni steadying him, but the two of them waved Savil off when she made a half-step in their direction.

:We're all right,: Donni Mindspoke. *:I'll get Mardic into bed myself, and then I'll come make up the bed in here again.:*

Savil turned her attention back to the boy, knowing she could trust Donni to deal with the situation if she had said she could.

"Come on, Vanyel," Andrel was saying, coaxingly. "Come on, lad, come back to us. Wake up, come out of it."

Vanyel blinked, blinked again, and sense came back into his eyes. He looked about him, momentarily confused, then the destruction about him seemed to register on him. He closed his eyes, a soft, hardly audible moan coming from the back of his throat.

And for one instant, Savil was nearly flattened beneath an overwhelming load of blackest despair, terrible guilt, and a grief so heavy she felt her knees start to give way beneath the weight of it.

Then it was gone; absolutely cut off, and so completely that for a moment even she doubted that she had felt it.

But one look at Andrel and Jaysen convinced her otherwise; the former was deeply shaken, and the latter white-lipped.

She expected tenderness and concern from Andrel— but strangely enough, it was Jaysen who carefully got the boy into a chair, wrapped in the comforter; and from the chair back into the bed when Donni had stripped it of the wet coverings and remade it. It was Jaysen who stayed beside him, leaving Savil free to see to it that Mardic was truly all right. Savil wasn't in a mood to ask questions about his apparent change of heart.

Mardic was fine, and relatively cheerful. "I'll have a godsawful headache," he told her; "Poor Van thought I was going to kill him, took me for an enemy in his dream. When he realized it *was* a dream, he pulled most of it—"

"*Most* of it?" Savil choked. "He flattened you, and he pulled *most* of it?"

"Near as I can tell." Mardic put both hands to his temples and massaged a little. "Well when he pulled the blow, the energy overflowed into those raw channels and hurt him, and he went over the edge; couldn't control *anything*. Then—I *think*—he lost his center and got lost in his own pain. Andrel had the right notion; physical shock is what gave him something to home in on."

"But you *are* going to be all right?"

He gave her half a grin. "If you'll let me get some sleep."

Savil took the statement as an unsubtle request and made a hasty exit.

She got back just in time to see Andrel give Vanyel some kind of sedative to drink. But it was Jaysen who sat with the boy until Andrel's sedative took effect. And it was Jaysen who righted the armor-stand, and picked up the broken-backed lute from the floor with a wince at seeing the fine instrument so ruined.

"I'll see to getting this fixed, if it can be," he said, when he saw Savil watching him before she knelt to put out the fire. They daren't have a fire here while Vanyel was asleep, nor candles burning, either—not unless Andrel could do something to keep him from going into another fit.

"Jays, what am I going to do with him?" she asked, quietly, standing up with a wince as a pulled muscle in her back told her what a fool she'd been. He motioned that she should precede him out the door, and she half turned to see his face as she walked past him. "He's sick with backlash, and he's getting sicker, not better. His channels are all raw; you can't Mindtouch him without doing *that* to him, throwing him into convulsions. That was what set all this off, Mardic trying to soothe him out of a bad dream. What am I going to do the *next* time he has a nightmare?"

Jaysen shrugged helplessly, and shut the door behind her. She made a circuit of the common room, setting candles erect and lighting them. "If you don't know, be damned if I do. Andy, can we keep him sedated long enough to heal?"

Andrel grimaced, looking as if he'd swallowed something sour. "With any other patient I'd tell you where to put that question—what I just gave the boy was argonel."

Jaysen and Savil both started with surprise, and in Savil's case the surprise was not unmixed with shock. "Great good gods, Andy!"

"Ease up; he's safe enough," Andrel interrupted her, throwing himself down on the couch with his usual lack of concern for the furniture. He groaned, stretched, and then raised an eyebrow at the Seneschal's Herald. "Jaysen, may I mention that you have lovely legs?"

Jaysen, who was attired only in shirt and hose and only just now really realized this, blushed a furious scarlet, but refused to be distracted. "Argonel, Andy—" he began, taking a chair and crossing his legs primly.

"He's burning it off at a respectable rate, or I wouldn't have given it to him," Andrel replied. "The benefit of it is that it's a muscle relaxant *and* a sedative; he won't be able to go into convulsions again even if you Mindtouch him. I *won't* speak for him tossing the Palace around, but he won't go into *physical* convulsions. As for him healing, well that depends entirely on what you mean."

Savil took another chair, flopping down into it with a tired *thud* as loud as the one Andrel had made connecting with the couch cushions.

"Physically," she said, flatly. "Pure physical healing. Backlash symptoms, exhaustion, blood loss. I'll worry about raw channels later."

"Yes, I can keep him sedated long enough for the effects of backlash to wear off, for his physical energy to recover and for him to replace the blood he lost. I can combine the argonel with jervain, and dull out all the Gift-senses enough so that they aren't so sensitive. That *might* let the channels heal. I don't know for sure; I've never seen nor read of anything like this, Gifts being blasted open like his were."

"Mentally?" Jaysen prodded, frowning. "Emotionally?"

"At this point I don't think even Lance can help him," Andrel replied sadly. "You both felt—"

Jaysen nodded, ruefully. "That's—I think perhaps I picked up something more than either of you," he said, a shadow of guilt crossing his face. "He—he thinks that everything he touches is doomed, cursed. Because of—what he and 'Lendel were. And I know *exactly* where he got that particularly poisonous little thought. Only it isn't a 'little thought' anymore. It's as much an obsession as Tylendel's was."

He hung his head, and wouldn't look at her. "I never

thought—" he faltered. "I never guessed—I thought he was just a user—"

Savil was not feeling charitable just now. "Damn right, you never thought," she snapped. "You never thought at all! You and your damned provincial—"

"Savil," Andrel said, warningly, his head turned slightly to the side, nodding at the door to Vanyel's room.

She subsided. If she got angry, Van might pick it up; it might set him off again. "Sorry, Jays," she finally said grudgingly, not feeling sorry at all.

"At least you didn't send somebody out to cut their wrists," he answered unhappily.

She winced. "No—I just—hell, this isn't getting us anywhere. Andy, you think you can get him *physically* recovered, right?"

Candlelight reflected in his eyes, which had gone inward-looking. "I would say yes, cautiously."

"Let's worry about that, then, for a couple of days. I have a germ of an idea, but whether or not I can pull it off is going to depend very strongly on whether or not *you* can get Vanyel fit to ride."

"If I can't get him to that point in the next couple of weeks or so, it's never going to happen," Andrel replied.

"What's the chance we can do something about the way he's barricading himself—or even help him get some of his power under his own control?"

He pondered her question while the fire crackled beside him. "Why don't you ask your Companions? He may be able to barricade against you, but I doubt he can do much against Yfandes."

She pressed her hand to her eyes and shook her head. "Gods, why in hell didn't I think of that?" And at the same time, Mindsent *:Kellan?:* knowing that Jaysen was doing the same with Felar.

:Here,: came the reply, immediately.

She sent their dilemma in a complicated thought-burst, and waited while Kellan digested the information, and possibly conferred with Felar and Yfandes.

:Yfandes says that the bonding is weak,: came the reply, flavored with the acid tang of concern. *:It fades in*

and out—and it hurts the boy, sometimes, to speak with her.:

:*Can we do anything about that?:* Jaysen fell into the rapport, and if there was anything other than genuine distress there on Vanyel's behalf, Savil couldn't feel it. Through him, she could Hear Felar.

:*Physical contact,:* Felar said shortly.

Kellan agreed. :*As much as possible. That is what strengthens the bonding; now she cannot help him to get control of what he does.:*

:*And if the bond is strengthened?:* Jaysen asked.

:*Perhaps,:* said Felar.

:*A hope,:* added Kellan.

Jaysen looked into Savil's eyes from across the room, and nodded, a little grimly. At this point they would accept even a hope, however tenuous.

Nothing hurt much, now, not since he'd drunk that fiery stuff the red-haired Healer had given him. Those places inside him, the mind-things, that had burned so— they still burned, but remotely, as if the hurting belonged to somebody else. He couldn't concentrate on much of anything for very long, and none of it really seemed to matter.

Only the empty place in him was pretty much the same; only that continued to ache in a way the Healer's potions couldn't seem to touch. The place where Tylendel had been—and now—

But the potions let him sleep, a sleep without dreams. And he'd had the snow-dreams again—that was what had thrown him into that fit.

Oh, gods—he'd thought—he'd thought they'd never come again. He'd thought 'Lendel had driven them away.

But they weren't the dreams about being walled in by ice, so maybe 'Lendel had—

Maybe not. He couldn't tell. It was the other dream, anyway. Clear, vivid as no other dream he'd dreamed had ever been, and much more detailed than the last time he'd had it.

He'd been in a canyon, a narrow mountain pass with walls that were peculiarly smooth. He'd known, in the dream, that this was no real pass—that this passage had been *created,* cut armlength by armlength, by magic.

He'd known, too, that the magic had been wrong, skewed. It had an aura of pain and death about it, as if every thumblength of that canyon had been paid for in spilled blood.

It had been night; cloudy, with a smell of snow on the wind. Where he stood the canyon had narrowed momentarily, choked by avalanches on either side. He'd been very cold, despite the heavy weight of a fur cloak on his shoulders; his feet had been like blocks of the ice that edged the canyon walls.

He had felt a feeling of grim satisfaction, when he'd seen that at this one point the passage was wide enough for two men, but no more. And he knew that *he* had somehow caused those blockages, to create a place where one man could, conceivably, hold off an army.

Because an army was what was coming down that canyon.

He'd sent for help, sent Yfandes and Tylendel—

Tylendel? But Tylendel was dead—

—but he'd also known that help was unlikely to arrive in time.

He had waited until they were almost on him, suspecting nothing, and knowing that they could not see him yet because he willed it so. Then he had raised his right hand high over his head, and a mage-light had flared on it; so bright that the front ranks of that terrible army winced back, and their shadows fell black as the heart of night on the snow behind them. He had said nothing; nothing needed to be said. He barred the way; that was all the challenge required.

They were heavily armored, those fighters; armor of some dull, black stuff, and helms of the same. They carried the weight of that armor as easily as Vanyel wore his own white fur cloak. They bore unornamented round shields, again of the same dull, black material, and carried long broadswords. For the rest, what could be seen of their clothing under the armor and their cloaks over it, they were a motley lot. But they *moved* with a kind of sensitivity to the presence of the next-in-line that had told

Vanyel in the dream that they had been drilled together
by a hand more merciless than ever Jervis had been.

They stared at him, and none of them moved for a very
long time—

Until the front ranks parted, and the wizard stepped
through.

Wizard he was, and no doubt; Vanyel could feel the
Power heavy within him. But it was Power of the same
kind as that which had cut this canyon; paid for in agony.
And when it was gone, there would be no more until the
wizard could torture and kill again. Vanyel had all the
power of life itself behind him; the power of the sleeping
earth, of the living forest—

He spread his arms, and the life-energy flowed from
him, creating a barricade across the valley—

—*like the barricade across his heart*—

—and a shield behind which he could shelter. He faced
the wizard, head held high, defiance in the slightest
movement, daring him to try and pass.

But the ranks of the fighters parted again, and the first
wizard was joined by a second, and a third. And Vanyel
felt his heart sinking, seeing his own death sentence written in those three-to-one odds.

Still, he had stood his ground—

Until Mardic touched his mind.

It had *hurt,* that touch; salt on raw flesh. He'd inter-
preted it as an attack of the wizards, and had struck back,
struck to kill, and only as he'd made his strike had realized that—

—*a dream, oh, gods—it's a dream, it isn't real, and
that's Mardic—*

And had tried to pull the blow; *had* pulled the blow,
but that sent the aborted power coursing back down
places that burned in agony when it touched them. And
he'd tried to stop the flow, but that had only twisted things
up inside him, until he was a thrashing knot of anguish
and he didn't know where he was or what he was doing.
It all hurt, everything hurt, everything burned, and he
was trapped in the pain, in the torment, crying out and
knowing no one could hear him, and lost—he couldn't

feel his body anymore, couldn't hear or see; he was foundering in a sea of agony—

Then a shock—like being struck—

He found himself gasping for breath, frozen to his
teeth, but back in a normal body that hurt in a normal
way.

Then he had blacked out for a moment; came to with
the Healer shaking him, talking to him.

He was soaking wet, and shivering.

Mardic? What about Mardic?

The Herald Jaysen was holding him upright, more than
half supporting him—

*Tylendel, dead, crumpled at Jaysen's feet. My fault,
oh, gods, my fault—*

The grieving came down on him, full force; but somewhere at the back of his mind he *knew* that *they* were
feeling what *he* was feeling and he clamped down on it—
closed that line off—

In the stunned, mental silence he heard Jaysen's anguished thoughts, as clearly and intimately as if he was
speaking them into Vanyel's ear.

*:Gods—oh, gods, I didn't know, I didn't guess—I
thought he was playing with the boy, I thought he was—
oh, gods, what have I done?:*

He shuddered away from the unwanted sympathy, from
the mind-words that were like acid in his wounds, and
blocked *that* line just as ruthlessly.

Then had come the potions—and the numbness. The
blessed *unfeeling*. He drifted, nothing to hold him, not
even his worry for Mardic. It was pitchy dark, they hadn't
left a single flame in the room, which under the circumstances was probably wise. Scraps of what he now knew
were thoughts drifted over to him; now Savil's mind-
voice, now Jaysen's (dark with guilt, and Vanyel wondered why), now Mardic's.

If he had been on his feet, he would have staggered
with relief at hearing that last. *I didn't kill him—thank
the gods, I didn't kill him.*

He drifted farther, until he couldn't hear anything anymore. Until he lost even his own thoughts. Until there

was nothing left but sleep, and the sorrow that never, ever left him.

Savil stood beside the garden door with one hand on the frame, and prayed. She didn't pray often; most Heralds didn't. Praying usually meant asking for something—and the kind of person that became a Herald tended to be the kind that didn't look outside of himself for help until the last hope had been exhausted.

For Savil, at least, it had gotten to that point.

Just beyond the window, bundled in quilts and blankets and half-lying against Yfandes' side, Vanyel dozed in the sun, still kept in a sleepy half-daze by Andrel's potions. Jaysen had carried him out there, with his own mind so tightly shielded against leaking his thoughts that Savil fair Saw him quivering under the strain. Jaysen would be back for the boy in another two candlemarks, which was all Andrel would allow in this cold. This was the third day of the routine; there had been no real repetition of the crisis that had precipitated it, but Savil more than half expected one every night.

Vanyel sighed in sleep, and one arm stole out of the blankets to circle around Yfandes' neck. The Companion nuzzled his ear, and instead of pulling away, he cuddled *closer* to her.

But before Savil had a chance to really take in this first, positive sign that the Herald-Companion bond was taking root in the boy, someone *pounded* on her outer door. She half-turned, and heard Donni pattering across the common room to answer it. There was a murmur too indistinct to make out.

The voice from outside the door strengthened. "Please, I'm Van's sister—let me at least talk to my aunt—"

Savil started, and strode quickly across Vanyel's room, pulling open the door. There could only be one of Vanyel's sisters likely to show up on her doorstep at this point, the one that had fostered out in hopes of a career in the Guard.

"Let her in, Donni," Savil said—and blinked in surprise. The girl in the doorway could have been herself at seventeen or eighteen.

God help her—no wonder she went for the Guard, Savil thought irrelevantly. *She's got that damned Ashkevron nose.*

Evidently the same thought was running through the girl's mind. "You must be my Aunt Savil," she said forthrightly, standing at what was almost "attention" in the doorway. "You have the nose. I'm Lissa. Can I help?"

Savil decided that she liked this blunt girl. "Perhaps, I don't know yet," she replied. "First, Lissa, come in and tell me what you've heard."

Lissa turned away from the garden door with a shudder. "He looks like he's been dragged through the nine hells facedown," she said.

"And at that he looks better than he did three days ago," Savil replied. She would have said more, but there was another pounding on the suite door and a voice she knew only too well rumbled angrily when Donni answered it.

"Like bloody hell she's too busy," Lord Withen Ashkevron snarled. "I didn't bloody ride my best horse to foundering to be put off with a 'too damned busy!' Now where in hell is she?"

Savil, with Lissa at her side, strode across to the door, flung it open, and stood facing Withen with her back poker-straight, feet slightly apart, arms crossed over her chest.

"What do you want, Withen?" she asked flatly, narrowing her eyes in mingled annoyance and apprehension.

"What the hell do you think I want?" he growled, ignoring Lissa and Donni as if they weren't there, placing his fists on his hips, and taking an aggressive, widelegged stance. "I want to know what the hell you've been doing with the boy I sent you! I sent him down here for you to make a *man* out of him, not turn him into a perverted little catamite!" His face darkened and his voice rose with every word. "I—"

"*I* think that's more than enough, Withen," she snapped, cutting him off before he could build up to whatever climax he had in mind. "I, I, I—dammit, you blustering peabrain, is *that* all you ever think of? Yourself? Vanyel almost *died* four days ago, he almost died *again* three days ago, and he could die *or* go mad in the next candlemark, and all *you* can think of is that he did something your back-country prejudices don't approve of! Gods above and below, you can't even call him by his bloody name, just 'the boy'!''

She advanced on him with such anger in her face that he actually fell back a pace, alarm and surprise chasing themselves across his eyes. Lissa moved with her, and stood beside her with every muscle tensed, and her fists clenched into hard knots.

"You come storming in here when we've maybe—*maybe*—got him stable, without so much as a 'please' or a 'may I,' you don't even ask if he's in any shape to put two words together in a sensible fashion! Oh, no, all *you* can do is scream that *I've* made him into a catamite when you sent him to be made into a man. A *man!*" She laughed, a harsh cawing sound that clawed its way up out of her throat. "My *gods*—what the hell did you think he was? Tell me, Withen, what kind of a *man* would send his son into strange hands just because the poor thing didn't happen to fit his image of masculinity?''

Savil ran out of things to say—but Lissa hadn't.

"What kind of a *man* would let a brutal bully break his son's arm for *no damned reason?*" the girl snarled. "What kind of a *man* would drive his son into becoming an emotional eunuch because every damned time the boy looked for a little bit of paternal love he got slapped in the face? What kind of a *man* would take *anyone's* word over his son's with *no cause* to *ever* think the boy was a liar?'' Lissa faced down her father as if he had become her enemy. "You tell *me*, Father! What right do you have to demand *anything* of him? What did you ever give him but scorn? When did you *ever* give him a single thing he really needed or wanted? When did you ever tell him he'd done well? When did you *ever* say you loved him?''

Withen backed up another two paces, his back against the wall beside the door, his expression that of someone who has just been poleaxed.

Savil found her tongue again. "A *man*—may all the

gods give you what you deserve, you fathead! *What kind of a man would care more for his own reputation than his son's life?''* She was backing him into the corner now, unleashing on Withen all the pain and frustration and anger she'd been keeping bottled up inside her over the past week. He had gone pale—and started to try to say something, but she cut him off.

"Let me tell you this, Withen," she hissed. "Everything that Vanyel's become, *you* had a hand in making—and mostly because *you* didn't want a son, you just wanted a little toy copy of yourself to parade around so that people could congratulate you on your bedroom prowess. You helped make him what he is—gave him a set of values so distorted it's a wonder he even recognized love when he saw it, and taught him that he had to keep everything he felt secret because adults couldn't be trusted. And *now* I have one boy dead, and one a hair from dying, and all you care about is that somebody *might* think you weren't *manly* enough to father *manly* sons! Oh, get out of here, get out of my sight—"

She turned away from him before he could see the tears in her eyes. Lissa put a steadying hand on her shoulder and glared at her father as if she would be perfectly happy to take a piece out of him if he said one wrong word.

"S-s-savil—I—I—" he stammered. "They said—but I didn't believe—is Vanyel—"

"One wrong word, one wrong move, and he will die, Withen," she said flatly, her eyes shut tightly as she reestablished control over herself. "One wrong *thought* almost killed him. He slit his wrists because he discovered that someone he trusted believed that his *love* was the reason Tylendel died. Are you pleased with what you made? It was certainly the *honorable* thing for him to do, wasn't it?"

"I—I—"

"I am very gratified to be able to tell you that he *isn't* yours anymore, Withen, he's mine. He's been Chosen—if he lives that long, he'll be a Herald-trainee, and as such, he is *my* charge. You've forfeited any claim on him. So you can have what you've always wanted—little Mekeal can be your heir-designate, and you can wash your hands of Vanyel with a clear conscience.''

Withen flinched at her pitilessly accurate words, and seemed to almost shrink in size.

"Savil—I didn't mean—I didn't want—"

"You didn't?" She raised an ironic eyebrow.

He winced. "Savil, can I—see him? I won't hurt him, I—dammit, he's still my son!''

"Lissa, do you think we should?"

Lissa looked at her father as one looks at a not-particularly-trustworthy stranger. "I don't know that he can behave himself.''

Withen's face darkened. "You ungrateful little—"

Lissa shrugged, and said to Savil, "See what I mean?"

Savil nodded. "I see—but he has a point. Maybe he ought to see his handiwork." She nodded toward the door to Vanyel's room. "Follow me, Withen. And keep a rein on that mouth of yours, or I'll have you thrown out.''

He stopped dead at the garden door, and pressed his hands and face against the glass in stunned disbelief. "My *gods*—" he gasped. "They said—but I didn't believe them. Savil, I've seen men dead a week that looked better than that!''

Lissa snorted. Savil pushed him away from the door impatiently, and opened it, flinching a bit as the cold air hit her. She looked back at him; he'd made no move to follow. "Are you coming, or not?" she asked, keeping her voice low so as not to startle Vanyel.

He swallowed, his own face set and very white, and followed her with slow, hesitant steps. She walked quickly to the patch of sheltered, sun-gilded brown grass where the boy was lying with Yfandes; he hadn't moved since she'd left. He didn't seem to notice she was there as she knelt in the harsh, dry grass that prickled her knees through the cloth of her breeches and hose.

"Van—Van, wake up a little, can you?" she said softly, not touching him at all, either with hand or mind. "Van?"

He moved his head a little, and blinked in a kind of half-dazed parody of sleepiness. "A-aunt?" he murmured.

"Your father's here—Withen—he wants to see you. Vanyel, he can't take you home, he has no power over you now that you're Chosen. You don't have to see him if you don't want to."

Vanyel blinked again, showing a little more alertness. "N-no. S'all right. 'Fandes says s'all right; says I should."

Savil rose quickly and returned to where Withen waited uncertainly on the worn path, halfway between the door and where the boy lay. "Go ahead," she said roughly. "Don't raise your voice, and speak slowly. We've got him pretty heavily drugged, so keep that in mind. You might trigger more than you want to hear if you aren't careful."

She followed a few steps behind him, with Lissa behind her, and remained within earshot as he knelt heavily in the dry grass and started to reach out to touch Vanyel's shoulder. She very nearly snapped at him, but Vanyel roused a bit more, and waved the blunt fingers away.

"Vanyel—" the man said, seeming at a complete loss for words. "Vanyel, I—I heard you were sick—"

Vanyel gave a pitiful little croak of a laugh. "You h-heard I was playin' ewe t' 'Lendel's ram, y'mean. Don' lie t' me, Father. You lied t' me all m'life an' I couldn' prove it, but I *know* when people lie t'me now."

Withen flushed, but Vanyel wasn't through yet.

"Y're thinkin' now that—I—I'm perv'rt'd, unclean or somethin', an' that I—I'm just bad an' ungrateful an' I n-never p-p-pleased you an'—*dammit*, all I ev' wanted was f'r you t' tell me I did *somethin'* right! Just *once*, Father, j-j-just one time! An' all *you* ever d-d-did was let J-J-Jervis knock me flat, an' then kick me y'rself! 'Lendel *loved* me, an' I loved *him* an' you can *stop* thinkin' those—god—damned—*rotten—things*—"

Withen pulled back and started to his feet—opened his mouth like he was about to roar at his son—

But that was as far as he got. Vanyel's eyes blazed; his face went masklike with rage. And before Withen could utter a single syllable, Vanyel surged up out of his cocoon of blankets and knocked Withen head over heels into the bushes with the untrained, half-drugged power of his mind alone.

Withen struggled up. Vanyel knocked him flat. Lissa made as if to go to one or the other of them, but Savil caught her arm.

"Look at Yfandes," she said. "She's calm, she hasn't even moved. Let them have this out. Between us I think Yfandes and I could keep the lad from killing his father, but that isn't what he wants to do."

Twice more Withen tried to get his feet, and twice more Vanyel flung him back. He was crying now, silent, unnoticed tears streaking his white cheeks. "How's it *feel*, Father? Am I *strong* enough now? How's it *feel* t' get knocked down an' stepped on by somethin' you can't reason with an' can't fight? You *happy?* I'm as big a bully as J-J-Jervis now—*does that make you bloody happy?*"

Withen's mouth worked, but no sound came out of it.

Vanyel stared at him, then the angry light faded from his eyes and was replaced by a disgusted bitterness. "It doesn't make *me* happy, Father," he said, quietly, and clearly; the last of the drug-haze gone from his speech. "Knowing I can do this to you just makes me sick. *Nothing* makes me happy anymore. Nothing ever will again."

He sank back down to the ground, pulled his blankets around himself, and turned his face into Yfandes' shoulder. "Go away, Father," he said, voice muffled. "Just go away."

Withen got slowly and awkwardly to his feet. He stood; shaken and pale, looking down at his son for a long time.

"Would it make any difference if I said I was sorry?" he asked, finally; from the bewildered expression on his face, acutely troubled—and more than that, vaguely aware that he had just had his entire world knocked head-over-heels, and was entirely uncertain of what to do or say or even *be* next.

"Maybe—someday," came the voice, thickened with tears. "Not now. Go *away*, Father. Please—leave me alone."

Dear Withen: I think you are right for once in your life. The boy is not a boy anymore. He never was *the boy you*

*thought he was. If you can adapt yourself to treating him
as an adult and an acquaintance rather than your offspring,
I think you can come to some kind of a reconciliation
with him eventually.*

"Savil?"

Savil looked up. Mardic peeked around Savil's half-
open door, uncertainty in his very posture.

Huh. I'm getting better at reading people.

She gave a quick glance out her window. Vanyel was
sitting on the bench just outside it, talking with Lissa,
Yfandes hovering over both of them.

Bless the child; I don't know what I'd do without her.

For a moment she forgot Mardic; a terrible weariness
bowed down her shoulders like a too-heavy cloak.

*Gods. What am I going to do? He's not getting better,
just a little stronger. He keeps trying to make me or Liss
into a substitute for 'Lendel, into someone else to follow.
I can't let him do that. It'll just make things ultimately
worse. But when we try and push him into standing on
his own feet, he goes into a sulk.* She sighed. *It makes
me so angry at him that I want to slap him into next week.
And he's had too much of* that *already. He doesn't really
deserve it, either. Hellfires, those sulks are the closest
he's ever gotten to* normal *behavior! Oh, gods—*

Mardic cleared his throat, and she jumped. "I'm sorry,
lad, I'm woolgathering. Must be getting old. Come on
in."

He edged into the room, crabwise. "Savil, Donni and
I want to ask you something," he faltered, hands behind
his back, rubbing his left foot against his right ankle.
"We—Savil, you're the best there is, but—Vanyel needs
you more than we do."

"Gods," she sighed, rubbing her right temple. "I have
been shorting you two—I am sorry—"

"No, really, we don't mind," Donni interrupted, poking her curly head past the edge of the door just behind
Mardic's shoulder.

"I was wondering when you'd put in your silver-
worth," Savil replied.

"We *do* come as a set," she pointed out. "No, Savil,
you haven't been shorting us. It's more that we're afraid

you're going to split yourself in half, trying to do too many things. *Vanyel* needs you; we've finally *got* what we needed from you—there wasn't anybody else likely to be able to teach us to work in concert, but look—''

Mardic moved farther into the room; Donni stayed by the door. They reached out to one another, arms extended, and hands not *quite* touching, and—

Where there had been two auras there was now one; a golden-green flow over and around them that was seamless—and considerably *more* than either aura had been alone. Savil blinked in surprise. ''Just when did you two start to do that?'' she asked.

''The night—when we had to get the Temple open,'' Mardic supplied. ''When we had to get the arrow up, and then even more when we meshed in the Healing-meld. That's when what you'd been showing us sort of fell into place. So, well, now any Herald-Mage could teach us, and really, given what we do together, it probably ought to be Jaysen, or Lancir. But Jaysen hasn't got anyone right now.''

''Piffle. You'd make a three-hour tale of a limerick,'' Donni sniffed. ''Savil, we asked Jaysen; he said he'd take us if you allow it.''

Savil put down her pen, and closed her gaping mouth. ''I think I may kiss you both,'' she replied, as Donni gave Mardic an ''I told you so'' grin. ''I was trying to think of a way to get you another mentor and coming up blank because I'm the only one who knows how to teach concert work. Bless you, loves.''

She rose and took both of them in her arms; they returned the embrace, their support as much mental as physical.

''Savil,'' Donni said quietly, as she released them with real reluctance. ''What are you going to do with Vanyel? He's—he's still so broken—and everything here has just *got* to keep reminding him of 'Lendel. It's too bad you can't take him somewhere really different.''

''Gods, that's only too true,'' she replied.

—really different—gods—oh, gods, thank you for bright little proteges!

''Donni,'' she said slowly, ''I think you may just have

found my answer for me. Now I'm even more grateful to you for finding yourselves a new teacher.''

''You've got an idea?''

Savil nodded. ''And kill two birds with one stone. Those things the Leshara had brought in—they *had* to be from the Pelagirs, just like what 'Lendel conjured in retribution. I'd have had to go out there anyway, to find out who's been tampering. So—what I'm going to do is take Vanyel there to some friends of mine, the Hawkbrothers. They're self-appointed guardians of the Pelagirs, so they should be told if there's been a mage tampering with their creatures. And they follow a different discipline; maybe they can help Van. And if they can't, I know they can at least contain him.''

''But you really think they can help him?'' Donni asked hopefully.

''Well, *I* can't; I know for a fact that Starwind is better than I am. Besides, if we keep Van drugged much longer, Andrel is afraid he'll become addicted, but if we take him off—''

''He could wreck the Palace.'' Mardic nodded solemnly. ''When are you taking him?''

''When—within the next few days, I think. The sooner the better.'' She looked over his head, to the Wingsister talisman on her wall. ''The only problem is that to find Starwind k'Treva and Moondance k'Treva I'll have to go to *them*—because they don't *ever* come out of the Pelagirs. That means two things. I'll have to build a Gate, and I'll have to hope that I still know *how* to find them.''

Eleven

"**G**ods, I *hate* Gating," Savil muttered to Andrel, squinting against the glare of sun on snow as she scanned the sky for even a hint of cloud.

"Why? Other than the recent rotten associations—"

"It's damned dangerous at the best of times. It plays fast and loose with local weather systems, for one thing; it's a spell that sets up a local energy field, a kind that disrupts any kind of high-energy weather pattern that's around it. Usually for the worse." She closed her eyes, centered and grounded, and extended her Mage-Gift sense up and out, looking farther afield for anything that *might* move in while she had the Gate up. To her vast relief there didn't seem to be anything of consequence anywhere nearby; the only energy-patterns she could read were a few rising air currents over warm spots, too small to be any hazard.

She sighed. "Well, the weather's not going to cause any problems. How was the lad?"

"Drugged to his teeth, and I would stake my arm that he won't be able to count to one before some time tonight. And I am damned glad you told me that you were planning on Gating out of here." Andrel tucked his long, sensitive hands inside his cloak, and peered across the open Field through the sunlight. "Since it was Gate-energy that blew his channels open—"

"Probably," Savil interrupted.

"All right, *probably* blew his channels open—he's going to be doubly sensitive to it for the rest of his life. He'll likely know when someone's opening a Gate within

257

a league of him. And actually going through one *may* touch off another fit. Which is why—''

''—you drugged him to the teeth. I have no objection; it's a little awkward, but that's why we have the kind of saddles for our Companions that we do.''

They crunched their way across Companion's Field, now covered with the first snowfall of the season. Savil repeated a quieting exercise for every step she made, for she knew she needed to establish absolute calm within herself; she would be Gating to her absolute physical limits (in terms of the distance she planned to cover) and that would take every reserve she had.

In light of that, she had turned everything (other than establishing the Gate itself) over to the hands of others. Mardic and Donni had done all her packing, Lissa had taken care of Vanyel's, and Lissa had taken charge of the boy once Andrel was finished with him. They were all waiting at the Grove Temple at this very moment.

''So why else don't you like Gating?'' Andrel asked, while the Field around them glowed under the sun.

''Because when I get there, I'm going to be pretty damned worthless,'' she replied dryly, ''And I'd better hope the Talisman performs the way Starwind claimed it was supposed to, or we'll be a pretty pathetically helpless pair, Vanyel and I.''

''Why don't you do what Tylendel did, use someone else's energy?''

''Because I don't really know what he did,'' she said, after a long pause that was punctuated only by the sound of their footsteps breaking through the light crust of snow. ''None of us do. That may be why we ended up feeding the energy back through poor Van instead of grounding and dissipating it. I personally do not care to take the chance of doing that to another living soul and neither do any of the others. Vanyel lived through it; someone else might not. And it may well be that you have to have a lifebound pair to carry it off at all. So,'' she shrugged, ''we do this the hard way, and I fall on my nose on the other side.''

They entered the Grove, the leafless trees making a lacework of dark branches against the bright blue sky.

The peace of the Grove never left it, no matter what the season was. That was one reason why Savil had chosen to set up the Gate here. The other was that it was the safest place on the Palace grounds that she could put a Gate; no one but Heralds ever came here without invitation. There should be no accidents caused by a stranger wandering by at the wrong moment.

The group waiting by the Temple, which looked today as if it had been newly-made of the same pure snow that covered the ground around it, was a small one. Jaysen, Donni and Mardic, and Lissa. There were only two Companions there; Kellan and Yfandes. Companions tended to avoid the Grove except when a Herald died. Vanyel was slumped over in Yfandes' saddle, wrapped in the warmest cloak Savil could find and strapped down securely enough that his Companion could fight or flee without losing him.

Avert— Savil thought, a little superstitiously. *Let there be no reason for her to* have *to fight. We've had enough bad fortune without that.*

She went first to his side; his hands had been loosely tied together at the wrist and the bindings were hooked over the pommel of the saddle. The stirrup-irons were gone, probably stored in one of the packs bundled behind his saddle; the stirrup-leathers had been turned into straps binding his calves to the saddle itself. He was belted twice at the waist; once to the pommel, once to the high cantle, using rings on the saddle meant for exactly that purpose. He was *not* going to come off.

Andrel reached her side; he reached up and pried open one of Vanyel's eyelids. The boy didn't react at all, and his pupils were mere pinpoints. The Healer's eye unfocused for a moment as he "read" the boy; then he nodded with satisfaction.

"He should be all right, Savil. No more drugs, though, after this. Not even if those friends of yours—"

Savil shook her head. "They don't like this kind of drug. Not for any reason. Drugs like you've been giving him are too easy to abuse."

"I don't like them either, but there are times you've got no other choice, and this was one of them." Andrel touched the boy's hand; his green eyes darkened as he brooded for a moment. "Gods. I hope you're right about these people. His channels haven't healed at all, not really."

"If they can't help us, no one can." Savil turned her back on her semi-conscious charge and faced the door of the Temple, and put herself into the right mindset to invoke her spell.

To build a Gate—

It was the most personal of spells. Only one person could build a Gate, because only one mind could direct the energy needed to build it. The spell-wielder had to have a very exact notion of *where* the Gate was to exit, and no two people ever had precisely the same mental image of a place. In any event, only Savil had ever been in the k'Treva territory of the Pelagirs. She couldn't be "fed" by another Herald-Mage, since she would need every bit of her attention for the Gate itself and would have none to spare to channel incoming energy. Lastly, because the energy had to be so intimately directed, it could come from only one place—

From *within* the builder of the Gate. Or—perhaps—one soul-bound to the builder of the Gate? A lifebond was at such a deep level that it wasn't conscious, so perhaps that was why Tylendel had succeeded in using Vanyel as his source of energy.

The kind of power needed to build a Gate was the kind that *could* be stored, could be planned for. But like a vessel that could only hold so much liquid, a mage could only hold so much energy within himself. Savil had prepared for this; she could replenish herself within a day when the spell was completed and the Gate dismissed. But for that critical period of twenty-four candlemarks she would be exhausted—physically, mentally, and magically.

No time to think of that. Get to it, woman. First, the Portal, then the Weaving.

The Temple door had been used so many times before as one end of a Gate that it needed no special preparation. She needed only to—reach—

She raised her hands, closed her eyes, and centered

herself so exactly that everything about her vanished from her attention. There was only the power within her, and the place where the Gate would begin.

I call upon the Portal—

She molded the power into a frame upon the physical frame of the doorway; building it layer upon layer until it was strong enough to act as an anchor to hold *this* place when she warped space back upon itself.

Then she began spinning out threads of energy from the framework; they drifted outward, seeking.

This is the place, she told them, silently willing them to find the real-world counterpart of the image in her mind. *Where the rocks are* so *and the trees grow* thus *and the feel of the earth is in* this *manner—*

They spun out, longer, finer, more attenuated. When they weakened, she fed them from within herself, spinning her own substance out and feeling it drawn out of her.

Now she was losing strength; it felt exactly as if she were bleeding from an open wound. And the power was not merely draining from her anymore, it was being *pulled* from her by the Gate itself. This was the point of greatest danger for a Herald-Mage; she was having to fight the Gate to keep from being drained right down to unconsciousness.

Then one of those questing power-threads caught on something, out beyond the farthest range of her sensing; another followed—

There was a silent explosion of light that she could see even through her closed lids, and the Gate Wove itself in an instant into a temporary, but stable, whole.

She dropped her hands, opened her eyes, and swayed with uttermost exhaustion; Kellan was there beside her in time for her to catch the pommel of her saddle to keep from falling.

The door of the Temple was no longer within the door-frame. Instead, the white marble—glowing now, even in the bright sunlight—framed a strange and twisted bit of landscape.

"*That's* where you're going?" Jaysen said doubtfully, looking at the weird shapes of rock, snow and sand that

!ay beyond the portal. It was snowing there, from black, lowering clouds; fat flakes drifting down through still, dark air. Savil nodded.

"That's it; that's the edge of the Pelagirs near Starwind's territory. The other end is a cave entrance, so we'll have some shelter on the other side until Starwind and Moondance get there."

"And if they don't?" Jaysen asked. "Savil, I don't like to think of you two alone out in a place like that. The boy is next to useless, and you're exhausted."

"Jays, it's quite possible that they'd take one look at you and kill you if they didn't see me right there with you," she said, clinging to the saddle and trying to muster enough strength to climb into it. "They're unbelievably territorial and secretive, and for good reasons—think for a minute, will you? They *have* to have known someone was tampering, stealing creatures they thought safely locked up. If they see a stranger and Sense he's Mage-Gifted, they're likely to strike first and ask questions of the corpse. And I mean that literally. I'm taking enough risk bringing the boy in, and he's plainly in need of help, and branded as *mine.*"

She gave up trying to be self-sufficient. "Boost me up, will you?" she asked humbly.

Jaysen went her one better; with the help of Andrel he *lifted* her into place. "Have you got everything you need?"

"I think so." In actual fact, she was too tired to think; it was all she could do to keep her mind on the next step of the journey. "Toss the firewood through."

Four heavy bundles of dry, seasoned wood went through the Gate to land in the snow on the other side.

Vanyel whimpered beside her; she could see his face was creased with lines of pain. *He's feeling it, like Andy thought he might. Better hurry.*

"Mardic—" she said quietly. "Donni—"

Savil's proteges came solemnly to her stirrup; she held out her hands to them, and shared a moment of mind-melded intimacy with them that was more than "farewell"; it was a sharing of gifts. Her pride in them and love and blessing—and their love and well-wishing for her.

"Lissa—"

The girl came to stand beside her students.

"I can't begin to thank you," Savil began, awkward, as ever, with words.

"Thank me by bringing Van home well," Lissa replied earnestly. "That's all I want." She reached up and squeezed Savil's hand once, then backed away.

The youngsters moved out of the way, and Jaysen and Andrel came to take their place without any prompting. She gave a hand to each, closing her eyes again, and opening herself to them in a melding even more intimate than she had shared with her students, for there were no secrets among the three of them, and nothing held back. What she had not told Mardic and Donni was that there might be no returning from this journey. If she failed with Vanyel, he might well destroy both of them, his Gifts were that powerful. Even now he moaned again in his drug-induced slumber, feeling the Gate energies despite a dose of narcotic that would have rendered a less sensitive Gifted unconscious for a week.

For a moment, she was angry. *He could kill us, and do it without knowing what he was doing. Oh, gods. Gods, you* owe *him, dammit! You've taken his love—at the least give him something in return.*

But she was too tired, too depleted to sustain even her anger at Fate or the gods or—whatever. Especially when this might *really* be farewell.

So this was a moment when she asked forgiveness of her friends for anything she might have done in the past— and they asked for and received the same from her.

When she raised her heavy, weary head, the two pairs of eyes, green and gray, that met hers were bright with tears that would not be shed—at least not now. She squeezed their hands, and let go; they stepped away from her as she straightened in her saddle, took a deep breath, and faced the Gate and the gray landscape beyond it. It looked no more welcoming now than it had before, and dallying wasn't going to make the leaving easier.

:All right, Kellan,: she Mindspoke. *:Let's go.:*

And they rode into the stomach-churning vertigo she had come to hate.

Savil huddled beside the fire with her legs curled under her, forcing herself to stay awake. There was, thank the gods, no wind; the cave was warming fairly quickly. It smelled of damp, though, and of the musty taint of the half-rotten leaves that had blown in here with the autumn winds. That damp meant that if she let the fire die, it would chill down very quickly, a chill that would penetrate even their thick wool cloaks.

Once she'd taken the Gate down, she'd had just enough strength to lay the fire, and start it with the coal she'd brought in a fire-safe. After that she'd sunk to the sand next to it, pulling Vanyel close in beside her. He was curled up against her now, bundled with her inside her cloak, his head in her lap; he shook like a reed in the wind. From time to time he moaned and his hand groped for something that seemed to elude him; she soothed him back into sleep, stroking his hair until he finally recognized that she was still with him and calmed a little.

The Gate-crossing had been hard on him, as hard as she'd feared. When she'd gone to take him from Yfandes' back, he'd been half-roused out of his drugged daze; his eyes had been wide open, his jaws clenched. He had been held paralyzed, not by the drugs, but by unfocused and overwhelming terror and pain. It had taken a candlemark to get him soothed down again.

Somewhere just outside were Kellan and Yfandes, standing a watchful guard in the falling snow. Still in their tack, poor things—she'd barely been able to get Vanyel unstrapped from the saddle before collapsing beside him. She had nearly forgotten to activate the Wingsister Talisman. It had taken Kellan's sharp reminder to shake her out of her fog of exhaustion long enough to stab her finger and let the prescribed three drops of her blood fall on it.

Memory came, then, as sharply defined as if she had bid farewell to the Hawkbrothers scant days ago instead of years.

* * *

"Blood calls to blood, and heart to heart," Starwind told her gravely, his ice-blue eyes focused inward. He held his slashed palm above the Wingsister Talisman of silver wire and crystals, and his blood dripped onto the heart-stone of the piece, dyeing the clear crystal a vivid ruby.

Savil watched, silently, feeling the power flowing and weaving itself into the intricate design of rainbow crystal and silver wire.

This was nothing like the kind of magic she was used to using; it really wasn't much like that the Hawkbrothers had taught her, either. This was older magic, much older, dating, perhaps, from the times of the Mage Wars, the wars that had wrecked the world and left the Pelagirs a twisted, magic-riddled ruin. She shivered a little, and Starwind looked up, one of his brief and infrequent smiles lighting his face for a moment.

He closed his hand; Moondance touched the back of it, and he opened it again. The slash in his palm had been Healed with the speed of a thought. At eighteen the young outlander now calling himself "Moondance" was well on his way to becoming that rarest of mages, a Healer-Adept.

Starwind fixed the Talisman in its place on the mask of feathers and crystal beads; it resembled a palm-sized diadem perched on the brow of the mask above the eye-slits. He handed the whole mask to her, and nodded at the Talisman. "When you need us again, come to us, and let three drops of your own blood fall upon the heart-stone. I shall know, and come to you."

In all those years since, the heart-stone's bright scarlet had not faded. She only hoped that the set-spell had not faded either. It did seem to her that the heart-stone began pulsing with a dim, inner light from the moment that her blood touched it. But that could have been the flickering of the fire, or the wavering of her own vision; she was too spent to tell, and too drained to begin to sense power even if it was moving under her own nose.

Vanyel stirred at her side, curling his knees tighter

against his chest. She shifted a bit, glad that the floor of
the cave was covered in several inches of dry, soft sand.

Poor child, she thought, her mind dark with despair.
*I'm at a loss for what to do with you. You keep reaching
out to me for support, and I want to give it to you, and
I can't, I mustn't. If I do, you'll just fall right back into
the pattern you danced with poor 'Lendel.* She stroked
the fine, silky hair beneath her hand, and her heart ached
for him. *You don't know what to think anymore, do you?
You're afraid to touch again, afraid to open yourself,
you're full of such fear and such pain—gods, when you
told Withen that nothing would ever make you happy
again—*

She swallowed the lump in her throat that threatened
to choke her, and blinked at the dancing flames, then
closed her stinging eyes and felt tears bead up on her
lashes. *Starwind, old friend*, she thought desperately,
*where are you? I'm out of my depth; I don't know what
to do. I need your help—*

:And you have it, sister-of-my-heart.:

She started. There was a swirl of snow at the cave
entrance, white-gold and shadow in the dancing firelight.
There had been no alert from either Companion—

But when the snow settled and cleared, he was there.

He hadn't changed, not at all.

The sword of ice, she had called him when she'd first
seen him. Flowing silver hair still reached past his waist
when he put back the hood of his white cloak and let the
silky mass of it tumble free. There still were no wrinkles
in his face, not even around the obliquely-slanting, ice-
blue eyes; he was still tall and unbent, still slender as a
boy. Only the cool deeps of his eyes showed his age, and
the aura of power that pulsed about him. No mage would
ever have any doubts that this was an Adept, and a powerful one.

He smiled at her, and held out his hands. "Welcome,
heart-sister, Wingsister Savil," he said in the liquid *Tayledras* tongue, gliding to her to take the hands she held
up to him in his own. "Always welcome, and well come
thou art."

"Starwind, *shaydra*," her sight darkened for a moment, and when it cleared, the *Tayledras* Adept was kneeling at her side, holding her upright.

"Savil, you stubborn, headstrong woman," he chided, as she felt an inrushing of energy from his center to hers. She swayed a little, and he held her upright. "What need could possibly have been so great that you drain yourself to a wraith to Gate yourself here?"

"This need—" She pulled back her cloak to show him the boy curled against her side, his face taut with pain.

"God of my fathers—" He reached out with his free hand and barely touched Vanyel's brow. He pulled back his hand as if it had been burned. "Goddess of my mothers! What have you brought me, sister?"

"I don't know," she said, slumping wearily against him. "He's been blasted open, and he can't heal—more than that—I'm too tired to tell you right now. So much has happened, and to both of us—I just can't think what to do anymore. All I know is that he's hurting, and I can't help him, and if I'd left him where he was he'd have destroyed himself at the best, and half the capital at the worst."

"There is nothing wrong with your judgment, I pledge you that," Starwind replied, sitting back on his heels and regarding the boy dubiously. "There is such potential there—he frightens me. And such darkness of the soul—no, Wingsister, not *evil;* there is nothing evil in him. Just—darkness. Despair is a part of it, but—denial of what he is and must become is another. Self-willed darkness; he wills himself not to see, I think."

"You see more than I do," she told him, rubbing her aching forehead. "I haven't the right to ask it of you, but—will you help me with him? *Can* you help me?"

The firelight turned the ice of his eyes to blue-gold flame. "You have the right, sister to brother, to ask what you will of me. Did you not gift me with the greatest of all gifts, in the person of my *shay'kreth'ashke?*"

She had to smile a little at that. Bringing Starwind another boy long ago had been one of the few unalloyed good things she'd ever done. "Where is Moondance, anyway?"

:Moondance stands in the snow, defending his head

*and his lifeblood. Telling the stranger-*lasha'Kaladra *not to eat me,:* came the laughter-flavored reply. *:I frightened her. She does not trust me, I think.:*

:Kellan—: Savil Mindspoke tiredly.

:He popped up right under Yfandes' nose and scared the liver out of her, Chosen,: Kellan replied apologetically. *:She went for him before we knew who it was. It's all right now, he's just making amends.:*

:Bright Havens, Kell, you *know him, at least!:* she snapped, her tiredness making her impatient.

:Not anymore—:

"I fear I have greatly changed, Wingsister," Moondance said contritely from the entrance. "And I also fear I had forgotten the fact."

Savil looked over Starwind's shoulder and felt her mouth gaping. Starwind put one finger beneath her chin, and shut it for her with a chuckle.

"Great good gods!" she said after a moment of stunned silence. "You *have* changed!"

The Moondance she had known—he hadn't had the name "Moondance" for long at that point—had been brown-haired and brown-eyed and as ordinary as a peasant hut. Not surprising for one of peasant stock. But now—now the hair was as long and as silver and the eyes as ice-blue as Starwind's. The lines of his face were still the same; square to Starwind's triangle, but the cheekbones were far more prominent than Savil remembered, and the body had grown out of adolescent gawkiness and into a slender grace so like Starwind's that they could have been brothers by birth instead of by blood.

:He even smells *different,:* Kellan complained.

"How did you *do* that?" Savil demanded.

Moondance made a fluid shrug, and tossed the sides of his white cape over his shoulders, showing that he wore only thin gray breeches and a sleeveless gray leather jerkin with matching boots. Savil shivered at this reminder that the *Tayledras* never seemed to notice the cold. "It's the magic we use," he said. "It makes us into what it wants us to be. I think."

"As always, an oversimplification," Starwind corrected him fondly. *"Ka'sheeleth.* Savil has brought us a problem. Come look at this boy—''

Moondance drifted over to Savil's other side, sat on his heels beside her, and studied Vanyel's face for several breaths.

"Hai'yasha,'' he breathed. *"Shay'a'chern,* hmm? And Lovelost? No, it goes deeper than that.'' He reached out as Starwind had, and touched Vanyel's forehead, but unlike Starwind, did not pull away. *"Ai'she'va*—Holiest Mothers! The *pain!''* His jaw tightened and the pupils of his eyes contracted to pinpoints. "Reft and bereft of *shay'kreth'ashke.''* His face took on the tranquillity of a statue. "Pawn he is now—pawn he has been—'' he said, his tone flat, his voice dropping half an octave. "Pawn to what he is and what he wills not to be. But will or no, the pawn is in play—and the play is a trial—''

"And what of the game?'' Starwind asked in a whisper.

Moondance hesitated, then life came back to his face as he shrugged again, and his pupils went back to normal. "No way of knowing,'' he replied, slowly taking his hand from Vanyel's forehead. "That depends entirely upon whether he is willing to become more than a pawn. But yours to be the Teaching, I think,'' he said, looking up sharply at the Adept. "It is like your powers that he holds. As for Healing, I think that half of it will be his doing—if he Heals at all—''

"And the other half yours,'' the Adept stated with an ironic smile.

Moondance turned Vanyel's wrist up, showing the scar across it—then turned over his own hand, and the firelight picked out the scar that ran from the gold-skinned hand halfway to the elbow, a scar that followed the course of the blue vein pulsing beneath the skin. "Who better?'' he asked. "We have something in common, I think.''

Savil swayed again, caught in a sudden dizziness, and Starwind took hold of her shoulders to steady her. "You need rest,'' he said in concern. "Will you have it here, or can you ride?''

Savil thought longingly of just lying down where she was, and then reflected on being able to do so in a bed.

And also on the Companions, out there in the snow and cold, and still in their harnesses.

"The Companions can and will carry double," she sighed, feeling just about ready to fade away. "If you're willing to ride them. Or strap us in, I don't much care which. But I'd like *them* in the warm."

"Then we ride," Starwind said, as Moondance scooped Vanyel up in his arms as if he weighed next to nothing. The older Adept rose to his feet and offered her his hand, and it took every scrap of will she had left to her to stumble erect. "It is not far, Wingsister."

"I hope not," she told him earnestly, staggering out into the snow, while Moondance put the fire out with a single backward glance. "Because if it isn't, you're going to be carrying me as well as the boy."

First there was darkness, and the peace that came with being so drugged that there was no thought at all. It was the only time he felt anything like peace, these days, and he welcomed the drugs and the red-haired Healer who brought them. There were times without counting when he hoped that *this* time the Healer had miscalculated—that *this* time he wouldn't wake.

Then there was pain; unfocused, but somewhere near at hand. Like the touch of sun on skin already reddened and burned. It got past the drugs, somehow; he tried to push it away, but it continued to throb in those half-healed places in his mind, promising him more pain to come.

Then—nothing *but* pain; fire in his veins and under his skin, flames dancing along his nerves and scorching his mind. Gate-fire, Gate-energy—it was unmistakable, and unbearable, and yet it continued long past the moment he thought his sanity would shatter or his heart stop. He screamed, or thought he did. He was lost in it, and there was no way out—not even death, for the pain would not let him die.

Then it was gone. But it left him aching, all the channels burned raw again, and worse, all the memories replaying themselves over and over—Gala dying, Tylendel throwing himself from the Tower, Tylendel lying in state in the Temple—

Then, without warning, the Dream.

He stood blocking the way, a one-mage barricade across Crook-Back Pass. Mage-light from his upraised hand reflected from the impassive faces and hollow, empty eyes of the three wizards who opposed him.

This was *not* like the old dream—the dream of being alone in the ice. This was—something else. He could sense things, shards of meaning, just under the surface of it, but couldn't seem to bring them out to where he could read them.

But it felt—real. Fearfully real.

"Why do you bother with this nonsense?"

The voice from behind the wizards was sweet, lilting. One more figure paced forward as the ranks of the army backing the wizards parted to let him pass.

"You are quite alone, Herald-Mage Vanyel." One of the wizards stepped two paces to the side to allow the newcomer through to the center, to face Vanyel.

He was beautiful; there was no other word for him. A perfectly sculptured face and body, hair and eyes of twilight shadow, a confidence, poise and power so complete they were works of art.

Except for the dark eyes, he could have been Vanyel's brother; except that he was too perfect, he could almost have been a younger Vanyel.

He was clad in dull black armor, like his soldiers, but carried no weapon. He didn't need one; he was a weapon. He was a weapon with no other purpose than the destruction and death he molded into his power. Unlike the knife which could cut to heal or harm, this weapon would never serve any other purpose than pain. Vanyel knew that as well as he knew himself.

"You are," the beautiful young man repeated; smiling, choosing his words to hurt, "quite alone."

Vanyel nodded. *"You tell me nothing I was not already aware of. I know you. You are Leareth."* The word meant—

"Darkness." Leareth laughed. "I am. Darkness. And these are my servants. A quaint conceit, don't you think?"

Vanyel said nothing. Every moment he kept Leareth

here was one more moment speeding Yfandes down the road with Tylendel—

—but Tylendel was dead—

"You need not remain alone," Leareth continued, *moistening his lips with his tongue, sensuously. "You have only to stretch out your hand to me, Vanyel, and take my Darkness to you—and you would never be alone again. We could accomplish much together, we two. Or if you wish—I could even—"* he stepped forward a pace; two. *"I could even bring back your long-lost love to you. Think of him, Vanyel. Think of Tylendel—alive, and once more at your side."*

"NO!"

He struck at the terrible, beautiful face, struck with all the power at his command—and wept as he struck.

:*Dreams, young Vanyel.*: A blue-green voice froze him in mid-strike. :*Nothing but dreams. They vanish into mist if you will it.*:

The army, the pass, Leareth, all whirled away from him into another kind of darkness; this was a darkness that soothed, and he embraced it as eagerly as he had repudiated the other.

Cool, green-gold music threaded into the darkness; not dispelling it, but complementing it. It wound its way into his mind, and wherever it went, it left healing behind it; in all the raw, bleeding places, in all the burning channels. It flowed through him and he sank into it, drifting, drifting, and content to drift. It surrounded him, bathed him in balm, until there was nothing left of hurt in him—

—except the place Tylendel had left behind—the place that still ached so emptily—

The green-gold music was joined by another, a blue-green harmony like the voice that had spoken to dispel the dream. And this music was no longer letting him drift aimlessly. It was leading him; it had wound around his soul and he had no choice but to follow where it wanted him to go.

The blue-green music took the melody, the green-gold faded to a descant, and the voice spoke in his dreams again. :*Look; you wish control— here is your center— so to center and so to ground—:*

The music led him in a dance wherein he found a balance he hadn't known he craved until he found it. The music spun him around; he spun with it, and he knew that having found this point of equilibrium he would not lose it again.

:*So, so, so*, exactly *so,:* the music chuckled. :*Now, you would protect yourself*—thus *the barrier, see? Dense, and it keeps all out, flexible to your will. Always your will, young Vanyel, it is will and nothing less—*

It spun him walls to keep others out of his mind; he saw the way of it and spun them thicker, harder—then raveled them again down to the thinnest of barricades, knowing he could build them up again when he wanted to.

Then the blue-green music faded, leaving the green-gold to carry the melody alone. It sang to him then, sang of rest, sang of peace, and he dreamed. Dreamed of waking, moving to another's will, to drink and care for himself and sleep again. But no more dreams that hurt, only dreams full of the verdant music.

Then he woke—truly woke, not dreams of waking—to the sound of it; breathy, haunting notes that wandered into and out of melodies that he half recognized, but couldn't identify. There was a scent of ferns; a smell of growing things, a whiff of freshly-turned earth, and a hint of something metallic. Behind the music, he heard the sound of gently falling water.

He was no longer drugged. And the mind-channels within him no longer burned and tormented him.

He opened his eyes, slowly.

He thought for one mad moment that he was somehow suspended in a tree. He was surrounded on all sides by greenery, and luxuriantly-leaved branches hung over his head. Then he saw that while the branches were real, and the leaves, they were not the same organism. The branches supported huge ferns whose fronds draped down like a living canopy over his bed, and the greenery about him was a curtaining of multi-layered, multi-shaded green fabric hung from a framework of more branches, each layer as light and transparent as a spiderweb, and cut to resemble a cascade of leaf shapes. He had never in his life imagined that there could be so many colors of green.

Weak beams of sunlight threaded past the fern fronds. The blankets—if that was what they were—were a darker green, like moss, and felt as soft as velvet, but were thick and heavy.

He tried to sit up, and discovered that he couldn't. He was absolutely spent, with no strength left at all.

The music beyond the curtains finished with a breathless, upward-spiraling run, and a few moments later, the curtains parted.

Vanyel blinked in surprise at the young man who stood there, framed by the green of the curtain material; he knew he was staring, and rudely, but he couldn't help himself. He'd never seen anyone who looked like this—

A young man—silver-haired as any oldster, with hair longer than most women had, and with eyes of light blue that measured and weighed him, full of secrets and thoughts that Vanyel couldn't begin to read. He wore a sleeveless green jerkin, and breeches of a darker green, and in the hand that held back the curtains there was a white flute that looked as if it had been carved from luminescent, opaque crystal.

Vanyel suddenly realized that, indeed, he *couldn't* read the young man's thoughts; there was *presence* there, but nothing spilling over into his own mind.

He stammered out the first things in his mind—not terribly clever, and certainly not original but—"W-w-where am I? W-w-who are you?"

The young man tilted his head to one side a little, and Vanyel saw a faint hint of smile as he replied, very slowly and with a strange accent, "Well. 'Where am I?' you ask me—better than I had feared. I had half dreaded hearing '*who* am I?' young Vanyel." He tilted his head the other way, and this time the smile was definite. "You are in k'Treva territory in the Pelagir Hills, and before you ask, your aunt, our Wingsister Savil, brought you here. We are her friends; she asked us to help her with your troubles. I am Moondance k'Treva; I am *Tayledras*, and I have been your Healer. That is my bed you are lying in. Do you like it? Starwind says it is a foolish piece of conceit, but *I* think that this is only because he did not think of it first.''

Vanyel could only blink at him in bewilderment.

Moondance shook his head, ruefully. "I go too fast for you. Simple things first. Are you hungry? Thirsty? Would you like to bathe?''

All at once he *was* hungry—and thirsty—and disgustingly aware that his skin was crawling with the need for a bath.

"All three," he said, a little hesitantly.

"Then we remedy all three." Moondance pulled the curtains back to the foot and the head of the bed, and—

—and reached to pull off the blankets. At which point Vanyel realized that he was quite nude beneath the bed-coverings. He flushed, and clutched at the blanket.

Moondance gave him an amused look. "Who do you think it was that undressed you and put you where you are?" he asked. "I pledge you, it was not the Eastern Wind.''

Vanyel flushed again, but did not release the blanket.

"So, so—here, my modest one—" Moondance reached up to one side among the hangings, and detached something which he tossed onto the blankets. Vanyel reached for it—a wrap-robe of something green and silken that was, thankfully, much more substantial than the hangings. As Moondance pointedly turned his back, he eased out of the bed and wrapped it around himself.

And reached for one of the bed-supports as dizziness made the room spin around him.

"That will *never* do." There was a cool touch between his eyes, and the room steadied.

"Come," Moondance was just in front of him, holding out his hands encouragingly. "Keep your eyes on me—yes. A step. Another. You have been long abed, young Vanyel, you must almost learn to walk again.''

The *Tayledras* Healer walked backward, slowly, as Vanyel followed, looking only at his eyes. But he did not move to give the boy support in any way, except the one time Vanyel stumbled and nearly fell. Then Moondance caught him; held him until he could find his balance again, and only when Vanyel was standing firmly again did he draw away.

Vanyel was vaguely aware that they had crossed a threshold into another room, but just *walking* was costing him so much sweating, concentrated effort he didn't dare look around any. It seemed to take years before Moondance stopped, caught his elbow, and guided him to a seat on a smooth rock ledge that rimmed a raised pool of water so hot that it steamed.

"Now, look about you." Moondance waved at the pool and the rest of the room. "This is the pool for washing. Here is soap. When you are clean, go *there*, the pool for resting."

Though the pool Vanyel was sitting beside was deep, it was quite small. Next to the "pool for washing" was another, much larger, much deeper, and slightly above it, with an opening in the side that spilled hot water down into this pool. Both pools looked natural; rock-sided and sandy-bottomed.

"I think even weak as you are, you shall be able to find your way there. I shall return with food and drink." The young man hesitated a moment—then with the swiftness of a stooping hawk, leaned over and kissed Vanyel full on the lips. "You are very welcome, young Vanyel," he said, before Vanyel had a chance to get over his surprise. "We are pleased to have you, Starwind and I, and not just for the sake of Wingsister Savil."

He vanished before Vanyel had a chance to react.

Vanyel found that if he moved slowly and carefully he didn't exhaust himself. He shed the robe and eased himself into the water with a sigh, and soaped and rinsed until he *finally* felt clean again. His pool emptied itself over the side and down a channel in the floor—and where the water went from there he couldn't say. He had figured by now that this was some kind of hot spring, which accounted for the metallic tang in the air.

With Moondance gone, he had a chance to get a good look around while trying to sort himself out. There didn't appear to be any "doors" as such in this dwelling; just doorways. This bathing room was multileveled; highest level was the "pool for resting" which cascaded to the next level and the "pool for washing," which in turn was above the "floor" and the channel carrying the water away that was cut into it. There were no windows in the walls of natural rock; the whole was lit by a skylight taking up the entire ceiling, and there were green and flowering plants and ferns standing and hanging everywhere. There was only one entrance into this room—that led back to the bedroom, also rock-walled and roofed with a skylight, from what Vanyel could see of it.

The ledge between the pools was *not* that high, though it took far more of Vanyel's strength to get over it than he would have believed. Once in the larger pool he discovered that his surmise was right; crystalline hot water bubbled up from the sand in the center of the pool; someone had improved on nature by forming the rock of the pool sides below the waterline into smooth benches.

It was wonderful; the water was about as hot as was comfortable, and was forcing him to relax whether or not he wanted to. He closed his eyes and sat back, deliberately thinking of absolutely nothing, and only opened them again when he heard light footsteps crossing the stone floor below him.

It was, as he expected, Moondance, who had brought with him an earthenware beaker of what proved to be cider and a plate of sliced bread and cheeses and fruit.

"Eat lightly," the young man warned, climbing to Vanyel's level and setting his burdens down on the rim of the pool at Vanyel's right hand. "You have been three weeks without true food, and spent more than one of those days drugged."

"Three weeks?"

Moondance shrugged. "You needed Healing, of a kind your good Healer Andrel could not give you. I think perhaps no Healer among your folk could have given you such Healing; they know nothing of the Healing of hurts caused by magic, only of illness and wounding. *That* is a study only a few have made, and most of those few *Tayledras.* Eat, young Vanyel. There are herbs in the bread and the drink to strengthen you."

"Where—where is Savil?" he asked, suddenly a little worried at being alone with a stranger.

"With Starwind. She was very weary, both in body and in soul. This—thing that has happened. It has been a deep grief to her, as well to you. Her heart is as sore, I think. They are old friends, my *shay'kreth'ashke* and Savil, and there are no secrets between them, and much love. She has need of such love. Perhaps more than you, for *she* has had no one to lend her support."

Vanyel had looked up at him sharply at that—with the word *ashke* striking him with the force of a cold slap in the face, making his heart pound painfully.

Moondance looked down at him, something speculative in his glance. He weighed Vanyel for a moment, then cleared his throat and looked away, deliberately. "I have a thing to say to you, a thing I wish you to think upon."

Vanyel put down his cider, and waited, apprehensively, to hear the rest.

"I have shared your thoughts; I know more of you than anyone, except, perhaps, your *shay'kreth'ashke.*"

Moondance changed his position so that he was sitting with his back to the pool, leaning his weight against his hands and staring up at the clouds visible through the skylight. He was being very careful *not* to look at Vanyel.

"As you have guessed from my words," he said, "I am *shay'a'chern.* As is Starwind. As you." Now he gave Vanyel a very brief, sidelong glance. "I am a Healer-Adept and I Heal more than people—I Heal *places.* I know the natural world as only one who wishes to restore it to its rightful balances can. This is the thing I wish to tell you; in all the world, there are more creatures than just man that make lifetime matings. Among them, some of the noblest—wolves, swans, geese, the great raptors—all creatures man could do worse than emulate, in many, many ways. And with all of them, *all,* there are those pairings, from time to time, within the same gender. Not often, but not unheard of either."

Vanyel found himself unable to move, and unable to anticipate the direction this was taking.

Now Moondance dropped his eyes to catch and hold Vanyel's in a joining of glances and wills that was unbreakable.

"There is in you a fear, a shame, placed there by your

own doubts and the thoughts of one who knew no better. I tell you to think on this: the *shay'a'chern* pairing occurs *in nature*. How then, 'unnatural'? *Usual*, no; and not desirable for the species, else it would die out for lack of offspring. But not *unnatural*. The beasts of the fields are innocent as man can never be, who has the knowledge of good and evil and the choice between, and they do not cast out of their ranks the *shay'a'chern*. There was between you and your *shay'kreth'ashke* much love—only love. There is no shame in loving.''

Vanyel couldn't breathe; he could only see those ice-blue eyes.

''This I think I have learned: where there is love, the form does not matter, and the gods are pleased. This I have observed: what occurs in nature, comes by the hand of nature, and if the gods did not approve, it would not be there. I give you these things as food for your heart and mind.''

Once again, before Vanyel could move, he bent deliberately and kissed him, but this time on the forehead.

''I leave you for a moment with both kinds of nourishment.'' He smiled, and gave Vanyel a slow wink. ''Since you are not to stay in the pool forever, I must needs find you clothing. *I* would not mind, but your aunt grows anxious and wishes to see you awake and aware, and we would not wish to put her to the blush, hmm?''

And with that, he jumped down from the pool ledge to the floor, and vanished again.

Twelve

"Here." Moondance, a crease of worry between his brows, was back in a few moments with a towel and what looked like folded clothing; green, like his own. "You shall have to care for yourself, I fear. There is trouble, and I have been called to deal with it. Starwind and Savil will be with you shortly." He hesitated a moment, visibly torn. "Forgive me, I *must* go."

He put his burdens down on the pool edge and ran back out the doorway before Vanyel could do more than blink.

Gods—I feel like somebody in a tale, going to sleep and waking up a hundred years later. It seems so hard to think—like I'm still half asleep.

He dressed slowly, trying to collect his thoughts, and making heavy work of it. He *did* remember—vaguely—Savil telling him that he was too ill for Andrel to help; and he definitely remembered—despite the fog of drugs about the words—being told that she was going to take him to some friends of hers. He hadn't much cared what was happening at that point. He'd either been too drugged to care, or been hurting too much.

Presumably Moondance, and the absent Starwind, were the friends she meant. They were fully as strange as those weird masks of beads and feathers that Savil had on her wall. As was this place. Wherever it was.

He pulled the deep green tunic over his head, and suddenly realized something. He wasn't drugged—and he wasn't hurting, either. Those places in his mind that had burned—he could still feel them, but they weren't giving him pain.

Moondance said he Healed me. Is that why it feels like I halfway know him? Tayledras. *Didn't Aunt Savil tell us stories about them? I thought that was all those were— stories. Not real.* He looked around at the strange room, half-structure, half-natural, each half fitting into the other so well he could scarcely tell where the hand of nature left off and the hand of man began. *Real. Gods, if I were to describe this place, nobody would ever believe me. This—it's all so different. I even feel different.*

He could sense some kind of barrier around him, around his thoughts. At first it made him wary, but he tested it, tentatively, and found that it was a barrier that *he* could control. When he thinned it, he became aware of presences, what must be minds, out beyond the limits of this room. Animals, surely, and birds, for their thoughts were dim and *here*-centered. Then two close together—very bright, but opaque and unreadable. One "felt" like Savil and the other must be the mysterious Starwind. Then two more; just as bright, just as opaque— but one he recognized by the "feel" as being Yfandes. Then a scattering of others. . . .

Yfandes. A Companion. My Companion.

So—it was no hallucination, then. He *had* somehow gotten Herald-Gifts and a Companion.

Gifts I never wanted, at a cost I never thought I'd pay. I'd trade them and half my life to have—him—back again.

That hit like a blow to the gut. He descended from the level of the uppermost pool to the floor and sat heavily on one of the stone benches around the edge of the room, too tired and depressed to move.

Oh, 'Lendel . . . gods, he thought, bleak despair overcoming him. *What am I doing here? Why didn't they just let me die?*

:Do you hate me, Chosen?: said a bright, reproachful voice in his mind, *:Do you hate me for wishing you to live?:*

:Yfandes?: He remembered what Savil had said, about how his Companion would pine herself to death if he died, and sagged with guilt. *:Oh, gods, Yfandes, no—no, I'm sorry—I just—:*

He'd been able to not-think about it when he'd been

drugged. He'd been able to concentrate on nothing more complicated than the next moment. Now—now his mind was only too clear. He couldn't ignore the reality of Tylendel being gone, and there were no drugs to keep him in a vague fog of forgetting.

:You miss him.: she replied, gently. *:You need him, and you miss him.:*

:Like my arm. Like my heart. I just can't imagine going on without him. I don't know what to do with myself; where to go, what to do next.:

If Yfandes had a reply, he never heard it; just at that moment Savil and a second *Tayledras*, this one in white breeches, soft, low boots and jerkin, entered the room. Vanyel started to stand; Savil motioned for him to stay where he was. She and the stranger walked slowly across the stone floor and took places on the bench beside him.

Vanyel was shocked at her appearance. Although her hair had always been a pure silvery white, she'd never looked *old* before. Now she did; she looked every year of her age and more. He recalled what Moondance had said about Tylendel's death being as hard on her as it was on Vanyel. Now he believed it.

"Aunt Savil," he said, hesitantly, as she and the stranger arranged themselves comfortably beside him. "Are you all right? I mean—"

"Looking particularly haglike, am I?" she asked dryly. "No, don't bother to apologize; I've got a mirror. I don't bounce back from strain the way I used to."

He flushed, embarrassed, and feeling guilty.

"Van, this is Starwind k'Treva," she continued. "He and Moondance are the *Tayledras* Adepts I told you younglings about a time or two. This," she waved her hand around her, "is his, mostly, being as he's k'Treva Speaker."

"In so much as any *Tayledras* can own the land," Starwind noted with one raised eyebrow, his voice calling up images of ancient rocks and deep, still water. "It wou'd be as correct, Wingsister, to say that this place owns me."

"Point taken. This is k'Treva's *voorthayshen*—that s— how would you translate that, *shayana?*"

The *Tayledras* at her side had a triangular face, and his long hair was arranged with two plaits at each temple, instead of one, like Moondance—and he *felt* older, somehow. At least, that was how he felt to Vanyel.

"Clan Keep, I think would be closest," Starwind said, "Although k'Treva is not a clan as your people know the meaning of the word. It is closer to the Shin'a'in notion of 'Clan.' "

His voice was a little deeper in pitch than Moondance's and after a moment Vanyel recognized the "feel" of him as being the same as the "blue-green music" in his dreams.

"My lord," Vanyel began hesitantly.

"There are no 'lords,' here, young Vanyel," the Adept replied. "I speak for k'Treva, but each k'Treva rises or falls on his own."

Vanyel nodded awkwardly. "Why am I here, sir?" he asked—then added, apprehensively, "What did you do to me? I—forgive me for being rude, but I *know* you did something. I feel—different."

"You are here because you have very powerful Mage-Gifts, awakened painfully, awakened late, and out of control," the Adept replied. His expression was calm, but grave, and held just a hint of worry. "Your aunt decided, and rightly, that there was no way in which you could be taught by the Heralds that would not pose a danger to you and those about you. Moondance and I are used to containing dangerous magics; we do this constantly, it is part of *what* we do. We can keep you contained, and Savil believes we can teach you effectively. And if we cannot teach you control, then she knows that we can and *will* contain you in such a way that you will pose no danger to others."

Moondance had not looked like this—so impersonal, so implacable. Vanyel shivered at the detached calm in Starwind's eyes; he wasn't certain what the Adept meant by "containing" him, but he wasn't eager to find out.

"As to what we have done with you—Moondance Healed your channels, which are the conduits through which you direct energy. And I have taught you, a little, while you were in Healing trance. I could not teach you a great deal in trance, but what I have given you is very important, and will go a great way toward making you safe around others. I have taught you where your center is, how to ground yourself, and how to shield. So that now, at least, you are no longer out of balance, and you may guard yourself against outside thoughts and keep your own inside your mind where they belong. And there will be no more shaking of the earth because of dreams."

So *that* was what had happened—with the music, the colors—and this new barricade around his mind.

Starwind leaned forward a little, and his expression became far more human; concerned, and earnest. "Young Vanyel, we, Moondance and I, we are perfectly pleased to have you with us, to help you. But that is *all* we can do; to help you. *You* must learn control; we cannot force it upon you. *You* must learn the use of your Gifts, or most assuredly they will use you. Magic is that kind of force; I beg you to believe me, for I know this to be true. If you do not use it, it will use you. And if it begins to use you," his eyes grew very cold, "it must be dealt with."

Vanyel shrank back from that chill.

"But this is neither the place nor the time to speak of such things," Starwind concluded, rising. "We have you under shield, and you are too drained to cause any problems for the nonce. Youngling, can you walk? If you can, you would do well with exercise and air, and I would take you to a vantage to show you our home, and tell you a little of what we do here."

Vanyel nodded, not eager to be left to his aching memories again; he found on rising that he was feeling considerably stronger than he had thought. He couldn't move very fast, but as long as Starwind and Savil stayed at a slow walk, he could keep up with them.

They went from the bathing room back through the bedroom; it looked even more like a natural grotto than the bathing room had. Vanyel almost couldn't distinguish the real foliage from the fabric around the bed, and the "furniture," irregularly shaped chairs, benches and tables with thick green cushions and frames of bent branches, fitted in with the plants so well as to frequently seem part of them. There was a curtained alcove (with more of those leaf-mimicking curtains) that seemed to be a wardrobe, for the curtains had been drawn back at one side enough to display a bit of clothing.

From there they passed into a third, most peculiar room. There was no furniture, and in the center of it, growing up from the stone floor, was the living trunk of a tree, one a dozen people could not have encircled with their arms. Attached to the trunk was a kind of spiral staircase. They climbed this—Vanyel feeling weak at the knees and clinging to the railing for most of the climb— to a kind of covered balcony that gave them a vantage point to see all of Starwind's little kingdom.

This was a valley—no, a *canyon;* the walls were nearly perpendicular—of hot springs; Vanyel saw steam rising from the lush growth in more places than he could count. Although there was snow rimming the lip of the canyon high above, vegetation within the bowl ran riot.

"K'Treva," Starwind said, indicating the entire valley with a wave of his hand. "Though mostly only Moondance and I dwell here-below. Beneath, the living-spaces for the *hertasi* and those who do not wish the trees."

Vanyel looked over the edge of the balcony; below him was a collection of rooms, mostly windowless, but with skylights, the whole too random to be called a "house."

"There are other living places above—which is where most of us dwell," Starwind continued, with an ironic smile. "Moondance is not *Tayledras* enough to be comfortable above the ground. The *hertasi* you may or may not see; they serve us, we protect them and allow them to dwell here. They are shy of strangers—even of *Tayledras;* really, only Moondance is a friend to all of them. They are something like a large lizard, but they are full human in wit. If you should see one, I pray you strive not to frighten it. And although you may go where you will here-below, pray do not come here-above without invitation."

Vanyel looked up, but couldn't see any sign of these "living places"—only the staircase spiraling farther up the trunk and vanishing into the branches. The very thought of being up that high was dizzying, and he thought it was likely to take a great deal more than an invitation to get him to climb above.

"Tchah—I stand on Moondance's side," Savil replied. "I remember the first time I was here, and you made me try to sleep up in one of your perches. Never again, my friend."

"You have no sense of adventure," Starwind countered, putting his palms down on the rail and leaning forward a little. "The last thing, one that you may sense, so that you know it is indeed there—the barrier about the vale. It protects us from that which we would not have pass within and it keeps the vale always warm and sheltered. So—this is k'Treva. What we do here—two things. Firstly, we make places where the magic creatures of the Pelagirs may live in peace. Secondly, we take the magic out of those places where they do not live, making the land safe for man. We use the magic we take to make boundaries about the places of refuge, so that none may pass who do not belong. That is what the k'Varda, the Mage-Clans of the *Tayledras*, do. We guard the Pelagirs from despoilers as our cousins, the *Shin'a'in*, guard the Dhorisha Plains."

"As I keep saying, you're like we are. You guard the Pelagirs as the Heralds guard Valdemar," Savil said.

Starwind nodded, his braids swaying. "Aye, save that your Heralds concern themselves with the people, and the *Tayledras* with the land."

"Valdemar *is* the people; we could pack up and flee again, as we did at the founding, and still be Valdemar. I suspect the same would be true of you, if you'd only admit it."

"Na, the *Tayledras* are bound to the land, cannot live outside the Pelagirs; we must—" Starwind was interrupted by the scream of a hawk somewhere above his head. He threw up his forearm, and a large, white raptor plunged down out of the canopy of leaves to land on Starwind's arm. Vanyel winced, then saw that the *Tayledras* wore white leather forearm guards, which served to keep the wicked talons from his flesh.

It was a gyrefalcon; its wings beat the air for a moment before it settled, its golden eyes fixed on Starwind's face.

The *Tayledras* smoothed its head with one finger, then stared into the hawk's eyes for a long, long time, seeming to be reading something there.

Then, without warning, he flung up his arm, launching it back into the air from his wrist. The falcon's wings beat against the thick, damp air, then it gained height and vanished back up into the tree branches.

"Bad news?" Savil asked.

"Nay—good. The situation is not so evil as we feared. Moondance is wearied, but he shall return by sunrise."

"I'm glad to hear something is going right for someone," Savil replied, sighing.

"Indeed," the Adept replied, turning those strange, unreadable eyes on Vanyel. "Indeed. Young Vanyel, I would advise you to walk about, regain your health, eat and rest. When Moondance returns and is at full strength, your schooling will begin."

So he did as he was told to do; exploring what Starwind called "the vale" from one end to the other. It was shaped like a teardrop, and smaller than it seemed; there were so many pools and springs, waterfalls and geysers, and all cloaked in incredible greenery that effectively hid paths that came within whispering distance of each other, that it gave the illusion of being an endless wilderland.

It kept him occupied, at least. The vale was so exotic, so strange, that he could lose himself in it for hours—and forget, in watching the brightly colored birds and fish, how very much alone he was.

Half of him longed for the time—before Tylendel. The isolation of that dream-scape. The other half shrank from it. He no longer knew what he wanted, anymore, or what he was.

He certainly didn't know what to do about Yfandes; he needed her, he loved her, but that very affection was a point of vulnerability, another place waiting to be hurt. She seemed to sense his confusion, and kept herself nearby, but not at hand, Mindspeaking only when he initiated the contact.

Savil was staying clear of him, which helped. When Moondance finally made an appearance, he made some friendly overtures, but didn't go beyond them; Vanyel was perfectly content to leave things that way.

When he asked, the younger *Tayledras* acted as a kind of guide around the vale, pointing out things Vanyel had missed, explaining how the mage-barrier kept the cold—and other things—out of the vale.

The elusive *hertasi* never appeared, although their handiwork was everywhere. Clothing vanished and returned cleaned and mended, food appeared at regular intervals, rooms seemed to sweep themselves.

When the vale became too familiar, Vanyel tried to catch a glimpse of them. Anything to keep from thinking.

Then he was given something else to think about.

:You fail,: Starwind said in clear Mindspeech. He was seated cross-legged on the rock of the floor beyond the glowing blue-green barrier, imperturbable as a glacier. *:Again, youngling.:*

:But—: Vanyel protested from the midst of the barrier-circle the Adept had cast around him, *:I—:* He was having a hard time shaping his thoughts into Mindspeech.

:You,: Starwind nodded. *:Exactly so. Only you. Until you match your barrier and merge it with mine, mine will remain. And while mine remains, you cannot pass it, and I will not take you from this room.:*

Vanyel drooped with weariness; it seemed that the *Tayledras* mage had been schooling him, without pause or pity, for days, not mere hours. This was the seventh—or was it eighth?—such test the Adept had put him to. Starwind would go *into* his head, somehow, show him what was to be done. Once. Then Vanyel fumbled his way through whatever it was. As quickly as Vanyel mastered something, the Adept sprang a trial of it on him.

There was no sign of exit or entrance in this barren, rock-walled room where he'd been taken, and no clue as to where in the complex of ground-level rooms it was. There was only Starwind, his pointed face as expressionless as the rock walls.

Vanyel didn't know what to think anymore. These new senses of his—they told him things he wasn't sure he wanted to know. For instance—there was something in this valley. A power—a living power. It throbbed in his mind, in time with his own pulse. He had told Savil, thinking he must be ill and imagining it. She had just nodded and told him not to worry about it.

He hadn't asked her much, or gone to her often. *If I don't touch, I can't be hurt again.* The half-unconscious litany was the same, but the meaning was different. *If I don't open myself, I won't be open to loss either.*

The *Tayledras,* Starwind and Moondance, alternately frightened and fascinated him. They were like no one he'd ever known before, and he couldn't read them. Starwind in particular was an enigma. Moondance seemed easier to reach.

But there was always that danger. *Don't reach; don't touch,* whispered the part of him that still hurt. *Don't try.*

There had been a point back at Haven when he'd tried to reach out, first to Savil, then to Lissa. He'd wanted someone to depend on, to tell him what to do, but the moment he'd tried to get them to make his decisions for him, they'd pushed him gently away.

Now—no more; all he wanted was to be left alone.

It seemed, however, that the *Tayledras* had other plans.

Savil had come to get him in the morning, after several days of wandering about on his own, reminding him of what Starwind had said about being schooled in controlling these unwanted powers of his. He'd followed her through three or four rooms he hadn't seen before into—

—something—

He wasn't sure what it was; it had felt a little like a Gate, but there was no portal, just a spot marked on the floor. He'd stumbled across it, whatever it was, and found himself on the floor of this room, a room with no doorways.

Savil had appeared behind him, but before he could say anything, she'd just given him a troubled look, said to Starwind, "Don't hurt him, *shayana,*" and left. Stepped into thin air and was gone. Left him alone with this—this madman. This unpredictable creature who'd been forcing him all morning to do things he didn't un-

derstand, using the powers he hadn't even come to terms
with possessing, much less comprehending.

"Why are you doing this to me?" he cried, ready to
weep with weariness. Starwind ignored the words as if
they had never been spoken.

:Mindspeech, Chosen,: came Yfandes' calm thought,
:That is part of his testing. Use Mindspeech.:

He braced himself, sharpened his thoughts into a kind
of dagger, and *flung* them at Starwind's mind.

:Why are you DOING this to me?:

:Gently,: came the unruffled reply. *:Gently, or I shall
not answer you.:*

Well, that was more than he'd gotten out of the Adept
in hours. *:Why?:* he pleaded.

:You are a heap of dry tinder,: Starwind replied serenely. *:You are a danger to yourself and those around
you. It requires only a spark to send you into an uncontrolled blaze. I teach you control, so that the fires in you
come when you will and where you will.:* He stared at
Vanyel across the shimmering mage-barrier. *:Would you
have this again?:*

He flung into Vanyel's face memories that could only
have come from Savil—a clutch of Herald-trainees weeping hysterically, infected with *his* grief; Mardic flying
through the air, hitting the wall, and sliding down it to
land in an unconscious heap; the very foundations of the
Palace shaking—

:No—: he shuddered.

:There could be worse—: Starwind showed him what
he meant by "worse." A vivid picture of Withen dead—
crushed like a beetle beneath a boot—by the powers Vanyel did not yet comprehend and could not direct.

:NO!: He tried to deny the very possibility that he could
do anything of the kind, rejecting the image with a vio-
lence that—

—that made the floor beneath him tremble.

:You see?: Starwind said, still unperturbed. *:You see?
Without control, without understanding, you can—and
will—kill, without ever meaning to. Now—:*

Vanyel hung his head, and wearily tried to match the
barrier one more time.

* * *

Savil ran for the pass-through, in response to Starwind's urgent summons, Moondance a bare pace behind her. She hit the permanent set-spell, a kind of low-power Gate, at a run; there was the usual eyeblink of vertigo, and she stumbled onto the slate floor of Starwind's Work Room and right into the middle of a royal mess.

Starwind was only now picking himself up off the floor behind her; there was a smell of scorched rock and the acrid taint of ozone in the air. And small wonder; the area around all around Vanyel in the center of the Work Room was burned black.

Lying sprawled at one side of the burned area was the boy himself, scorched and unconscious.

Moondance popped through the pass-through, glanced from one fallen body to the other, and made for the boy as needing him the most. That left Starwind to Savil.

She gave him her hands and helped him to his feet; he shook his head to clear it, then pulled his hair back over his shoulders. "God of my fathers," he said, passing his hand over his brow. "I feel as if I have been kicked across a river."

Savil ran a quick check over him, noted a channel-pulse and cleared it for him. "What happened?" she asked urgently, keeping one hand on his elbow to steady him. "It looks like a mage-war in here."

"I believe I badly frightened the boy," Starwind said, unhappily, checking his hands for damage. "I intended to frighten him a little, but not so badly as I did. He was supposed to be calling lightning and he was balking. He plainly refused to use the power he had called. I grew impatient with him—and I cast the image of *wyrsa* at him. He panicked; and not only threw his own power, he pulled power from the valley-node. Then he realized what he had done and aborted it the only way he could at that point, pulling it back on himself." Starwind gave her a reproachful glance. "You told me he could sense the node, but you did not tell me he could pull from it."

"I didn't know he could, myself. Great good gods—*shayana*, it was *wyrsa* that his *shay'kreth'ashke* called down on his enemies, didn't I tell you?" Savil's gut went

cold; she bit her lip, and looked over her shoulder at
Moondance and his patient. The Healer-Adept was
kneeling beside the boy with both hands held just above
his brow. "Lord and Lady, no wonder he nearly blew the
place apart!"

Starwind looked stricken to the heart, as Moondance
took his hands away from the boy's forehead and put his
arm under Vanyel's shoulder to pick him up and support
him in a half-sitting position. "You told me—but I had
forgotten. Goddess of my mothers, what did I do to the
poor child?"

"Ashke, what did you do?" Moondance called wor-
riedly, one hand now *on* Vanyel's forehead, the other arm
holding him. "The child's mind is in shock."

"Only the worst possible," Starwind groaned. "I
threw at him an image of the things his love called for
vengeance."

"Shethka. Well, no help for it; what is done cannot be
unmade. *Ashke,* I will put him to bed, and call his Companion, and we will deal with him. We will see what
comes of this." He picked the boy up, and strode through
the pass-through without a backward glance.

"Ah, gods—this was going well, until this moment,"
Starwind mourned. "He was gaining true control. Gods,
how could I have been so *stupid?"*

"It happens," Savil sighed, "And with Van more so
than with anyone else, it seems. He almost seems to attract ill luck. *Shayana,* why did you throw anything at
him, much less *wyrsa?"*

"He finally is willing enough to learn the controls, the
defensive exercises, but *not* the offensive." Starwind put
his palms to his temples and massaged for a moment, a
pain-crease between his eyebrows. "And if he does not
master the offensive—"

"The offensive magics will *remain* without control,"
Savil said grimly, the smell of scorched rock still strong
about her. "Like Tylendel. I couldn't get past his trauma
to get those magics fully under conscious lock. I should
have brought *him* to you."

"Wingsister, hindsight is ever perfect," Starwind
spared a moment to send a thread of wordless compas-

sion her way, and she smiled wanly. "The thing with this boy—I told you, he *had* the lightnings in his hand, I could see him holding them, but he would not cast them. I thought to frighten him into taking the offense." He lowered his hands and looked helplessly at Savil. "He is a puzzle to me; I cannot fathom why he will not fully utilize his powers."

"Because he still doesn't understand why he should, I suppose," Savil brooded, rocking back and forth on her heels. "He can't see any reason to use those powers. He doesn't want to help anyone, all he wants now is to be left alone."

Starwind looked aghast. "But—so *strong*—how can he *not*—"

"He hasn't got the hunger yet, *shayana,* or if he's got it, everything else he's feeling has so overwhelmed him that all he can register is his own pain." Savil shook her head. "That, mostly, would be my guess. Maybe it's that he hasn't ever seen a reason to care for anyone he doesn't personally know. Maybe it's that right now he has no energy to care for anyone but himself. Kellan tells me Yfandes would go through fire and flood for him, so there has to be *something* there. Maybe Moondance can get through to him."

"Only if he survives what we do to him," Starwind replied, motioning her to precede him into the pass-through, and sunk in gloom.

Vanyel woke with an ache in his heart and tears on his face; the image of the *wyrsa* had called up everything he wanted most to forget.

He could tell that he was lying on his bed, still clothed, but his hands and forearms felt like they'd been bandaged and the skin of his face hurt and felt hot and tight.

The full moon sent silver light down through the skylight above his head. He saw the white rondel of it clearly through the fronds of the ferns. His head hurt, and his burned hands, but not so much as the empty place inside him, or the guilt—the terrible guilt.

'Lendel, 'Lendel—my fault.

He heard someone breathing beside him; a Mindtouch

confirmed that it was Moondance. He did not want to talk with anyone right now; he just wanted to be left alone. He started to turn his face to the wall, when the soft, oddly young-sounding voice froze him in place.

"I would tell you of a thing—"

Vanyel wet his lips, and turned his head on the pillow to look at the argent-and-black figure seated beside him on one of the strange "chairs" he favored.

Moondance might have been a statue; a silvered god sitting with one leg curled beneath him, resting his crossed arms on his upraised knee, face tilted up to the moon. Moonlight flowed over him in a flood of liquid silver.

"There was a boy," Moondance said, quietly. "His name was Tallo. His parents were farmers, simple people, good people in their way, really. Very tied to their ways, to their land, to the cycle of the seasons. This Tallo . . . was not. He felt things inside him that were at odds with the life they had. They did not understand their son, who wanted more than just the fields and the harvests. They did love him, though. They tried to understand. They got him learning, as best they could; they tried to interest the priest in him. They didn't know that what the boy felt inside himself was something other than a vocation. It was power, but power of another sort than the priest's. The boy learned at last from the books that the priest found for him that what he had was what was commonly called magic, and from those few books and the tales he heard, he tried to learn what to do with it. This made him—very different from his former friends, and he began to walk alone. His parents did not understand this need for solitude, they did not understand the strange paths he had begun to walk, and they tried to force him back to the ways of his fathers. There were—arguments. Anger, a great deal of it, on both sides. And there was another thing. They wished him to wed and begin a family. But the boy Tallo had no yearning toward young women—but young *men*—that was another tale."

Moondance sighed, and in the moonlight Vanyel saw something glittering wetly on his eyelashes. "Then, the summer of the worst of the arguments, there came a

troupe of gleemen to the village. And there was a young
man among them, a very handsome young man, and the
boy Tallo found that he was not the only young man in
the world who had yearnings for his own sex. They
quickly became lovers—Tallo thought he had never been
so happy. He planned to leave with the gleemen, to run
away and join them when they left his village, and his
lover encouraged this. But it happened that they were
found together. The parents, the priest, the entire village
was most wroth, for such a thing as *shay'a'chern* was
forbidden even to speak of, much less to be. They—beat
Tallo, very badly; they beat the young gleeman, then they
cast Tallo and his lover out of the village. Then it was
that the young gleeman spurned Tallo, said in anger and
in pain what he did not truly mean, that he wanted nothing of him. And Tallo became wild with rage. He, too,
was in pain; he had suffered for this lover, been cast out
of home and family for his sake, and now he had been
rejected—and he called the lightning down with his half-
learned magic. He did not mean to do anything more
than frighten the young man—but that was not what happened. He killed him; struck him dead with the power
that he could not control.''

   Moonlight sparkled silver on the tears that slowly crept
down Moondance's face.

   ''Tallo had heard his lover's thoughts, and knew that
the young man had not meant in truth the hurtful things
he had said. Tallo had wanted only for the boy to say
with words what he had heard in the other's mind. So he
called the lightning to frighten him, but he learned that
the lightning would not obey him when called by anger,
and not by skill. And he heard the boy crying out his
name as he died. Crying out in fear and terrible pain,
and Tallo unable to save him. Tallo could not live with
what he had done. With the dagger from his lover's belt,
he slashed his own wrist and waited to die, for he felt
that only with his own death could he atone for murder-
ing his love.''

   Moondance raised his left arm to push some of his
heavy hair back from his face, and the moon picked out

the white scar that ran from his wrist halfway to his elbow.

"There was, however, a stranger on the road; an outlander who had sensed the surge of power and read the
signs and knew that it was uncontrolled. She came as
quickly as she could—though not quickly enough to save
both. She found the young men, one dead, one nearly—
she saved the one she could, and brought him to a friend
who she thought might understand."

Moondance was so silent and for so long, that Vanyel
thought he was through speaking. He stared up at the
moon, eyes and cheeks shining wetly, like a marble statue
in the rain.

Then he spoke again, and every syllable carried with
it a sense of terrible pain. "So here is the paradox. If the
boy Tallo had not misused his fledgling powers and struck
down his lover, they would have gone off together, and,
in time, parted. Tallo would likely have been found by a
Mage and taught, or—who knows?—gotten as far as Valdemar and been taken by a Companion. Those with the
power are not left long to themselves. It might even have
been that the Mage that found him was a dark one, and
Tallo might have turned for a time or for all time to evil.
But that is not what happened. The boy killed—murdered
in ignorance—and was brought to k'Treva. And in
k'Treva he found forgiveness, and the learning he needed
as the seed needs the spring rain—and one thing more.
He found his *shay'kreth'ashke.* In your tongue, that
means 'lifebonded.' "

Vanyel started. Moondance nodded without turning to
look at him. "You see? Paradox. Had things not fallen
as they did, Tallo would never have met with Starwind.
The *Tayledras* are very secretive and Wingsister Savil is
one of the first to see one of us, much less to see k'Treva,
in years beyond counting. The two meant to be lifebonded would never have found each other. There would
be no Healer-Adept in k'Treva, and much *Tayledras* work
would have gone undone because of that. So—much good
has come of this, and much love—but it has its roots in
murder. Murder unintentional, but murder all the same."

Moondance sighed again. "So what is the boy Tallo to

think? Starwind's solution was to declare the boy Tallo dead by his own hand, a fitting expiation for his guilt, and to bring to life a new person altogether, one Moondance k'Treva. So there is no more Tallo, and there is one that magic has changed into a man so like *Tayledras* that he might have been born to the blood. But sometimes the boy Tallo stirs in the heart of Moondance—and he wonders—and he weeps—and he mourns for the wrongs he has done.''

He turned his head, then, and held out his hand to Vanyel. *''Ke'chara,* would you share grief with Tallo? Weeping alone brings no comfort, and your heart is as sore as mine.''

Vanyel started to reach for that hand, then hesitated.

If I don't touch—

''If you do not touch,'' said Moondance, as if he read Vanyel's thought, ''You do not *live.* If you seal yourself away inside your barriers, you seal out the love with the pain. And though love sometimes brings pain, you have no way of knowing if the pain you feel now might not bring you to love again.''

''Tylendel's dead.'' There; he'd said it, said it out loud. It was real—and couldn't be changed. The tight, burned skin on his face hurt as he held back tears. *''Nothing* is going to bring him back. I'll *never* be anything but alone.''

Moondance nodded, slowly, and left his hand resting on the edge of the bed; Vanyel couldn't see his face, shadowed as it was by the white wing of his hair.

''The great love is gone. There are still little loves— friend to friend, brother to sister, student to teacher. Will you deny yourself comfort at the hearthfire of a cottage because you may no longer sit by the fireplace of a palace? Will you deny yourself to those who reach out to *you* in hopes of warming themselves at your hearthfire? That is cruel, and I had not thought you to be cruel, Vanyel. And what of Yfandes? She loves you with all her being. Would you lock her out of your regard as well? That is something more than cruel.''

''Why are you telling me, asking me this?'' The words were torn out of him, unwilling.

"Because I nearly followed the road you are walking."
The *Tayledras* shifted slightly in his chair and Vanyel
heard the wood creak a little. "Better, I thought, not to
touch at all than to touch and bring hurt upon myself and
others. Better to do nothing than to make a move and
have it be the wrong one. But even deciding to not touch
or to be nothing is a decision, Vanyel, and by deciding
not to touch, so as to avoid hurt, I then hurt those who
tried to touch me." He waited, but Vanyel could not
bring himself to answer him.

Moondance's expression grew alien, unreadable, and
he shrugged again. "It is your decision; it is your life.
A Healer cannot live so; it may be that you can."

He uncoiled himself from his chair and in a kind of
seamless motion was standing on his feet, shaking back
his hair. The tears were gone from his eyes, and his expression was as serene as if they had never been there as
he looked down on Vanyel. "If you are in pain, Mindcall, and I shall come."

Before Vanyel could blink, he was gone.

Morning came—but the expected summons to Starwind's Work Room did not. The sun rose, he wandered
from room to empty room, in the small area that he knew,
without finding anyone. He began to wonder if his rejec-
tion of Moondance last night had led them all to abandon
him here.

Finally he found a way out into the valley itself, and
stood by the rock-arch of the doorway, blinking a little
at the bright sunlight, unfiltered by the tinted skylight.
There were ferns the size of a small room, bushes and
small trees with leaves he could have used as a rain shelter, and the larger trees, while not matching the one
growing up through the middle of the "house" in girth,
were still large enough that it would take five people to
encircle their trunks with their arms.

:Yfandes?: he Mindcalled tentatively. He wasn't at all
sure he'd get a reply.

But he did. *:Here,:* she said—and a few moments later,
she came frisking through the undergrowth, tail and spir-

its held banner-high. She nuzzled his cheek. :*Are your hands better?*:

He had unwrapped them this morning from their bandages, and aside from a little soreness, they seemed fine—certainly nothing near as painful as they had been last night.

:*I think so.*: He rested his forehead against her neck. It was incredibly comforting just to be in her presence, and hard to remember to barricade himself around her. :*Where is everybody?*:

:*Savil is up above, in Starwind's place.*: She gave him a mental picture of a kind of many-windowed room perched in the limbs of what could only be the tree growing up through the center of the "house." :*She doesn't much care for it, and having her up there makes Kellan nervy, but he was upset over the accident yesterday and he feels happier up in the boughs. They're talking.*:

:*With the other k'Treva?*:

:*I think perhaps.*:

:*Where's Moondance?*:

:*By himself. Thinking,*: Yfandes said.

:*'Fandes—did I—*: He swallowed. :*Did I do something wrong last night?*:

She looked at him reproachfully. :*Yes. I think you ought to talk to him. You hurt him more deeply last night than he showed. He's never told that story to anyone; Savil and Starwind know it, but he never* told *them. And he's never even told Starwind how badly he still* feels. *It cost him a great deal to tell it to you.*:

His first reaction was guilt. His second was anger.

By his own admission, Moondance's tragic affair had been nothing more than that—an affair doomed to be brief. How could he even *begin* to compare his hurt with Vanyel's? Moondance wasn't alone—

Moondance hadn't murdered Starwind—just some stupid gleeman, who would have passed out of his life in a few weeks. A common player, and no great love.

Moondance still had Starwind. Would always have Starwind. Vanyel would be alone forever. So how *could* Moondance compare the two of them?

Yfandes seemed to sense something of what was going

on in his mind; she pulled away from him, a little, and looked—or was it *felt?*—offended.

That only made him angrier.

Without another word, spoken or thought, he turned on his heel and ran—away from her, away from the *Tayledras*—away from all of them. Ran to a little corner at the end of the vale, a sullen grove of dark, fleshy-leaved trees and ferns, where very little light ever came. He pushed his way in among them, and curled up around his misery and his anger, his stomach churning, his eyes stinging.

They don't give a damn about me—just about what I can do. They don't care how much I hurt, all they want is for me to do what I'm told. Savil just wants to see me tricked into being a Herald, that's all. They don't any of them understand! They don't any of them know how much—I—

He began crying silently. *'Lendel, 'Lendel, they don't know how much of me died with you. All I want is to be left alone. Why can't they leave me alone? Why can't they stop trying to make me do what they want? They're all alike, dammit, they're just like Father, the only thing different is what they want out of me! Oh 'Lendel—I need you so much—*

He stayed there, crying off and on, until full dark—then crept as silently as he could back to the building—part of him hoping to find them waiting for him.

Only to find it as vacant as when he'd left it. In fact, only the night-lamps were burning, and those were only left for the benefit of any of the *Tayledras* who might care to come down to the ground during the night. It didn't even look as if he'd been missed.

They don't care, he thought forlornly, surveying the empty, ill-lit rooms. *They really* don't *care. Oh, gods—*

His stomach knotted up into a hard, squirming ball.

No one cares. No one ever did except 'Lendel. And no one ever will again.

His shoulders slumped, and a second hard lump clogged his throat. He made another circuit of the rooms, but they stayed achingly, echoingly empty. No sign of anyone. No sign anyone would ever come back.

After pacing through the place until the echoes of his own footsteps were about to drive him into tears, he finally crawled into bed.

And cried himself to sleep.

Thirteen

Leareth laughed; his icy laughter echoed off the cliffs as he held up one hand and made the simplest of gestures. A mage-storm swirled into being precisely at the edge of Vanyel's defenses. Vanyel poured power into his shielding; this was the last, the very last of his protections. He was drained, the energy-sources were drained, and he himself had taken far more damage in the duel than he would allow Leareth to know.

He was no match for the scouring blast that peeled his shields away faster than he could replace them. Leareth smiled behind his mage-storm, as if he knew that Vanyel was weakening by the moment. Sweat ran into his eyes and started to freeze there; he went to his knees, still fighting, and knowing he was going to lose. Leareth seemed not even wearied.

A final blast struck down the last of his protections. Vanyel screamed as agony such as he'd never known before arced through his body—

Vanyel woke up; the bed was soaking with sweat, and he was shaking so hard the ferns over his head quivered. He was afraid that he had screamed out loud.

But when no one came running into the room, he knew that he hadn't; that everything had been in the dream. At least this time he hadn't awakened anyone, and hadn't been trapped in the dream.

Dream. Oh, gods, it isn't just a dream. He shivered, despite the warmth of the room, and stared up through the fern fronds at the descending moon. The nightmare had him in a grasp of iron claws and would not let him

302

go. *This is going to be real, it feels real. It's ForeSight. It has to be. Leareth calls me "Herald-Mage Vanyel," and I'm in Whites. I'm dreaming my own death. This is what is going to happen to me, how I'm going to die, if I become a Herald. Alone. In terrible pain, and all alone, fighting a doomed battle.*

He shivered harder, chilled by the cold of the dream, chilled even more with fear. He finally threw the covers back, grabbed his robe, and padded into the room with the hot pools, finding his way by moonlight and habit.

For this was not the first time he'd awakened in the middle of the night, dream-chilled and needing warmth. This was just the first time since he'd arrived here that the dream had been clear enough to remember.

He climbed into the uppermost pool, easing himself down into the hot water with a sigh and a shiver. *Oh, gods. I don't want to die like that. They can't want me to have to face that, can they? If they knew about this dream, would they still want me to be a Herald? Gods, I know the answer to that—*

He eased a little farther down into the hot water, until it lapped at his chin. He was fighting blind, unreasoning panic, and losing. *What am I going to do? Oh, gods—I can't think—*

I have to get away. I can't stay here. If I do, they'll try and talk me around. Where can I go? I don't even know where "home" is from here. But I can't stay—I'll just go, I'll just pack up and go, and hope something turns up, it's all I can do. It means leaving Yfandes—

For a moment that thought was more than he could bear. But—fear was stronger. *It's lose her, or lose my life. No. I can't. I can't face an end like that. Besides,* he choked on a sob, *she just wants me to be a Herald, too—*

He looked up, judging the hour by the moon. *I've got a few hours until dawn. I can be out of the valley and well away before they even start looking for me. And they might not—Starwind still isn't ready to deal with me again; they might just think I've gone off somewhere to be alone, especially if I block Yfandes out* now *and keep her out.*

He climbed out of the pool and dried himself with his robe; he knew exactly where the clothing he'd arrived in was hung—the far end of Moondance's closet. He pulled it on as quickly as he could, taking the heavy cloak and draping it over one arm. One of the packs was in there, too, the one with the rest of his winter clothes. They were too warm to wear in the valley, so he'd never unpacked them, wearing instead Moondance's outgrown things. There was always food out in the room beside the one with the staircase; *Tayledras* sometimes kept odd hours. He filched enough bread and cheese to last several days and stuffed it into the pack with his clothing.

It took him most of a candlemark to reach the entrance to the valley. If it hadn't been snowing, he might have turned back at that moment—but it was, lightly, enough to cover his tracks. He swung the heavy cloak over his shoulders, braced himself for the shock of the temperature change, and stepped out into the dark and cold, remembering just in time to put up a shield so that he could not be tracked by his own aura.

"Two steps forward, one step back," Moondance's voice drifted up the ladder—Savil refused to call anything that steep a "staircase"—to Starwind's *ekele;* it was a good three breaths before Moondance himself appeared. His head poked through the hatchway in the gleaming wooden floor just as a gust of wind made the whole tree sway and creak.

Savil gulped, and gripped the arms of her low chair, looking resolutely away from the windows and their view of the birds flying by *below* them. Starwind never would tell her what it was they used in those windows instead of glass—which wouldn't have lasted ten breaths in a high wind. It was the same thing they used for the skylights, only thinner. Some kind of tough, flexible, transparent membrane—and Savil could not bring herself to believe that it would hold if you fell against it. The *ekele* creaked again, and she shuddered as she saw the window-stuff ripple a little with the warping of the window frames.

"Would you mind explaining that cryptic remark?"

she asked, as the rest of Moondance emerged from the "entrance."

"Oh, thy pupil, Wingsister," he said, at his most formal, closing the hatchway against another gust of chill air. The ladder was sheltered, but not entirely enclosed—that would have been impractical—and Starwind couldn't see wasting a mage-barrier on the entrance to his "nest" when the hatchway served perfectly well most of the time. "Bright the day, Master-*ashke*."

"Wind to thy wings," Starwind replied automatically, turning away from the window, his gloom brightening a little. *"Shay'kreth'ashke*, there is no 'Master' here for thee."

"Nay, till the day thy wings bear thee upwards, thou'rt my Master." Moondance glided across the unsteady floor to Starwind's side, as surefooted as a sailor on a moving deck.

"Enough, I'm drowning," Savil groaned. "Gods, life-bonded—it's enough to make me celibate. What about my pupil? And will you *please* come away from that window? I keep thinking the next gust is going to pitch you out."

"The window would hold. Besides, no *Tayledras* has fallen from his *ekele* in years beyond counting, Wingsister," Starwind said, turning his back to the window and leaning on the ledge.

"So the time is long past for it to happen, and I don't want it to be you, all right?" Another gust made the whole tree groan, and she clutched at the arms of the chair, her knuckles going white.

"Very well," Starwind was actually smiling as he stepped away from the window and folded himself bonelessly into one of the chairs bolted to the floor of his *ekele*. He got a certain amount of pleasure out of teasing Savil about her acrophobia.

Each *ekele* was something like an elaborate treehouse; there was one for each major branch of the King Tree, some twenty in all. Not all were tenanted, and they were mostly used for meditation, sleeping, teaching, and recreation. For everything else, the "place below" served far better. But when a *Tayledras* needed to think, he frequently retreated to his *ekele,* sometimes for weeks, touching foot to ground only when he needed to.

An *ekele* consisted of a single windowed room, varying in size, made of polished wood so light in color that it was almost white, and furnished at most with a few chairs bolted to the floor, a table likewise bolted, and rolled pads stored in one corner for sleeping. Starwind's was one of the highest, hence, one of the smallest. The view was majestic. It was wasted on Savil.

Moondance took a third chair, and sat in it sideways, legs draped over the arms. "Well?" Savil demanded. "Are you going to explain yourself?"

"Your pupil. First, we strive to bring him to not depend upon others. So—then he pulls in upon himself, confiding not even in his Companion, hiding his pain within. Then I try to bring him to confess the pain, to share it, to reach out—"

"So?"

Moondance shrugged, and Savil sensed he hadn't told everything.

"What did you tell him?"

Moondance's moods could be read from his eyes; they were a murky gray-blue. "I—told him of myself. I thought if he could see that he is not the only soul in the world that feels pain, he might be brought to share it."

Savil's eyes narrowed; Moondance was unhappy. "*Shayana,* did he hurt you? If he did—"

"Na, the only one who hurt me was myself." His eyes cleared, and he gave her a wry smile. "He only pushed me away, is all. So, he hides all day, and this morning he is hiding again. His bed is empty, the *hertasi* say he went to the end of the vale, and his Companion says he has blocked her out entirely. To put it rudely, Wingsister, he is sulking."

Savil sighed, forgetting to clutch the arms of the chair. "Gods, what are we to do with him?"

Starwind's expression sobered again, and he began to answer—but was interrupted. Both *Tayledras* snapped to attention; their heads swung to face the window as if a single string had pulled them in that direction.

Two birds shot up from below and hovered there, just

outside that window; the white gyrefalcon, and a second, of normal plumage. Starwind leaped out of his chair and flung the window open; the birds swirled in on the blast of wind that entered, and he slammed the window shut again.

Moondance had jumped to his feet, holding both arms out, ready for the birds, the moment Starwind went for the window. The falcons homed for him unerringly and were settling on the leather guards on his forearms before Starwind had finished latching the window closed.

The elder *Tayledras* held out his arm, and the buff falcon lofted to his forearm with a flutter of pinions, settling immediately.

Both *Tayledras* stared into their birds' eyes in silent communion. Savil kept as still as she could; while the bond between Hawkbrother and his birds was a strong one, and the magic-bred birds *were* considerably more than their wild brethren, their minds were something less than that of a very young child, perhaps a trifle superior to a cat, and it didn't take much to distract them.

The white falcon mantled; the buff cried. The *Tayledras'* eyes refocused, and Savil read "trouble" in the grim lines of their mouths.

"What?" she asked.

"First—tampering, as you had reported it to us, but this time on *our* ground and not on k'Vala," Starwind said, soothing his bird by stroking its breast-feathers. "A clutch of colddrakes, from the look of it. Something has *made* them move, so when we deal with the drakes, we shall have to look farther afield; there are folk settled in that direction under k'Treva protection. This is the first time we have caught the culprit in the act, and I do not intend to take this lightly."

"I hope you're counting me in that 'we'; a clutch of drakes needs every mage you can muster," she said, getting carefully to her feet and bracing herself against the sway of the *ekele*.

"If you would—you would be welcome." Starwind looked relieved. "But Vanyel—"

"If he's hiding, he'll only come out when he's ready.

He's not going to come to any harm while he's in the vale. How far are these monsters, anyway?''

"Half a day's footpace; perhaps less," Moondance replied, "The which I do not like. It speaks for them being harried, or even Gated. In which case, why and who?"

"Good questions, both of them," Savil agreed. "Who can we count on?"

"Nothing under an Adept, not with drakes; not even Journeymen should handle drake-swarms, at least not to my mind. *Shethka.*"

"Don't tell me, we're the only three in any shape to take them on, right?"

"Sunsong is still recovering from moving the firebirds to sanctuary, Brightwind is too old to travel, Stormwing is pregnant."

"Lord and Lady—*lock* her up!" Savil exclaimed.

"No fear, she's steadied since she reached Adept. No more headlong races into danger just for the thrill. So— Rainstar is out already, with another call from the *kyree*, as is Fireflight. And that is the total of k'Treva Adepts." Starwind grimaced. "If this were summer . . . ."

"If this were summer, it wouldn't be colddrakes, *ashke,*" Moondance reminded him. "We work with what we have, and grateful that Wingsister Savil is with us."

"Let's get on with it," Savil said, steadying herself for the long climb down, as the *Tayledras* transferred their birds from forearm to shoulder for the descent. "So far as *I'm* concerned, I'll take a colddrake over your be-damned ladder any time!"

The snow cleared just before dawn, and the sun rose, pale and glorious, shining through the bare branches of the trees. The forest was filled with light; with the light came a resurgence of Vanyel's good sense.

He sat down on a stump, tired and winded, and suddenly seemed to wake out of the hold of his nightmare. *What am I doing out here?* he thought, panting. *I don't know where I'm going, I don't know what I'm going to do when I get there, I have no idea where I am! I just— hared off into nowhere, like a complete idiot!*

He put his pack down at his feet and scooped up some

of the new snow in his mitten and ate it; it numbed his tongue, but it didn't do much for his thirst. *I can't believe I did anything this stupid.*

He wrapped his cloak tighter, and tucked his knees up under his chin, staring at the delicate tracery of white branches against the painfully blue sky. He began to think things through, slowly; one small, painful step at a time.

He flushed with shame. *I can't believe I did this. Dammit, I know how much Savil loves me, I've felt it—and Yfandes, and—damn, I am a rotten fool. Moondance was just trying to say that it's—easier to have other people around who hurt when you hurt, not that he thought he hurt worse than me. I hurt him by pushing him away.*

His blush deepened. *Worst of it is, he'll likely forgive me without my asking. They didn't abandon me yesterday; they were busy—probably over my welfare. They gave me exactly what I wanted; to be left alone. I should have been knocked up against a wall.*

He brooded, watching the birch branches swaying in the breeze. He was alone, completely alone, as he had not been since he left Forst Reach. The only thing breaking the silence was the whisper of the breeze and the occasional call of a winter bird. It was the kind of solitude he had sought—and not found—in the ice-dream. And now that he had it, he didn't want it.

Not that this place wasn't peaceful—but a sanctuary, as he had discovered with his little hideaway at the keep, could all too easily become a prison.

When you lock things out, he thought slowly, *you lock yourself in. I think maybe that was what Moondance was trying to tell me.*

He stared at the white branches, not seeing them, and not really thinking; just letting things turn over in the back of his mind. There was a half-formed thought back there, an important one. But it wasn't quite ready to come out yet.

Finally he sighed, and turned his thoughts back to his own stupidity. *Even if that dream is ForeSight, there's probably ways around it. Nobody's going to force me into being a Herald. I could probably stay here if I asked to. There was no reason to go running off into the wilderness*

*with nothing but what I could carry and no weapons.
Gods, what a fool I am!*

He swiveled around to look down his backtrail. Even
as he watched, the brisk breeze was filling in the last of
his tracks with the light, powdery snow.

He groaned aloud. *Oh, fine. Just fine. I probably won't
be able to find my way back now! I don't need teachers,
I need nursemaids!*

Then he blinked, caught in sudden astonishment at the
tone of his own thoughts. He sat up a little straighter and
took stock of himself, and found that he was—feeling
alive again. Feeling ready to *be* alive.

*It's like I've been sick, fevered, and the fever just broke.
Like I've been broken inside, somehow, and I'm finally
starting to feel healed. I haven't felt this—good—since
Tylendel—died—*

He closed his eyes, expecting pain at that thought.
There *was* pain, but not the debilitating agony of loss it
had been.

'Lendel, he thought with a tinge of wonder, *I still miss
you. It still hurts, you not being here. But I guess Moondance was right. I have to get on with my life, even though
you aren't here to share it.*

He opened his eyes on the snow-sparkling forest, and
actually managed a weak smile at his own folly. "I really
am an idiot, a right royal moon calf. And you'd have been
the first to laugh at me, wouldn't you, 'Lendel?" He
shook his head at himself. "All right, I guess I'd better
figure out how to find my way back without a trail to
follow."

Then the answer came to him, and he laughed at his
own stupidity. "Lord and Lady, it's a good thing you take
care of fools. All I have to do is look for *mages*. It's not
like there's too many enclaves of mages out here, after
all! The power should be there for even a dunderhead
like *me* to see."

He closed his eyes again, and took a deep breath of the
cold, crisp air. *Center—ground—and open—well, just
like I figured, there they are—*

The surge of Gate-energy hit him with a shock, knocking him senseless.

* * *

When Vanyel came to again, the sun was high overhead, shining down on his cheek; it was noon, or nearly. He was lying where he'd fallen, on his side, braced between his pack and the stump. He'd curled up around the pack, and the roots from the stump were digging into his side and leg. His ears were ringing—or was it his head? Whatever; it felt as if he'd been graced with one of Jervis' better efforts.

Gods. He glanced up at the sun, and winced. *That was a Gate. Nothing else feels like that. Oh, I hurt. It's a good thing I was wrapped up in this cloak when I fell over, or I'd have frozen.*

He pushed the pack away, and rolled over onto his stomach. That at least got the sun out of his eyes. He got his knees under him, and pushed himself up off the snow with his arms; he was stiff and cold, but otherwise intact. Only his head hurt, and that in the peculiar "inside" way that meant he'd "bruised" those new senses of his. He knelt where he was for a moment, then pushed his hood back and looked around. It looked as if he'd fallen right over sideways when the shock hit him.

Guess I'd better get moving. Before I turn into a snow-statue. He pulled himself to his feet with the help of the stump, then stamped around the snow for several moments, trying to get his blood moving again.

I hope nobody noticed I'm gone. I hope that Gate wasn't somebody out looking for me. I feel enough of a fool as it is.

He hitched his pack over his shoulder, and took his bearings. *All right, let's try again. Center—and ground—and open—and If I find out that Moondance had anything to do with this I'll—*

His head rang again, and he swayed and almost fell, but this time the shock was a clear, urgent, and unmistakable wordless cry for help. It sobered him as quickly as Andrel's bucket of cold water.

There was no "presence" to the cry, not like any of the Gifted or the *Tayledras* had; it was just simple and desperate. This was no trained mage or Herald. It could only be an ordinary person in mortal fear.

Gods! His head swiveled toward the source of the cry as a needle to a lodestone. And without any clear notion of *why* he was doing so, except that it was a cry for help, and he *had* to answer it, Vanyel began stumbling toward the source at a clumsy run.

He had been following a game-trail; now he was right off any path. He ran into a tangle of bushes, and could find no way around it. Driven nearly frantic by the call in his head, he finally shoved his way through it. Then he was in a beech grove; there was little or no growth between the straight, white columns of the trunks, and he picked up his pace until he was at an all-out run.

But the clear, growth-free area was too soon passed; his breath was burning in his lungs as the forest floor became rougher, liberally strewn with tangles of briar and rocks, and hillier as well. His cloak kept hanging up on things, no matter how hard he tried to keep it close to his body. He tripped; stumbled wildly into the trunk of a tree, and picked himself up only to trip a second time and fall flat in the snow. The breath was knocked out of him for a moment, but that panicked, pleading voice in his "ear within" would not let him give up. He scrambled to his feet, pulled his cloak loose from a bramble, and started running again.

He must have tripped and fallen a good dozen times over obstacles hidden in the snow, and he surely made enough noise to have warned anything that wasn't deaf of his coming.

Anything that wasn't deaf—or very busy.

Winded, floundering blindly, and unable to focus on anything more than a few feet ahead of him, he fell over a root just as he reached the crest of a low hill, and dropped into a thicket of bushes that crowned it.

He saw the danger before he got up and broke through their protective cover. He froze where he was. The "danger" was too intent on its victims to have paid any attention to the racket he'd been making. Likely an entire cavalry troupe could have come on it unawares.

This was the very edge of the cleared lands of some smallholder; a fertile river-valley, well-watered, sheltered from the worst of the winter weather and summer storms. Arable land like this could well tempt an enterprising farmer out into the possible perils of the Pelagirs. There had been a stockade around the house and barns to guard against those hazards that could be foreseen.

But the stockade, of whole tree trunks planted in a ring around the buildings, was flattened and uprooted. It could not have held more than a few moments against what had come at the settlers out of the bright winter morning.

Vanyel had never seen a colddrake, but he knew what it was from descriptions in far too many songs and tales to count.

Less like a lizard, and more like a snake with short, stubby legs, it was the largest living creature Vanyel had ever seen. From nose to tail it was easily as long as six carts placed end-to-end. Its equine head was the size of a wine barrel; it had row upon row of silvery needle-sharp spines along its crest and down its back, and more spines formed a frill around its neck. It snarled silently, baring teeth as long as Vanyel's hand, and white and sharp as icicles. Its wickedly curved claws had torn the earth around it. Vanyel knew what *those* looked like; Moondance had a dagger made from one. Those claws were *longer* than his hand, and as sharp as the teeth. Huge, deep-purple eyes, like perfect cabochon amethysts, were fixed unwaveringly upon its prey, a young woman and her two children. It was a pure silver-white, like the cleanest of snow, and its scales sparkled in the sunlight; it was at least as beautiful as it was deadly.

As one mangled body beneath its forefeet testified, the creature knew very well how to use its wickedly sharp claws and teeth.

But neither tail nor fangs and claws was what held the terrified woman and her two children paralyzed almost within reach. It was the colddrake's *primary* weapon— the hypnotic power of its eyes.

It stared at them in complete silence, a silence so absolute that Vanyel could hear the woman panting in fear where he lay. The drake was not moving; it was going to bring its prey to within easy reaching distance of it.

Vanyel hadn't reshielded since he'd first been impaled upon that dreadful dagger of the woman's fear. He could still sense her thoughts—incoherent, hysteric, and hope-less. Her mind wailed and scratched at the walls that the colddrake's violet gaze had set up around it. She was trapped, *they* were trapped, their wills gone, their bodies no longer obeying them.

That was how her husband, the children's father, had died; walking right into the creature's grasp, his body obedient to *its* will, not his own. The beast was *slow,* that was the true horror of it—if they could just distract it for a crucial moment, break its gaze, they could escape it.

Vanyel could "hear" other minds, too—out there on the opposite side of the clearing. The *rest* of the extended family—there must have been dozens of them—had made it past the slow-moving drake to the safety and shelter of the woods. Only these four had not; the woman, bur-dened with her toddlers, and the man, staying to protect them. He could "hear" bits of their anguish, like a chorus wailing beneath the woman's keening fear.

Vanyel stared at the trapped three, just as paralyzed as they were. His mouth was dry, and his heart hammered with fear. He couldn't seem to think; it was as if those violet eyes were holding *him* captive, too.

There was movement at the edge of his field of vision.

No—not all had fled to the woods. From around the corner of the barn came a man; limping, painfully, slowly, but moving so quietly that the snow didn't even creak beneath his boots. He was stalking the drake. A new set of thoughts invaded Vanyel's mind, fragmentary, but enough to tell him what the man was about.

:—*get close enough to stick 'im*—:

It was an *old* man, a tired, old man; it was the woman's grandfather. He'd been caught in the barn when the thing attacked and knocked the stockade flat, and he'd seen his granddaughter's husband walk into the thing's jaws. He'd recognized the drake for what it was, and he'd armed himself with the only weapon he could find. A pitchfork. Ridiculous against a colddrake.

:—*get them eyes off 'er an' she kin run fer it*—:

The colddrake was paying no attention to anything except the prey right before it. The old man crept up behind it without it ever noticing he was there.

The old man knew, with calm certainty, that he was going to die. He knew that his attack was never going to do anything more than anger the creature. But it *would* break the thing's concentration; it *would* make it turn its head away for one crucial moment.

His attack was suicidal, but it would give his grand-daughter and her children a chance to live.

He came within an arm's length of the colddrake—he poised the pitchfork as casually as if he were about to stab a haybale—and he struck, burying the pitchfork tines in the colddrake's side with a sound like a knife burying itself to the hilt in a block of wood.

The drake screamed; its whistling shriek shattered the dreadful silence, and nearly shattered Vanyel's eardrums. It whipped its head around on its long, snaky neck, and it seized the old man before he even let go of the pitch-fork. With a snap of its jaws that echoed even above its shrill screeching, it bit the old man's head neatly off his shoulders.

Vanyel screamed as he felt the old man die—and the oldster's desperate courage proved to be too much of a goad for him to resist.

Anger, fear, other emotions he couldn't even name, all caught him up, raised him to his feet, drove him out into the open and exploded out of him with a force that dwarfed the explosion he'd caused when Starwind had tried to make him call lightning.

He was thinking just enough to throw up a shield around the woman and her children with one shouted word. Then he hit the drake with everything he had in him. The blast of raw power caught the drake in the side and sent it hurtling up over the roof of the house—high into the sky—and held it suspended there for one agoniz-ing moment while Vanyel's insides felt as if they were tearing loose.

Then the power ran out, and it fell to the earth, bleed-ing in a hundred places, every bone in its body shattered.

And Vanyel dropped to his knees, then his hands, then collapsed completely, to lie spent in the open field under the pale winter sun, gasping for breath and wondering what he had done.

Savil surveyed the last of the colddrake carcasses, and turned to Starwind, biting her lip in anxiety. "Where's the queen-drake?"

"No sign of her," he replied, shortly, holding to his feet with pure will. He'd taken the brunt of the attack, and he was dizzy and weak from the effort of holding the center while Savil and Moondance closed the jaws of the trap about the colddrake swarm.

"I have not seen her, either," Moondance called up the hill. He was checking each carcass in case one should prove to be an immature queen. It was unlikely to see a swarm with a juvenile queen, but it wasn't unheard of, either.

Yfandes had consented to carry the *Tayledras* double— the need to get to the place where the drake swarm was before the swarm reached inhabited areas was too great for any other consideration. Starwind had then served as the "bait" afoot, while Moondance on Yfandes and Savil on Kellan had been the arms of the trap.

"No queens," he said, flatly, having checked the sixth and final body.

The fight had stripped the snow from the hilltop, exposing the blackened slope. The six drakes lay upon the scorched turf in twisted silver heaps, like the baroque silver ornaments of a careless giantess strewn across black velvet.

"*Ashke*, are you well?" Moondance asked anxiously, leaving the last of the bodies and climbing the hill with a certain amount of haste. Starwind looked as if his legs were going to give out on him at any moment, and Yfandes had moved up to lend him her shoulder as support. He leaned on it with a murmur of gratitude as the Healer-Adept reached his side.

"I will do well enough, once I have a chance to breathe," the elder *Tayledras* replied, as Moondance added his support to Yfandes'. "I am more worried that we did not find the queen."

"Do you suppose," Savil began—

Then all three of them felt an incredible surge of raw, wild power—and it had Vanyel's "presence" laced through it.

"M'lord?"

Someone was tugging at his shoulder. Vanyel lifted his head from his arms; that was just about the limit of his capabilities right now.

"Gods," he said, dazedly, as the stocky young cloak-shrouded woman at his side tried to get him to sit up. "Oh, please—just—don't do that right now."

"M'lord? Ye be hurt?" she asked, thick brows knitting with concern. "Ye bain't hurt, best ye get inside fore 'nother them things comes."

"Aren't . . . anymore," he replied heavily, giving in to her urging and hauling himself into a sitting position. The sun seemed very bright and and just on the verge of being painful to his watering eyes.

Gods, it's one of the holders. She's going to lay into me for not coming sooner, he thought, squinting at her, and already wincing in anticipation of harsh words. *She's going to want to know why I didn't save the old man, or come in time to save the young one. What can I tell her? How can I tell her it was because I was too scared to move until the old man threw himself at the thing?*

"Ye saved us, m'lord," she said, brown eyes wide, the awe in her voice plain even to Vanyel's exhausted ears. "Ye came t' save us, I dunno how ye knew, but, m'lord, I bain't got no way t' thank ye."

He stared at her in amazement. "But—"

"Be ye with the bird-lords, m'lord? Ye bain't their look, but they be the only mages abaht that give a bent nail fer folks' good."

"Bird-lords?" he repeated stupidly.

"Tchah, Menfree, 'tis only a boy an' he's flat paid out!" The newcomer was an older woman, a bit wrinkled and weathered, but with a kindly, if careworn, face. She bunched her cloak around her arms and bent over him. "Na, lad, ye come in, ye get warm an' less a'muddled, an' then ye tell yer tale, hmm?"

She took Vanyel's elbow, and he perforce had to get

up, or else pull her down beside him. The next thing he knew, he was being guided across the ruts of the plowed field, past the carcass of the colddrake (he shuddered as he saw the *size* of it up close) up to the battered porch of the house and into the shadowed doorway.

He was not only confused with exhaustion, but he was feeling more than a little awkward and out of place. These were the kind of people he had most tried to avoid at home—those mysterious, inscrutable peasant-farmers, whose needs and ways he did not understand.

Surely they would turn on him in a moment for not being there when they needed help.

But they didn't.

The older woman pushed him down onto a stool beside the enormous fireplace at the heart of the kitchen, the younger took his cloak and pack, and a boy brought him hot, sweetened tea. When one of the bearded, dark-clad men started to question him, the older woman shooed him away, pulling off her own dun cloak and throwing it over a bench.

"Ye leave th' boy be fer a bit, Magnus; I seen this b'fore with one a' them bird-laddies. They does the magickin', then they's a-maundered a whiles." She patted Vanyel on the head, in a rather proprietary sort of fashion. "He said there bain't no more critters, so ye git on with takin' care a' poor old Kern an' Tansy's man an' let this lad get hisself sorted."

Vanyel huddled on the stool and watched them, blinking in the half-dark of the kitchen, as they got their lives put back together with a minimum of fuss. Someone went to deal with the bodies, someone saw to the hysterical young mother, someone else planned of rites. *Yes*, they were mourning the deaths; simply and sincerely, without any of the kind of hysterics he'd half feared. But they were not allowing their grief to get in the way of getting on with their lives, not were they allowing it to cripple their efforts at getting their protections back in place.

Their simple courage made him, somehow feel very ashamed of himself.

It was in that introspective mood that the others found him.

* * *

"—I know it was a stupid thing to do, to run off like that, but—" Vanyel shrugged. "I won't make any excuses. I've been doing a lot of stupid things lately. I wasn't thinking."

"Well, don't be too hard on yourself. ForeSight dreams have a way of doing that to people," Savil said, crossing her legs and settling back on her stool beside the hearth. "They tend to get you on the boil and then lock up your ability to think. You wouldn't be the first to go charging off in some wild-hare direction after waking up with one, and you probably won't be the last. No, thank you, Megan," she said to the wide-eyed child who offered her tea. "We're fine."

If the settlers had been awed by Vanyel, they'd been struck near speechless by the sight of the *Tayledras*. They didn't know a Herald from a birch tree, but they knew who and what the Hawkbrothers were, and had accorded them the deference due a crowned head.

All three of the adults were weary, and relief at finding both that Vanyel was intact and that the queen-drake was indisputably deceased had them just about ready to collapse. So they'd taken the settlers' hospitality with gratitude; settling in beside the hearth and accepting tea and shelter without demur.

Vanyel had waited just long enough for them to get settled before launching into a full confession.

"So when I finally managed to acquire some sense," he continued, "I figured the best way to find my way *back* would be to look for where all the mage-energy was. I did everything like you told me, Master Starwind, and I opened up—and the next thing I knew it was nearly noon. Somebody'd opened up a Gate—I think somewhere nearby—and it knocked me out cold."

"Ha—I *told* you those things were Gated in!" Savil exclaimed. "Sorry, lad, I didn't mean to interrupt you. Then what?"

"Well, I didn't think there was anyone around here but *Tayledras*, so I thought one of them had done it. I started to open up again to find the vale, and I heard a call for help. I got here, and when I saw that colddrake—kill the old man—I just—I just couldn't stand by and not do anything. I didn't even think about it. I wish I had, I think I overdid it.''

"With a colddrake, particularly a queen, better overkill,'' Savil replied, exchanging a look of veiled satisfaction with Starwind. "You may have acted a fool, but it put you in the right place at the right time, and I am not going to berate you for it.''

"Aunt Savil, I,'' he flushed, and hunched himself up a little, "I got here before the old man came out. I didn't *do* anything until he—I mean—I was just hiding in the bushes. I guess,'' he said, in a very small voice, "I guess Father's right. I *am* a coward. I could have saved him, and I didn't.''

"Did you *know* you could have saved him?'' Moondance asked, quietly, his square face still. "Did you *know* that your mage-powers would work against the drake?''

"Well—no.''

"You ran *toward* the danger when you Mindheard the call for help, right?'' Savil asked. "Not *away?*''

"Well—yes.''

"And you simply froze when you saw the strange monster. You did not flee?'' Starwind raised one long eyebrow.

"I guess that's what happened.''

"I think perhaps you have mistaken inexperience for cowardice, young Vanyel,'' Starwind said with conviction. "A coward would have run away from a plea for help. A coward would have fled at the first glimpse of the drake. You were *indecisive*—but you remained. It is experience that makes one decisive, and you have precious little of that.''

"M'lord Starwind?'' One of the homespun-clad men of the settlement was standing diffidently at the *Tayledras'* elbow.

"Phellip, I *wish* you would not call me 'lord,' '' Starwind sighed, shaking his head. "You hold your lands under our protection, yes, but it is a simple matter of barter, foodstuffs for guardianship, and no more than that.''

"Aye, m'—Master Starwind. Master, this drake—she just be chance-come, or be there anythin' more to it?"

Starwind turned to look at him more closely, and with some interest. "Why do you ask that?"

Phellip coughed, and flushed. "Well, m'lord, I was born 'n' bred west a' here. M'people held land a' Mage-lord Grenvis—*he* were all right, but—well, when 'is neighbors had a notion t' play war, they useta bring in drakes an' th' like aforehand."

"And you think something of the sort might be in the offing? Phellip, I congratulate you on your foresight. The thought had only just occurred to me—"

"Da?" One of the boys couldn't contain himself any longer, and bounced up beside his father. "Da, there gonna be a war? With fightin' an' magic an'—"

Phellip grabbed the loose cloth of the boy's tunic and pulled him close. "Jo—I want ye t' *lissen* t' what m'lord Starwind is gonna tell ye—m'lord, *you* tell 'im; 'e don' believe 'is ol' man that fightin' ain't good fer nothin' but fillin' up graveyards."

"Young man," Starwind fixed the boy with an earnest stare. "There is *nothing* 'fine' about warfare. There is nothing 'glorious' about battle. All that a war means to such as you and I is that people we know and love will die, probably senselessly; others will be crippled for life—and the fools who began it all will sit back in their high castles and plot a way to get back what *they* lost. If there *were* to be a war—which, trust me, Phellip, I shall try most earnestly to prevent—the very *best* you could hope for, young man, would be to see these lovely fields around you put to the torch so that you would face a very hungry winter. *That* is what warfare is all about. The only justifiable fight is a defensive one, and in *any* fight it is the innocents who ultimately suffer the most."

The boy didn't look convinced.

Vanyel cleared his throat, and the boy shot a look at him. "Pretty exciting, the way that drake just nipped off that fool old man's head, wasn't it, Starwind?" he drawled, in exaggerated imitation of some of the young courtiers of his own circle.

The boy paled, then reddened—but before he could

burst into either tears or angry words, Vanyel looked him straight in the eyes so fiercely that he could not look away.

"That's what you'll see in a war, Jo," he said, harshly. "Not people in tales getting killed—*your* people getting killed. Younglings, oldsters—everybody. And some fool at the rear crowing about how *exciting* it all is. *That's* what it's about."

Now Jo looked stricken—and, perhaps, convinced. Out of the corner of his eye Vanyel saw the farmer nodding in approval.

Out of nowhere, Vanyel felt a sudden rush of kindred feeling for these people. Suddenly they weren't faceless, inscrutable monoliths anymore—suddenly they were *people.* People who were in some ways a great deal more like him than his own relatives were. They had lives— and loves and cares.

Their outlook on warfare was certainly closer to his than that of any of his blood relations.

They aren't that much different than me. Except— except that I can do something they can't. I can—I can protect them when they can't protect themselves. And they can do things I can't. But I could learn to grow a carrot if I had to. It probably wouldn't be a very good carrot, but I could grow one. They won't ever be able to blast a colddrake.

What does that mean, really? What does that say about my life? Why can I do these things, and not someone else—and what about the people out there who—who send drake-swarms out to eat helpless farmers? If I can protect people like this from people like them—doesn't that mean—that I really have to?

He looked up and saw his aunt's eyes; she was watching the children at their chores, cleaning and chopping vegetables for a stew. Her expression was at once protective and worried.

It's the way Savil feels—it's got to be. That's why she's a Herald.

And suddenly Tylendel's words came back to him; so clearly that it seemed for a moment as if Tylendel were sitting beside him again, murmuring into his ear.

"... *it's a kind of hunger. I can't help it. I've got these abilities, these Gifts, and I can't not use them. I couldn't sit here, knowing that there were people out there who need exactly the kind of help I can give them and not make the effort to find them and take care of them.*"

Now he understood those words. Oh, the irony of it; this part of Tylendel that he had never been able to comprehend—*now* it was clear. Now that Tylendel was gone—*now* he understood.

Oh, gods—

He closed his eyes against the sting of tears.

Oh, yes— *now* he understood. Because now he felt that way, too.

Too late to share it.

Fourteen

:**W**ell?: To all appearances, Savil was asleep beside the settlers' stone hearth as she Mindspoke Starwind in Private-mode. In actuality, despite her weariness she was anything but sleepy, and was watching the fire through half-slitted eyes as she waited for the opportunity to confer with him. Her single word contained a world of overtones that she was fairly certain he'd pick up.

:*Interesting, on several levels*,: he replied. He was lying on his back, arms beneath his head, his eyes also closed.

The settlers—Savil had learned before the evening was over that they were calling their lands "Garthhold," and that there were seven loosely-related families in the group—had offered the *Tayledras* and their friends unlimited hospitality. All four of them were bone-tired even after rest and tea, and it was agreed among the three adults that it would be no bad thing to take them up on it. They refused, however, to put anyone out of his bed. So after a dinner of bread and stew, they made it plain that they intended to sleep by the fireside. The four of them were currently rolled up in their cloaks, on sacks of straw to keep them off the stone of the floor, beside the glowing coals of the kitchen hearth.

Vanyel was genuinely asleep. Savil wasn't certain of Moondance; he was curled on his side, his face to the fire, as peaceful and serene as a child's.

By all rights, he should really be asleep. There'd been several injuries related to the colddrake's attack and the hasty escapes, and Moondance had had his hands full

Healing them. Then he had delegated himself magical assistant to getting the stockade back up. It had saved the Garthholders no end of effort to have the logs spell-raised back into place. He *should* have been exhausted.

So Savil thought, until he Mindspoke both of them. *:May I enter the conversation? I assume there is one.:*

So much for Moondance being weary.

:Be welcome, but keep it in private,: she replied, *:Among other things, we're discussing the boy. Starwind, go on please.:*

:From the small things to the great—I think perhaps *you may cease to fear for the boy. I think he now feels the hunger you spoke of, and understanding has been attained. Herein the question is if the boy can conquer his fears.:*

:I wondered about that. He's been wearing a very odd look on his face this evening, and I've never *known him to be as friendly with common folk as he was tonight.:* She opened her eyes wide and stared at the glowing embers of the hearth without really seeing them. *:Poor Van. If that dream of his is ForeSight—that's a hell of a burden to carry around.:*

:It still may never come to be,: Moondance reminded them, and the straw of his bedding crackled as he shifted. *:We still See only the thing most likely at this moment. And the moment is always changing. I would change the subject. We have a more urgent consideration. Those colddrakes were Gated here. That speaks of—:*

:—great trouble to come,: Starwind replied, his mind-voice dark and grim. *:There is no doubt in my mind at this moment that the drakes were sent to harry this area in advance of a fighting force.:* The fire popped once. *:This has gone beyond tampering. There was a village to the west of here under tacit k'Treva protection. I can no longer sense it; it is under a foreign shield.:*

:Someone moved in and took it over, hmm?: Savil brooded on that a moment. *:What would you say to us organizing a little surprise for whoever sent those drakes? I doubt anyone is expecting k'Treva response this soon. By rights, dividing the swarm should have kept us busy for a week.:*

Starwind's mind-voice was troubled. *:I would say that you are not k'Treva—:*

:And I would reply that I am Wingsister, which makes me just as much k'Treva as Moondance. I would say also that two mages tampering in this area is a very unlikely coincidence. It is far more likely that this is the same mage who was hired by the Leshara of Valdemar. Which makes it the more my fight.:

More straw rustled, and Savil moved her head slightly; just enough to see Starwind's ironic gaze bent on her for a long moment.

:And I,: Moondance put in, *:would say that my shay'kreth'ashke is unlikely to win a battle of wills with such a stubborn one as I know the Wingsister to be. I would also say that three Adepts are better in this than two.:*

Starwind sighed. *:I fear I am defeated ere I begin. What do we do with the boy, then? We cannot leave him here, and I mislike taking the time to take him back to the vale. That will lose us the element of surprise.:*

:He may prove useful,: Moondance said unexpectedly. *:He did defeat the queen-drake.:*

:We bring him, I suppose,: Savil agreed, though with some misgiving. *:Surely Yfandes can be counted on to keep him out of serious trouble.:*

:I cannot like it, but I must agree,: Starwind replied reluctantly. *:This is a great deal of danger to be taking one so untested and so newly-healed into.:*

:I know,: Savil said, wishing the coals burning in the fireplace didn't look so much like a burning town. *:Believe me, I know.:*

It had been snowing all day, not heavily, but steadily. The air felt almost warm. The Companions moved like white spirits through the drifts of flurries, each carrying double. White horses, white riders—all but one; the one riding pillion behind the second Companion was in smoky black and dark gray, a shadow to a ghost.

"You all look like Heralds," Vanyel said, from the pillion-pad behind Moondance. "Everyone does except me."

"How so?" Moondance asked, somewhat surprised.

"It's your white outfits," Savil supplied, as Kellan lagged a little so that she could reply without having to turn her head. "Heralds always wear white uniforms when they're on duty."

"Ah—youngling, *Tayledras* always wear the colors best suited to blend into the treetops. In winter—white. In summer, obviously, green." Moondance was carefully plaiting a new bowstring using both hands; he wasn't even bothering with the reins, he had those looped up on the pommel of the saddle. Vanyel didn't much care for riding pillion, but it wasn't bad behind Moondance; the younger *Tayledras* didn't mind talking to him. As Vanyel had suspected, he had forgiven Vanyel even before he made his apology to the *Tayledras*. Which he had done as soon as he could get Moondance alone; it only seemed right. Now it was as if the incident had never occurred; Moondance even seemed to welcome his questions and encouraged him to ask them.

They'd talked about Vanyel's Gifts, mostly. Vanyel hadn't actually *talked* about them to anyone; Savil hadn't had much opportunity to do so, and Starwind had just gone directly into his head, showed him what to do, and then expected him to do it.

"So, what were we up to?" Moondance asked.

"ForeSight." Vanyel shivered. "Moondance, I don't like it. I don't *want* to know what's going to happen. Is there any way I can block it?"

"Now that it is active? Not to my knowledge. But you must not let it cripple you, *ke'chara*. You are not seeing the *irrevocable* future, you see the future as it may be if nothing changes. The most likely at this moment. These things may change; *you* can change them."

"I can?" Vanyel perked up at this.

"Assuredly. But it may be that the cost of such a change is to dissolve a friendship or a love you would not willingly forgo. You may feel such a bond is worth the price." He smiled crookedly back over his shoulder. "If I were to have the certain knowledge that my lifebond to Starwind would send me to my death tomorrow, I would go willingly to that fate. But I would not tell Starwind of my foreknowledge. Think on that, if you will.''

Vanyel did brood on that for several furlongs.

It was Moondance in Yfandes' saddle and not Vanyel, because if they were surprised by an attack, Vanyel had been ordered to drop off the pillion pad and stay out of the fight.

It was humiliating—but sensible. Vanyel was rather more acutely interested in ''sensible'' than in ''humiliating'' at the moment. If an attack came, he'd obey those orders. He'd learned his lesson with the colddrake.

''Well, are there no more questions, *ke'chara?*''

Vanyel shook his head.

''Then I have one for you. Starwind has said that when you were frightened in practice you pulled power from the valley-node. Is this true?''

''What's the valley-node?''

''Savil did not tell you?'' Moondance made a face. ''No patience, that one. You surely have felt that all things have energy about them, yes?''

''Even rocks—''

''Ge'teva, if you sense that, then your Mage-Gift is a most strong one! Even I have some difficulty with seeing that. So; have you seen that this energy flows along lines, as rainwater to streams?''

Vanyel hadn't, but when he closed his eyes and *extended* he could see that Moondance was right.

''I do now.''

''Then follow a stream to the place where it meets another.''

He did. There was a kind of—knot. A concentration of power. He told Moondance so.

''That is a node.'' Moondance nodded. *''Tayledras* can direct the course of these streams on occasion, which is how we take the magic from places where the wars left it and move it to a place where it is useful. We build our strongholds over places where two or more powerful streams meet; nodes. The energy of the node is such that all of us can use it, but we have found that a-many outland mages not only cannot sense the streams, they cannot sense nor use the nodes. This may be something only

those outsiders at the level of our Adepts do well; I think
it is perhaps unique to the *Tayledras* that all of us, from
the time we start to feel our Gifts awaken, manipulate
this energy as easily as a child plays with building bricks.
There was a time—*very* long ago—when the *Tayledras*
adopted outlanders very commonly, and it is said that
these outlanders changed even as I have. I think that the
key to change is using this magic under the direction of
Tayledras born. So; of outland Adepts we have known,
only Wingsister Savil can link into the nodes as well as
Tayledras; her Gift is very strong. So, it seems, is
yours.

Vanyel was confused as to where all this was leading.
"But what does that mean, Moondance?"

"For now—you exhausted yourself when you killed the
colddrake. That is something you need not do *quite* so
quickly, if you remember that you can pull from the life-
energy nodes within your sensing range. When *they* are
drained—*then* you use your own strength."

:That's what I've been trying to tell you,: Yfandes said
unexpectedly in his mind.

That gave him food for thought for several more candlemarks.

They'd journeyed westward from Garthhold with the
rising of the sun, stopping three times on the way to
question folk Starwind knew. The first had been a fur
trapper, who'd told them of rumors of a renegade wizard,
who was half-human, half-Pelagir changeling and had
sorcerous skills and a taste for worldly power. The second
was a *kyree,* a wolflike creature with a mind fully the
equal of any human. *He* stopped *them;* Mindspeaking to
warn them of of the same wizard, but his stories were
more than mere rumors; to his certain knowledge the
changeling was planning to carve himself a realm of his
own as quickly as he could, and had already begun that
task.

The third *had been* one of k'Treva's border-guards—
not *Tayledras* herself, but another of the Pelagir change-
lings, a *tervardi,* a kind of flightless bird-woman.

She was no longer among the living.

When Starwind had been unable to Mindcall her, they

had detoured to the grove of trees that held her *ekele*. There was no sign of a struggle, but they found the fragile, white-plumaged wraith in her *ekele*, dead, without a mark upon her, but with her bow in her hand, bowstring snapped, and her empty, glazed eyes wide with what Vanyel assumed was fear.

Starwind spent some moments beside the body, working some kind of subtle magic. Vanyel could feel things stirring, even if he couldn't yet read them. What it was Starwind found, he would not tell Vanyel, but the three adults grew very grim—and Moondance took the bow and its arrows when they left.

They had been riding all day, cutting cross-country at the ground-eating pace only a Companion could maintain; it was nearing sunset when they slowed, on coming to what looked to be a fairly well-traveled road.

Savil and Kellan halted while they were still within the cover of the forest, and Yfandes came up beside them as silently as it was possible for something the size and weight of a Companion to do. The snow-laden branches of an enormous evergreen shielded them from the view of anyone on that road, although the road itself looked deserted. There didn't seem to be any new tracks on it, and all the old ones had been softened with a layer of new, undisturbed snow. The road was lined on both sides by a row of these evergreens, though, and anything could lie in wait undetected behind them.

"The village of Covia lies a few furlongs up that road," Starwind whispered, as the sun sank in sullen glory ahead of them. "There is still a shield upon it, and I do not like the feel of the power behind that shield. I do not, however, sense that the power is presently in the village."

"Nor I," replied Savil, after a moment.

:Nothing,: Yfandes said to Vanyel.

" 'Fandes says she doesn't feel anything either," he reported, feeling rather in the way.

"My thought is to enter the village and see how much is amiss—and what the people know. Then—Vanyel, it is in my mind to leave you with the villagers. You have enough mage-training to be some protection to them, and they may be of some physical protection to you."

"I—yes, Master Starwind," he replied, not much liking the idea, but not seeing any other choice. "What about 'Fandes?"

:I don't like it, but I'll go with them,: Yfandes said reluctantly. *:If you need me, I'll know, and they need a second mount.:*

Vanyel reported Yfandes' words with a sinking heart. Starwind nodded. "I think she has the right of it; we can cover more ground mounted. Well." He peered up the road through the gathering evening gloom. "I think it is time to see the handiwork of our enemy."

Vanyel was doing his best not to be sick. Again. He'd already lost control over his stomach once, just outside of Covia, when they'd found the wizard's—warn-off.

It was well after sundown, and pitchy dark outside of the village square. The entire population of the village, upwards of seventy people, was jammed into the tiny square. Many of them had brought lanterns and torches. They were crowding about the four strangers and two Companions, like baby chicks seeking the shelter of the hen's wings—although they were paying scant attention to Savil and less than that to Vanyel and the Companions. The Herald was a dubious and unknown quantity, and the boy and the "horses" were being dismissed out of hand.

The party had made a kind of impromptu dais out of the low porch of the Temple, which was barely large enough to hold the four humans; the Companions were serving as living barricades on either side, to keep them from being totally overwhelmed. As it was it was getting a little cramped, behind the two *Tayledras*. But Vanyel was beginning to be rather glad he was being ignored. Between the tales the villagers were telling Starwind—and the physical evidences they were displaying in the flickering of the torchlight to substantiate those stories—it wasn't easy for Vanyel to control his nausea.

This *had* been a pleasant little village, as safe as any place inside the Pelagirs. People could feel comfortable about raising children; had time for celebrations now and again.

It was no longer pleasant, nor safe. It was now a place under siege, with no way out.

Two weeks ago a stranger had come to the village, mounted on something that was *not* a horse, and accompanied by a retinue of some of the Pelagirs' least attractive denizens. He had announced that the town and its inhabitants were now *his,* and had helped himself to whatever he wanted. After one demonstration of his power had left a heap of ash where the village inn had once stood, these folk had more sense than to resist—but they *had* attempted to send for help. The remains of their messenger were found the next morning, impaled on a stake in the middle of the outbound road. The frozen corpse was still there; the Companions had passed it on the way in. From the look of the man, simple impalement had come as a relief.

He had come back about every other night, each time taking both goods and victims. The villagers told Starwind that they had been praying for help; they assumed he was the answer to those prayers. He seemed, to Vanyel at least, to be agreeing with that assumption.

Vanyel was just grateful that the fitful torchlight wasn't bright enough for him to see much of the details of what had been done to some of the wizard's victims. He was equally grateful that he was in the dark at the back of the porch, behind Savil.

"—this's the last, Master Starwind," the swarthy, unshaven headman said, wearily, his red-rimmed eyes those of one who had seen far too much of horror in the past few days. "This girl."

He pushed a mousy blonde female right up onto the porch, where Vanyel couldn't avoid looking at her. The young woman would still have been attractive—if she hadn't been vacant-eyed and drooling. She was filthy, her hair matted and hanging in lank snarls. Starwind flinched at the sight of her, but Moondance fearlessly took her face in both his slender hands and gazed into her blank brown eyes for a long time.

When he finally released her, his face and voice were tight with anger. "I think that Brightwind may be able to bring her mind back,'' he said, slowly and carefully, as if he was trying to keep from saying something he had rather not speak aloud. ''It will require many months— and she will never be able to bear the touch of a man; she has been too far hurt within. Even so, all those channels meant for pleasure have been warped, and now can only carry pain. I do not know if even I can Heal that. I do not think that anything will be able to Heal her heart and soul of what was done to her; not entirely. It may be it is better not to try; it may be that it is better to wipe all away and begin with her as with a small child.''

The balding headman nodded as if that was what he had expected to hear. ''She was one of the first he took,'' he said heavily, ''Her and her mother. Her father was the messenger we sent—we never found anything of her mother.''

''And he grows stronger, this Krebain, with every person he takes?'' Starwind asked.

The torches wavered in the wind, casting weird shadows across the man's hollow-cheeked face as he nodded. Vanyel could scent the coming of more snow in that wind. ''He seems to. Seems to me he's doing blood-magic, wouldn't you say, Master Starwind?''

Starwind nodded, and narrowed his eyes in thought. ''Aye, Gallen; you know your lore well, I think. So. This Krebain has retreated to whatever place he has made for a fastness, and it is bound to be somewhere near; I think we shall continue with my original plan. Gallen, I shall leave young Vanyel here with you. He knows something of material strategy and warfare; he is also Mage-Gifted.''

Vanyel shivered at the thought of being left alone here. The headman cast one doubtful look at him and ventured a protest; Vanyel didn't much blame him. ''Master Starwind—I beg you—this is only a boy—''

''He destroyed a queen colddrake, alone and unaided,'' Moondance said quietly, pushing Vanyel forward and putting one hand on Vanyel's shoulder. ''It is in my mind that he could deal with more than you would reckon.''

''He did?'' This time the look Headman Gallen gave

him was a little less doubtful, but it was still not overly confident.

"Gallen, I do not expect Vanyel to have to defend you from this Krebain," Starwind said patiently. "He could never be a match for a blood-bound Adept, and I would not expect it of him. I expect him to have to deal with some of this renegade's creatures at worst. My thought is that the three of us shall find Krebain and deal with him—and that when his control over his slaves is gone, some of them may think to attack here. I see no reason why, among you, you folk and Vanyel could not defend yourselves against such lesser dangers. Does that content you?"

It didn't—that was obvious. But it was all that Headman Gallen was going to get, and he well knew it. Vanyel attempted to put himself into the mindset of a warleader. He didn't feel particularly successful at it.

"Van, see what you can do about organizing these folk," Savil said quietly. "You know most of those old ballads by heart, and there's lots of good advice in them; that's why we make you learn them. I don't want you to try anything more than a token defense if something does come at you that you can't handle. Just call Yfandes for help and delay things as long as you can. For the rest— the creatures they've described are strong, but not particularly bright. Barricades across the road and fire should keep most of them at bay. You took that queen colddrake; remember that. You can take just about anything else except this Krebain himself so long as it isn't a small army."

Vanyel gulped, and tried to look competent and brave. *This is what it all comes down to, doesn't it? This is what I have to do; I have to, like 'Lendel said. Because these people need me.* "Yes, Aunt," he said carefully. "Barricades and fire."

Savil looked worried and preoccupied. "Do your best, lad. Remember that 'voice' I used to stop you and 'Lendel fighting? It makes people listen; goes right to their guts. Imitate that if you can." She mounted Kellan from the porch; Starwind took Yfandes' saddle, but Moondance hesitated a moment before taking the pillion behind him.

"Vanyel, *ke'chara,* remember what I told you about the nodes. *Use* them. There are—" he paused, and his eyes unfocused for a moment. "There are three that I can sense that you should be able to use. I wish you could reach the valley-node as we can, but I think it is beyond your strength for now. None of the three nearby are as strong as the valley-node, but taken together they should serve." He took Vanyel's face between his hands and kissed him on the forehead. "Gods be with you, youngling. With fortune, this will be no more than an interesting exercise for you."

He mounted behind Starwind, and the crowd of villagers parted to let them through. Vanyel watched them vanish into the darkness with a heavy heart.

If he hadn't been so frightened himself, he'd have lost his temper a dozen times over. He had to keep explaining to these people, time and time again, exactly *what* he wanted of them and *why* he wanted it—and would turn his back on one group, thinking that he had *finally* gotten through to them, only to return to find they'd abandoned the project and were staring apprehensively off into the darkness.

It wasn't that they were stupid; it was that they were so completely without hope. They couldn't see any *chance* of holding off anything, and so they had abandoned any thought of being able to do so. After all, *their* best efforts hadn't done anything but get folks killed. Vanyel, who was counting on *them* to be as much protection for him as he would be for them, was nearly frantic. It took hours before he was finally able to get them going under their own power.

Then there was the matter of defense.

When dawn came and he asked for their weaponry, he got as ill-used and motley an assortment of near-junk as he'd ever seen, and there wasn't a one of them who knew how to use any of it. These were farmers born and farmers bred; most of them off lands held of lords or mage-lords who were bound to protect *them*. The k'Treva had bartered protection for made-stuffs and foodstuffs, and they had never thought they'd need to raise a blade in their own defense.

So Vanyel was faced with the task of showing rank amateurs the way of the sword. *Forget* teaching them point-work; *forget* the finer points of defense. In the end he padded them to the eyebrows and set them to bashing at each other. Teach them to hold something long and poke with it, or hold something heavy and smash with it—and if it was something with an edge, hope that the edge, rather than the flat, connected.

By the second day of this he was tired to the bone, half-mad with frustration, and frantic with the fear he dared not show. So when Veth, Gallen's half-grown son, came at him wide open for the hundredth time, he lost his temper completely and hit him with a full force blow he had not consciously intended to deliver. And tried to pull it too late to do any good.

He knocked the boy halfway across the square.

Veth landed sprawled on his back—and didn't move—

And Vanyel's heart stopped—

And in his mind he saw—Jervis—standing over *him*—

Oh, gods!

Vanyel's sword went flying; his helm followed it as he ran to kneel at Veth's side in the cold dust of the square.

Oh, gods—oh, gods—I've done to him what Jervis did to me. Oh, please, gods, please don't let me have hurt him—

He unlaced the boy's helm and pulled it off; about then Veth blinked up at him and started to sit up of himself, and Vanyel nearly cried with relief.

"Veth—please, Veth, I'm sorry, I—I lost my temper—I didn't mean it—"

The boy looked at him with bewilderment. "Eh, Master Van, I be all right. I been kicked by our old mule worse nor this—just let me get a bit of a drink, eh?"

Vanyel sagged back on his heels, shutting his eyes against the harsh sunlight, limp with relief. The boy got gingerly to his feet.

Oh, gods. I—I'm as bad as Jervis. I'm worse than Jervis; I know better. Oh, gods—

"Vanyel, young sir—"

He looked up; it was Reva, Veth's mother, her tired face anxious. He winced, and waited for her to give him the tongue-lashing he deserved.

It didn't come. If you'll forgive me for being an interfering old hen," she said, with a little quirk of her mouth, "I think you've about worn yourself into uselessness, young sir. I know you haven't eaten since last night. Now here—"

She offered him her hand; astounded, he took it, and to his utter befuddlement she hauled him to his feet. "Now," she put one arm around his shoulders, the other about Veth's, "I think it's time you both got a bit of food in you. The time it takes to eat won't make Veth a better fighter, nor you a better teacher." She hugged them both, as if they were both her sons, then released them.

The words he had thrown into Withen's face—was it only a year ago?—came back to shame him further.

"Let every man that must go to battle fight within his talents, and not be forced to any one school."

I've been treating them exactly the way Jervis treated me. Forcing them to use things they don't know, to go outside of their talents. I am a complete and incompetent fool.

Vanyel blushed. And stammered. "I—I'm no kind of a teacher, Mistress Reva, or I'd not have chosen what I did to teach." He raised his voice so the rest of those practicing in the square could hear him. "This is getting us nowhere. It's like you trying to teach me to—to plow and spin, for a Midsummer contest a week away. We haven't the time, and I'm a fool. Now, please, what are your *real* weapons? Any of you know the use of bow? Or sling? Boar-spear, maybe?"

It was not his imagination; there were looks of real relief all across the square—and the beginnings of smiles.

But in the end, all his preparations were in vain.

The villagers willing to fight were on the barricades; there were really only two blockades—there was only one road going through the village, and it led directly through the pounded-dirt square. The square itself was fairly defensible now; not even a colddrake would have been able to get past the buildings. The folk too frightened or unable to defend themselves had faded away into the shadows as they did every night to scatter and hide in the cellars and attics of the buildings around the square. Headman Gallen had by now come to the conclusion that Vanyel knew something of what he was about; he and two or three of the other folk not too cowed to take a stand (including the old herb-witch, who took a dim view of this young upstart wizard taking over *her* village) were having a hasty conference with Vanyel on supplies—when a surge of Gate-energy invoked practically under Vanyel's nose knocked him to his knees and very nearly knocked him out.

The only thing that saved him from unconsciousness this time was that he was completely under shield. He found himself gasping for breath, and completely disoriented for a moment. His eyes had flashing lights in front of them, and he shook his head to try and clear it. *That* was a mistake; his head reacted poorly to the abrupt movement.

He could hardly think, much less see. *Gods—what in—*

"What do we have here?"

The clear, musical tenor voice sounded amused—and Vanyel froze. The voice carried clearly; the petrified silence in the square was as deep as the Nine Pits.

He looked up when his eyes cleared, and found that all he could see were the backs of people. The members of his erstwhile war-council were standing huddled together as if to keep him hidden in the shadows behind them. Vanyel got hold of the splintery side of the storehouse and pulled himself cautiously to his feet, ducking his head behind Gallen's and standing on tiptoe to peek over the shoulders of the men in front of him. His gut went cold when he saw the flamboyantly dressed stranger in the middle of the cleared square.

This could *only* be the wizard Krebain.

The torches falling from the hands of the stunned villagers were unneeded; the wizard had brought his own mage-light with him. It hung over his head, a tiny green-yellow sun. People were slowly backing away until they ran into the walls and the barricades, leaving the stranger standing in arrogant isolation in the exact center of the dusty square.

The wizard was a gaudy sight; he wore scarlet and gold; skin-tight breeches, close-cut gold-embroidered velvet tunic, scarlet cloak with cloth-of-gold lining. Even his boots and velvet gloves were scarlet. He had a scarlet helm that was more than half mask, ornamented with a preposterous crest of a rampant dragon in gold. With one hand on his hip, he tapped at his chin with a gloved finger as he turned to survey the people surrounding the square.

"A rebellion—I do believe this is a rebellion! How *droll!*" He laughed; it had a nasty sound to it.

He was graceful, slim, and very tall. White-blond hair tumbled from beneath the helm in wavy, shining cascades. What could be seen of his face was like elegantly sculptured marble. Vanyel found himself caught by the wizard's sheer charismatic beauty. None of the villagers had said anything about *that*.

Vanyel felt almost sick. Evil such as had been described to him *shouldn't* be—beautiful!

But then he thought, *Artificial—that really is what he is. He's changed himself, I'm sure of it, like—painting his face, only more so. If I had a lot of power and didn't care how I used it, I suppose I'd make myself beautiful, too.*

"I wonder what could have roused you worms to think to stand against me?" Krebain mused aloud. "None of you had half an ounce of courage before this. But then— none of you smelled of the mage-born before this, either, other than that foolish old witch of yours over there." He smiled slyly. "I think I detect a stranger among you— hmm? Now where have you hidden him?"

Ice crawled up Vanyel's spine. *All they have to do is point a finger at me—and even if they don't, if I call Yfandes fo* help, he'll know where I am. Oh, gods, can I hide? I can't challenge him! They can't expect it of me— I'm no match for him!*

But to his surprise, not a single one of those remaining in the square answered the wizard's question. In fact, the men standing in front of Vanyel moved closer together, as if to shield him from the wizard's chance sight.

The wizard's voice sharpened with impatience. "I grow weary, curs. Where is the stranger I sensed?"

Silence.

Except for the herb-witch, who whispered back at Vanyel, with the merest breath—"Stay quiet, boy. You're no fit opponent for him, and we know it. Won't do any of us any good for you to get caught, and he just may take us apart for spite even if he gets you. Maybe if he gets bored, he'll go away."

"I *said*, I want to know where the stranger is." The wizard looked about him, both hands on his hips now, and anger in his pose. "Very well. I see it's time you learned another lesson." He turned slightly, so that he was staring right at the group clustered in front of Vanyel, and raised his left hand. "You—Gallen." He made a little summoning motion. "Come here. . . ."

Gallen made a staggering step, then another. He was fighting the wizard with his will, but losing. Sweat popped out all over his brow, and he made a whimpering noise in the back of his throat.

Behind him, the group closed ranks, still shielding Vanyel from view. Before him, the wizard grinned sadistically. "You really haven't a hope of fighting me, you know," he said pleasantly. "It's like a babe challenging an armed warrior. Come along, there's a good dog."

Gallen ran the last few steps, coming to a trembling halt at the wizard's side. Krebain strolled around him, looking him over carefully. The mage-light followed in faithful attendance above his head. "Let's see—I believe you have a wife." He swept his gaze over the rest of the villagers. "Yes, indeed—and there she is. Reva—my goodness. A would-be sword-lady, are you? Come here, my dear."

He crooked his finger, and dusky Reva stumbled out of the group at the barricade on the west road, still clutching her improvised pike of a knife strapped to the end of a staff. Her face was strained, white—and a mask of despair.

Krebain shook his head. "Really, my dear, you have no use for a weapon like that. Take it from her, Gallen."

Gallen did not move; sweat poured down his face, glistening in the mage-light.

"I said, *take it*." Krebain's voice sharpened with command, and Gallen's gnarled hands slowly reached forward to take the pike from his wife.

"Now—just rest the point of that wicked little knife on her stomach, why don't you." Gallen his face reflecting his agony, lowered the pike until the point of the blade touched his wife's stomach. He whimpered again as Krebain's will made him brace it. Krebain's smile grew broader. "Of course, Reva, it would be very painful if you were to walk forward just now—"

Vanyel couldn't bear it. He gathered what little there was of his courage, and shouted, his voice breaking.

"Stop it!"

He pushed his protectors aside and walked out from behind them to stand in the open, a pace or two in front of them.

And in the moment when Krebain turned to face him, licking his lips, he Mindcalled with all his strength—

:Yfandes! The mage—he's here! 'Fandes—:

"That's enough, child."

Vanyel felt a barrier close down around the village, a barrier that allowed no thought to escape, and no further call for help.

He raised his chin with the same bleak defiance that had served him against his father.

"Let them alone, wizard," he said, his voice trembling despite his efforts to keep it steady. He could feel sweat trickling coldly down the back of his neck and his mouth was dry and sour with fear. "I'm the one you wanted."

Krebain made a dismissing gesture, and Reva and Gallen staggered as his hold over them was released. Gallen threw down the pike and seized her shoulders, and together they melted into the crowd at Krebain's back.

"Come where I can see you," the wizard said, mildly.

Vanyel walked, with slow and hesitant steps, into the area where the mage-light was striking.

"What a *pleasant* surprise—"

Unless Krebain was feigning it—which was possible—he *was* surprised.

And—pleased.

If Vanyel could keep him in that mood, maybe he could keep them all safe a little longer. He began to feel a tiny stirring of hope.

"What a truly pleasant surprise. My would-be enemy is a *beautiful* young man. What is your name, lovely one?"

Vanyel saw no reason not to answer him. If nothing else—if Yfandes had heard him, he'd be buying time for help to arrive. He allowed himself a moment to hope a little more, then replied, "Vanyel Ashkevron."

"Vanyel—I do *not* believe this—Vanyel Ashkevron?" The wizard laughed, throwing back his head. "What a joke! What a magnificent *jest!* I come a-hunting you, and *you* walk unarmed into my very hand!"

Vanyel shook his head, bewildered.

The wizard grinned. "Dear, lovely boy. You have enemies, you know, enemies with no appreciation of beauty and a great deal of coin to spend. Wester Leshara holds you to blame for the death of his cousin Evan, didn't you know that? He sent me an additional commission to deal with you as I had with young Staven Frelennye. *I* had thought to attend to my own pursuits a while here, then deal with you at my leisure, allowing matters to cool first. But—now I don't know that I am going to oblige him by killing you. Not when you turn out to be so very beautiful. Come closer, would you?"

Vanyel felt no magical coercion, which rather surprised *him.* "If you don't mind," he said carefully, "I'd really rather not."

This time Krebain's smile held a hint of real humor. "Then I shall have to come to you, beautiful Vanyel."

He paced gracefully across the pounded dirt of the village square, taking each step as though he walked on a carpet of petals strewn especially for his benefit. The mage-light continued to follow him faithfully. He strolled around Vanyel as he had walked around Gallen, but his expression this time was less cruelly cheerful and more acquisitive. His path was an inward-turning spiral, with Vanyel as the center, so that he completed his circuit facing Vanyel and less than a handspan away. He reached out with one crimson-gloved hand, ignoring the presence of everyone in the square as if he and Vanyel were alone together, and laid it along Vanyel's cheek. Vanyel looked steadily into his blue-black eyes within the shadowed eye-holes of the helm-mask and did not flinch away. Those eyes were the first indication he had seen that the wizard was something other than human. Those dark and frightening eyes were slitted like a cat's—and under the velvet of the glove, Vanyel could feel something very sharp and talonlike resting on his cheek.

"My goodness," Krebain breathed, "Silver eyes. Rare and beautiful, Vanyel Ashkevron. How wonderful, and how strange, that you should be here, at this moment. And I wonder, now—given what I know of Tylendel Frelennye—were you only the *friend* of Tylendel, or were you something more than friend?"

Still ignoring everyone else, he leaned forward and kissed Vanyel passionately and deeply.

Vanyel trembled with an unexpected reaction comprised of both revulsion and desire.

Half of him wanted to pull away and strike at this creature who could casually force a man to stab his own wife, who could regard the villagers about them so lightly as to totally ignore them at this moment.

The other half of him wanted to melt into the wizard's arms.

He fought the temptation to yield. *This—dammit, it's nothing but sex, that's all it is. I know what real love feels like—and this—isn't—close.*

He closed his eyes, as his knees went to water.

A dream-flash—

"Surrender to me, Herald-Mage Vanyel," Leareth said. "Take my darkness to you."

Had that dream been, not ForeSight, but a warning?

He fought to think clearly, battling silently, but daring to give no outward sign of his struggle. It was at that moment that he realized that whatever other powers this wizard had, he did *not* share Vanyel's Mind-Gifts. Like—

Thought-sensing, for instance. The shield over the village was spellcast, not mindcast. Which meant that Vanyel should be able to read the wizard, without Krebain knowing he was being read.

Krebain finally brought an end to the kiss, pulling away slowly and reluctantly, taking his hand from Vanyel's cheek with a tender caress of his velvet-clad fingers.

"Oh," he whispered, his eyes half-shut, the slits in them narrowed to near-invisibility. "Oh, beautiful and rare, *lovely* Vanyel. Come with me. Come with me, be my love. I can teach you more than you have ever dreamed. I could carve you a kingdom, give you power, pleasure—anything you desired. Name it, and it would be yours."

The temptation was incredible. And the thought—*I could guide him. I could bring him to compassion. He doesn't have to be this way. I could make him into something better. Couldn't I? Even if I don't love him— wouldn't that be worthwhile? Wouldn't that be a worthy goal? And I don't love him—but I could care for him, I think. There's a mutual need—isn't that enough?*

His heart raced. *I have to know—what is Krebain truly made of? If there's something there to work with— something I can influence—*

Krebain smiled. "I could even," he whispered, "grant you the finest revenge upon Wester Leshara the world has ever witnessed. A revenge so complete that it would even satisfy Tylendel's lover."

The wizard's mind was open to Vanyel's at that crucial instant; completely open and unguarded.

Vanyel saw *how* Krebain had gotten his power; how— and from what—he had learned it. And the uses he had put it to. And how he had *enjoyed* what he had done. There was nothing there that was human or humane.

Gods! Never—never would I give myself to that!

Utter revulsion killed all trace of desire—and *now* Vanyel flinched away, his nausea plain for anyone to read.

Krebain stepped back an involuntary pace, his face flushed. He frowned with anger, and his expression hardened. "I will have you, Vanyel Ashkevron—with or *without* a mind."

Vanyel had that much warning to get a shield up; had that much warning to scream *"Run—"* at the villagers.

At least, he *thought* he screamed that warning at them. They certainly scattered as quickly as if he had, scrambling up and over the barricades that they had built to keep the menace out, leaving him alone with the wizard.

Who called the lightnings down on him.

Vanyel's body screamed with pain, despite the shielding; his hair stood on end, and fire ran along his nerves. He went to his knees beneath the onslaught; reinforced his shielding and felt it weakening—and then remembered what Moondance had said about the power-nodes.

He reached, desperately; found them, tapped into them, and felt their power flowing into him, giving him a heady surge of strength, driving out the pain and renewing the will to *fight* this monster in human guise.

He staggered to his feet, backed up a pace, and deflected Krebain's own lightnings back into his face.

The fires arced across the square and the wizard retreated, getting his own shields up just in time. Vanyel did not give him a chance to recover from his surprise, but launched an attack of his own; not lightnings this time, but a vise of power, a glowing shroud that he closed around the wizard and began tightening.

But Krebain broke it after a moment's struggle, and countered with a circle of flame that roared up about him and began eating its way inward. Vanyel could smell his boot-soles scorching, and his skin tightened and hurt.

Vanyel in his turn, sweating with the heat, and his fear and effort, called upon the dust of the square to rise and snuff the flames.

This time Krebain gave him no chance to invoke a counterattack, but summoned a mage-storm like the one in Vanyel's dream. It howled down out of the night sky and surrounded him in a cloud of wind and energy, crackling with it, screaming with it.

And like the one in Vanyel's dream, this one ate away at his shields as fast as he could bring them up.

The whirlwind howled and raged, obscuring sight—he couldn't see—couldn't see anything anymore, just the flickering storm of power shrieking around him, coming closer by the moment.

One by one the nodes went drained and dead; now there was only his own strength left.

He went to his knees, holding the last of his shields up with little more than desperation left to sustain him—

—and a final hammer-blow blew the storm away and *smashed* him to the earth.

Vanyel lay stunned in the sudden silence of the square, broken and bleeding.

He was sprawled half on his back, and the silence howled in his ears as the storm had. The square was deserted now, but for the silent scarlet figure of the wizard.

Vanyel was utterly spent, and everything hurt so much he could hardly think. He coughed, and tasted blood, and when he tried to breathe, he felt stabbing pains in his chest and back.

He was oddly conscious of little things, of a pebble digging into his cheek, of his ankle bending the wrong way, of a strand of hair tickling his nose, of blood running into his eyes—of a single flake of snow spiraling down into the mage-light.

His vision began to darken as Krebain strode toward him from across the square; he seemed to be seeing things through a shadowy mist.

The wizard stood over him.

And strangely, he felt like laughing. *Gods. All that being afraid of that dream, for nothing.* He saw the wizard's expression, and sobered. *So. This is what it comes to. This is how it ends. At least—he looks a little tired. At least I put up some kind of a fight.*

He thought he heard someone, something, whimper. *Please, gods—let those people have gotten away. Don't let this have been for nothing. Let the others come in time to save them.*

"I told you, Vanyel Ashkevron, that I would have you with or without a mind," Krebain said softly. "But I would rather you were mine wholly, and of your own will. You see? I can be merciful. I can be kind to those I love. I give you another chance, beautiful Vanyel. Surrender to me, and I will heal your hurts, and give you all that I promised you. Will you come with me now?''

No. Not ever. Not at the cost of my life. He looked up at those inhuman, chillingly cold eyes. *And it will be at the cost of my life. But—gods—I can't let it cost more lives than my own!*

He reached, as far as he could, hoping for a tiny bit of energy left in the power-nodes—hoping to find another node, undrained—

—and touched the valley-node instead.

Gods—it isn't possible!

For a moment he thought he saw a way out, not only for the villagers, but for himself. But when he assessed his own capabilities, he saw that to use the raw, elemental force of the vale *would* surely kill him. He no longer had the strength to control it. The effect would be like what he had done to himself in practice with Starwind—only a hundred times worse.

He could die painlessly, letting the wizard destroy his mind and soul—or he could die in agony, saving the people of Covia.

I was willing to die before, for 'Lendel—why would I be afraid of pain and dying now? he thought, with a catch in his throat. *I surely owe a price for not stopping 'Lendel. All right. Gods, let this be my expiation. Give me this last strength to stop him.*

"No," he breathed. "Never."

The wizard's face twisted with anger, and he stepped back to deliver the final blow. Vanyel closed his eyes and *reached*—

In this last moment, peace came to him. A strange and heart-tight inner stillness, born of total acceptance that what he was about to do would kill him without Moondance near to heal what he would do to himself. With a feeling oddly like the lifting of his heart, he opened himself to the valley-node—and focused—

And the raw power poured through him and blasted from his eyes.

He screamed in agony, but his own cry was lost in the shriek Krebain made as the bolt of power caught him unshielded, in the face.

Then Vanyel fell, into true peace, and darkness.

"Oh, 'Lendel, wherever you are, I'm coming. Please, please be there—

Dear Withen; I think you would be very proud of your son today—

A faint sound from the fern-canopied bed beside her made Savil set down her pen and paper beside her chair, unwrap herself from her cloak, rise, and draw the silky hangings aside.

Vanyel—bandaged, splinted and bruised, and looking very pale against the dark green of Moondance's bedding—moved his head again on the pillow, and opened dazed eyes.

Savil swallowed hard; he looked so battered, so bewildered.

Oh, my little love, we so nearly lost you this time—so close, so close. I half expect you to ask me to let you stay here, sheltered and safe. And the gods know, you've earned it.

He blinked, as if he didn't quite believe what he saw.

"Aunt—Savil?" he said faintly. "Are you—real?"

She sat carefully on the edge of the bed, and touched his cheek, giving him a faint smile. "That real enough for you?"

He nodded, and blinked again. "The people—the villagers—Gallen and Reva—are they all right?"

"They're fine, *ke'chara,*" she replied, her heart filling with pride and love at the question. *His first thought—for others. There's no doubt; Starwind was right. There is no doubt of him.* "We got there just in time for Moondance to keep you from getting away from us. Gods—it's a good thing that bastard wasn't still alive. I don't think I've ever seen him so angry in my life, and Yfandes was white-hot with rage. There wasn't much left for us to do. Basically all *I* did was make a Gate to get us all back to k'Treva so Moondance could put you back together again."

"Then everyone's all right?" he asked insistently, as if he didn't quite dare to believe her. "Are they protected now? Are you and Starwind and Moondance all right, too? That wizard—he was the one *Leshara* hired—he told me so. He told me—''

''Later,'' she soothed. ''Tell me all that later. We're all fine. K'Treva sent out some of the Journeyman *Tay-ledras* to help get Covia back on its collective feet and give the region a little more in the way of protections. *You're* the only one who sustained any damage, love.'' She glanced up at the skylight to gauge the time. ''I expect Moondance will be along any moment to give you another Healing.''

He sighed, and made a tiny choking sound. She looked down, and saw to her confusion that he was crying.

''Vanyel,'' she asked, bewildered by the tears, and the strange, lost look in his eyes, ''Van, what's wrong?''

''I—'' he choked hopelessly. ''I—after 'Lendel—they won't want me. The Heralds—they won't want me—''

''Oh, Van—'' She closed her eyes against a surge of tears of her own, but these were born of joy. *Child—oh, child, you rise above my expectations. That was the very last thing I ever thought I'd hear from your lips right now.* ''Van—*ke'chara*—the Heralds *will* want you. How can they not want you? You *are* a Herald already.''

''I—am? I am?'' He stared at her, bewildered, clearly unable to believe her.

She reached over to the chair and pulled her white cloak from it, draping it carefully over him. He clutched it, his eyes wide, his face reflecting all of his changing emotions, as he moved from hopelessness through surprise, to a joy that equaled her own.

''—there. There's your Whites to prove it. You have a bit more to learn; we'll be staying here for a few moons yet while Starwind teaches you—but Vanyel, what makes a Herald is the *heart*. A caring heart, that cares for others before itself. And *you are* a Herald.''

He smiled then, a smile so sweet and so *happy* that it stopped her breath, and closed his eyes in absolute contentment, falling asleep with one hand still clutching the cloak to him.

—yes, Withen. You would be very proud. I know I am.

MERCEDES LACKEY

The Novels of Valdemar

To Order Call: 1-800-788-6262
www.dawbooks.com

DAW 25